A DROP OF VENOM

SAJNI PATEL

WITHDRAWN

A DROP OF VENOM

SAJNI PATEL

HYPERION

LOS ANGELES   NEW YORK

First Edition, January 2024
10 9 8 7 6 5 4 3 2 1
FAC-004510-23327
Printed in the United States of America

Stock images: snake (title page and chapter openers):
1986352829; snake (breaks): 735297934/Shutterstock
This book is set in Garamond Pro/Monotype
Designed by Phil Buchanan

Library of Congress Control Number: 2023010972
ISBN 978-1-368-09268-5

Reinforced binding

Follow @ReadRiordan
Visit www.HyperionTeens.com

SUSTAINABLE FORESTRY INITIATIVE Certified Sourcing
www.forests.org
SFI-01681

Logo Applies to Text Stock Only

For all the girls the world has tried to silence

THE EYES OF THE GORGON

IF YOU HAD THE POWER TO TAKE REVENGE ON THOSE WHO hurt you, would you make them suffer as you suffered—an eye for an eye? If so, would this bring you closure?

These are grim questions, not easy to talk about. But for survivors of sexual violence, they can resonate powerfully. Often, healing feels impossible, much less finding closure. Justice feels out of reach, much less retribution. In *A Drop of Venom*, these questions are not hypothetical. This is the story of a young woman who survives sexual violence and becomes strong enough to take terrible revenge. But in doing so, will she become as much of a monster as her abuser?

In blending the Medusa myth with Indian folklore to build a new, vibrant fantasy world, Sajni Patel offers us the story *behind* the myth—a tale of abuse and healing, of survival and rebirth, of a woman claiming power in a world dominated by men, in which heroes and villains are not so easy to distinguish. As a friend tells our protagonist Manisha at her lowest point in the novel: "those in power seek to control what they fear." In Manisha's world, as in our own, what some men in power fear most are powerful women who will hold them accountable for their misdeeds. *A Drop of Venom* is Medusa's story from Medusa's point of view, but it is also a story for every survivor in every age and in every world.

Why address a problem like sexual violence in a young adult fantasy novel? For the same reason the issue was addressed in mythology thousands of years ago: Sexual violence has been with us always. It affects a huge number of people in every generation. According to the Centers for Disease Control, over half of women and almost one third of men have experienced some form of sexual violence during their lifetimes. Transgender, queer, and nonbinary people are four times more likely than their cisgender peers to suffer from all forms of violence, including sexual, according to a study by the Williams Institute at UCLA. And according to RAINN (the Rape, Abuse & Incest National Network), youth are at particular risk. Almost 70 percent of sexual violence survivors are people between the ages of twelve and thirty-four. The most powerful way to combat the problem is to break through the silence. Stories like *A Drop of Venom* give voice to survivors, while provoking all of us to think about what it means to be a hero, a monster, a good person.

This is not, however, just a story about an important topic. It is an epic, page-turning, fantastic adventure that deals with important topics. Patel is a master worldbuilder, weaving a tapestry of cultures, history, magic, and myth so believable and instinctively *true* you might get a sense of déjà vu. Her world feels like a place we should have known about, one that we must have experienced before, perhaps lurking just under the surface of our own reality.

We follow the stories of two young people, Manisha and Pratyush, as they struggle against the expectations of their societies. Manisha is a nagin, her people hunted as monsters and rebels by the kingdom. To stay alive, Manisha must pretend to be a human orphan. She enters the service of the kingdom's great temple, where she hides her true identity and tries to rise in rank, going deep "undercover" in the hopes that she may someday bring down the system from the inside.

Pratyush is the last slayer, a hero born with epic strength and skill, who has his own reasons for disliking the kingdom, but who sees no choice except to honor his debt to the King and protect the kingdom from monsters. When Manisha and Pratyush meet, the chemistry between them is immediate, but love between them would be strictly forbidden. Priestesses cannot allow a man to touch them. Slayers cannot marry. They each have clearly defined roles in life, and they are expected to stick to them.

As the King tells Pratyush: "You don't exist to feel; leave that to poets. You don't exist to think; leave that to scholars. You don't exist to rule; leave that to me. Your only purpose is to kill. So, kill. And if you cannot do the one thing you were born to do, then what good are you?"

Neither Pratyush nor Manisha are content with their roles. Neither like being controlled. But does a love story between two young outsiders have any hope when the entire weight of the kingdom seems bent on making them enemies—Pratyush a hero, Manisha a monster?

Rick Riordan Presents has published many important stories. *A Drop of Venom* is, for me, perhaps one of the *most* important, because it deals with issues that so many young readers will face in one way or another during their lives: fighting societal expectations, speaking truth to power, finding your authentic self, surviving trauma, claiming agency. Most of all, it asks the questions: If you had the power, would you be better than those who use power against you? What makes a monster, and what makes a hero?

So go ahead and look into the eyes of the gorgon, the nagin, the fearsome woman who is said to turn men to stone. You may find that she's not who you think she is. There may be a reason the King does not want you to behold her face. You may see truth there, and truth can be the most dangerous weapon of all.

Rick Riordan

A Note from Sajni

I'VE BEEN ENAMORED WITH MYTHOLOGY FOR AS LONG AS I can remember, particularly with the tragic backgrounds of legendary figures. Medusa being one of them, with one of the most devastating and lingering tales still told to this day.

She was haunting and felt incomplete. She'd been silenced. She is given a short story amid the vast landscape of mythology, and little is known of this once-beautiful temple priestess. If you should ask anyone about Medusa, they'd most likely recognize her as a snake-haired monster who turns men into stone. But behind that fearsome facade, the one history would rather tell, is underlying trauma. I would be remiss if I didn't warn you of the following potentially triggering subjects.

This novel heavily involves sexual assault, rape culture, misogyny, violence, and gore. Please be advised that these elements are presented in both discussion and on-page scenes. These are issues that I considered with great care and are vital elements in shaping Medusa, and thus Manisha. The story could not be told without them.

Beyond that, this is a tale of epic adventure that pushes back the veil so that you may judge for yourself what it truly means to be a monster.

PROLOGUE

HERE, THERE WERE MONSTERS.

As integral to life as breathing. They prowled through the shadows all around. Eyes as cavernous as the Blood River. Talons sharper than winter-steel swords. Minds as adept as any human's. Plotting behind dense foliage. Stalking from the jungle canopy. Lurking in the depths of calm waters.

Calculating, cunning, and deadly. Make no mistake. Monsters, contrary to popular belief, were intelligent.

These were tales as old as creation, of beings born from nightmares: those who crawled through dimensions, said to have no souls, preying on humans if only to wreak havoc and satiate their bloodlust. Legend said these monsters originated from the depths of the universe where light had never reached, born in inky shadows and drawn to this world to hunt weaker creatures: humans.

To bring balance, the vidyadhara gifted these weak mortals aid from their abode in the heavens—the floating mountains.

But mortal kings schemed to gain celestial knowledge from them, forbidden truths that could lead to unnatural things. They bided their time, and on the deathbed of the first king, his sons enslaved the vidyadhara, clipped their wings, and stole their wisdom. Anarchy ensued. Imbalance spread across the realm, stretching as far as the glistening sea, as deep as the shadowy chasms, and as high as the speckled night sky.

As humans evolved and villages joined other villages to rise in defense, something new was born. They were the slayers: warriors who trained from childhood to hunt and kill monsters. They were men of fame, adored by all, envied and desired, and lavishly celebrated by the kings of this new realm.

Their weapons gleamed as they razed the land like an angry scythe. Fires set the world ablaze, and venom rose from its ashes.

The slayers were said to be immortal: For every monster slain, a lifetime was added to their own. Monsters were said to be inherently evil—deserving of death upon first sight.

But that was the thing about myths and legends.

There was so much to get wrong, and so little one knew of their true origins.

ONE

Manisha
(FIVE YEARS AGO)

All monsters and heroes have beginnings. This is mine.

Silt and cinder covered Manisha's face, gray snowflakes burdening her lashes and sloughing from her feet as she scrambled up a tree. She wasn't trying to flee or hide (nagin did *not* run); she searched for an opening to unleash a counterattack.

The roar of the Fire Wars was blistering and deafening. Chaos unfurled—meant to destroy, even when it couldn't obliterate resilience. The realm sat on the brink of oblivion, crumbling at the hands of the men who had forged its beginnings. *A world built in blood shall drown in blood.* And so the Nightmare Realm flowed red, a waterway of slain bodies carving through its heart. But today was *not* the day Manisha and her family would be sent down the Blood River. Not if they could help it.

Her eldest sister, Eshani—the most levelheaded of the three—came crashing through the jungle ferns, half kneeling, half squatting on the back of her giant tiger, Lekha. Eshani plucked an arrow from her quiver and unleashed it into the thicket, earning screams from invading soldiers. Her arrows never missed, not when the winter-steel tips hungered for vengeance.

Lekha roared, flashing razor-edged teeth and a mighty jaw. The ground shuddered like thunderclaps threatening to smite all in their path, Lekha's big paws pounding the ground like a battle drum.

Eshani backflipped off, landing on her haunches at the base of the tree her youngest sister climbed.

"Manisha!" Eshani called.

But Manisha was scampering higher, coughing as the sizzling air turned hotter by the minute and ignoring how every breath scorched her insides.

In the near distance, a row of the King's army fought the remnants of the once-mighty naga. Manisha's mother and aunts and second-eldest sister, Sithara, stood among the resistance. They were wild and wonderful, goddesses in their own right, wielding every weapon they could carry. Tridents and spears, swords and knives, arrows and axes.

The battle raged on, erupting with showers of arrows, clashing daggers, and a cacophony of wails. The blood of Manisha's people splattered against the green and brown of the forest, dusted with ashes. Her eyes brimmed with tears. A scream trapped itself in her chest. They couldn't die like this! They just wanted freedom. Why couldn't the King leave them alone? Hadn't he contributed enough bodies to the Blood River without adding theirs?

A soldier struck Mama. A vicious rage exploded through Manisha. She might've only been eleven, but she wasn't a stranger to violence— or the need to defend her loved ones. Papa wasn't here anymore to help protect Mama, so the sisters had to.

Manisha released an arrow. The one arrow split into three. Two hit the soldiers advancing on Mama. The third arrow careened into the main attacker's forehead, slitting all the way through his skull. The squelching sound made her shudder. But better him than her mother.

Papa had said naga arrow tips were made from winter-steel, the strongest metal in the land. Razor sharp and dipped in the blood of their foremothers, said to be more poisonous than any cobra, the naga people's namesake.

"What are you doing?" Eshani snapped, her hand suddenly on Manisha's shoulder.

"I had to save her," Manisha protested.

"She'd want you to save yourself first!" Eshani tugged her arm and, together, they darted across tree limbs.

A quake rocked the land. A shrill pierced the air, nearly knocking them from the canopy. A horde of giant, angry boars rushed through the battle, bigger than tigers, with skin too thick for even winter-steel to pierce. They bared sharp teeth and even sharper fangs. Their eyes bulged dark red like clotted blood.

The boars gored soldiers with their two-foot-long tusks. Screams filled the air, already stifled by chaotic ruin. They ran off into the smoky distance, writhing soldiers impaled on carmine-stained tusks.

Manisha shook at the sight, but she couldn't pity those sent to kill her family.

"Let's go!" Eshani screamed as the branch broke beneath them.

Falling was always a thrilling moment, one that seemed to pass in slow motion. Manisha caught glimpses of the floating mountains through the jungle canopy. She used to jump from higher and higher ledges, pretending to fly. Legends said the ancient ones could fly. Manisha wondered if they ever fell. If they ever twisted ankles and bruised knees and scraped cheeks. If they ever fell on their sisters and trapped them against jagged tree limbs and crooked roots.

She moaned, rolling off Eshani, her back screaming in pain. She bit her lip to keep from crying. Warriors didn't cry over a few sprains, she reminded herself.

Eshani groaned louder with every movement. "You weigh a thousand suns," she mumbled.

"Oh no!" Manisha knelt beside her, helping her to sit up beneath a trio of weeping willow trees.

"It's okay, little one," Eshani grunted, even though she was only two years older than Manisha. She clutched her side. "Hide. Into the ditches."

Manisha eyed the shallow graves before scuttling down and wrapping her dupatta around her face.

"Make sure you cover your entire head. Don't move until someone digs you out, do you understand?" Eshani said, her words rushed.

"Yes," Manisha whimpered, fighting instincts to lie in a curled position on the loose timber platform in the center. The grave was meant for a boy who'd died from his wounds. Nothing about this felt okay.

Eshani dropped banana leaves on top of her sister, long enough to cover her entire body, and then dirt.

As darkness descended around Manisha, her breathing turned ragged, harsh inside the cloth. The earth was hard and smelled of dirt and grass. The pocket of air was both cold from the clutches of the ground and warm from her labored breathing.

She stilled, ignoring the cramping in her legs and back, and clenched her eyes tight. Heat seeped into the ground as the fires raged. She took slow breaths, harnessing the meditation rites of her people to be anywhere except here. Her body went slack. Her mind drifted to a different plane, a place where she sat with her foremothers as they regaled her with the legend of the naga.

As Manisha listened to them drive off the distant, muffled sounds of war, she cradled her bangle to her chest. The band of four gold coils around an oval stone glowed in the dim. She brought it to her face. The small amber stone pulsated as a tiny serpent writhed inside. She glanced up in bewilderment, a dozen questions sitting on her tongue. In the distance, shadows broke and came to life.

"You will not die here," her ancestors told her. "You are the daughter of Padma, the grandchild of Padmavati. You have the blood of your foremothers in you, the will of great queens," they hissed, their eyes turning into glinting diamonds, their forms changing into specters with long, winding tails, their hair frostbitten white.

They spoke of the naga legends in haunting whispers, of how their people were special, significant. But Manisha supposed everyone said that of their own kind.

One voice rose above the others, as clear as day when she spoke. "The naga are meant to be great and unifying, ruled by queens who will rise from morbid origins."

Manisha frowned. She'd never believed in kismet and karma. How could she when her people didn't deserve this fate?

Her foremothers swarmed around her in a rush of winds, spiraling higher and higher into a hooded cobra made from a mass of a hundred upon a hundred serpents.

"Heed our wisdom," they hissed as one. "Retribution will come from resilience. A reckoning as inevitable as *venom*."

MANISHA GASPED WHEN SHE CAME TO, PANIC WEDGED DEEP in her aching bones. But there was no room to thrash around, no place to escape.

"Hurry," Sithara said, her voice distant and yet so close. "Is she all right?"

"She's stronger than she knows," their mother replied, prying through the darkness like a goddess of light.

Manisha rose from a grave of ashes, reaching out for the imploring hands of her sisters. Mama wept, clutching Manisha in her arms while her sisters embraced them.

She touched her mother's face—gashes across her brows and cheeks, skin covered in dirt and ash, hair riddled with debris—and cried. Her mother, although she'd never admit it, must've been in so much pain. In a matter of years, she'd transformed from a gardener who merrily picked herbs, armed with a trowel and basket, to queen of the avenged, dripping in the blood of her enemies.

"Don't cry, beta," Mama said, wiping away Manisha's tears. "War is the invention of the power-hungry and soulless. *We* are *naga*. We fight to our last breath. And even the grave cannot silence us. Our righteous fury will manifest in formidable cries, reaching our enemies from the Nightmare Realm itself. We will *not* be annihilated. Or forgotten."

They trekked north, walking in solemnity, bodies aching and thoughts cluttered with grief, anger. They left death behind. Ash-ridden trees had turned into cylinders of cinder, the bodies of their people and wild animals burned in the fires like nightmarish sacrifices. Manisha wept for them all.

Eventually, the embers of dead jungle gave way to untouched vegetation as they crept closer to the floating mountains, a place war would never reach. The glint of their underbellies hovered high above like marbled stars, perfect and mysterious and perpetually unattainable.

At the river, Mama took Manisha by the shoulders, her dupatta slipping from her head. Her face was caked with blood and dirt. "You have to pretend that you are not part of the naga people, that you're a lost village girl."

"Why? What's happening?" Manisha asked, terror surging through her.

"We have to send you away."

Her sisters stood against a tree, annoyed, angry, anything but happy. Her lips quivered when she asked, "Did I do something wrong? I'm sorry if I did. Please don't send me away."

"Oh, my precious beta." Mama hugged her tight and trembled, hiccupping on her next breath. "I have to keep you safe."

"I'm safer with you."

"No." Mama glanced up at the floating mountains, the behemoth in the clouds casting icy shadows over them. "It is safest where violence cannot reach."

Manisha swallowed and shook her head, tears streaming down her face.

Eshani limped toward Manisha and knelt beside her with a softened grunt. She took her youngest sister's hand in hers, her haunting jade eyes glistening, and explained, "They won't take three sisters. Only one. I'm the eldest, and I have to protect you." She glanced over her shoulder at her twin. "And Sithara is . . . too unruly."

"Mama, please. I want to stay with you."

Their mother caressed her cheek. "Listen to me and obey."

Manisha whimpered.

"Do as you're told, hah? I need you to live. I need you to survive."

"Why do they want us dead? Just because we won't live by their laws?"

"They're men," Mama replied bitterly. "They follow a cruel king who follows the cruelty set by kings before him. We'll come for you. You must be a brave girl now, braver than ever."

She cupped Manisha's cheeks and kissed her forehead. "You must pretend to be a simple, lost girl from the kingdom villages."

Manisha nodded, her body turning heavy and numb, but she wouldn't cry. Warriors didn't cry.

"You must pretend not to know anything about us, about the world. You must pretend not to be too smart. You must pretend not to know what a weapon is or how to wield one—but keep practicing in secrecy. You must pretend to be . . . submissive to the temple priestesses and kind to the men who go there," she added with clenched teeth.

"I don't understand, Mama."

Eshani said, "You must act like them, okay? Act like you believe in their teachings. Act like you're not sad. Pretend not to know about us, how our forefathers are brave naga, our foremothers great nagin."

Manisha hiccupped, her lips trembling, her hands shaking. She wanted to plead, beg to stay with her mother and sisters.

Sithara pushed away from the tree she'd been leaning on. She flinched with every other step, held out her hand, and pulled Manisha to her feet. She pushed her little sister's shoulders back and lifted her chin. Sithara tilted her head to the side, looking awfully formidable with the harsh lines of her cheeks and jaw, the fury in her brows, her emerald eyes glinting in the morning light.

"You are nagin," she stated, "daughter of our mother, a sister to us. You have a lot to live up to, but you won't have a chance to prove yourself if you die, will you?"

Manisha shook her head.

"We don't come from mothers and sisters who cower and plead, do we?"

"No," she said quietly.

"We are strong and fearless and adaptable. We do what needs to be done, don't we?"

"Yes."

Sithara touched a knuckle to Manisha's chin. "We're going to meet again one day when our time comes. When it's safe. And you're going to be fiercer than any of us, aren't you?"

She smiled softly. "Yes."

"Be brave, little one."

"Be cunning," added Eshani.

"Be strong," concluded their mother.

Manisha blew out a breath, feeling the blood of her foremothers flow and burn in her veins like venom—powerful and present.

"Quickly now," Mama said.

They rushed to bathe Manisha. Rose petals in her hair for fragrance.

Kohl lining, made from soot, for her eyes. The blood of berries for her lips. A clean-as-could-be salwar kameez and a dupatta wrapped around her head for modesty.

"I'll take her," Eshani offered, and then looked to Manisha. "But that means you have to ride with me."

"No fear," Sithara reminded. "Besides, Lekha is just a big, soft cat."

"A *cat...*" Manisha echoed.

Mama hugged Manisha to her chest, as if letting go might end her. "I love you, beta."

"I love you, too, Mama," Manisha said, holding back sobs and memorizing every facet of her mother's features. She didn't want them to ever fade away, but she knew they would.

Sithara hugged her next as Lekha emerged from the brush, one giant paw after another. She licked blood from her lips and snarled.

"Who's a good girl?" Eshani said, petting the five-foot-tall golden tiger.

Lekha trained her honey eyes on Manisha and yawned.

The girls climbed onto the tiger's back. Lekha rose.

Mama held her hands to her chest, tears cascading down her cheeks. Sithara gave a small but reassuring smile, a fist to her chest to ensure strength and heart in their journey. With a final farewell nod from Mama, Lekha took off, charging through the jungle faster than lightning, it seemed. And Manisha's entire world and family faded behind her. She trapped sobs deep within her chest, her body convulsing.

Lekha slowed down, prowling toward turquoise waterfalls pouring from the floating mountains in broken streams. Above, a flat cliff protruded from the jungle canopy.

"Hurry," Eshani said, dismounting and urging Manisha to walk faster toward the cliff. When two priestesses appeared, Eshani and Lekha hid, fading into the jungle.

Manisha approached them, resisting the urge to glance back at her sister, fighting the longing to run to her.

"Where did you come from?" the older woman asked, her poise so proper and elegant, her sari glimmering in threads of gold and scarlet.

"I'm lost," Manisha replied.

The women regarded her. The second snickered. "Your parents?"

"I have no family," Manisha responded, biting her tongue to keep the truth trapped. Lies tasted bitter.

"Head Priestess, we should sell her to the soldiers," said the one who'd snickered, keeping her glare on Manisha.

"She looks very young, Sita," the Head Priestess countered.

"Girls marry young. If nothing else, we can groom her and sell her to the highest bidder," Sita replied.

The Head Priestess responded, "You were fourteen when I took you in. Would you rather have been married off or sold to soldiers?"

"No."

"Where is your kindness, then?" She turned to Manisha and said, "You would be quite beautiful if we cleaned you up and taught you proper ways. Would you like to come with us and serve in the world's most elite, most revered temple, high on the sacred floating mountains?"

No, she wouldn't. But she nodded anyway.

"We shall give meaning to your life. We'll pair you with Arya. She's about your age and without family. Come . . ." She extended her hand and took Manisha to the platform, lifting the pleats of her sari to climb the stone steps.

Manisha went with them—these strangers, these enemies—to a foreign land, with an agonizing heaviness in her heart. It took everything in her not to look back.

She gulped when they reached the top, marveling at the flying peacocks—the fabled mayura. They were as large as rhinos and as fierce as tigers, yet too beautiful to gaze upon. They shuddered, with feathers made of emeralds and sapphires, gold and bronze.

The birds cawed into the heavens, shaking the ground beneath her feet. They spat fire as brilliant as rubies shimmering against the afternoon sun.

Manisha craned her head back to glimpse one of the massive creatures, shielding her eyes from the brilliance of its feathers. It turned its head to stare at her with deep onyx eyes, sending a stiff breeze.

Manisha stumbled back. Sita snickered. But the Head Priestess landed a gentle hand on Manisha's shoulder, urging her forward. A much older girl in a dark-blue-and-gold salwar kameez smiled down at Manisha from atop the beast. She offered a hand.

Manisha took that hand. She took the ride of her life, her breath escaping in rapid pants as the bird soared into the air. She finally knew what it was like to fly, to see the jungle from above, a mass of entangled green without regard for the beings who suffered within its clutches.

The air turned chilly and thin as they rose through low-lying clouds. She squinted from the sudden glare of the full breadth of the sun, warmth seeping into her skin. The surface of the floating mountains came into view, buildings like palaces, orchards dotted in pinks, meandering streams, and scattered clusters of women.

When she dismounted, she found her footing as quickly as she'd lost it and followed the Head Priestess toward the towering pillars of the greatest temple in the world.

"How do the mountains float?" Manisha asked. Her curiosity, ignited by the majesty around her, was outweighed only by grief.

"They're strung by stars and sit on pillars made of moonlight," said the Head Priestess.

"Who built these temples?"

"Why, the gods themselves. Here you must always be on your best behavior and heed the rules. The ancient ones roam freely, sometimes showing themselves to us if we're special. They live all around as invisible beings, always watching. You must never bring shame."

Manisha studied the intricately carved depictions on a pillar—magnificent peacocks and monstrous elephants, elegant snakes and mysterious turtles.

Images of winged people had been carved throughout the scenes. They floated along, grasping the stone cloth that ballooned above their heads, catching on an unseen wind.

"The vidyadhara," the Head Priestess explained. "The gods of the kingdom. The ones you will now serve with your whole heart and soul."

Manisha kept her mouth shut. She'd only ever heard about the vidyadhara as an ancient race of people who could fly—and who were later enslaved by the first king.

This temple, in all its beauty and finery, was a lie. Just like the kingdom was a lie. And the King a liar.

TWO

PRATYUSH
(NINE YEARS AGO)

All heroes and monsters have breaking points. This is mine.

"They say every sla—every man *like me* . . . has a breaking point," Papa whispered to Ma. They sat before a crackling fire, Papa poking the embers. Sparks flew up into the chimney, as bright as tiny suns, darkening as they cooled and floating back down as ash.

Ma rubbed his back and hugged him from the side, soothing him like she did her children. Ma was a great woman, full of compassion and empathy, resilience and great strength. And even though Pratyush was young, he knew he wanted to be that way, too.

He crouched on the stairs, hidden in the shadows, and listened. He had his father's blood, and with it inherited an unruly lineage and all its cursed blessings.

He didn't understand why his father called these gifts a stain on their humanity. Thanks to them, he could use one ear to listen to his older sister's breathing as she slept in her room at the top of the steps. With the other, he heard his parents' hushed conversation as clear as a calm day. Despite the distance between them. Despite the storm raging outside.

Pratyush's little fingers dug into the hem of his kurta as he leaned over, trying to make sense of what his father was saying.

"This is why we've remained hidden, is it not?" Ma asked, running her fingers through Papa's hair.

"Hah," he conceded.

"Is it not enough living in the borderlands? This far from the King, on the edge of civilization? Any farther and we'd be ... in *their* territory."

"We're too close as it is. The beasts haven't attacked because they don't know what I am. Nor do they suspect Pratyush. But one inkling, *one* suspicion of the truth, and our lives here are done for."

Ma sighed, her breath a heavy fog hitting the flames as she nestled deeper into the blanket around her shoulders. "When will you tell him?" she asked, her voice soft, sad.

Pratyush knitted his brows together. What did they mean? Tell him what?

Papa straightened his back and pushed out his chest. "It's time. He must know, prepare."

Ma clutched his arm. "But you said—"

"I know what I said. I thought we could hide, that all would be well. Perhaps that's still the case. But kismet has a way of finding you, of dragging people to their destinies. Fate has a fury when you try to deny it. It's better that he's prepared when the time comes. He's already eight and skilled in many things, but he's far behind on proper training. And that is my fault."

"I don't like this for him," Ma contested.

"We knew this could happen when we conceived. His blood is more precious than gold, his abilities more coveted than riches. Kingdoms are built on our backs. He must be strong, cunning. He *must* be prepared. Or the world will use him and leave him for dead."

Ma released another sigh and nodded, wiping her tears.

A thunderclap roared across the sky, shaking the house. Pratyush jumped, his little heart palpitating.

Even Ma startled. But not his father. Papa was never afraid or caught off guard.

"What about our little girl?" Ma asked solemnly.

"Pritika will have to be highly protected. This is why my kind avoid marriage. Every loved one can be used against us." He took her hand and kissed the back. "I apologize, my love. My words are harsh but true. I will never regret this life we've chosen together—or our children. I will do my best to protect you all."

"I know," she said. "But what I meant was . . . does she, too, carry the bloodline?"

"Possibly. I can't tell if she's a . . ." His voice drifted off, as if speaking that one last word was forbidden.

"What troubles you? Why are you suddenly so worried about being found out?" she asked.

He closed his eyes and breathed. "The voices are building in my head. I can't contain them. They get louder by the day, screaming, torturing. When I was in town a few weeks ago, men were chattering on about another . . . you know what. From a faraway place, under the King's thumb, being worked to the bone.

"The Famed One, they called him. They said he went mad from the voices, from seeing the beasts he'd slain come back in his sleep. The townsmen made it sound like a haunting. They said his most recent kill appeared to him as she had in life. A withered woman in white, with long black hair covering her face, her neck perpetually bent downward. Her bony hands kept reaching for him, but he was always able to move in time. After all, one cannot be killed by something that has already been slain.

"Yet he was found dead. The King seemed perplexed. He tried to keep it hidden, maybe because we're supposed to live a lifetime for every monster we slay, and the Famed One had killed plenty. People think we're immortal, and the King prefers this myth to continue. It wouldn't end well for anyone to know that we can be killed—perhaps not so easily, but still. . . .

"The townsfolk said the Famed One went mad without sleep, peeling off his flesh as he lay in bed, dying by his own hands, the only way he *could* die. Others said the monster he killed returned and slit his throat while he was unable to move."

Ma gasped, a hand to her mouth. "Do you think she escaped the Nightmare Realm, that the dead were able to come back for vengeance?"

He hushed her. "Do not speak about that god-awful hell. It's probably nothing more than lore."

She lowered her hand to touch his face. "But aren't *you* lore, my love?"

Papa kissed her palm. "Nonetheless, he's dead, and now the King will search harder for me to replace him."

Pratyush shuddered, imagining what it had been like for the Famed One, to be awake but unable to move—and even worse with a monster coming at him!

A noise caught his attention. It wasn't Pritika, who could obviously sleep through anything, but a faraway, muted disturbance. Something out of place in the thunderous storm, something with a different cadence than the pouring rain.

By the time Pratyush stood to check on Pritika, Papa was already at the window, pulling back the curtain and searching the darkness. Had he heard it, too?

"What is it?" Ma asked.

"Get the children into the cellar," Papa ordered, his stern, steady voice rippling across the frigid air.

Pratyush immediately rushed to his sister's room, where a candle cast dancing shadows in the small space. He stilled, dragging his gaze across the room, his heart beating harder.

He took one step after another, looking everywhere: up, down across the wooden planks and boards, past the dresser, and to the cot where Pritika yawned awake and squinted up at him.

He let out a breath. She was okay. Even though she was two years older than him, he tried to take care of her the way he'd seen his father take care of her. He wanted to be just like him—smart, kind, funny, and, above all, a protector of the family. Pratyush was hardly ever scared when his father was around, and he wanted to be brave like him.

Something muttered to his right. His head jerked toward the sound, as if someone had whispered something right into his ear. But there wasn't anyone else here.

He crept toward the window. Rain smashed so heavily against the glass that all he could see was serpentine rivulets of water.

A thunderclap hit like a roaring lion. Lightning struck, illuminating the entire world in startling shades of gray. A hand grabbed him.

Pratyush yelped.

"Shh," his mother said, placing a trembling finger to her lips, bending to meet him at eye level. Her gaze whipped to the cot as his sister sat up and rubbed her eyes.

"Come. Quickly." Ma reached out for her, wiggling her fingers.

Pritika didn't ask questions. She didn't hesitate. After all, they'd been trained for emergencies early on. She grabbed a coat and slipped it on as Ma rushed them out of the room.

Pratyush took Ma's hand, her flesh cold and shivering. "What's happening?" he asked, his voice timid.

"We must hide in the cellar, where it's safe. Quite a storm out there," she replied, smiling. But Pratyush made out the slight quiver in her lips and the unease of her stiff movements. He heard the pounding of her pulse at her temple, could see the beads of sweat pushing out of her pores, her skin turning warmer as blood rushed to the surface.

What was she so afraid of?

Ma released him so she could hold Pritika's hand in her left hand and took a lantern in her right, hurrying them down the steps. They quickly slipped into shoes and were almost at the door when something crashed through the front wall, an explosion of splintered wood and shattered stone.

Ma screamed, moving the children behind her with her hip. She shoved the lantern up, as if light would ward off the attack.

"Get them out of here!" Papa ordered, sliding to the edge of the debris.

In his hands, he wielded his legendary parashu—a behemoth battle-axe said to be gifted by the gods. The gleam of its blade cut through the darkness like an angry shard. Rain pounded the ground, blown in by wind and wetting the house in a gush of water. Every few seconds, lightning and thunder paired up in a discord of shrieking.

And in those deafening, chilling moments, when the entire house sparked to life in blazes of light, Pratyush saw it all.

His eyes went wide in disbelief, his body unyielding.

He'd heard the stories. Of monsters larger than buildings. With teeth as big as hands and as sharp as daggers. With toxic spit dripping like tar. Talons for hands and blades for nails. Taut muscles. And above all, the most dangerous thing—intelligence.

Papa said there were monsters, and that monsters were smart.

But even the wildest of stories hadn't prepared him for this. Now one of those fabled monsters stood a few feet from him. Growling at Papa as if he'd come all this way in a storm just for him.

In the blink of an eye, Papa grunted and lunged for the beast. Pratyush flinched, holding his breath, but then slowly opened his eyes.

His father hadn't died in one swift blow. His father . . . was fighting.

Like a famed master. Swiping and dodging and attacking and gliding. Kicking with powerful blows and striking with precision. Inky blood gushed from the monster, dousing the furniture and walls and splintered wood with sickening, viscous fluid.

The smell of rain and metallic blood floated in the air, surging through Pratyush's senses, and awakened a terrifying chill. Goose bumps skittered across his flesh, and the hairs on the back of his neck stood up as something more horrifying stepped into the room.

This beast was even bigger, its eyes crimson like the deepest-colored roses. It smashed down what remained of the wall. The entire house shook, and pieces of timber crumbled.

Ma yelped as she pushed the children out a side door clinging lifelessly to its hinges.

"What about Papa?" Pratyush asked, blood rushing through his veins like fire, heating his skin, telling him to turn back, to fight.

Rain slammed against them as soon as they were outside. In an instant, they were soaking wet.

"He knows what he's doing. We have to make sure you two are safe!" Ma cried above the howling wind and pounding rain. "Come!"

A loud thunder rocked the skies, masking the crash of a tree trunk swinging through the house and hitting the porch pillars. One pillar snapped into three, falling onto Ma. She stumbled from the force, dropping the lantern and pushing the children forward as her face smashed against the slippery porch.

"Ma!" Pratyush cried, skidding to a stop in front of her as Pritika held on to his shirt.

Ma clenched her jaw and squirmed while Pratyush, crying, tried to move the pillar. "No!" she said, wincing and clutching her bleeding leg. "It's gone through me. Don't move it. Don't waste your time! Take your sister and hide in the cellar!"

She offered herself like a sacrifice to cruel gods, struggling to get free but commanding them to run. Pratyush took Pritika's icy hand, tugging her away. He pushed water-laden hair from his forehead. He grabbed the lantern, fear clawing up his throat, deadening his legs. But he willed himself to move, to run, to make it to the cellar.

He didn't look back once, heaving and grunting and struggling and sloshing across a small field. He set the lantern beside the cellar as Pritika crouched and looked around. He gripped the handle of the cellar door and pulled. He tried and tried, tears streaming down his face, glancing at Pritika as she spat up water and clenched her eyes against the rain.

In the far distance, something new rumbled across the fields. Faint lights flickered in the storm. An army. Hope.

With his sister's help, Pratyush yanked the door with all his might. It finally opened! He urged Pritika down first, following her with quick steps. He grabbed blankets from a basket in the corner and wrapped her up as their father would have.

"Sit here," he said, moving her by her convulsing shoulders to sit in a chair. He brought over a sickle from the wall and placed it in her lap. Then he set the lantern nearby at her feet.

"Wh-where are you going?" she asked, her teeth chattering.

He kissed her forehead, muttering, "Everything will be all right. Stay here, okay?"

"But—"

Pratyush had already bounded up the cellar steps before Pritika could protest. All he could think about was how afraid his parents were that she would be found.

He slammed the door shut and ran toward the house just as the night sky lit up with fiery white lightning. He shielded his eyes, stumbling over rocks and slipping in mud when a bolt of lightning branched off and hit the house, setting it ablaze.

Pratyush screamed, frozen on the spot as flames came roaring to life. For a moment that felt like forever, his mind went blank. He . . . didn't know what to do, where to go, how to react.

The army would be here soon. They'd help. They had to!

His mother's screams cut through his thoughts. Without thinking, he ran for her, for the house, toward this heaving, fiery monster.

Heat incinerated pieces of his clothes, charred his shoes, but he didn't feel it.

Flames lapped at his skin, brighter than the sun, but he wasn't blinded by them.

Ma wasn't where he'd left her. She'd been dragged inside, a trail of blood in her wake.

Pratyush leapt into the fire, ducking into a pocket of air, and emerged in what was once the front room. The fire raged, greedily devouring the remnants of Pratyush's home and sucking out the air.

To his right, one of the monsters lay in a pool of inky blood, its head dismantled and guts oozing from its stomach. Papa was heaving beside it, on one knee, his flesh torn to the bones. He gripped his battle-axe, grimy with dark blood, and dragged it toward the other beast.

To his left, the bigger monster had Ma by the hair as she frantically fought.

Pratyush went for her at the same time his father lunged for the beast. But Papa had seen him, his eyes widening, and for a moment, he lost focus.

A moment was all a monster needed. It lashed out into Papa's already-open wounds. Its talons went straight for his throat.

In a few calculated strikes . . . his father collapsed.

"Run," Papa gurgled through bloody lips.

"Run," Ma uttered, her face pushed into the broken floorboards.

A boy as young as Pratyush should've run.

A boy with the blood of his father—roaring to life like a million sparks igniting in his bones—did not.

He went to his father, skidding on blood and water, and grabbed the parashu. The beast turned its back, stepping toward Ma, unthreatened by this small child.

Pratyush, filled with rage and confusion and loss and chaos, let out a cry as he ran for the monster. He hurled himself into the air, raising the battle-axe above his head and landing on the beast's horn-spiked back. A strength he never knew he had ached through him.

Consumed by his bloodlines, engulfed by the silent, haunting wails of his slain parents, Pratyush slammed the battle-axe into the beast. Using his foot for leverage, he yanked the battle-axe out and carved it into the beast's skull. Over and over. No matter how much his little body hurt. No matter how much the monster moved or tried to yank him from its back. No matter how much fire and rain and blood covered him.

He couldn't stop, not until the monster was slain.

But as the beast crumpled beneath him, an uncanny stream of whispers flooded into his thoughts, driving him backward. He slipped off, bruising his elbows on jagged pieces of broken wood. He clutched his head, clenched his eyes, and seethed, keeping in a scream that rippled through his chest.

Pratyush rolled onto his side, his mind filled with torment and hatred and worry. He felt the final thoughts of the monster inside him, felt the final skull-splitting blows as if his own head were being torn apart.

He fought a mental battle, shoving the monster's wails aside and into a trunk in the corner of his mind. As much as he wanted to lie there and cry, he couldn't. Not with the fire growing.

"Ma!" he grunted, crawling toward his mother. He grabbed her scarred hand, crusted with burned flesh, but his grip was slippery.

She didn't respond. She lay limp, motionless, even as Pratyush dragged her out of the house, fumbling with each step. He went back for Papa, pulling him out of the crumbling house, too.

With the heat of the fire singeing his back, Pratyush collapsed to his knees between his parents. They had been mutilated beyond recognition. The scourge of anger fled from him, leaving an overwhelming force of sadness as he dropped his head. He hugged his mother and lifted a hand to touch his father . . . and wept enough tears to last lifetimes.

"WHERE'S MY SISTER?" PRATYUSH NERVOUSLY ASKED THE soldier ahead of him.

"She's being taken care of. Don't worry about her. You're about to meet the King. Best get prepared for that instead," the soldier replied, adjusting the sheath of his dagger at his waist.

Pratyush wiped his nose with the back of his sleeve and looked up at the towering ceiling of the palace, laced with gold and jewels and decadent murals. The place smelled like incense and roses and nutty sweets.

The doors opened to a giant room where a tall, finely dressed man grinned down at Pratyush.

The soldier nudged him and commanded, "Bow before your king."

Pratyush bent at the waist.

"Have you enjoyed your food and bath and nice, new clothes, eh?" the King asked.

Pratyush nodded, rubbing the side of his leggings. His hands shook, his eyes flitting back and forth in this strange place with no signs of

Pritika. He didn't care about clothes and food. He just wanted to be with his sister.

The King studied him, his gaze lingering over Pratyush's face and hands. "They said you were in the fire that destroyed your house, that you were covered in burns. Today, you stand before me without a trace of affliction. There's no denying what you are. Come."

Pratyush and the soldier followed him into a courtyard where dozens of soldiers sparred and practiced, metal clanking against metal.

The King smiled and said, "Show me what you can do." He held out a hand and the soldiers on the field paused to witness him.

Pratyush fiddled with the hem of his beige-and-blue kurta, itchy and smelling nothing like his mother's soaps.

When he didn't respond, the King asked, "Are you mute?"

He shook his head.

"Then speak," he growled.

"I—I don't understand."

"Show me how you fight."

Pratyush glanced at trained soldiers, at full-grown men. "I don't know how to fight."

The King chuckled. "No? You've just slain a monster. You fight like . . . your father. Is that where he's been hiding all this time?"

"Wh-what?" he asked, confused.

The King scowled. "Don't you know what you are?"

Pratyush swallowed and shook his head. "A s-son to a—a farmer."

The King chuckled again and then glanced at the soldier beside Pratyush before his smile slipped. He looked down at Pratyush and said, his voice deep and even, "You, my dear boy, are the greatest gift to the kingdom after kings and queens. You are a slayer. And as far as I know, *the* slayer, last of your kind, and so you shall be called henceforth. That is your destiny, and you cannot escape it. It's the only thing you're meant for."

Pratyush clenched and unclenched his fists at his sides, shivering in the afternoon sun. The word *slayer* echoed in his thoughts. The stuff of legends and lore. Monster hunters and killers of beasts. Famed warriors.

The King tilted his head to the side and flashed a smile. "Do you know what happened?"

Pratyush shook his head.

"I saved you. My men will train you. After all, slaying is all you're good for, and we need to make sure you're capable. I shall raise you as my own. You owe your life to me, your unfailing loyalty. Don't you? As long as you listen to me, you and your sister will be taken care of."

Pratyush's trembling stilled as he gazed deep into the King's narrow brown eyes. The black centers expanded. Sweat trickled across his royal brow in tiny beads pushed up from his skin. The vein in his thick neck, just above the jewel-encrusted coat, pulsated, the gush of blood as loud as morning birds.

The King was lying.

THREE

MANISHA
(ONE YEAR AGO)

Manisha often struggled to fit in at the temple. There was so much competition instilled in the girls, and there were so many faults they found with her. Her fingers too thick to gently pluck strings or arrange delicate art, her voice too unsteady to sing properly, and her gait too purposeful to be considered elegant. Outright ridicule was prohibited, but stares and quieted snickers followed her like a shadow, along with Sita's constant disdain for her. There were times Manisha wanted to give up and cry, but she couldn't. She'd told her mother and sisters that she would be strong.

She was best equipped to work in the fields, but she had been declared a temple girl. Soon after, when the Head Priestess promoted her to apsara, she'd been just as surprised as anyone.

Still, no matter how the other girls adjusted their view of her—after all, apsara were respected and valued—she couldn't trust anyone. Not when they were constantly taught unquestioning obedience to this religion and unerring loyalty to the King.

Being careful made for a lonely existence. She'd never realized how intertwined she'd been with her family and her people. She'd been part of a whole, a beloved and important thread in an ever-greater tapestry. Meaning. Acceptance. Even when she was fleeing for her life, she'd been part of a team that she had literally killed for and would have died for.

The apsara insisted that theirs was a famed sisterhood of incredible proportions, but those were putrid lies. Or perhaps they simply didn't understand what a true sisterhood was.

While the other girls found refuge and friendships in one another and had taken to the temple lifestyle, Manisha found solace in books. Pretending that Papa read to her as she snuggled against his side on a cot had become a regular habit.

In the few spare minutes of her day, she could be found sequestered in a magnificent library of endless shelves, a rolling ladder, and more books than one could count. She'd never known the world could be so vast and history so deep. But there was never enough time to read, and taking books from the library was frowned upon. Despite attending classes all day, apsara education seemed shallow at times and left her hollow, aching for more knowledge.

Late one evening, Manisha walked alone in the dark. She'd been so mesmerized by an astronomy book that she hadn't realized how late it had gotten. Flames danced in large sconces to light the way to the main building; moonlight shone bright, like a white fire in the night sky.

Manisha walked past marble stairs and imposing pillars, toward the grand hall in the center of the temple. Taking a shortcut, she strolled through the grand hall. She knew it wasn't allowed, but these little rebellions were the only things keeping her soul alive when the apsara had all but smothered the spark inside her.

In the middle was the kingdom's famed altar. Set against a mosaic of swirling colors meant to represent the cosmos, the vast and infinite, speckles of shimmering diamonds signified stars against the pinks and blues of clustered galaxies. The eternal flames of a hundred diya, having burned since the beginning of the ancient ones' arrival, floated around the mosaic.

At its center was the shrine—a dark shadow where light couldn't enter, surrounded by pikes of crystal. Called the holiest of places, it had a magnetic pull, where droplets of night air hung suspended around the edges of the shadow, ambiguous in shape and matter.

Manisha wondered why the jagged tips of the spikes faced toward the dark shadow. Shouldn't the spikes have faced outward to prevent anyone from going into the shadowy door? Or were the spikes meant to prevent someone—or some*thing*—from emerging?

She walked carefully around the platform altar, checking over her shoulder to make sure she was alone, when the moonlight caught on something above. The walls, all marble, had been carved into intricately detailed scenes of the vidyadhara, stories about the cosmos, what looked like other worlds, myths, and so on.

The hall itself was taller than a palace, and she had to crane her neck all the way back to see to the top. The domed roof ended at a ledge above lines of orbs, with the walls of larger-than-life carvings below. Manisha had always assumed the orbs were a decoration, but something had been calling to her lately—something no one else on the floating mountains seemed to notice.

She pressed a hand against the carvings—also forbidden, but, well, just about everything seemed to be against the rules here. The wall was cold. Thanks to the sculptures, there were many nooks and grooves, perfect for climbing with her fingers and toes. So, she did. Feeling like her old self, the freedom of shucking off proper etiquette, reminded her of how her cousins would climb the outer walls of their city, resulting in many bruises, scrapes, and broken bones.

Manisha slipped, her breath aching in her chest as she grasped the hooves of a carved animal. She clung to the wall, afraid to move, to fall. Sithara had taught her how to climb. A neighborhood boy had tossed one of her toys onto a rooftop. She'd tried to fetch it—so her parents wouldn't know she'd lost it—and fell. The boy had laughed at her, and Sithara found out.

"Don't ever give up," Sithara had told her.

Manisha grunted and hoisted herself to the lines of orbs. She gripped the ledge above them and crawled onto the platform, huffing. She sat, her legs dangling over the edge, and gulped. She was so far up. A fall from here would break bones.

Reaching down, she touched an orb, only to realize it was the end of a scroll. She pulled it out and reverently unrolled the cloth, reading the ancient text in the full light of the moon.

Did anyone know the scrolls were here? How could they? The apsara didn't have ladders this tall. The domed roof prevented anyone from climbing down. And surely no one else here knew how to scale walls.

What was so important that the vidyadhara had hidden scrolls here?

Manisha spent a long while trying to understand the text. She'd been taught the language of the ancient ones, though she wasn't perfect at it. Drawings were helpful. Like this one of an island on the back of a gigantic sea turtle. Myth or reality? Was this what the world looked like beyond Yamuna—the Great River, emptying into a lake as large as a sea filled with monsters of the deep? Here and there were dark, flat doors connecting vast distances across the world, the galaxy, and even realms.

The only realm that came to mind was Patala—the Nightmare Realm. A strange bridge where nightmares were born, where the dead traveled along the Blood River for final judgment.

There was a picture of another flat door with obscure edges and no handle. The shadowy door looked very much like the one beneath Manisha's feet. She rolled up the scroll and replaced it, then proceeded to carefully, achingly, climb down.

Her curiosity got the best of her. Manisha approached the altar and did the forbidden, stretching over the ledge separating mere mortals from the holiest of holy places.

Water droplets touched her finger and trickled upward. She smiled, mesmerized.

Manisha... a familiar voice whispered into the room.

She gasped, pulling her hand back, and looked around the hall. Her heart spasmed. But she was alone. Everyone else was confined to their quarters for the night.

Manisha... the voice called again, haunting the room, echoing against the walls.

She gulped and slowly turned to face the altar. Had she invoked the gods? No, no—that couldn't be. These were false gods spun by cruel kings. Had she set off a trap of some kind with all the rules she'd broken tonight?

The voice came from the shadow and sounded so much like Eshani. Manisha stood immobile with fear, but her heart rose with hope as she lent an ear, desperate to hear her sister again.

She did the unthinkable and crossed the barrier, her bare feet stepping off the chilled marble floor and onto a strangely warm surface. The shadow door seemed to breathe, expanding and contracting. The crystal pikes glowed, the tips crackling. Welcoming her? Warning her?

As she neared, the magnetic pull began lifting her off the ground, and in her panic, Manisha scurried back, past the threshold, and ran all the way to her room. The darkness welcomed her, cradled her, as she curled up on her bed, clutching her fists to her ears. Instead of her sister's voice, she started to hear the voices of a thousand slain naga cursing her existence. Maybe that hadn't been Eshani calling after all, but the mourning dead of her people.

Why should you continue on when our lives have been taken? Even the serpent-wrapped pillars of her home had crumbled. Manisha might've been the only thing to survive.

"I don't know," she intoned to the fading accusations as she nearly broke down crying. But she couldn't. She wasn't allowed to.

Manisha eventually drifted off to sleep to face nightmares she could barely remember. When morning light eased into her room, she dragged herself out of bed and went to the balcony. Icicles had formed overnight on the golden roof edges of the temple buildings, glimmering like multifaceted gems.

She slid a finger over her bangle's four bands, remembering how happy her grandmother had been gifting her the bracelet—something passed from generation to generation. Mama had received a ring, Eshani a necklace, and Sithara an arm cuff.

Manisha thought of her gifting ceremony, the simple diya, prayers, and sweets. Her finger followed the curved center around an amber oval as she wondered how many more days until her sisters came for her. She tapped the bangle's center, once small and slightly raised, now the size of an almond. It was as if the egg-shaped gem had grown, counting the years. *Four years.* Four years she'd been here without a word from her family.

She thought back to the grave of ashes and the vision her ancestors had bestowed. They'd shown her a tiny serpent squirming inside the stone. Closing her eyes, she could almost feel a pulse. It was probably her imagination, or her own pulse, but Manisha liked to think the vision was true. Anything to link her to home, anything to gather these floating, torn memories and piece them together before they completely wilted.

Had her family forgotten about her? Was her fate to remain here forever, serving this foreign temple and these false gods for the barbaric King?

No. She couldn't think that, because then all hope would be lost.

"I miss you so much," she whispered into the chilling breeze.

But she couldn't allow herself to feel sad, because if she went down that road, she'd wonder if the rest of her family had died. And there was no coming back from that. Hope was all she had.

Manisha went about the day as usual, starting with a quick bath and dressing in her assigned jade-and-gold salwar kameez, meeting others in the main hall for morning worship before breakfast and classes.

In music, Manisha practiced the sitar, her fingers nimble against stiff strings after years of frustrating, bloody practice. It helped to imagine herself plucking arrows and pulling against a taut bow at the King's army instead of playing this thing. Or better yet, arrows aimed right at the King's head. Winter-steel to meet his winter hair.

These classes were as boring as wilting grain, but she did as Eshani would've done—pretend to be perfect and accomplished to stay alive, living just beyond anyone's scrutiny. If Manisha excelled, acting as if she wholeheartedly believed this foreign religion of winged gods and cosmic entities who spun golden threads of kismet and punished through karma, then she would climb the temple hierarchy. She would have some semblance of authority.

Eshani would've been proud, nudging Manisha with a shoulder and smiling with approval. And Sithara? Even as the cold cut of her jaw blurred from memory, Manisha knew the roughest of the three sisters would nod with admiration. Not at the blending in, but at Manisha's ability to maneuver through the court of priestesses and rise from a floor-scrubbing temple girl to a priestess worthy of command. She still had a long way to go—and, for now, plenty of classes.

"Dance like this," an instructor would say as she flicked her wrist.

"Always be poised, smiling, and well-mannered," another said, standing straight and pulling her shoulders back.

"Prepare sweets as if they are art," yet another would say as she sprinkled dried rose petals over concoctions drenched in cane syrup.

And the most tedious class of all? Learning how to flatter the men and boys who visited the temple. Giggling at their jokes. Fawning over their accomplishments, no matter how insignificant. Why were they so needy for constant validation from the very girls they refused to respect?

"Converse with men with gentle amiability, keeping your opinions to yourself," the teacher had said. "But don't speak with one too long. You might mislead him."

Manisha had rolled her eyes so hard, she thought they might actually get lodged in the back of her head. That might solve a problem— no man wanted to be in the presence of a temple girl who couldn't see him to tell him how handsome he was.

She continued playing in perfect harmony with the rest of the class, despite her mind being elsewhere.

"Very well done," the Head Priestess commented on Manisha's sitar playing.

"You could use more practice," Sita added in that maliciously sweet tone. "You wouldn't want to disgrace us."

Manisha bowed her head, wondering what she'd done to make Sita dislike her. Arya gave Manisha a reassuring nod. Some of the other girls smiled smugly. It was easy to see who sided with Sita. Manisha supposed that was court politics, to side with the one in power to gain their favor. Small gestures like these, passive comments, snide looks ... all seemed trivial in comparison to running for one's life in the Fire Wars. Yet, like water dripping on stone, it slowly, impercep-tibly eroded.

During Manisha's first days here, Sita had *accidentally* shoved her onto the pebble pathway in the gardens and blamed Manisha for stepping in her way. Manisha had licked the blood from her lip, her chest to the ground, and dug her hands into the dirt. It took a long time to learn how to balance outward submission with the inner strength of her naga heritage. But now? Manisha wondered if she wasn't just as hollow as the other girls, a vessel to be filled with unquestioning obedience or concealed animosity.

She feared how much of her heritage had slipped away. She was afraid of being scared and left behind like a burden, afraid of second-guessing herself after years of Sita constantly assigning her blame.

First, her voice had been silenced.

Then her skills had been suppressed.

Her personality stripped.

All Manisha had left were her thoughts, and she turned them harder than stone. Sita would *not* reach her mind, no matter what. But without another to confide in, her resolve teetered. She had to find a way out of here.

The Head Priestess turned from them, coughing into a handkerchief.

"Are you all right?" Manisha asked.

"Just a little ill, nothing to worry about . . ." the Head Priestess replied.

They moved to the next group as Arya excitedly grasped Manisha's arm and dreamily said, "A compliment from the Head Priestess! She favors you, you know. Imagine if she selected you to move up to daivika one day."

That *was* the plan. A girl didn't keep herself trapped in a floating prison, waiting on others, without a backup. She couldn't sit around feeling sorry for herself; she had to be strong for when she met her sisters again.

It had seemed like a straight shot to ask to train as a rider. Instead, the Head Priestess had assigned her to the temple because she was considered beautiful. Never before had Manisha hated her own beauty, and she'd even been tempted to slash her face if it meant becoming a rider. But she didn't have access to anything sharp for a long time, and by the time she did, her assignment had been finalized.

She'd been given the title of laukika—the worldly apsara, the thirty-four priestesses of the lower ranks who upheld the temple. The daivika, the heavenly apsara of ten, were the court of commanding priestesses who could do whatever they wanted, including flying to the ground. They controlled the floating mountains, thus the most powerful place in the kingdom. Maybe what her mother had wanted was not for Manisha to simply hide here, but to take it over?

It was a lot to expect from a young girl who had no power— impossible, even. At least it gave Manisha something to focus on until she was free. Because if she could gain control, she could leave whenever she wanted and even bring her family here, to safety. They could be together again. She could protect them. And these flying peacocks used solely for transport? Didn't anyone know that they could be used to conquer? They could douse the King and his palace in a rain of fire, the way he'd done to her family and home.

But how does a runaway girl overthrow a powerful man? She hadn't figured that part out yet.

After class, Manisha went to the grand hall to prepare for guests, casting a glance over her shoulder at the shrine, but Eshani's voice didn't return. Above, the light no longer caught on the orbs, as if they'd disappeared. Maybe that night had been a feverish dream.

Disappointed, she set up the sweets table. Flattening out a pale pink silk covering, she arranged banana leaf plates for servings of sweet coconut rice wrapped in lotus leaves, steamed to perfection. Visitors enjoyed decadent food, much like a wedding or large festivity for the naga. The only thing missing was jalebi. Manisha smiled. The sweet, gooey orange treat had been a favorite among the kids growing up and never lasted long enough.

When guests arrived, Sita shooed Manisha and Arya behind the lattice walls, into a secret hallway between the grand hall and the wall facing the kitchens and residences. Manisha frowned but didn't argue. After all this time, she still couldn't interact with guests. It didn't matter. She didn't like socializing anyway.

She covered her head with her jade-tinted dupatta, slipping into the cool recesses. The latticework inner wall allowed the girls to view the grand hall while remaining hidden from guests.

"Who do you think is here that's so important?" Arya asked, nearly poking her nose through a swirl-shaped hole in the marble wall. Billowing light from the hall cut through the carvings, covering her in an illuminating pattern of light and shadow.

"Why do you ask that?" Manisha countered, peering through the carved holes.

"Sita only hides you away when there's someone important, or had you not noticed?"

Manisha shrugged. "It's not as if they're royalty, right? Why doesn't the King ever visit?"

"He was here last year, but his visits are very guarded. No one knew until he left. I heard he dresses like any regular noble. He's so humble and wishes for us to treat him as any other."

Or was it so no one like Manisha could make a move? Although what would she have done? Asked about her frayed people? Gained his favor to get back to the ground and attack later? No. One look at his face and all she'd see would be the contorted, bloody faces of her slain kin. She'd probably go mad with anger and try to slit his throat, but she knew she wasn't fast enough.

The giggles of younger girls in the hidden hallway reverberated off the walls, their bare footfalls padding away as Arya shushed them. At least someone was having fun. Sita never bothered to use the darkened walkways, so this was probably the only place where the girls could play without being scolded. Manisha was tempted to join them, to run again, to laugh, and to let go of the shackles of proper etiquette.

A hush fell over the girls, drawing Manisha's attention back to the hall.

Three guests entered the main room like giants, faces hardened, postures rigid, and bodies sculpted by brutal battles.

An apsara welcomed them, lifting her hand toward the center for worship.

Manisha picked up on two pairs of soft, bare footfalls trekking across cold floors, and one pair of footsteps so muted, they were nearly imperceptible.

The apsara led the trio to offer prayers at the innermost shrine, the shadowy door inside the crystal pikes.

The apsara told them, "It is said that the ancient ones were born during the creation of the Akash Ganga. From the great sky river came both devas, the wise ones, and asuras, the monsters which you slay. The ancient ones came to us from the glimmer of faraway stars to battle the asuras who had escaped the faraway darkness. I suppose you must have a connection with them, since you battle on our behalf."

Two men nodded with an acquiescent hum, but the third was silent.

They knelt on red-and-gold pillows in front of the central altar. The light cast from the diya sprayed against the contours of their faces, sharpening the angles of their jaws like a fine blade. The quiet one, the tallest of the three, was just a boy.

Many boys had visited over the years, typically sons of noblemen and diplomats, even royalty—cousins of princes, mostly. They escorted their families. This one, however, arrived with commanding officers dressed in formal uniforms. Maybe he was the son of a famed commander?

Manisha was so focused on the guests that she startled when a strange magnetic pull drew her attention to the boy. A sense of curiosity. She wasn't sure how to feel about it. Flustered? Annoyed? Guarded? All three?

Arya clutched Manisha's wrist and pulled her away, whispering, "Don't get distracted by boys."

"I—I would never," she muttered. "Who is he?"

Whispers and excited conversations bubbled around them as all the girls glued themselves to the carved gaps to watch.

"They call him Pratyush. He's a famous warrior."

Manisha scrunched her brows, confused. "But he's just a boy."

Arya shrugged. "All warriors start out as boys. This one must be strong. The men he's with look like commanders, so he must be important."

Manisha intended to look away but couldn't seem to move.

The boy was handsome. Broad-shouldered with long black hair, the top half of which was tied back. So young and yet so commanding. Everyone flocked around him as if he were the most important person in the hall. The men he was with, the apsara at his beckoning, even Sita and the Head Priestess had come to greet him. More than that? He was allowed to light the prayer diya, an act reserved for the highest-ranking men and the apsara.

Instead of leaving the delicate holder on the altar as most would, he picked it up and . . . broke it. The fragile clay shattered in his hands.

A look of shock crossed his face . . . and just about everyone else's. The girls behind the wall gasped, their eyes bulging as the centuries-old antique crumbled in his palms.

Had any of the girls broken something so precious, Sita would've exiled them, kicking them off the floating mountains with nothing more than the clothes on their backs.

What would she do to this famed warrior boy?

Sita's face flared red, her lips pressing into a tight line. She fell to her knees to collect the destroyed remains from the floor.

Manisha cracked. A bubble of laughter tore through her. She immediately covered her mouth.

Arya shot her an incredulous glare, as if she'd been personally offended. Manisha cleared her throat. Only to end up cackling. She hadn't laughed since she'd arrived at the temple. She, in fact, didn't think laughter was even permitted by Sita.

Sita's look of horror and utter disbelief, tangled with the inability to do a single thing, was a moment to behold. But add a commanding warrior gaping at his mess like any other awkward boy... well, Manisha couldn't help it.

She was now covering her mouth with both hands, cackling up a muffled storm.

Her laughter must've escaped because Sita glared daggers of wrath at the lattice wall. All the girls took three careful steps away from Manisha.

The boy, whose face had been flustered, went from embarrassed to indifferent as he, too, looked at the lattice wall splattered with Manisha's laughter.

Sita, the Head Priestess, and the host apsara had gathered every last speck of the broken diya holder, reverently holding the pieces in their hands. The commanders shook their heads, rattled. Yet all they did was give the boy a pat on the back as if saying, *This is why we can't have nice things.*

"We should get to the kitchens to help with supper," Arya whispered, ushering the younger girls out of the walkway before they suffered Sita's wrath.

Manisha knew she should go, too, but she was rooted in place, unable to remove her stare from the boy. He kept glancing at the lattice wall. There was no way he could possibly see her, not with how the marble carvings had been designed to conceal persons in the recesses. But his intense focus made her question if he could.

She walked to the end of the hallway. Yet, when the boy looked up, his gaze immediately found her. She walked back, toward the entrance. Again, he found her. How was this possible?

When the prayers ended, the warrior boy meandered toward the sweets. A table and a wall were the only things separating them. He picked up a diamond-shaped kaju katli, made from the pistachios growing in the courtyard and dusted with edible silver.

He popped the entire sweet into his mouth and glanced over his shoulder. Then he dragged his gaze across the lattice wall until his eyes landed on Manisha. She stilled in the shadows.

He had the strangest-colored eyes, lavender and poetic. Such a stark contrast against dark brown skin and the harshness of warrior-worn clothes.

"It's not nice to laugh at someone, you know?" he said, his voice scratchy. He couldn't be older than sixteen.

How could he pinpoint her so easily?

"I know you're there," he added, the corner of his lips tipping upward. Suddenly, he seemed less like a grumpy warrior and more like a regular boy. "I smell your rose oil hair perfume and hear the crunch of a leaf under your foot."

She scowled, not having felt anything beneath her steps. But when she gingerly lifted her left foot, there it was ... a leaf.

How ... ?

"Someone's coming ... but I hope to see your face before I leave. You know, the girl who dared to laugh when I'm pretty sure Sita was about to beat me with a broom," he said with a grin and walked away.

Manisha's hand jerked to her mouth, trapping a giggle, because wouldn't that have been something to witness? Sita losing her composure over this boy!

In the next seconds, Arya returned and tugged Manisha away. "We're going to be late for supper duty."

"I'm coming."

In the kitchen, Manisha peeled potatoes and sliced vegetables with astonishing speed when she thought no one was looking. It was the only time she was allowed a knife. She tended to broths and oversaw lotus-leaf-wrapped dishes of rice and herbs, tossing items into pots from afar. How else could she train her precision?

Dinner came and went. Finally. A long day in the kitchens ended with scrubbing counters and floors until they sparkled like new. She ate leftovers before heading to her room. Outside, the bustle of the farewell ceremony had ignited to send the warrior boy and commanders on their way.

The sun eased lower, dipping beneath the clouds, casting magnificent rays of pink and purple across the sky. As Manisha walked, she pulled a crimson rose from one of many shrubs lining the walkway around the temple. She was so caught up reminiscing about how much Papa loved flowers that she nearly bumped into someone.

The boy who'd broken the antique diya holder was standing just inches from her. She stared into his unusual amethyst eyes, like thin lavender petals held up to the sun. Such an intense gaze from someone this young unnerved her so much that she had to blink a few times to make sure all the pieces aligned.

He was so strange to look at. A boy, probably around her age, but with the soul and severity of someone who'd gone through too much already. Manisha knew it well, that fatigue.

Fading light swept across a handsome face, even as she reminded herself she wasn't supposed to think so.

He was much taller than her. She raised her chin to look at him, although she was supposed to look at her feet. A warm, thick kurta covered his wide shoulders, the deep green reminiscent of the jungles below.

He cleared his throat and said, "Hello." But his voice came out raspy.

She tried not to giggle. As formidable as he looked, he sounded like any other boy.

"This way," the host apsara said from behind him.

He ignored her, his gaze never breaking from Manisha's as the sun set, flashing a final ray of light into her eyes. She squinted. Soon, the full strength of the stars and moon would light the world.

And just like the stars and moon and sun seemed to flow as one, each calling the other, the magnetic pull between Manisha and the warrior boy intensified. She didn't want to leave. Was this what the older girls back home spoke of? She'd often snuck into their gatherings and listened to them talk about boys, of new feelings and first love and strange attractions.

"The girl who dared to laugh?" he asked. But how could he have known? Even if he'd seen slivers of her through the lattice wall, they weren't enough to piece together an entire face.

"Your ride awaits," the apsara said, pointedly looking at Manisha from behind the boy as if this interaction was entirely her fault.

He turned to address his host, and Manisha took the chance to slip away, down the hall and through a door.

Her back hit the wall and she pressed the rose against her stomach. She didn't have time for nonsense feelings. While she enjoyed private quarters and plentiful food, her family was probably dirty and cold and hungry. They hadn't sacrificed themselves so that she could forget them, wrapped up in the attention of some boy.

She pushed off the wall and focused on more important things—like ascending to daivika. Besides, their paths couldn't possibly keep crossing.

Except... they did.

THE WARRIOR BOY RETURNED MANY TIMES OVER THE FOL-lowing months, more times than anyone else. And people noticed. Still, he'd become a highlight of a mundane life trapped on the floating mountains.

"He must be really religious," Arya said during his latest visit.

"Why do you think that?" Manisha asked, arranging blossoms in a vase as they watched their guests from afar, slipping in a technique she'd seen Papa use that added a burst of indulgent fuchsia because he loved color.

Arya shrugged. "Maybe he's seeking forgiveness for his violent ways in battle. Why else would someone visit the temple so often?"

Manisha swallowed. Yes, why else?

When she finished the arrangement, another apsara gracefully floated to the table, snatched the colorful flower from the vase, looked Manisha dead in the eye, and crushed it in her fist. "This isn't the right way," she said with the soft voice all the girls had been trained to speak in, no matter the emotion behind it.

Manisha's mouth hung open as the apsara walked away. Arya touched Manisha's arm and solemnly beckoned her to move on. The girls silently parted ways for their duties. Arya went to organize new clothes arriving from merchants. Manisha moved to an adjacent room, her heart heavy as if the apsara had crushed her father's memory.

With a pang in her chest, she helped an older apsara give a history lesson to a handful of children. Manisha put on her best practiced sweet voice and a painfully trained smile as she spoke. The children held on to her every word, even as her gaze wandered to the warrior boy sitting near the back, his gaze studious, curious. She began to wonder if he came here so often because he knew she was a serpent among hens. Was he planning on dragging her off to the King?

A young one raised a hand and asked, "Do you think the ancient ones could fly because they got used to living in the clouds? And if we lived here, we could fly, too?"

"Hah," another agreed without raising their hand. "Like how people become mermaids when they live in the water. One time, I saw one."

"Well, no, that's not actually how that works," the apsara explained as the children went into an argument about how it was the truth and all they had to do was jump off the edge to find out.

Manisha's heart stopped mid-beat imagining children leaping to their death because they wanted to fly. But then the warrior boy sighed, his shoulders deflating as he crossed his eyes and dramatically threw his head back. The man beside him scowled.

Manisha tamped down a smile.

The boy shook his head at the man and mumbled loud enough for her to hear, "Then don't raise stupid progeny."

Manisha's face turned hot as she tried her best not to guffaw and ended up coughing instead. Everyone was too focused on the escalating discussion among the children and their wild gesticulations to notice. Of course the warrior boy was watching her and shrugged as if to say, *You can't reason with children.*

With every visit, he edged closer and closer, and she minded less and less. He'd become her fleeting joy when her determination began cracking.

Once, in passing in the courtyard, all he said was "Hello."

She smiled and gave a bow of the head, jerking her chin toward Sita, who watched closely from the benches beneath a cluster of pistachio trees.

"Ah," he whispered. "Wouldn't want her to beat me with a broom. She still hasn't forgiven me for breaking the diya holder."

Another time, months later, he approached the sweets table when she was still setting up and asked, "What's your name?"

"You shouldn't ask," she muttered, checking over her shoulder in case Sita was nearby. She wasn't.

"Can I give you a compliment?"

She hurried through the rest of the setup, expecting him to comment on her appearance. What else could he possibly have to say?

"You speak well," he said instead, taking her by surprise.

"What?" she asked, finally looking into those strange eyes.

"During classes, you speak better than diplomats."

"Even when you think the children are stupid?"

He smirked. "Even more so."

Fortunately, his host interrupted to lead him back to worship, shooting a warning look at Manisha. Unfortunately, Manisha found herself noting the fluctuations in his changing voice and how, every time he visited, he seemed to grow a little taller, a little broader, and a little handsomer.

She watched them leave. He half glanced over his shoulder at her and she tilted her head. Curiosity sprouted, like seedlings pushing up through unobstructed meadows.

Arya approached and whispered, "The Head Priestess grows sicker, and everyone awaits her departure from this life soon."

Manisha knew. An apsara's passing meant a rearranging of the ranks. Anything was possible.

Her stomach turned queasy. This one woman was the only reason she'd been allowed onto the floating mountains, the reason she'd become an apsara instead of a temple girl ready to be sold, and the reason Sita hadn't done worse to her.

What would become of her now?

FOUR

MANISHA
(FIVE MONTHS AGO)

Apsara were known to be celestial dancers, the best in the realm. Rigorous practice allowed Manisha to work on balance. She imagined she could twirl on one leg, blindfolded, and shoot arrows.

Tonight's performance was like any other, except the slayer had been there. She kept thinking about how he had immediately turned his gaze to her, even though she'd been sent to dance in the very back. How she suddenly felt more awake. Even now, alone in her room, she found herself smiling at her reflection in the mirror, her stomach roiling in delightful waves.

Thunder rattled the sky. A storm was brewing. She inhaled the smell of approaching rain. For a moment, she was thrown back to the jungles below; her entire body and mind flooded with overwhelming longing. For a second, it was like she was home, happy and safe, and not here. Her soul ached with yearning, but she chased the sadness away before it overtook her—before anyone noticed.

Howling winds agitated the mayura. They refused to fly, much less return the guests to the ground below. They were stuck until the winds calmed.

She stared into the dimness of her room, the only light filtering in from the balcony in flashes of lightning. The wind pushed back the thin curtains as they flapped wildly. Sitting on the bed, she unwove her braid, letting silky hair fall down her back.

The storm intensified, and her shoulders relaxed. Something about the chaos reminded Manisha of being with family. Their lives had been tumultuous, but they'd been together. Here, the quiet was overwhelming. In her room, her posture withered with no one to scold her. Her walls came down with no one to pry. She felt like she'd been holding her breath all day and only now could breathe freely.

Pulling her bangle from a pocket sewn into her top, she slipped it on, shut her eyes, and imagined she was in the noisy city of Anand deep in the canyonlands. *Home.*

She laughed to herself. Her mother's voice a lingering whisper as she declared green vines signaled the best time to pick vegetables. Her aunts arguing to the ends of the world about following the harvest moon for better crops. Eshani going on and on about game strategy and Sithara never sitting still. Lekha lazily swatting at low-hanging vines and blankets drying on garden lines.

Manisha opened her eyes and blinked away tears. The oval stone beneath her finger was pulsating. It had softened over the past months. In the light of the candles, something was taking shape inside the stone, writhing in coils like the tiny snake from her vision.

Wouldn't that be wonderful?

She slid a finger over the bulging surface. The shape jerked beneath her touch.

"That's a nice bracelet," a slightly gritty voice spoke from the balcony.

Gasping, Manisha swiped beneath her pillow to grab her knife.

She tucked it into the waist of her skirt, jumped from the bed, and marched toward the curtains. There, a figure was sitting on the railing, facing her open room, his hands clutching the banister beneath him.

The warrior boy! He could've given her a heart attack!

Manisha shoved aside the curtains, annoyed with how they tangled themselves around her wrist in the increasing winds.

"What are you doing here?" she demanded, looking below to make sure no one could see him. Her heart was hammering in her chest. Why was he here? How would she be punished if anyone found out?

"I didn't get a chance to talk to you today. You danced well," he said, as if this was some casual conversation in a normal place.

"You're going to get yourself removed from the floating mountains. Is that what you want?" she hissed.

"What do *you* want?" he asked instead.

Even sitting on the pink granite railing, he loomed over her. A massive boy of great strength. So wide that he was twice her breadth. She couldn't believe how much he'd grown. Taller, a bit more muscular, his voice no longer raspy but deeper, smoother, more resonant.

She caught herself reaching toward him, her hand inches from his chest.

He chuckled. "I have that effect."

She scowled. "Forget touching, you're not even allowed to *be* here."

"But there's no rule saying that *you* can't touch *me*, is there?" His chest rose and fell. He cleared his throat as if he hadn't meant to be so bold.

Manisha's breath hitched as she looked up into his shadowed face. They'd never been alone together before. She could barely make him out, but his presence, his voice, his silhouette—it was undeniably him. "You know what I want to do? What I'm tempted beyond my control to do?"

"What's that?"

"To press my palms against your chest . . . and shove you off my balcony. You stupid boy! You're not supposed to be here!" She froze, realizing how un-apsara-like she was being, and braced for his scolding.

A scolding that did not come.

He chuckled again, but this wasn't amusing! "Other priestesses fawn over me, but you're ready to harm me? I thought violence was forbidden here."

"So is this." She gestured between them as if she couldn't be any clearer. Never had anyone triggered so many opposing emotions. Irritation and humor. Disbelief and familiarity. Things that shouldn't go together jumbled into one massive sense of comfort around him.

"Tell me who you are."

She scoffed, even as the storm's icy breeze cut her cheek. "Don't you know from all the times you've heard me speak?"

He lowered his chin and said, "I mean, where did you come from?"

"That's not important." She looked to the ground below. They were three stories high with no ladder in sight. In the distance, the mayura squawked. "How did you get up here?"

"I scaled the wall."

"That's impossible; these walls are smooth." She glanced up, but there were no ropes leading down from the roof, either.

"You don't know who I am, do you?" he asked, his face near hers. Suddenly, his scent of spices and rose oils was overwhelming.

"I—I don't care who you are, boy who visits too often and keeps trying to make conversation with me." She pushed out the words, hoping they sounded dismissive instead of nervous.

He studied her. "I always thought there was something different about you. You don't belong here, do you?"

"I'm not going to answer your absurd questions."

The breeze died, and the curtains calmed. The storm was fading into the distance. He scratched the back of his head. "They'll look for me soon."

She shrugged. "You'd better get going, then."

He pushed off the railing and stood at full height. An impressive figure and an entire head taller than Manisha. "You don't seem nervous to have me in your private presence."

"Why? Do most girls faint?"

"Well, yeah."

"I suggest you return to those who flounder at the sight of you if you expect a girl to swoon."

He laughed. "Wit and sarcasm and nothing like I'd expect from a temple princess."

"Priestess," she corrected.

"You don't seem intimidated at all."

"I've dealt with worse." Like man-eating creatures and centipedes that could shrivel her bones with one bite.

"You have the most beautiful eyes I've ever seen." He lifted a hand to touch her face but paused.

Manisha didn't step back.

"What would you do if I touched you?" he asked softly, almost shyly.

She bluffed, "Have you removed and never allowed to return."

Muffled voices called out below, searching for the warrior boy.

Manisha didn't know if it was the way he welcomed her quips, or how he made her feel strangely comfortable, but something pushed her to test her boundaries. "And maybe a mayura will burp flames up your backside as you walk away in your humiliation."

She steadily met his eyes, thinking his impassiveness would crack into anger. In her experience, men who visited the temple didn't like being talked back to. She steeled herself for his words, even for his hands. Then he would be annoyed with her and never try this again.

It took a few seconds, but his impassiveness did crack. Into *amusement*. He wagged a finger and laughed. "You *are* different. I knew I smelled it on you. Maybe we can see more of each other next time."

"I doubt it."

He straddled the railing—did he not fear falling off?—and said, "By the way. It's rude, you know? To keep watching me every time I visit."

She trapped a gasp, her cheeks burning. "Do you want me to push you on your way?"

He grinned. A slice of moonlight cut across his face, revealing dimples and white teeth, a few with sharp, glinting points. "But touching is forbidden," he teased.

He jumped, quietly landing on the ground with ease. By the time Manisha reached the banister, he'd disappeared. By the sound of distant voices and impatient cawing, he'd met the others to fly back to the world below.

She heaved out a breath, annoyed yet exhilarated.

Stupid boy.

A WEEK LATER, THE APSARA GATHERED DRESSED IN FUNERAL white. Onstage, Sita clasped her hands at her waist and solemnly announced, "Our dear Head Priestess has passed away. It is with both sadness and joy that I take her role as your new Head Priestess, as were her wishes. After much thought and discussion with our late Head Priestess in the past months, I'm honored to announce our new second-in-command, who will one day take my place. Sethal. Please approach."

Soft applause welcomed her.

Sita went on, "Additionally, because the passing of our late Head Priestess leaves an opening among the ranks, I shall also announce a new daivika—a divine apsara—to complete our group of ten. Our late Head Priestess had many discussions with me about whom she'd like chosen, and it's my privilege to carry out her wisest selection."

Manisha had been shaking but stilled with bated breath, looking up at Sita from her position on a pillow. But hope slowly dissolved into disappointment.

Sita had taken absolute control. It didn't matter what the Head Priestess had wanted or said, because in this moment Sita lifted her hand to someone else.

Manisha's heart plummeted into her stomach as she watched her plan unravel. It had been a desperate plan, but now there was nothing to hold on to.

What had she been thinking? She was so stupid. Sita would never assign her to a higher position. Sita had never liked her, and never would.

Her thoughts raced through new routes, other strategies, but there was really only one thing she could do. She had to leave against the rules if she wanted to search for her family, risking every punishment if it meant freedom. She had to think quickly, before every thread of fading hope slipped from her grasp.

She waited a few days' time for the mourning phase to pass and approached one of the riders who prepared to take flight, running a hand down the side of a mayura. If one thought regular peacocks were easily agitated, these giants were a dozen times worse.

"Funny how they aren't easily annoyed by you," the rider said.

Manisha smiled and said, "I wanted to be a rider when I first arrived here. How long did you train to be one?"

"Many harrowing years. They're very deadly, you know. One second in their flame, and you're dead. One fall from their backs, and you're as good as dead."

"Why aren't the rest of us allowed to ride? Once in a while, even?" Manisha tried to sound casual.

The rider said, "Like I mentioned, it's very dangerous. The Head Priestess wouldn't risk it. And I agree."

Manisha didn't respond. She *had* asked about flying several times over the years. No rider even hinted at breaking the rules for her. It wasn't as if she could just steal a bird and take off. They didn't let just anyone ride them, not that she had any idea how to do so. Maybe she could negotiate. What would a rider need, though?

"I should get going," the rider said, glancing at the sky around them. "Another storm approaches, and we have guests waiting."

"Who is it this time?"

"Soldiers and a warrior, I'm told."

By *warrior*, she meant the warrior boy. Why wasn't that surprising?

Manisha and the warrior boy went through the same routine, a familiar dance. He listened to her speak on history to a small group as thunderclaps rattled the sky. He indulged in sweets and supper, his gaze always finding her. And when evening descended, knowing that the mayura wouldn't fly in this weather, Manisha sat on the edge of her bed, facing the swaying balcony curtains, and waited.

A shadow appeared but hesitated. Manisha heaved out a sigh and went to the balcony, drawing back the curtains and setting her sights on the broad frame of this grinning boy.

"Were you expecting me?" he asked.

She crossed her arms and leaned against the doorframe, keeping her distance. "You'll get kicked out, you know."

"They won't kick me out."

"You're a bit cocky, aren't you?"

"Very. You know, I've requested you as my host several times now, to the point where it's embarrassing," he admitted. "Sita finds an excuse to deny me the privilege every time."

Instead of acknowledging the flutter in her chest or wondering what Sita made of his insistence (and if she would punish her for it),

Manisha said, "You ask me the same questions every time. So allow me to speed up the process. I won't tell you my name, although if you've requested me, I'm sure you already know."

He grinned at that.

"I won't tell you anything about myself, although you say you can *smell* it on me. Where do we go from here?" She tapped her chin, feigning intense thought. "Oh yes. Here's the part in our dance where I'm inclined to shove you off the balcony, and you make some joke about me touching you."

His smile slipped. No witty comeback. No flirtatious circumvention. That was fine; she wasn't in the mood anyway. The heaviness of despair hadn't lifted from her chest. She wanted him to notice, to ask how she was, but he didn't. Manisha couldn't understand why that made her even sadder. She didn't expect anyone, much less a boy, to ask if she was okay.

He should hurry and get on his way before someone saw him. Who would protect her from Sita's anger now?

The warrior boy said, "Let's play a game."

"No," she replied weakly.

"I'll tell you something about my past, and you tell me something about yours."

Before she could decline, he went on. "I hate storms. Much less being in the middle of one in the sky. How do you live like this?"

She shrugged. "I enjoy storms. They're calming."

"They're chaos," he countered. "It was a stormy night the last time I saw my parents. The King's army had swarmed across our ranch hunting monsters."

Manisha froze.

He scratched the back of his neck and let his hand hang there. "It was the first monster I'd ever seen. A behemoth of extraordinary height and teeth. I was only eight, so maybe everything looked bigger.

There were two, which doubled the danger. Lightning struck our house and set it on fire while the monsters attacked."

Her heart sank into the pit of her stomach. She could guess how his story ended.

"My mother died trying to save me and my sister."

Manisha's heart tightened in her chest. "Oh . . . I'm so sorry."

He gave a weak smile. "My parents had always taught me to stand up for the oppressed, to avenge the fallen. My father died while battling the monsters. You think I lead with violence, but violence found me that day. I picked up his battle-axe and killed the beast."

"At . . . at eight years old?"

He nodded.

"And you've been killing ever since?" she asked, beginning to piece together this boy she'd refused to know more of.

He tilted his chin up, his head cocked to the side. "Slaying monsters like it's my job . . ."

Intrigued by his story, she asked, "What—what happened after that?"

"The King took me in, trained me with an elite army. I'm indebted to him. He promised my sister to a nobleman's son in a peace treaty, which elevated her status. The King said she would get married and live an easy life with everything a person could want. She was still young, though—too young to get married to someone years older than her. I hated this for her." He paused with a sad laugh. "She was kind and smart and better than me at everything. Even with daggers. I wanted her to be happy."

His eyes flashed, and his jaw hardened. "I hated myself for not being able to help her. If only I'd known how the King turned her into a shadow of herself."

Manisha listened quietly. She knew all too well how the King could warp people.

"I was *supposed* to help her. We were supposed to be there for each other; we didn't have anyone else. But I couldn't stop the engagement," he added with a wretchedness that made Manisha hurt for him.

He went on, "We were being watched, and our time together was limited more and more until I could barely see her. I told the King she didn't want the marriage. It made no difference. The King said this was how things were done, that girls married early and unions were arranged by higher authorities, and we should accept it as a blessing from him."

He stared into the distance as if the memories were getting the better of him. Manisha didn't push.

"Her betrothed treated her badly. Every time I stepped in, he took it out on her. The King then kept me from intervening. He said I was causing discord among the noblemen and teaching my sister to be disobedient."

She wanted to tell him never to believe such things when they came from the King but bit back the words.

"Also, I was ready to pummel her worthless betrothed's face into oblivion."

His fists tightened at his sides, but he eventually relaxed them. Manisha had the overwhelming urge to take his hands in hers. Of course, she didn't dare move.

"In the end, I guess I couldn't do much since I was always being sent away to fight one thing or another. I had no way to keep her safe even though I wanted to, no place of my own for her to stay, and I feel like I did wrong by her and let my parents down. She was the only family I had left."

"What happened to her?" Manisha asked quietly, bracing for an ugly answer.

"The King told me she got sick when I was away, and they'd already sent her off on a funeral pyre. I never got to say goodbye." He swallowed hard on those last words.

Manisha sucked in a deep breath. Her eyes misted, remembering her lost loved ones, too many to count, too many to bear. Maybe they weren't so different after all. They each had enough sorrows to fill the sky. "Life's unfair, isn't it?"

"Life is cruel," he corrected.

"Why are you telling me all this?" she asked quietly, wondering if he was trying to lower her guard.

He shrugged and looked away; his cheeks flushed. "I've kept that to myself for a long time, and I . . . Well, you don't make me feel like I have to be impervious and strong all the time. You make me feel . . . like a normal person."

Oh. She didn't know how to respond to that or what to make of it. People expected him to be perfect and unaffected, the same way they expected her to be submissive and delicate.

"Who are you, really?" Manisha finally asked, curiosity digging deep as the pieces of this warrior boy started to align.

"Do you really not know?"

She shook her head, even as key words fit together in her thoughts, things she'd forced herself to ignore to keep from knowing him.

He pushed off the balcony and took one long stride to stand over her. He looked down into her eyes and replied in that signature gritty tone, his voice rumbling like thunder, "I'm the slayer, last of my kind."

Manisha's breath hitched. This boy wasn't just any warrior.

He was lore.

Never had she thought, in all her years, that she would come face-to-face with the slayer of monsters.

FIVE

PRATYUSH
(PRESENT DAY)

Every slayer has a breaking point.

It was one of the last things Papa had said, and Pratyush couldn't get that night out of his head. He'd bang his skull on a rock if it meant he could forget. Out of all the horrors that had happened in that storm, he kept returning to the hushed conversation between his parents.

Those words stuck with him, and now he wondered what *his* breaking point would be.

It hadn't been years of training, fighting, being sent to war, and carrying out clandestine battles against monsters that no one else dared to hunt. It wasn't immeasurable loss or the ghosts in his head. Nah, because he was still here. Somehow. For some reason.

He was sure his breaking point was hovering around him. Because a sense of dread clawed at his thoughts, a heaviness thickening in his bones. It had taken up residence in his head, a nagging sensation, an added sense, something he couldn't shake off. Maybe a feeling that meant nothing. But what if it was an actual sense? What if his father was worried about his breaking point because he sensed it coming?

Would it happen to Pratyush, too? Or was this what having too many voices in one head did to a guy? No wonder the Famed One had peeled his own skin off.

Morbid to think about? Yep. Especially for a seventeen-year-old.

Well, he could think about his sanity later. Right now, he was about to face off with another adversary of the kingdom.

He huffed out a breath and waited in the brush, squatting on dirt, hidden among weeds and wheat. He'd paused on the threshold of danger.

The Flesh Fields were at his back. He was just out of reach of ravenous flowers stretching for his throat, of prickly vines snaking their way toward thrumming flesh, of plants filled with the curdling blood and crushed bones of two soldiers taken moments earlier.

Pratyush glanced at the remaining fighters to his right. A few were as young as sixteen, but most were in their late teens or early twenties. It was a weird position to be in, to be younger than those he commanded. But the King had taught him from an early age that he was different, a born leader bred to fight. Besides, very few challenged his lead, and the ones who did . . . found themselves dead by the very claws Pratyush was trying to save them from.

He kept telling himself he wasn't a hero. He was out here to slay monsters, not save everyone who came along. Were some careless? Yep. Did some deserve to die? Maybe. But he couldn't carry the burden of the voices in his head *and* the guilt of losing soldiers. Yet here he was, weighed down by the two who'd just died.

The others looked ahead.

Sweat riddled their skin, their eyes bulging, chests heaving. The only sound was the squelching of the flowers eating the dead. The survivors would definitely have nightmares after this. Well, hell, daymares, too! The Nightmare Realm would feast on their dreams, the River of Blood gorged with the newly slain.

They crouched in a narrow line. Danger at their backs and danger up ahead.

Pratyush skimmed the horizon. Waiting to give word to the others, his eyes fell to the gleam of his father's parashu, the same weapon he'd used to kill his first monster. The same weapon Papa was using when he'd died. It was a heavy memory in hand, holding both power and pain.

The handle was made of carved wood and a metal like gold but as strong as winter-steel. The battle-axe's blade touched the tall grass, marbled leaves of green and brown. The heartbeats of his fighters, the flutter of wings overhead, the scratch of marching ants, and his own pulse swooshing behind his ears pounded through his thoughts.

The sight of the blade, dabbled with drizzling raindrops and flashing in the sun, was a piece of beauty before the pandemonium. In these brief seconds, he felt one with his father, tethered to a lifeline, grounded.

Pratyush's glare flitted up and across the hill, toward an increasing hum. No, wait, not humming, but ... buzzing hives and hordes of a million flying insects, the flutter of their wings thrashing against his ears.

He looked to the soldiers, meeting a few shaken faces. He frowned, muttering, "Get your shit together."

He understood why they were rattled, but there was something far worse ahead.

He cocked his chin toward the hill. Slowly, quietly, he led them toward a massive cave on the hilltop. There, a woman of staggering height moved back and forth, her form quivering like heat on hot summer stones. As they approached, Pratyush adjusted his eyesight to the distance, honing on the bhramari.

She was ... covered in an armor of bees, hornets, and wasps buzzing and skittering with her movements. He couldn't tell what she truly looked like beneath her layer of yellow-and-black arthropods.

As the soldiers snuck up on her, clad in black cloth and metal armor, neither the bhramari nor her swarm noticed them. From far away, anyone would've thought she was just a person—maybe a little odd and fully covered, but not a threat.

She stilled, as did the buzzing. Like the calm before an angry storm. She turned toward the soldiers ever so slowly. As she faced them, the youngest of the fighters raised their weapons, always eager, always less experienced.

Not yet. Pratyush held his hand down.

Her bees swarmed around her, hovering off her form, revealing sharp pincers protruding from bony cheeks and vacant eyes the color of honey in a bottomless vat. The air around her quivered as dark whorls of gray and blue came to life in an agitated sky above.

"Now!" Pratyush yelled, leading the charge with the soldiers behind him.

The bhramari hissed, her jaws opening so wide that it split her face in half. Her gown of yellow hornets fanned out and attacked. Armies of them flew at the soldiers, stinging and pinching and attempting with all their might to dig into human flesh.

The soldiers had come prepared. Their armor was impenetrable, at least for now, to these small but powerful pincers and stingers.

While the fighters kept her attention, Pratyush lunged for her side, driving his sword into her form. The blade went straight through. Clean. No blood, no pressure against flesh or bone. How was this possible? Was she even real? Were they fighting a ghost? A colony of intensely organized arthropods? This didn't make sense. What *was* she?

The bhramari turned to him. She screeched through a gaping mouth of absolute darkness, a void of nothing, as hypnotizing as her scream was startling. The ground shook; the skies wailed. She jutted her arms at him, and a cloud of vicious hornets careened toward the soldiers. There were so many, as if her body was made entirely of endless bees. Clouds of them swooshed off her.

While Pratyush's armor steadily held up, the insects covered his glass visor, clouding his vision. These weren't average hornets and wasps like in the countryside. They weren't the plump, honey-producing bees merrily meandering from flower to flower in the meadows, either.

Their attacks dented armor. Glass visors cracked. The soldiers couldn't withstand the horde much longer.

"Keep her attention!" Pratyush cried.

The soldiers lunged at her. Ram was among them at barely sixteen. Pratyush had only taken the time to learn his name because he was sure Ram was still a child by the roundness of his face. He wanted to safeguard him as much as possible so he could grow into a stronger soldier for bigger battles. But Ram had desperately wanted to prove himself.

As if slicing through air, Ram fell into the bhramari, not expecting his sword to go right through. Although his sword pierced to the other side, he didn't. The sword fell to the ground as her writhing form engulfed his convulsing body.

"Ah!" another soldier cried, shoving his sword through her and hitting Ram.

Ram moved through the edge of her form, but the bhramari swallowed him back inside. He grasped the sharp end of the sword now stuck in his metal armor as he was rattled about.

Idiots. Pratyush was surrounded by idiots. No matter how he tried to train them, there were always the few who would never listen, never think before acting.

"Dev!" Pratyush called out to his trustiest and strongest fighter, the only one who'd never failed him, and easily the smartest of them all. "Backup plan!"

Dev followed Pratyush, rushing to the bhramari's cave, which didn't go unnoticed. She floated after them, slower now with Ram inside her. Pratyush shoved everything around, knocking items down, breaking ceramics, looking for wood and twigs and leaves and cloth, anything that could be burned.

He ran around the moldy dankness in a sort of dance, a jerking cadence avoiding her bees, until a strong enough flame flickered off his fire starter. The thrum of steel and flint gave way to the crackling of a raging fire as everything ignited.

The ten-foot-high hive, a mosaic of combs against the back wall, seemed to be important. Instead of fleeing for her life, the bhramari went straight for the hive as flames licked at its base. The cells were each a foot long, filled with larvae encased in a gooey fluid. Writhing masses of gray grubs pushed out—plump larvae bigger than Pratyush's head. They turned to face him and the flames with hideous, gaping eyes and tiny arms. Their mouths opened in cries that shook dirt and rocks from the walls, each one filled with circles of rotating teeth.

Well, *damn*. If these were the bhramari's offspring, then the world was better off without a dozen more of them.

The bhramari was obviously trying to protect her brood, but there was no room to err, no room for doubts. Monsters were monsters. As simple as that. Monsters had killed his parents and countless others. Monsters were the reason Pratyush was in servitude to a king he hated. They were dangerous and deadly, and killing them saved the world.

"Just do your job," the King would say to him. "You don't exist to feel; leave that to poets. You don't exist to think; leave that to scholars. You don't exist to rule; leave that to me. Your only purpose is to kill. So, kill. And if you cannot do the one thing you were born to do, then what good are you?"

Pratyush and Dev shoved everything they could at the bhramari and her brood. She had no choice except to release Ram so she could fend off the flames.

Freed from her unearthly body, Ram fell to his knees. Pratyush went for him so he could yank him out, no matter that he was still so close to the monster. But he wasn't fast enough. Ram coughed as the smoke infiltrated his armor and wafted into his helmet. If they didn't hurry, they'd all be smoked alive.

Ram hadn't even raised himself up before hunger-driven larvae peeled off from the combs and crawled onto him.

"Get out of there!" Pratyush yelled, a piece of timber falling in between him and Ram.

Pratyush jumped over it, scrambling to get to him.

The roaring flames muffled Ram's cries, burning everything on sight, fast and furious. Then there was the sound of gnashing, oscillating teeth drilling through his armor. Ram stumbled and fell, one hand fighting off the larvae, the other reaching out for the slayer.

Pratyush extended himself to get to the boy, gripping his hand and pulling, but the larvae's weight wouldn't allow Ram to budge. There were too many—crawling across his head, gnawing on his helmet, breaking his visor through sheer force. Another crawled across his shoulders and down his arm toward Pratyush.

Pratyush, grunting, drove his sword through it. The grotesque thing exploded into greenish goo, an acid that corroded Ram's armor enough for other larvae to chomp right through his arm.

Ram let out an agonizing scream.

No!

Pratyush fell back, still gripping Ram's hand, now fully detached from his body.

Ram was gone, covered in blood beneath a feeding frenzy. Between his severed arm and penetrated visor, the boy was as dead as the larvae themselves would be.

Pratyush scurried backward over the fallen timber and through the wall of flames until he stumbled out of the cave, heaving.

"Quick!" he called to Dev.

Together, they pushed a boulder against the opening, entombing the bhramari and her brood as the fire consumed them.

Pratyush pushed away from the scalding rock and glared at the closed-off cave, flinching at the high-pitched squeals of larvae dying.

He didn't even have a moment to feel anger or guilt for unintentionally unleashing the acidic blood onto Ram. Because the bhramari was dying. He braced himself, but no matter how many monsters he'd slain, he was never truly prepared to absorb their final thoughts.

He felt the flames like they were burning his own skin, felt the bhramari's distress over her offspring. Her hatred of humans screamed through his mind.

As her life force escaped her desperate grip, it crawled inside him, earning him another lifetime. A powerful hurl to his guts, a punch to his mind as her wails filled his head; a booming cry exploding inside his skull.

He kept himself from falling, instead pushing through the pain and the ghostly presence trapped in his head.

He clenched his jaw and let her pass through him, dizzy, defeated, and eventually locked away in the corner of his mind with the others. A chest of slain monsters, a conglomerate of fading memories, and a lifetime of lifetimes.

Were these the voices his father had heard? Were these the haunting whispers and screams that drove the Famed One mad?

"It's done," Dev declared, bending over to catch his breath, going for his helmet to remove it.

"I wouldn't do that just yet," Pratyush heaved out.

Dev paused before lowering his hands, his helmet staying in place.

A boy lurched toward them, cradling his injured arm against his chest. "Where's Ram?" he asked, his voice cracking, another young soldier.

"They got him," Pratyush said.

"Why didn't you save him?" he yelled, gripping the slayer's shoulders.

"Back off," Dev growled, and the soldier did.

A numbness crossed Pratyush's limbs. His arms went limp. "I—I had his hand. It tore from his body. Can only hope that the fire killed him faster than the feeding offspring."

"Offspring?" the soldier choked out.

"Yeah. You don't want the details," Pratyush grunted. He hardened his voice and said, "Keep your armor on until we're out of the Flesh Fields."

Pratyush and the surviving fighters trekked through the Flesh Fields in solemn silence, evading the plants still gorging on their companions with haunting, squelching sounds. Finally, they emerged into the dewy hillsides at the edge of the kingdom. To the distant left was a noticeable barrier of thorny, clawed twigs thicker than a man's breadth and taller than a house. These were said to be the overgrown ruins of a legendary labyrinth built by the gods.

"How do you keep so calm, young one?" Dev muttered, glancing at the exhausted soldiers behind them.

Pratyush squared his sore shoulders. "I'm desensitized." It was sort of the truth. "And *young one*? You're only two years older than me . . . old man."

Dev grunted. But he understood; he was the same desensitized way. "You and I are too similar."

Both a compliment and a burden.

He continued, "We've been training since we were kids, taken from our homes and trained to fight monsters. I guess it doesn't bother me so much anymore, either. I can't tell if that's a good thing or not."

Pratyush glanced at him. "That's a lie."

"Why would I ever lie to you, the master of calling out liars to a fault?"

"I think you're getting tired of killing."

Dev nodded once, but he'd never admit it. There were too many ears listening, too many young soldiers wanting to find favor with the General and the King by squashing rebellious talk.

Dev added, "I'm here to protect my people, my family. You're not."

Translation? *You can leave.* Except...Pratyush couldn't. He owed his life to the King, but more than that, he honestly wanted to save people. He wanted to save lives and prevent others from experiencing the sort of murderous loss that he'd experienced.

"You should tell me one day," Dev said, "how you got here."

Pratyush didn't respond. No one knew, except the King. How a small child killed his first monster trying to save parents who died anyway. How the slayer, a powerful being, feared and adored, ended up in forced servitude.

"You saw me that day," Pratyush said instead. "My first time on the training field."

"You were a gawky runt. I couldn't believe they paired us up together for practice. I pummeled you every day back then."

"Made me stronger."

"I felt bad, you know?"

Pratyush knew. He knew when he'd seen glimpses of Dev's backside at ten years old bleeding from lashes because he didn't want to keep beating up Pratyush. Dev had never said a word, never admitted to it, but that was how a quiet friendship had been forged. And that was how little Pratyush had quickly learned to fight.

"I'm still waiting for the day..." Dev side-eyed him.

"What day?"

"The day when you'll pummel me back."

Pratyush scoffed. "Hitting you is like hitting stone. I like my knuckles intact, thanks. Besides, you're the only one I can trust to have my back after nine years of fighting together."

Dev nodded.

"At least we'll be home soon," a nearby soldier said to the others.

Home. Everyone here had a home, except Pratyush. More than saving others, all he really wanted was a home. And more than that—impossible, in fact—he wanted his family. He didn't want to be alone and wondered if this was why his father had evaded the King for so long. Did Papa have to slip away into the borderlands just to be free and have a family and home of his own? Had he requested freedom first?

"At least we get a bed," Dev grumbled with an irritated sigh. He'd much rather be with his bride in their faraway village.

A year ago, Dev had escaped to marry her during a mission when they'd traveled close to his homeland. Pratyush had diverted questioning, giving Dev as much time as possible. Although he'd been happy to help, it would've been nice to attend a wedding, to see two people in love, to truly celebrate and see something normal for once, without politics and blood.

Pratyush hadn't had a home since his parents died, but for a while, at least, he had had one thing to look forward to when returning to the palace. Time with his sister, though brief, had become the highlight of his life. They were never together for long, as the King always found a way to shove him into slayer duties.

Pritika would light up whenever she saw him.

"I don't want you to leave again," she'd told him once.

"I'm just a child. I don't have a choice," he'd responded, his voice higher back then. He'd seen one too many who fled from the King, only to be captured and their families killed.

"We can run away together," she'd suggested, hope filling her eyes. She was thirteen then, and he eleven. "They found out that I've begun to bleed."

Pratyush didn't know what that meant. Was she hurt? Was she ill?

She'd shaken her head and explained, "It means I'm of age to be considered for engagement. The Queen said I was like a princess . . . well, a far-off cousin of a princess . . . but meant to be negotiated into engagement with someone of high rank. She said it was an honor and the union would solidify houses, all good for the kingdom, but I don't want to be given away like . . . like *property*."

"But if you're married, your husband will take care of you," he'd said with some level of excitement. Maybe Pritika would be happy then, with a garden and a library and living away from the court. "You can have your own house and a family . . . rebuild what we lost. We were happy with our parents on our ranch. I bet you'll be happy if you have that again."

Her shoulders had slumped. "You're too young to understand. We were happy because our parents were happy. It's not something that just happens because you get married. Marriage here isn't like what our parents had. I haven't seen one happy couple. It's all about politics and selfish interests. If two people like each other, it never lasts." She'd added in a whisper, "I don't think these people even know what love is."

Pratyush had nodded. "I'll do whatever you ask me. Whatever makes you happy and keeps you safe."

"Promise?" she'd said with a weak smile and teary eyes.

He'd nodded and she'd hugged him so tight that he felt her worries through the embrace.

But he'd broken that promise—he'd failed her—and now Pritika was gone. Returning to the palace had become a numbing, dark experience. He merely went through the motions, his heart dead and his soul crushed into nothing worth saving.

In a few days' time, they'd reach the safety of the kingdom said to be above all others in known history, a place where monsters didn't exist.

Supposedly.

SIX

MANISHA
(THIRTY-SEVEN DAYS AGO)

A chilling breeze swept through the halls of the grand temple. The other girls shivered, but the cold had never bothered Manisha. It helped to harden her outer self when she stole moments to remember. Like how she saw her mother in the lotus blooms in shallow streams alongside the sidewalks, light pinks that Mama had loved.

Sita clapped her hands and the apsara took their places in line, dressed in the finest gold-and-pink silks, their long hair braided down to the waist and fitted with strings of jasmine blooms and one red rose. It had been four months since Sita had become Head Priestess, and Manisha still hadn't found a way off the floating mountains.

"Do not give men a reason to covet you," Sita instructed as they readied themselves for guests. "Keep your eyes downcast, your voices low, your opinions silent, your bodies covered, and distance maintained. You must desire nothing, and you must never cause others to desire you. Men are easily sparked, and as priestesses we must never tempt them."

The diyas, drenched in ghee and arranged in beautiful rangoli-style patterns, were ready to be lit at a moment's notice, as soon as the favored priestess met the visitors. To this day, Manisha couldn't look at a diya holder and not want to giggle remembering the day a young warrior boy had broken one.

Although cloudy below, the sun shone bright throughout the temple, setting everything aglow. The girls walked through a shimmering haze.

"The famed warrior is here," Sita announced with a double snap of her fingers, as if she were a queen and the others her ladies-in-waiting.

It had been a while.

Manisha's lips quirked up at the corners. The slayer's visits had become the only exciting thing in this place, a distraction from her failure to escape. Knowing that he was here, anticipating his flirting, made Manisha's insides roll in an unexpected, unfamiliar way. She didn't understand this feeling—a little terrifying but also sensationally pleasant.

She waited for Sita to call the name of one of her favorites, expecting that the slayer would find her afterward to continue their forbidden encounters. As soon as Sita announced a name, Manisha would disappear into the shadows.

"Manisha," Sita proclaimed, albeit begrudgingly.

It took a moment to realize she'd called *Manisha's* name. Arya glanced at her, also confused.

"Wh-what?" Manisha stuttered.

Sita scowled. She didn't like repeating herself, and she didn't have patience for stuttering girls.

Manisha shook her head and gave a short bow. "I mean, of course."

"Follow me." Sita held her chin high, leading Manisha down the wide hallway between marble pillars speckled with gold and silver.

"Are you prepared?" Sita asked from ahead.

"Yes." Manisha eyed her suspiciously.

Why would Sita allow her to attend to the slayer after all this time?

Did Sita know about their secret conversations? Or worse... her intentions of leaving? She internally flinched. How would she be punished for this?

Maybe she could just ask Sita if she could leave? Sita didn't want her here anyway, so there was nothing for her to lose. The kingdom was full of girls wanting to escape into temple life. She'd gladly exchange places with any of them.

No. On second thought, Sita probably wouldn't help. If anything, she'd demote Manisha to temple girl and sell her to a soldier.

For now, Manisha would follow the rules and serve their guest to perfection. It wasn't that difficult, to be honest. She'd gone over this routine so many times that she could perform it in her sleep, all without believing a single word.

Before they emerged into the courtyard—an open area where visitors waited beneath trellises of blooming vines—Sita turned to her, scrutinizing every detail.

Manisha stood still, her gaze listing off to the right. There wasn't a single thing Sita could adjust or reprimand. Not a single fold of her sari was out of place, not a single inch of flesh seen above her ankles or past her elbows, neither a hair astray nor a jasmine flower tilted.

Sita tried hard to find something to complain about. She ripped off the pleated section of sari from Manisha's waist and shoved it back in, tugging her in the process.

"Don't you know by now how to tuck this in?" Sita snarled beneath her breath.

It didn't look much different than it had ten seconds ago, but Manisha held her tongue.

"Why he keeps asking for you, I have no idea," Sita spat, then paused. Taking a step back, she glared. "Have you interacted with him?"

Manisha's heart stilled and her thoughts raced to all their secret encounters. She steadied her nerves as she carefully equivocated, "I would not want to break the rules that safeguard us."

Sita studied Manisha's face, her reactions, but Manisha held on to impassiveness. Sita scowled. Disgust gleamed across the brown of her eyes, the sort of loathing Manisha hadn't seen since Sita first suggested selling her off to soldiers all those years ago.

She would never help me.

"Hmm. Remember your oath. As long as you serve here—as long as you stand on these grounds—you must never allow a man to touch you."

"Of course."

"Because you know what happens to girls who are defiled and desecrate these holy mountains," Sita hissed. "Like broken vessels, they are of no further use; they get tossed out."

Manisha huffed out a breath, quivering. Yes, she knew all too well that her entire worth in this place depended on the Head Priestess.

"Go."

Manisha walked ahead, never happier to escape into service.

She tried to control her trembling, both from fear of what Sita might do to her and anger at herself for being afraid in the first place. Her sisters would be so disappointed.

She moved past the pillars. The sun blazed, and she squinted from the flash against the slayer's bronze-plated armor. She glanced down at the marbled floors, counting every step to the courtyard until she finally met his shoe-covered feet. He wasn't supposed to meet her halfway; Manisha was supposed to greet him first.

Flustered, she took a step back and proceeded anyway. She clasped her hands together, bowed, and said, "Welcome to the floating temple of the highest heavens. My name is Manisha."

"I know your name," he said, his voice throaty, raw, tired like he'd just come from battle. "But I'm glad to finally hear you tell me."

Manisha hated what his voice did to her, how it spun her insides like a tapestry manipulated by the fates. She hated that he kept coming here, risking her situation. She hated, most of all, that she was *enjoying* his attention.

She raised her eyes, catching the fine threads of his snow-colored kurta, a heavy shawl over his broad shoulders, and taking in his weary face. He'd grown so much in just a year—now over a head taller than her. She tilted her head back to see his face. Around them, pistachio trees bloomed with clusters of pink-and-cream-colored fruit. A mayura rose just past him, sweeping through the skies and releasing a pent-up breath of fire. The flames set the slayer's reflective armor ablaze with flashes of red.

Manisha saw why monsters thought this boy formidable. He simply was. Which meant *she* had to be careful. He wasn't just a boy who'd broken a diya holder and made her laugh.

He was dangerous.

He was extraordinary.

Built like a warrior who had trained since childhood, his clothes hugging the contours of hard-worked lean muscles, he was a picture of strength. His jaw a tight line, his face riddled with fresh scars. His violet eyes glowed, void of humor or solace, instead filled with ages of violent battles. The top half of his hair was neatly tied back while the bottom half swayed in the breeze, cutting across his neck.

She wanted to touch his cheek, run a thumb over the ridge of a fresh wound, and feel the years of the hunt. How unfair that he could be free and alive when so many couldn't.

He was heralded by the world below as a savior—a slayer of monsters. If he knew her origins, an enemy to his beloved king, then he'd see her as a monster, too. But even monsters deserved to be left alone, didn't they?

"It's healing," he said, his gaze dropping to her lifted hand.

She retracted her arm, her skin hot.

He smirked. "I have that effect."

Manisha frowned and said quietly, "If you're ready for prayer, you can follow me."

He nodded but held an arm out to stop the three men behind him. She'd only now noticed them. Noblemen? Assistants? Friends?

"Don't you want to be efficient with your time and have a group service?" she asked.

"I want a private service," he replied.

Ignoring the hungry look of the man to the right, the one with cavernous brown eyes and a deep scar across his jaw, Manisha turned to the group and said, "Another apsara will be sent for you."

"We should like to wait for you," the man with the scar replied, his stare turning dark.

The slayer looked back at him. "You'll ask for another."

The man stiffened his stubbled jaw but didn't respond. He was older than the slayer by at least several years, but he didn't argue. Maybe he was a soldier. She couldn't imagine someone as young as the slayer speaking back to a high-ranking official and not being reprimanded for it.

"Please remove your shoes," Manisha instructed and walked ahead, relieved to escape whoever that man was.

They went up the grand steps and into a hall as tall as the temple itself, with arches and crystal-and-ruby chandeliers. Elegant, detailed tapestries telling the stories of the gods decorated the walls. Ahead was the altar in all its glimmering splendor.

Above was the dome with its clear lack of orbs. Manisha hadn't tried to climb the walls since that night. Afraid that she'd done something to alarm the shadowy door, or that she'd been seen, because now someone walked through the grounds every night.

In the center of the altar, the dark shadow loomed. Every time

Manisha saw it, she pleaded to hear her sister again, but other than the one time, she hadn't. Maybe the voice had been in her head.

The slayer watched her from the corner of his eye. "Do you know what that is?"

She knew what she'd been told. "The gateway to the edge of the universe where the ancient ones arrived."

He scoffed. "It's a flat door."

"Made from air," she intoned. She may not believe in this religion, but she knew that wasn't just any door.

"Have you ever stepped through it?"

"You know no one is allowed near it, don't you?"

"Have you tried to approach it?"

Manisha looked at the shadow door and shook her head.

He leaned toward her and whispered, "Liar."

She stilled, swallowing, and felt his stare drop to her throat. He was the slayer; there was no point in lying to him. "Don't you want to know what's there?" she asked.

"No."

"Really?" She looked at him, and he eyed the shadow.

"In my experience, bad things hide in shadows. I don't want to know what's there."

"So...you don't believe the stories of the vidyadhara arriving through that door?"

He shrugged, unimpressed.

"I'll let you meditate," she said, lowering herself to a small burgundy pillow, her head bowed for prayer in hopes that he would follow suit.

He knelt beside her. "Are you done yet?"

She tilted away, opening her eyes, and whispered, "You're supposed to be in prayer."

"I'm not much of a religious guy," he whispered back.

"Slayer," Manisha said firmly, turning to him.

"Hmm?"

"You must meditate to get closer to the divine."

"We both know I don't come here to pray."

"Do you want to be removed?" she asked bluntly.

He raised his right brow, a sharp arch. Even when kneeling, he towered over Manisha. Despite the distance between them, the warmth of his body overpowered her, making it hard to think. "Do you speak to everyone this way?"

Her skin flushed. "Just you."

He smirked, as if knowing that meant so much more. "Do you want me to leave?"

"You're not used to being told no, are you?"

He grinned, and Manisha fought the temptation to look at his mouth. "No one tells me no unless they're begging for their life."

She scowled. "Don't speak about your violence here."

"My violence is what protects you and these mountains."

"The gods protect us," she replied, the meaningless words rolling easily off her tongue.

He snickered. Amusement glimmered in his soul-piercing gaze. A curl set his harsh mouth. "You think that? Who enforces the peace so danger doesn't come to this place?"

"These mountains are impenetrable. No one can reach us." *And no one can leave, either.*

"You think men can't build ladders tall enough?"

She grunted. "As tall as mountains?"

"Or build contraptions that can soar?"

"Unlikely."

"Or tame the flying peacocks?"

"I doubt that."

He waved a hand around. "You have no idea what the world below is like. You sit in your gold-and-jeweled temple like princesses in a palace."

No. Manisha knew. She knew because she and her people had hidden in the jungles, lived in caves lit by fireflies and glowworms for fear of people like him. Serpents had been her confidants and dirt had been her bed.

"*You* have no idea," she muttered. "Are you done insulting me?"

"What's that? Did the pious priestess reprimand me?"

"If you're done with prayer, you can make an offering," she said through gritted teeth, although she found herself enjoying this. He allowed her anger and comebacks. He welcomed real conversations without the stifling sweet voice and constant smile she was told to maintain. After being so emotionally starved and stilted, bickering felt like a wonderful dream.

"I have an offer for you. . . ." He stood and waited for her.

What sort of offer did he have? Did he know about her origins? Could he smell the jungle on her? Could he see the lineage buried in her bones? Maybe the reason he always found his prey was because he had enhanced senses, knew more than a person should. Maybe the legends were true—no prey could evade the slayer.

"Can you show me the gardens?" he asked, waiting for her to rise.

Manisha swallowed but agreed.

SEVEN

MANISHA
(THIRTY-SEVEN DAYS AGO)

"**W**hat happened to your bracelet?" the slayer asked as they strolled through the northern garden bursting with rainbow-colored flowers.

Manisha shrugged with sadness. That wondrous, magical, growing egg had detached itself from the coils of her bangle a few nights ago and rolled right into the thicket. She'd searched every chance she could get. But it was gone. A piece of herself went missing along with it.

They wandered beneath several identical balconies, surrounded by lotuses stretching up from the ponds. Almond blossoms rained down from ancient trees on this side of the temple where the sun blazed hottest.

"What's your offer?" she asked nervously.

"Are you cold?" He slipped off his shawl so fast that by the time Manisha realized his intentions, it was already draped around her.

"You can't touch me," she said, searching for watching eyes.

"I didn't touch you."

"You're not answering my questions. And this game you're playing will cost me."

"How?"

"If the Head Priestess finds out, I'll be—"

"What?" He quirked a brow and studied her slipping facade. "Do they beat you? In this place of nonviolence?"

"Of course not. It's just that . . . I've worked hard to get here. I won't let you, or anyone else, sabotage it for some pointless game. Now tell me, or I'll call a mayura to take you on your way."

He chuckled, displaying slim dimples and flashing fascinatingly sharp canines. He grinned down at Manisha with a smile that must've slain a hundred girls.

"What is it?" she pressed.

He sucked in a breath and said, "I offer my hand."

"What?"

He held out his hand, palm side up so that the callused flesh faced the sky.

Manisha blinked at it. "What does that mean?"

"Has no one spoken of offering hands?"

"No. Am I supposed to shake it? I thought I made it clear that you can't touch me."

He sighed. "Don't you know anything?"

She narrowed her eyes. "I know when a boy is patronizing me."

He cleared this throat. "Offering my hand means that I want to . . . marry you."

She choked on her next words. "I . . . thought slayers couldn't marry."

"I guess the right girl makes slayers marry." He scratched the back of his neck, his cheeks flushed. "I've loved you since you laughed at me for breaking the diya holder."

"Oh . . ." Heat singed her cheeks. *Love?* She didn't know what to say, what to do. She didn't know how to feel about his declaration. They'd only known one another in short intervals, but the idea of a domestic life with him wasn't terrible.

What was she thinking? Manisha was only sixteen. A future with a husband and children and whatever else adults did didn't matter. Not for her. All she could think of ever wanting was her family and a safe, peaceful place to live with them. Also, vengeance. That sounded about right. There was no future without dealing with the King and what he'd done.

Several seconds of silence slipped by, of the slayer waiting, of her stomach turning queasy but in an oddly pleasant way.

"Can I tell you something?" he asked, his tone soft, almost shy, but his look brooding.

"Sure."

He let out a rough breath. "I'm tired."

"Do you want to go inside and rest?"

"No. I mean I'm tired of life, of being a slayer. I've been training and battling since I was eight, and I'm exhausted. I just want some time off, to not fight, not train, not hunt. Maybe own a house and horses and . . . well, I don't know what else. Read a book, maybe? When I leave here, I'm going to ask the King for freedom, or at least some time off to have these things."

"Do you speak so openly with everyone?" She inclined her chin, searching the weary sadness on his face.

"No. I don't have a lot of people I can talk to."

"That sounds . . . lonely," she said, understanding but also surprised that a person as famous as the slayer didn't have a hundred friends and confidants.

His face twitched, and he quickly looked down. "Yeah. But you make me feel like I can tell you anything. Like maybe you won't laugh at me . . . although you laugh at me a lot."

Manisha found herself half smiling.

"Maybe you won't think I'm weak for feeling...things."

"I think they're called emotions."

He grinned at her. "Smart-ass."

She was full-on smiling now, something she hadn't done in a long while.

"You're easy to talk to, and I know I can trust you."

"How do you know?"

"A slayer knows."

She didn't mean to swallow, but she did, and his glance flitted to her throat.

"Maybe you don't tell me everything, but I know you're not untrustworthy."

She blew out a breath and confessed, "I like to listen."

His expression grew soft, which seemed like a rare thing.

"You've worked your wage for him, you know?" she said of his debt to the King.

The corner of his mouth quirked up. "You're so innocent."

"There you go patronizing me again," she muttered. "What will you do with all this freedom, anyway?"

"I want a home, a ranch, a family. I want a wife. I want you." He glanced at his feet.

"Aren't we young to get married?"

Apsara never married. Temple girls were occasionally sold. The only knowledge of marriage that Manisha had was glimpses of older girls and young women back home. She'd been young but aware that her parents and elders were married, but they'd seemed so past newly married. They were parents and educators and the foundations that held families and communities together. Manisha wasn't ready for that sort of responsibility, nor did she want it. She couldn't imagine wanting anything other than her family.

The slayer shrugged. "Lots of people get married young. I'm considered old, you know?"

Manisha smiled. "You look old."

He laughed. "Well, we don't have to marry right away."

She tugged at the edge of the shawl that smelled like him. She wished she could keep it. "I hear men get bored with their wives."

"You're cynical for a temple princess."

"Temple *priestess*. My servitude is to this place," she said out of habit.

Rejection weighed down his expression, a look so wretched that it made her believe him. "You're... turning me down? I never understood what a broken heart was until now."

Manisha fought the urge to cross her arms and roll her eyes. "It's not you. You're not the first to offer marriage."

He scoffed. "Who's asked to marry you? A minute ago, you didn't even know what offering a hand meant."

"Plenty of princes," she replied defensively.

He chuckled. "Are any of these princes older than ten?"

"That's beside the point."

"Who else has seen you? Besides these mighty princes in training."

"You've seen me plenty of times. Why were you always watching me from the corner of your eye when you were supposed to be bowed in prayer?" she chided.

"There's no focusing when you're anywhere near me."

"There would be if you had your eyes closed."

"You don't understand, I—" He paused.

"You what?"

"Nothing."

She looked past him, searching the balconies and windows again. "You come here to spy on priestesses."

"No! That's not it at all. I have... senses." He leaned toward her and took in a deep breath, his eyes closing. "You smell different."

Manisha froze.

They locked eyes. She wasn't sure what to make of his comments, so she held her breath, waiting. The unflinching, rigid lines of his jaw and brow implied that he wasn't lying, though.

His eyes glinted in the fading sunlight, keeping his stare pinned to hers. How could he go from boyish to intense so fast?

Her lips parted to probe for an answer, and his gaze slipped to her mouth. The evening bells rang. "This isn't a stormy evening, Slayer. Your time is almost up. We have supper and chai, if you'd like."

"Is there any chance that I could dine with you alone?" he asked. Absurd.

"No."

"Is there any chance that I could request that you sit beside me?" he asked, hopeful.

"No."

He blew out a defeated breath and asked, his voice quiet, "Do you really not want to marry me?"

His look of dejection wounded her. She'd never guessed that a warrior of his fame could be this saddened by the thought of a girl not wanting him. Surely, there had to be plenty of girls lined up for him.

"I hardly know you," Manisha told him.

"Then get to know me."

"We're barely allowed to talk. I'm not allowed to leave the temple. Getting to know one another is impossible."

"Then come with me."

She paused. Part of her wanted to go, but she knew better. "I may not know everything, but I'm not stupid."

But what if this was the only way off the floating mountains? Then what, once on the ground? He wouldn't just let her walk away. He was the realm's best hunter. He'd find her, and he would figure out what she was. Worse than that? What if he tracked her to her family? The King would know.

He tilted down to speak closer to her ear. "I would never desert you or get bored of you. I've been drawn to you since the day I smelled you."

"What do I smell like?" she asked, expecting the most generic response, one that he must've used on other girls.

"Like blossoms and fire and jungle and earth. You smell like heaven's raindrops mixed with the world below. You smell like sweet jungle fruit and tart roots, fireflies and glowworms."

She swallowed hard. A foreboding raged through her veins. A warning. He knew something.

"You don't smell like anyone I've ever come across. Your scent doesn't make sense," he said, frustrated.

Manisha forced a joking tone when she replied, "Maybe you're losing your touch. Maybe it *is* time for you to retire, old man."

He held a hand to his chest in feigned pain. "Now you've broken my heart twice."

"What do you know about love, anyway? Do you fall in love often?"

"And the pain continues." He held a fist to his chest. "Honestly? I've seen it with my parents."

"Your parents were loving?" It seemed hard to believe that a warrior boy, a slayer, came from a loving family.

"Papa would do anything for Ma, and vice versa. They rarely argued, and when they did, it was usually over philosophy or inventions," he said fondly. "Papa picked wildflowers for Ma every morning so she could enjoy them during breakfast. And Ma would grow roses so he could have rosewater baths."

Manisha found herself laughing. "They sound like they were very nice people."

His smile slipped. "I don't see that type of love around me much. I don't spend a lot of time with couples—or people in general, unless we're hunting. The way my father treated my mother is just one example of how I hope to be like him one day. So, you don't have to worry about me getting bored of you, or leaving you, or hurting you."

This all sounded nice, and she wanted to believe him, to fully trust the slayer. Maybe she could leave with him and then escape afterward? On one hand, he seemed kind; maybe he would keep his word. On the other, he was the slayer and would easily track her down.

"We should go to the dining hall before anyone gets suspicious." She handed him the shawl, holding on to it by a corner.

He took it, twisting his lips. "Would you really rather spend a lifetime alone here than live a life with me?"

She looked up at him. She didn't have many choices. "Even if I wanted to go with you, it's not that simple. It's not my choice. But . . . I'll consider it."

He smiled. "Be still my heart."

"All right . . ." she mumbled.

"When do you think you'll have an answer?" he asked, his cheeks flushed.

"When will you return?" Manisha countered.

"I have a mission, then I need to travel to the palace and ask the King's permission. Give me one month to get things in order. Is that enough time?" he asked, optimistic.

She nodded. One month was plenty of time to weigh her options . . . or lack thereof.

"If you decide you want to, then don't worry about anything on your end. If the King gives permission, Sita will have to obey," he added, as if he knew Manisha's concerns. Apsara didn't marry. This would be a first. But maybe the King would do something useful for once.

"We should get back." Manisha walked past him, wondering if he could smell her origins on her right now. Fireflies and glowworms and dirt were specific, and they weren't exactly romantic things to tell a girl.

Sita appeared between the pillars, her hands clasped primly and her expression both soft and infuriated. Manisha stilled, her heart racing.

"Manisha. Please attend to the kitchen," Sita said. Another apsara was standing beside Sita, her cheeks and lips tinged pink to match her immaculate sari. The gleam of malice hidden in her eyes slashed her beauty.

"But I'm in service," Manisha demurred. She hadn't had kitchen duties in months. Why *now*?

Sita lifted her chin in that quiet way that spoke louder than words.

"What about dinner?" the slayer asked.

Sita nodded toward the apsara beside her. "Supper is waiting in the dining hall for you. She will escort you and take care of the remainder of your visit."

"I mean with Manisha," he clarified.

Manisha's nostrils flared. If Sita hadn't been upset before, she had reason to be now. She tried to throw him a warning look, but the boy wouldn't heed it.

Sita replied, "We're in need of her talents in the kitchen."

Since when was washing dishes a talent? Manisha wanted to argue, but she couldn't. She wanted to voice how inappropriate this was, how uncalled for and embarrassing, but she knew her place. It didn't stop the slayer from voicing his thoughts—because he knew *his* place.

"With so many others, you need her?" he asked bluntly.

"Pardon me?" Sita said.

"There are forty-four apsara, plus at least a dozen attendants."

Manisha shook her head at him, horrified. This boy was really going to be the end of her.

"You're taking her away from service to an esteemed guest for ... kitchen duty?"

He might've been young, but he didn't hold back. He knew exactly who he was, and he was allowed to show it. Manisha found herself envying that about him.

Sita looked as flustered as Manisha felt.

"It's all right," Manisha assured him. "There'll be plenty of company for you."

He opened his mouth to protest when Manisha bowed her head and excused herself, hurrying away and not taking another breath until she was far from the slayer and his acute senses.

Her shoulders slumped the second she turned into the kitchen and saw the mess. Mounds of dishes and spilled sauces, a disarray of ingredients and forgotten utensils.

She immediately went to work, asking Arya, "Why are there so many dishes? This'll take hours to clean."

Arya replied, "I'm sorry. The Head Priestess dismissed the others early and instructed me not to touch anything. I cleaned some anyway; there was a lot more. She told me to leave when you arrived, but I can help."

"No," Manisha muttered. "You'll get into trouble."

Even though Arya had been the kindest person to her, Manisha couldn't fully trust that Arya wouldn't tell Sita anything if she asked. She'd learned her lesson: She'd once told another how she didn't like working in the kitchens. And for a year, all she did was work in the kitchens.

Arya nodded, leaving Manisha to work, to mull. It wasn't new for Sita to enforce more manual labor on Manisha than others, or to isolate her while doing so. It was fine. This gave her time to think.

Manisha scrubbed and plotted. Silence devoured the room. Her ears rang.

"Run," a voice said. Eshani's voice. The voice from the shadow door.

Manisha startled, dropping spoons into the water basin. She spun around. But she was alone.

Had minutes passed, or hours? The candles had burned to their ends and the sky had darkened.

Sithara had once told Manisha to follow her gut—the strange sensation that came from deep within and couldn't be explained. She'd always told her to hold on, to fight, to try again, to work through the pain if it meant reaching her goals, but never, ever deny the feeling from within.

Manisha didn't know where the voice had come from or if it had even been real, but she knew one thing for sure: The slayer was her only chance.

EIGHT

PRATYUSH
(PRESENT DAY)

O n a dirt road to the palace, villagers gathered to greet the returning army in a chorus of applause and chattering. Merchants
offered food, drink, even girls. Singers praised the slayer's skills,
chanting, "The woman of bees has burned!"

"I feel like a hero every time we return. Do you get tired of this?"
an awed soldier asked.

"Don't you wonder who pays for these things?" another asked,
brushing back the hair over his eyes. Beneath all the torn clothes,
grime, and battle wounds, he was no older than sixteen, and painfully
reminded Pratyush of Ram.

Pratyush scoffed. "Yeah, I'm tired. And the people pay." He yanked
an older soldier away from a basket of flatbread, admonishing, "Taking one for now is all right, but don't shove a dozen into your bag
for later."

"Hey!" the soldier retorted.

Pratyush growled, showing his canines. The man cowered, muttering apologies.

"Don't take more than what you need."

Pratyush turned to the young soldier and said, "You wanna know who pays for all these *free* things? Each person who gives them to us. Actually, we take them. By decree of the King. 'No soldier, upon arrival from battle or on his way out to war, should be denied food, drink, and rest,'" he recited. "These people are poor and hungry. They don't get reimbursed or paid for feeding us. What we take comes out of their mouths. Aren't your parents farmers? Don't you know this?"

The boy replied, "They never said we weren't given anything in return. They said it was our duty and honor."

In the distance, near the end of the dirt road lined with crumbling homes and carts, an older soldier had dismounted from his horse to harass a young—obviously too young—girl. While some men offered their daughters to soldiers—a well-known practice that Pratyush couldn't grasp—this girl's father hadn't. The man tried to intervene, stepping in front of his daughter, but the soldier pushed him back, knocking him against his home where pieces of the mud wall flicked off.

The father clasped his hands together and pleaded. Old age was apparent in his ashen hair, poverty in his worn and sullied clothes, and decades of hard work in his callused hands.

Pratyush dropped his head. Seriously, why was he surrounded by idiots?

They continued walking alongside the horses. Helmets and armor gently clanked, metal against metal, in the satchels hanging from the steeds with every step.

Pratyush kept an eye on the soldier ahead. He'd grabbed the girl's wrist. Images of his sister flashed across his thoughts in searing red. She'd been assaulted by her betrothed. Pratyush had been young, his every move watched. He'd been told that if he obeyed, Pritika would be taken care of. Where had he gone wrong? What could he have done differently? Whatever the reason, the way she'd been hurt, the fact that he couldn't help her, hadn't run off with her like she'd asked, hovered over him like a dark cloud.

Maybe he couldn't have done much then, but he could now.

With a snarl, Pratyush marched toward the soldier, took him by the neck, and dragged him back. The soldier's hands fell from the girl to grab Pratyush's wrists.

"What are you doing?" Pratyush snapped.

"Taking my due," the soldier grunted, trying to shove him off. Despite his training, his years, and his frame of solid muscle, the man shrank into himself. He might've intimidated most. But that was the thing about trying to go toe-to-toe with a slayer—you weren't going to win.

"Your *due* isn't with a child," Pratyush bit out.

"We're supposed to get whatever we want from these people. They only live because we die for them," the man shot back.

Pratyush released him. The soldier caught his breath, rubbing his swollen red neck.

"So, let me get this straight. One day, a soldier'll come through your village and take your daughter, and you'll just let him?" Pratyush asked.

The soldier choked out, "If he's fought so we can live, yes. We don't just fight. We see things, horrible things, and kill and suffer."

"Ah. I see. So that makes it right? Share the suffering? You'd allow the same thing to happen to your wife, your sister, mother, grandmother?"

"Yes," he said without a beat, without a fleck of remorse.

Pratyush pressed his lips together as others gathered around, waiting for his next move. He had to act carefully. While he had full authority over the soldiers, every action had a consequence, and sometimes that consequence was an uprising or a wave of dissent. "A soldier can take whatever he wants, huh?"

The man stood defiant. His chin in the air. "Yes."

Pratyush regarded him. Ah, hell. "Is this the hill you wanna die on?"

He swallowed with a nod, his eyes narrowing at his commander, readying for a fight as if he could win against a slayer. "Who is she to you?"

"I don't know her or owe her." Pratyush glanced at the trembling girl. She was probably a few years younger than him. In those terrified eyes, he saw Pritika. She wasn't just someone's sister or daughter, either. She was a person, one whose right to exist without harm outweighed this idiot's perceived right to abuse.

The soldier went on, "I've faced death for these strangers. I deserve this. If you want to take it from me, then send these old men and little girls into battle while I stay here and live."

"Ah. All right, then." Pratyush spoke loudly to the men around them, "Did you hear that? A soldier deserves to get whatever he desires."

The men murmured, cautious.

He jerked his chin at the girl. "You're making a choice, and choices have consequences. If you take her, I want you to remember what you just said."

The soldier took the girl and dragged her inside. The father pleaded and begged him not to take her, tears streaming down his face, but the soldier's heart was harder than stone.

"Are you really allowing this?" the young soldier at Pratyush's side asked, both appalled and infuriated, his hand on the hilt of his sword.

Pratyush's breaths came out hot and labored, his thoughts racing. He cocked his chin at Dev, a boy practically made from stone. When Dev cut through the crowd of soldiers and villagers, they instinctively moved out of his way. There was a reason people didn't cross him—or anyone from his village, really.

Dev was only nineteen, but he was as grisly and as hard as they came. He stood over six feet seven, head shaved and covered in black-and-green tattoos, and he was believed to be a cannibal. Silver barbells pierced his nose and brows and lip. His teeth had been filed sharp, following the traditions of his people. Rumor had it that those from the borderland village of Skanda tore meat from the bone without killing their prey first, much less cooking their meal. Dev kept his nails trimmed into sharp triangles like talons. His skin was the color of ash, gray like a depressing sky, and calcified—a trait shared among his people, hence the belief his kind were made from stone.

Dev stepped forward. The young soldier beside Pratyush stuttered over his next words, his mouth dropping open and his feet inching away from the boy who might've been part monster.

"You gotta understand how to get through to different kinds of people," Pratyush told him, still looking at the father who tore his shirt in shame. He wondered if *his* father would've done the same knowing how Pritika had been violated. No. Papa would've killed the man. Actually . . . Papa wouldn't have let it happen in the first place. He wouldn't have failed her the way Pratyush had.

Dev stomped past them to get inside the hut.

"What's your name?" Pratyush asked.

"R-Ras," the young soldier stuttered.

He patted Ras on the shoulder. "It's best to be smart and empathetic, but you also have to be calculating. Everything creates a reaction. I hope you never need an interference like this."

Ras shook his head. "No. *Nope.*"

"Good." Pratyush hurried to the small hut and helped the father up.

"Please," he begged, "please . . . she's my only child. I'll give you, and your men, anything else. Everything else, if you want."

"That won't be necessary," he said, pained by the man's desperation. It mirrored the sort of desperation he'd felt when he couldn't save his sister.

Pratyush pushed aside the cloth covering, a flimsy door to the small home, his stomach turning rancid. The girl was in the corner, terrified and immobile. For a moment, he was immobile, too, with thoughts of how Pritika might've been in this situation.

When the girl's eyes widened with a new terror—a hundred new horrors must've crossed her thoughts trapped with the three of them—Pratyush immediately gestured for her to go to the door as he took large strides away to give her space. She didn't deserve any of this, and he regretted that he hadn't acted faster.

She gasped, as if she'd been too scared to even breathe, and moved toward the exit. Dev went for the soldier before he could stop her. The soldier had barely looked over his shoulder by the time Dev shoved him face-first onto the floor.

The soldier fought to no avail, grunting and reaching for his sword. The girl, on her way to the door, kicked the weapon out of the soldier's reach. She gulped and stared at Pratyush, as if he might be upset enough to hit her.

He moved even farther away from the door, giving her as much space as possible. "I'm sorry this happened to you," he said softly, empathetically. "This is his own fault. You've done nothing wrong, but you should go."

She ran off, the cloth door covering rustling with the movement.

Pratyush squatted beside the soldier, who demanded, "What are you doing?"

"You said this was the hill you'd die on."

"No!"

"Oh? No? Not when you're the victim, huh? You said soldiers should be allowed whatever they desired, and I told you to remember those words. Do you know how much Dev desires to hurt you? Ever since you mocked him for his . . . what did he say to you?" Pratyush looked at Dev, one brow quirked.

Dev replied in that sullen, flat tone of his, "You said my mother was a hideous toad on stilts, and my sister so vile the thought of her made you vomit. That my kind was disgusting and revolting and that I smelled of rancid carcasses. That if not for the King, you'd kill me to put me out of my misery yourself." He leaned down. *"Now* who do you want to put out of their misery?"

"Okay! Fine!" the soldier cried. "I won't touch her!"

"No," Pratyush said, rubbing his temple in agitation. "You won't touch her, but you'll be upset. At who? At us, for doing this, and not at yourself for needing this sort of intervention. Do you think this is the world we fight for? Risk our lives battling monsters only to come home to different sorts of evil? You just don't understand what's wrong here; instead, you blame others. And I'm tired of telling you to behave. You're grown. You should understand words. But you don't. So! To help you learn empathy—that means compassion, by the way; that's, uh, a couple new words for you—here we go." He rubbed his hands together.

"What?" the man croaked.

Dev yanked down the soldier's pants. He squirmed, but it wouldn't help him now.

"It's a different terror when you're exposed like this, isn't it? This is what your victims feel. Imagine that these moments stay with them and their loved ones for years, eternity even. Some . . . go as far as ending their own lives." Pratyush swallowed on those last words.

"You do this to them and don't even care, going on with your life like nothing happened. You should've listened when I told you to stop. But if you're ever stupid enough to think about doing this again, remember this day. Is this why you put girls on their faces? It's hard to fight back, isn't it?" Pratyush's jaw clenched as he tried not to think about the bruises on Pritika's face from when her betrothed had pushed her facedown onto the floor.

Dev pulled out his dagger and pressed the hilt against the soldier's lower back, dragging it down. The soldier flinched and tried to crawl away.

"Please, don't!" he cried.

"I should let Dev have his way with you so you can learn another new word: *consent*. Also, Dev is a cannibal. Did you know that? Huh! The things you learn when you sit around a monster's beheaded corpse and chat."

"I beg you!" the soldier cried, and then *literally* cried.

"Why? Were you going to have mercy on that girl when she begged? You're special, then. And to think you're okay with even your mother and sister and wife and daughter experiencing this. One evil deed calls upon karma. Karma doesn't care if you're a man or rich or you've saved entire kingdoms with one kill. Karma knows the weight of your actions for equal return. I wonder how many evil deeds you've committed. How many times should Dev do this to repay you?" He stood and walked to the door, calling back to Dev, "Do what you want, my man, since apparently soldiers deserve whatever they desire. So, yeah, have at it, I guess."

Dev chortled and jammed the hilt of his dagger deep into the soldier's . . . lower back. Bones cracked. Dev clutched the soldier's hair and yanked him onto his side, inching so close to his face that he could lick him for a taste if he wanted.

"You are *lucky* that I'm not like you. I don't care for puny creatures masquerading as men or soldiers who piss themselves and cry at first sign of the sort of looming torture they inflict upon others. Most of all, I do not care to touch filth." Dev slammed the soldier's head into the ground and punched him in the crotch. The soldier howled, clutching himself and rolling onto his stomach.

Dev jerked him back onto his side. "I also detest weak men. They're beneath me. And the next time you even think of taking a girl, remember my fist." He punched him again. "And where this dagger will go next time, since you apparently like shoving things into places they don't belong."

Pratyush lifted the covering and stepped out. His fighters stood around as still as trees, in the exact horrified manner, in the exact positions he'd left them in. Oh, right. Cloth coverings didn't muffle much, did they?

"Let's be clear," Pratyush told them. "I may be young, but you listen to me or get off my team. I don't care what you've been taught is your *right*. If it violates someone else's rights, then you're trash. And we incinerate our trash, don't we?"

The others nodded, agreeing, and he was grateful not to find another look of defiance on this matter.

Dev emerged soon after, dragging the soldier out by his hair, past the petrified girl in the arms of her panicked father.

Dev shoved him forward so that the soldier fell to his knees in front of the girl.

"You got something to say?" Dev growled.

The soldier swallowed and muttered, "I'm sorry."

The "apology" wasn't enough, and it wasn't sincere, but his humiliation held some weight. He'd think twice before trying this again, and so would those witnessing this.

Dev kept the soldier in place, who pleaded apologies until the girl no longer seemed terrified. This man had taken power from her, and she deserved to take it back.

When the girl and her father relaxed, releasing the burdens of fear and shame, they thanked Pratyush and Dev, even the other soldiers who stood guard. The villagers watching should know these acts were violent crimes and would not be tolerated. That this girl had done nothing to bring shame, while this man on his knees had done all the wrong.

Dev dragged him to his feet, forcing him to walk, a limp with every painful step. The smell of piss wafted through the air.

"Now who stinks?" Dev snarled. "You rancid carcass."

NINE

MANISHA
(THIRTY-SEVEN DAYS AGO)

Manisha's sari was soaked through with dishwater. A sense of dread clawed up her spine like sharp talons carving her bones. She hurried outside to catch the slayer, to tell him *Yes, now, no time to waste, let's go!*

"Why are you running?" Sita demanded. "Apsara do not run!"

Manisha licked her lips and caught her breath. "The—the farewell."

"He's gone. You seem too eager to return to him."

"My service was incomplete, then." Her stomach lurched beneath Sita's glare.

By the gleam in Sita's narrowed eyes, the twist of her lips—she must've known that Manisha was planning something. There was no point in staying here, and another opportunity like the slayer's offer might never happen again. She was so stupid. She should've gone with him when he'd asked.

Her chest heaved as she prepared for Sita's punishment. The most common was scrubbing floors and picking up debris in the orchards. The worst was being sold to a soldier, but that usually happened to girls who'd been touched by men. Sometimes an accusation was all it took.

Sita wistfully looked off into the distance. "Get to bed. We have a long day tomorrow with the fig harvest, and I need you to oversee the preparation. My favorite time of the year, you know. The King pays handsomely for our chutney."

Manisha let out a thankful pant, taking a step forward. Sita moved in front of her to block off the path.

"You're dripping wet and unfit to walk through the temple like this. Such shame. Go through the back," Sita demanded.

"Y-yes, of course," Manisha muttered.

She turned from Sita and took another path, leaving the fiery sconces lighting the courtyard and wandering into the darkness. At least, since they were above the clouds, unobstructed starlight and moonlight shone brightly. It was never as dark as it was in the jungles below, and sometimes she missed the shadows. She missed her cave, sitting beside her mother and sisters beneath glowworms and flickering fireflies. Of course, back then she'd worried about being attacked by the army but never about being sold to a soldier. Somehow that seemed infinitely worse.

The damp silk of her sari clung to her waist and chest, turning colder by the second. She couldn't wait to change out of these wet clothes, warm up by the fire, and figure things out.

Something rustled in the brush behind her. Manisha paused, searching the darkness. There weren't many creatures to share the floating mountains with, but they did have some. Rabbits and owls, frogs that wandered from the ponds, birds that preferred the cold on their gossamer wings . . . but never a snake.

A golden serpent slithered out, so rare and brilliant that it glimmered like a hundred jewels in the moonlight, finer than anything the Queen could've owned.

"Such a beauty," Manisha said in awe, kneeling to offer a hand and giggling at the thought. "Don't worry, this isn't a gesture to marry you."

The snake, with curious speckled moss-colored eyes, slid around Manisha's wrist as she stood upright. She studied the serpent in the faint light, and the serpent studied her in return. Such mesmerizing eyes. Such exquisiteness. Such elegant movements. How anyone could fear or vilify serpents was beyond her.

She guessed the serpent was female based on the long, slender tail and said, "Should I name you...Noni?" She pronounced it "no-knee," which meant *small* in her mother tongue. It also referred to a fruit with green coloring that perfectly matched the serpent's eyes.

Noni reminded Manisha of the serpent-wrapped pillars of her homeland—of the creature her people were said to descend from. Her soft colors would've blended so well with the gardens hanging from balconies. She'd be right at home among the glowing vines growing around the pillars lining the road into the city of Anand, nestled in the heart of the canyonlands.

She basked in the same maternal affection she'd had for the writhing mass inside her bangle's oval egg. Could Noni be the serpent from her bracelet? The one from her vision? No. That was impossible. That wasn't how snakes were born.

But Noni didn't look like an ordinary serpent.

While Manisha was too enamored to notice a man walking toward her, Noni spotted him right away. She moved her head over Manisha's shoulder.

"Priestess," the man said, his voice gruff.

Manisha jumped and spun around, holding Noni to her chest. Her heart rattled against her ribs. "Wh-what are you doing here?"

"I'm afraid I'm lost."

She narrowed her eyes, her pulse raging. "The farewell is over. You shouldn't be here. The rules—"

"Aren't rules meant to be broken? Or at least bent?" He walked out from beneath the trees. He was the man who had accompanied the slayer, the one with a scar across his jaw. The hungry look in his eyes was gone, but they were still hard. Unyielding. This didn't feel right.

He explained, "I just wanted to see the night sky from this height. It's a shame guests aren't allowed to stay the night. You might have more patrons if that rule was changed, no?"

She watched him without a word, her legs like stone.

He sighed and added, "Maybe I'm a sap? When you see destruction and poverty, you can't help but to enjoy this serenity. You're fortunate."

"I can call a mayura for you," she said warily, shaking.

"Could I stay a moment longer? I'll never get this chance again." He took two steps toward her, but she couldn't seem to move. "What's in a moment?"

His question reverberated inside her head. She thought he'd step toward her again. Instead, he went around and cut through the temple perimeter.

"You aren't allowed there!" she called after him, but he ignored her and made his way toward the orchards.

Manisha looked back at the temple, but there wasn't anyone in sight. She couldn't just let him roam the grounds. Who would be able to find him then? And if she lost him, she'd surely get into trouble.

She vacillated between her options: run and tell Sita, or keep him in her sights? But as he disappeared into the shadows, she grunted and hurried after him, calling out, "Wait!"

He moved quickly for someone who wasn't running. His long legs took him faster and farther until she was running barefoot on fallen nutshells and twigs, flinching with every cut, all while holding the serpent against her and trying to keep the man in view. Noni made Manisha feel less alone in this strange, unsettling situation.

The man finally stopped at the very edge of the floating mountain, where a wall of waist-high shrubs acted as a reminder of the dangers beyond. He slipped through a narrow opening between the bushes and Manisha gasped. If he fell over, his blood would be on her hands!

As she ran after him, she kept searching for someone, anyone.

"Be careful!" she rasped, squeezing through the shrubs and traipsing over patches of grass and sprouts of wheat. She gulped when the wind surged upward, pushing her back. Her heartbeat fluttered with the sort of exhilaration she hadn't felt since before the Fire Wars, when she fell from heights just to know what it was like to fly. She did *not* want to fall from this high up.

"It's all right," he said, looking back at her before turning to the world beyond. "This is magnificent! Don't you think?"

Manisha gulped.

"Come. See where I live. Out that way, where fires create a circle around the lake." He pointed to the west, to a pair of lakes that marked the line between the old kingdom and the new.

"And this sky." He looked upward. "We are truly in heaven."

She dug her toes into the dirt. An invisible force stopped her from going any farther. Beneath the man's feet, pebbles and earth crumbled, falling thousands of feet below to the jungles.

"Please step back and return to the courtyard," she insisted.

"Don't fret," he replied, suddenly closing the gap between them. "But it's endearing that you worry over me."

Manisha had been so concerned about being this close to the edge that she didn't notice the serpent slithering around her neck and across her collarbone. Noni sat possessively on her shoulder.

"Are you done now?" she asked quietly, breathless.

Traces of hunger danced across his eyes as he looked down at the damp silk clinging to her chest. She crossed her arms, trying to make herself small. Every warning bell in her body sounded.

Run, the voice had told her. She'd thought the voice was telling her to run to the slayer, but had it been telling her to run from *this man?* Manisha couldn't move. Her legs had turned to mush, her body heavy with terror.

He wasn't as tall as the slayer, but he still stood at an intimidating height. He dragged his eyes back to hers. "The legends are true. You are of extraordinary beauty."

"What?" she mumbled.

"Legends of the apsara are well known. And the slayer won't *shut up* about you."

Heat rose to her face, her thoughts tumbling. Did the slayer really talk about her to others—to this disturbing man?

"He goes on and *on* about your eyes and lips and skin. . . ."

She gulped. Was the slayer so crass?

He was reaching out to her when Noni hissed. "What a nasty thing around your neck."

She wanted to spit, *A rare and valuable creature, actually, and friendlier than you. I insist you return to the courtyard now.* But her throat dried up and her words vanished.

"Come lie with me," he said softly.

"What?" she croaked, her heart skipping several beats, her eyes blooming wide. Terrified was an understatement.

"Take me to your room."

She dropped her arms, her fists balling up at her sides. Hot air rushed up her lungs. "You—you know that isn't allowed. Leave. Please." Her words came out quiet, insecure.

"But I am a *god* who walks among the temple grounds," he boomed, so bold that he could've fooled most.

"Blasphemy," she whispered.

Anger lit his face on fire, his eyes bulging as he bellowed, "You dare to question a god!"

Manisha flinched, hoping others were nearby and had heard. Hoping someone would come running to her aid. Even then, her brain fell back into the survivor mode she'd been so accustomed to in the jungles. How fast could she run? How hard could she hit? Where was the closest weapon?

She replied, buying time, stepping back, "If—if I question a god, he'll show patience in dealing with me." *If I question a man . . . he'll throw a tantrum.*

His nostrils flared large, dragging in copious amounts of air to fill his head. He took three monstrous steps toward her, looming just half a head taller, and snarled. "What will you do now?"

"Please leave," she whimpered.

"And if I do not leave?"

Her chest ached from the power of her ricocheting heart. She nearly choked on the adrenaline raging up her throat.

"You can't deny me, can you?" he asked, gripping her wrist.

Manisha yelped. Birds in the canopy trilled behind them. Noni lunged at him, fangs bared and determined to bite. But he was fast. He grabbed Noni in midair and flung her over the edge.

"No!" Manisha shrieked, running past him to reach out. But the poor creature fell from such a grueling height that all Manisha could see was utter darkness.

"No more screaming," he growled from behind her as cloth fell over her face.

In the tightest grip imaginable, he pulled the fabric to the back of Manisha's head. She couldn't see. She couldn't breathe. She couldn't scream.

She clutched at the cloth, trying to yank it off even the slightest bit, but he had a deadly grip. She panicked, gulping for air, her skin hot while he shoved her to the ground. She fell onto her face, the last of her breath knocked out of her.

One hand felt the edge of the mountain while the other gripped the fabric, desperate to get even one finger under to let in air. She needed more hands . . . to fight him off, to keep her sari down, to pry open his fist at the back of her head where his hold tightened the cloth, to punch and slap and gouge out his eyes.

But Manisha *didn't* have enough hands. And in this second, she didn't have enough air and it seemed that she also had a finite number of rib-bruising heartbeats left. But perhaps that was a blessing in this spiraling nightmare.

In a world where monsters were hunted and warriors were honored, how was it that the two could converge and no one had known?

Unspeakable panic clashed with ineffable pain. Manisha's mind shut down, went dark as her final breaths withered in her lungs. His every movement sent her closer to the edge until her cheek scraped the floating mountain's outermost pebbles. Howling winds from below clawed at her tightly covered face. The cloth dampened with her tears and saliva as she choked.

It wasn't until the last of his thrusts that he released his hold on the cloth. It unwound itself from her face and fluttered below in a dizzying haze. Her skin was fire and ice, her head hanging off a crumbling ledge.

In the most surreal minutes of her life, she felt nothing and everything at the same time. She saw both her past and future collide in the darkness that went in and out of blurred vision. The entire world splintered like the inside of her throat. The vast sky ripped apart like the fabric of her sari. The expanse of the universe pulled asunder like her weakened body.

Manisha was both flesh and ghost. She felt the ground beneath her and the burn inside of her, but she also floated above herself, watching in a frozen strangeness. This depraved man squatted over her body, which lay like a corpse beneath him. He stroked her hair and plucked a jasmine from her braid, tucking it into his pocket like a disturbing keepsake.

As she gulped in a breath, her ghostly remains seemed to fly back into her body. She wheezed and struggled to turn over. A figure emerged from the orchards, watching from over the shrubs.

"General?" Sita gasped. "You were only supposed to touch her."

She looked at Manisha. Was she appalled by the sight? Or was she worried Manisha had seen her? Her own Head Priestess had delivered her into the violent hands of this monster.

Manisha wasn't sure why she expected Sita's help, but she was desperate for it.

Sita's thin lips curled into a snarl, her words vile. "You have desecrated these holy grounds."

Manisha whimpered, tears streaming down her face.

"You came here cursed, and you shall leave cursed. Your beauty destroyed, your bones broken, and your spirit shattered."

Manisha spat the taste of blood from her mouth and wept, "What did I ever do to you?"

Sita's eyes, filled with a hatred Manisha had never seen, stayed firm on her. "The Nightmare Realm kept coming to me. It demanded I release you. You are of darkness. You don't belong here." Then she glared at the General. "This is more than a *compromising position*."

He grinned like the demons themselves. "I couldn't help myself. Now there's no question. She's defiled."

Oh no. Defiled girls were sold. Had—had Sita sold her to *him*?

The General looked down at Manisha and said, "Loose ends always need to be tied up."

With those words, he sent a swift and powerful kick to her stomach.

Both her flailing body and her piercing screams flew over the edge of the floating mountain, the place everyone believed was a refuge from the world's cruelty. The descent passed slowly as her insides churned into themselves. The mountain transformed into the rock that Manisha had seen from below. The clouds swallowed it whole while the jungle reclaimed her.

Her back hit branches and trees. Thorns shredded her skin to rags and blood poured out in rivulets. Grunts and warped cries escaped her mouth. Bones crunched, entombed inside her skin. Until she finally hit her grave.

It wasn't as hard and shattering as it should've been. There was a disturbing squirming softness beneath her.

Snakes. Serpents. Vipers.

Hundreds of them in all sizes, coiled and lashing. Agitated and ravenous.

As Manisha lay there, nearly dead but not quite, unable to move, unable to whimper, unable to even close her eyes, a pit of snakes rose like a dark wave. Hissing and striking, sinking fangs into every inch of her flesh until her blood turned as toxic as their venom.

They slithered over her, consuming her in a mass of writhing bodies, biting, contracting, until the mass seemed to swallow her whole. As if Manisha and this wild tangle of countless serpents had become a singular, ghastly beast.

A point came when pain and fear overpowered Manisha with such immeasurability that they no longer meant anything. She'd crossed that threshold, from pure terror to absolute numbness.

To stave off bone-chilling, bloodcurdling agony, her mind detached itself and drifted off to the plane where her foremothers waited with open arms. It had been so long since she'd last seen them, since the terrifying night before she left her family for the floating mountains—the night she was buried in a shallow ash grave. She was supposed to be safe in the heavens, but even heaven had a dark side.

Her foremothers spoke, but she couldn't hear them above the serpents' hissing. They took her hand and led her across windy pastures to the water. She'd never seen the sea, but Mama had said it was like an endless river filled with strange creatures, beautiful and deadly.

Manisha tugged away as they led her into the water, but the sand and rocks sank beneath her weight, drawing her forward. She fought and panicked as water rose to her knees, her hips, her shoulders, her chin, her nose...

She held her breath, her chest burning and spasming with the need to breathe, her body convulsing as her lungs finally took in water. Something so pertinent to life had become the deadliest thing of all.

She begged her ancestors to save her, but they merely watched empathetically.

"See where your people have fled," they hissed as one. "For one cannot reassemble the lost without knowing where to find them."

One voice rose above the others, intoning, "Three of three to lead them. Crowns of fang, thorn, and glass, molded by fire and as inescapable as *venom*."

Manisha gasped and choked as water filled her body. Her ancestors turned blurry as water rose above her.

This, she thought, *must be death*.

TEN

MANISHA
(THIRTY-ONE DAYS AGO)

Manisha's entire body thrummed, every inch screaming, humming in an onslaught of sensations. Her bones hurt and crackled. Her blood burned rivers beneath her skin. Her eyes ached as she slowly opened them.

She'd slept upon a mass of slumbering serpents, some coiled, some entangled. They breathed in and out as if one being.

Her grogginess made the world seem to shudder, surreal, and made it hard to wake up. She swallowed, her throat dry and her mouth tasting like metallic blood. She licked dry, cracked lips, turning parched, dizzy.

Her body shifted forward into a sitting position, but it wasn't her doing. The serpents beneath her pushed her up, creating a throne of scales and muscles and fangs. They watched her, alert but subdued, nothing like the aggravated mass she'd fallen into.

What was happening? How could she still be alive?

Manisha yelped in pain as her bones shifted back into place, tears sliding down her face. She jerked with every fracture realigning, every snap. To feel bones return to their ligaments and tendons, to have torn muscles and blood vessels fuse together, to have skin snap back into place—they were wildly unsettling sensations scurrying through her. A body filled with creepy, crawly things. Even breathing seemed to be bruising her ribs.

The serpents kept her in place while her body fixed itself. Somehow. Nothing made sense. Snakes didn't lie together in giant clusters. They didn't support a person this way. And a body didn't survive a fall like that, much less mend itself this quickly.

Above, the night sky twinkled around the underside of the floating mountain. Had she been asleep for hours, days, months? The moon came in and out of view behind clouds. Two entire phases had passed, which meant she'd slept for six days.

How is any of this possible?

The world kept spinning, noises buzzing and echoing, muffled inside her skull like wailing ghosts.

All around, the jungle glowed in iridescence. Vines snaking up trees sparkled with budding leaves. Mushrooms bloomed in pale yellow. Midnight flowers burst open in dazzling pinks and purples. Shimmering green outlined ferns.

Manisha squeezed her eyes shut and opened them again. Was this real?

With a groan, she moved forward, fighting through every motion. She gripped a rock over the edge of the pit. A wave of backbones clicked into place, and she winced, holding on even tighter. When she opened her eyes, the rock in her hand had crumbled into dust.

Her hands shook. Was this even her body? She panted, her thoughts delirious, trying to make sense of everything.

Ridges and craters from a thousand snakebites had created a new layer of skin, no longer smooth, but a map of welts, a new Manisha. Tears prickled her eyes.

She crawled out of the pit. The serpents gently pushed Manisha the rest of the way until she was on her knees. Her ripped sari was stained with blood, smeared with dirt, and caught beneath every crawl until she stood. She gathered the fabric that had unwound and slowly, painfully, wrapped it around herself again. She had to lean against a tree for support.

For the longest time, she went in and out of dizziness. A whooshing sound, a foggy sensation, filled her head, so loud when all else was eerily quiet. She'd never been so alone. She'd never felt this helpless. This worthless. What was the point of going on?

Everything was a struggle, an unending fight. Every thought, every breath, every movement.

A hissing sound had her searching the bioluminescence.

A snake slithered down the tree, its tail wrapped around the limb right above her.

"Noni?" Manisha rasped, the vibration scratching her throat.

She stretched out her hands. Tears fell for an entirely new reason. A friend, a connection to her people, something of comfort in a sea of chaos.

Surely this was the snake from the temple with her shimmering golden scales and moss-colored eyes. But Noni was twice the size.

"Have you grown? And how did you survive that fall? Poor beta," she said, working through the pain in her throat.

Noni stared at her and tilted her head, as if asking Manisha how *she'd* survived that fall.

"Point well made." She draped Noni over her shoulder and hugged the familiar creature to her chest. At least she wasn't completely alone.

Owls hooted in the distance and crickets played their songs. Fireflies danced across the jungle as Manisha pushed herself off the tree and walked, cringing with every step. She didn't know where she was going or what she should do. She just walked.

"Some people despise snakes, you know?" Manisha said aloud.

"But you remind me of home, like we're one step closer to my family. Thank you."

It seemed like a silly thing to try to hold a conversation with an animal, but the silence was worse. The mental and emotional isolation she'd been wading through in the temple had amplified now that there wasn't another person for miles. The quiet was a ringing in her ears. For the first time ever, Manisha was truly alone. And she couldn't determine if any of this was freeing or terrifying. No one waited to scold her, yet every small noise made her jump.

She traveled for two days, painfully picking fruit and nuts and drinking what little water she found hidden in reddish pitcher plants. Noni stayed nestled loosely around her neck, watching everything Manisha did.

Snakes were awfully soundless, adding to a quietude ripe for drawing out haunting thoughts. Memories of that dreadful night, flickers of terror, sparks of agony. She just wanted to get out of her head, out of this nightmare.

As dawn rose, the bioluminescence of the jungle fractured with morning warbles. It took forever before Manisha reached a river. She dropped to her knees at the water's edge and drank and drank. She carefully washed her tender face and arms, imagining how daunting it would be to wash the rest of her body. How bruised and broken she was, not because of the fall, but because of an attacker...

She crouched off to the side of the river, her body aching and screaming, so dirty, so...defiled. She wanted to scrub her skin off, crawl out of her body, anything to get away from the pain. But she wasn't ready. Not yet.

Exhaustion set in. She tried to climb a tree and failed. She tried over and over, unable to grip the trunk, unable to find the strength to hoist herself up, scraping her palms and legs, catching her sari. This had once been so easy, and now it had become a grueling effort. The more Manisha tried, the more she failed, and the more she failed, the more she lost any hold of her emotions.

Her chest was burning hotter and hotter. Her skin felt like scorching coals. Her eyes burned and her head throbbed. All in an effort to hold it in. But she couldn't keep it contained.

A sea of tears, of sadness, isolation, helplessness, of everything that made her feel worthless crashed into her until she was slumped against the tree on the dirty ground, utterly defeated and hiccupping through her sobs. She pulled her knees to her chest and wept a million tears.

MANISHA STRETCHED IN THE MORNING LIGHT. NONI WAS wrapped around her arm when she reached up to grab an orange-and-pink fruit that tasted like mangoes and berries. Swallowing still hurt, a hundred jagged knives skidding down her throat.

After eating a few ripe fruits, aware of the taste but overall numb to thoughts, Manisha went for the bath she so desperately needed. She picked plumeria along the way, to add oil and fragrance to smooth her skin and maybe erase the stink of that man. The General. That was what Sita had called him.

The sounds and smells of the jungle crept back from her memory. The smell of dirt and leaves. The sensation of pebbles underneath angry soles. Being back in the jungle brought a sense of urgency to flee, to constantly be aware of her surroundings, but Manisha also felt a little more like herself. Freedom. To move, breathe, look, and behave how she wanted to, and run to find her family.

She let her shoulders slump, throwing proper posture to the wind. A small, rebellious thing felt so liberating.

How was she going to find anyone in this vast wilderness? She'd waited so long for this moment, but now what?

Pushing aside undergrowth, Manisha walked along the river until she saw a secluded area, a small cove where maybe the current wasn't as strong. The river was so vast that she could hardly make out the trees on the other side. This had to be Yamuna—the Great River. All she knew was that the water moved south, toward home at the southern border. The ground beneath her feet changed from dirt and mud to fine sand and pebbles. Sand was a good exfoliator. Maybe she could scrub the General's touch off her.

Noni slithered off, behind rocks. Manisha let her roam freely—not that she had any say over the creature. Still, she knew Noni would always find her. It was a strange but comforting sense.

Ahead, a woman appeared past the brush, her back to Manisha as she faced the river's sparkling, rippling surface. She was near the murkier spots, which usually meant deeper and more dangerous areas. She disrobed, her dress falling from her shoulders.

Sunlight penetrated the canopy around Manisha, but there was nothing above the woman to prevent the full light of day from hitting her dewy skin: a creamy dark brown, the color of sandalwood.

Manisha immediately looked around, searching for others. Women never bathed in the open alone. Her instincts told her everything was a danger, but she desperately wanted someone to . . . she wasn't sure. Talk to? Confide in? Cry with? Hug?

Apsara didn't touch; Manisha hadn't had any physical affection since her mother and sisters had last embraced her.

This was the first person she'd seen in days. The world hadn't abandoned her! But was this woman friend or foe? She let out a sigh.

The woman at the riverbank turned around, the motion a jarring movement in the surrounding stillness. She glared at Manisha, her eyes dripping with anger.

Manisha swallowed and looked away.

"What are you doing here?" the woman demanded, her voice carrying over the water like a yell.

"I—I'm sorry. I'm lost." Manisha worked her jaw, as if learning to speak again. "I'm looking for my family. Or anyone, really. I was just about to bathe. I'll go farther down the river."

"Why aren't you looking at me? Does my nudity make you uncomfortable?" the woman asked, her voice so confident and self-assured that she sounded like a royal.

Manisha kept her stare at the ground but listened to every creak and crunch and movement in case there were others nearby. "Your privacy belongs to you."

"Hmm."

There was movement in the water and then rustling. A moment later, the woman announced, "I'm dressed," as she adjusted her garment around her. The hem dipped in the water, turning damp.

She was wearing a simple, flowing, pale yellow dress that reached her ankles. Bell sleeves covered her elbows. Her dress was the color of daffodils and fit perfectly into the color palette of pastures and prairies. Maybe she lived in a meadow. That seemed more fitting for her type of dress.

"What happened to you?" the woman asked, jerking her chin at Manisha's dirty, torn clothes.

A few weeks after Manisha had first arrived at the temple, she stood in the shadows as the then–Head Priestess declared a temple girl unclean. A single accusation was all it took. The priestesses cast her out.

"Being defiled is a reflection on you," Sita had hissed. "Your blame, your shame, and your burden to carry. Why were you walking alone? What were you wearing? Did you maintain distance? Did you look him in the eye for too long, smile too eagerly, give him any indication that he should touch you? You have no place among clean girls, much less a heavenly place such as this."

What if the defilement had been Manisha's fault? She couldn't remember clearly enough to know if she'd led him on. If only she'd cleaned the dishes quicker. If only she hadn't run after him. If only she'd reacted faster.

The apsara said this sort of thing was dishonorable, never to be discussed—a secret to keep, a disgrace to take to the grave. Yet Manisha found herself desperately wanting to tell someone.

"I was defiled," Manisha said quietly. She meant to say it with anger, but the words came out hoarse, almost unsure.

She braced for the woman's shocked expression. Maybe remorse, maybe a frown dismissing her situation, maybe judgment. Maybe even cruelty, apathy.

The woman expressed none of those things. She gasped, her impassiveness melting into compassion. Her entire demeanor changed. Her rigidness, her features, and her tone softened. "Do you mean you were violated? Raped?"

Manisha didn't know. The kingdom used words like *defiled, unclean, unworthy, broken, dirty, used*. But *violated*? That sounded violent, with a perpetrator and a victim. Not as one-sided as the apsara had taught.

"What is . . . rape?"

The woman kindly explained, "It's when one person sexually violates another, without the other person's consent. Is that what happened?"

Manisha bit her lip and nodded, tears flooding her eyes.

"Oh . . . I'm so, so sorry. Are you all right?"

Such simple words, and yet so kind that they almost made Manisha break down. She wanted to sob.

Manisha wasn't all right. She was filled with pain and confusion, but most of all, fear. Her thoughts raced with vulgar flashbacks. Her bones ached. Her skin burned. Her privacy had been ripped apart. The urge for violence—the very thing that she'd been taught to abhor for the past five years—gurgled up from the pit of her soul and consumed her. She wanted to lash out at her attacker. She wanted to be violence itself.

Manisha was not enraged. She *was* rage. She'd never wanted to be so destructive, even as upended as she felt. "As all right as one can be," she finally replied, her apsara training still in control of her emotions.

The woman watched her. She didn't seem convinced. "It's okay if you're not. You can feel whatever you feel."

Manisha didn't respond.

"What happened to him?"

She shrugged. "I don't know. He kicked me off a cliff and I went unconscious in a ditch for a while. By the phase of the moon, maybe several days."

"You survived days like that?"

"It seems so."

"What a resilient young woman you are. Impressive and worthy, and never think less."

Manisha's eyes widened. She'd never been referred to as a woman, always a girl. A girl who was subservient and young and needed another to direct her. Out of all the words this stranger said, *woman* was the most complimentary, and it made Manisha feel a little stronger.

"What are you going to do about him?" the woman asked, her voice hard.

"What do you mean?"

The woman lowered her chin and her voice. "I mean... what are you going to do about the man who violated you?"

Manisha shook her head, confused. She'd never heard anyone ask such a question. "I don't know. I—I have no idea where to find him. And if I did, I don't know what I *could* do."

The woman released her intensity and said, "Sometimes we don't need to do anything about them, but you should do something for yourself."

"I don't understand."

"Whatever you need to heal."

"Right now, all I want is a safe bath, food, water, and to find my family."

The woman's voice softened. "I understand. You can bathe here. It's safe; I promise. Otherwise, I wouldn't be here alone."

"Why *are* you alone? Where's your village?"

She pointed at the river, into the murky depths. "My name's Kumari. I'm a yakshini, a protector of this river. I live in the underwater city of Yamun."

Ripples moved back and forth in the water behind Kumari. Something *very* large lurked beneath the surface.

Kumari followed Manisha's gaze. "Oh, don't worry. That's just my makara."

Manisha stumbled over the word, repeating, "Ma-makara?"

Kumari smiled. "Mm-hmm. He's a beautiful one. If you'd like to travel the river, he can take you wherever you'd like."

Manisha stayed frozen to the spot. "No, thank you."

Kumari shrugged and walked into the jungle. "Suit yourself. I'll find you some food while you bathe." She leaned back into view from behind the ferns. "Are you strictly vegetarian?"

Manisha hadn't been before the temples. She shook her head.

The yakshini beamed. "Delightful! My makara will fetch some fish for us. He'll find the plumpest trout!" And off she went.

Manisha eyed the shadow of the makara moving away as she kept toward the small cove, partially cut off by boulders, where the water reached her waist. Noni appeared behind a tree and watched the giant, spectral mass of a water dragon from overhead.

After another search of the area, Manisha stripped off her clothes and knelt in the water with a fistful of flowers and another fistful of sand. Waves lapped at her shoulders and ebbed forward and away.

She scrubbed. Hard. Shuddering until she finally broke down into sobs. She cleaned every part of herself, unable to control her crying. Her fingertips ran over the new ridges of her body. They were everywhere, little entryways that had deposited streams of poison into her flesh.

She didn't understand how a person could have survived that fall—or an attack from so many vipers. She should be dead, not engorged with venom. Trying to make sense of it all hurt her head.

The plentiful bites didn't scab or bleed or leave open puncture wounds. They'd healed in sealed welts. She wished that the rest of her had healed this quickly.

Every time her hand moved closer to clean her privates, she jerked back and wept. She was too nervous to touch, to feel how battered she was, to remember someone else violently touching there. Until it was the only section left. She couldn't put it off forever, not when she'd been so desperate for this bath.

Her fingers trembled as she gently touched the area, her tears masked by the river water. The ache was gone, but the memory lingered, haunting like a scalding ghost. She brought her hand to the surface. Her fingers shook as blood trickled away.

Manisha cried until there were no tears left.

The only thing she wanted right now, more than vengeance, more than turning back time, was her mother and her sisters.

The shadow of the floating mountains could no longer reach her. She was finally free. She'd waited too long for this moment, this untethering, to let it float away with her tears and sorrows. She had to press forward and never stop until her mother and sisters were in her arms again. Until they were finally safe.

ELEVEN

PRATYUSH
(PRESENT DAY)

The King had always said slayers were the kingdom's treasure. But unlike the kingdom's other "treasures"—queens and jewels and rare artifacts—slayers weren't kept safe or held on display for others to appreciate. Nope. Just revered as heroes while forced into servitude.

It made sense at the time, not that Pratyush had much of a choice, orphaned and wanting to take care of his sister. It had seemed honorable. Protecting the kingdom from monsters protected everyone... well, except the monsters. But when he'd killed so often that the sight of blood didn't deter his appetite, when constant fighting didn't keep him awake at night, when life and death bled together into one endless nightmare, it was, eh, not such a great deal after all.

He thought he'd stayed for Pritika. Now he knew he'd never had a choice to begin with.

Pratyush had at least discovered a new frontier. It wasn't a monster or an adventure or riches. It was far more valuable.

He swallowed, seeing everything and everyone in front of him and yet not really seeing them at all. He wished his sister were here for him to talk to, about the voices in his head, about their parents, about matters of the heart. Was he doing any of this right? She'd been the one person who kept him grounded when he wanted to run off into the darkness. He hadn't felt that sort of levelheaded focus since. Until he smelled Manisha. She had him feeling like there was light in the darkness.

Sometimes, Pritika would sneak out of her room by climbing down from her balcony. A thing considered unladylike, and that could've gotten her into serious trouble, but she'd been quick and quiet. She'd hide sweets in her dupatta, tied around her waist like a warrior, and outmaneuver the guards to find Pratyush in a training field. They'd run off, Pritika giggling and showing him the best places to watch the stars. She'd tell him every detail of her time since they'd last seen each other. She'd express how she couldn't say these things to others for fear the Queen would find out, and then urge Pratyush to spill his thoughts.

He knew she spent her days in classes learning etiquette, sewing, music, and various other things. Pritika loved to learn, and he'd been happy to see her find joy in their situation. Ma used to say that people couldn't always control situations, but they could bend circumstances.

"I found a library under the palace," Pritika had whispered to him once, clamping her mouth shut, her eyes big and gleeful like this was her best secret.

"Okay . . ." Pratyush had said, not knowing what was so fantastic about a library.

"It's filled with gilded books. Not even scrolls," she'd said with awe. "Written in the ancient language. And there are passageways underneath the library. I hear sounds down there."

He'd scowled. "You have to be careful." But also, he'd been happy to see life coming back into his sister. She'd been mischievous before, finding anything their parents had hidden, pushing her boundaries, and venturing as far into the borderlands as she could with nothing more than a knife. Pratyush had been considered a serious boy who wanted to be just like their father. But Pritika had the free spirit and wanderlust of their mother, a soul meant for great adventures.

She'd turned the palace from a prison to an adventure.

She was the one person he wanted to tell about Manisha. How Manisha made him feel safe and unjudged, like he didn't have a million shortcomings. But also, how he was afraid that no apsara, much less Manisha, would want anything to do with him.

Glasses clinked in the massive banquet hall where the King, Queen, and noblemen sat for a feast whenever Pratyush and his fighters returned from conquest. The Queen, arrayed in the finest robed lehenga, draped in gold and jewels, roses around her bun, and a crown on her head worth more than entire villages, ate quietly like her required presence was an annoyance. Did she have better things to do than appreciate those who kept her from being clawed open by ravenous monsters?

She looked bored, and Pratyush wondered what the hell she did all day. She had servants for everything and, being married to someone as controlling as the King, didn't have say in any important matters and was removed from most people. Guess he'd be bored, too.

And the King? He was just annoying to look at. Food splattered across his beard, like he hadn't eaten in ages. Pratyush grimaced. Even monsters had better table manners.

"You look exhausted," the King commented around a mouthful of food. Gross.

Pratyush harrumphed. The King would be exhausted, too, if he'd just returned from slaying monsters. Anyway, Pratyush was at least enjoying a jamun lassi: dark plums mixed with water buffalo yogurt to create a sweet and tart creamy lavender drink topped with purple petals. He had three.

The King leaned back, his belly so round that he'd grown bigger than the pregnant Queen. Purple silks and beads of pearls hung from his neck; rubies coddled his fingers. Such luxury while so much of his kingdom starved, while others fought his battles. What would happen if Pratyush usurped him right here and now? He could slit his throat—a slayer was so fast that no one would notice until the King's giant head hit the table.

He was too tired to try.

The soldiers, assigned by the King, had gone out with Pratyush at a full force of fifty. They returned a weary dozen but ate enough for their fallen brothers-in-arms.

In the banquet room alone, the abundance of food and decadence overflowed like a raging monsoon river. The King's silver-and-gold plate remained full. Every time he took a bite, he was given more. Meanwhile, those in the villages were frail and starving.

Pratyush finished his food to the last morsel and had seconds. Another plate of lush rice turned golden with saffron and speckled with green tulsi, dried apricots, and crushed cashews. Alongside that, a piping-hot bowl of sambar filled with moringa pods, tomato slices, and eggplant. Slaying had taken its toll, and he'd been so famished that he thought his stomach would eat itself. To be honest, that wouldn't be the worst way to go.

When the General entered the room, the court applauded as if he'd done anything. The soldiers were too tired to reciprocate the energy. They watched him with weary eyes, shoveling food into their mouths and slouching back into their chairs. Why was anyone clapping, anyway? Where had he even been?

"Ah! The great slayer!" The General slapped Pratyush's back.

"You're late," the King growled.

"Forgive me. The court needed attention, and loose ends had to be tied up," he said with a bow before offering his usual obsequious flattery to the royals.

"Sit," the King ordered, downing his goblet of wine.

"Of course." The General sat beside Pratyush so that Pratyush was between the two. But because the royals liked their space, there was enough room between him and the King for an empty seat.

A rush of servants placed smaller plates in front of them.

Pratyush did a double take at the elegantly arranged assortment of buttery, nutty sweets topped with fragrant pink plumeria and sprinkled with toasted coconut shavings, luscious orange-red saffron, and gold flecks.

The last time Pratyush had seen these intricately made desserts was on the floating mountains in a pile for offerings. In the most sacred of sacred temples. The temple where *she* resided.

Manisha. Her name, an intoxicating drop on his tongue, tasted forbidden but so good that he wanted to say it again.

He took a deep breath filled with the aromas of sugar, cardamom, saffron, and cinnamon. Funny how a scent could throw a person into another lifetime harder than any blow. Suddenly, he wasn't in a crowded room flanked by annoyance but stepping barefoot on chilly marble floors, his shoulders wrapped in a warm shawl, quietly walking toward the sweets after prayer. Manisha's back to him. Her long, braided hair as black as the night sky, decorated with pearl-white flowers like twinkling stars. Her sari accentuating every curve, her skin smelling of rose oil and gardenias.

There was something about her that made him want to talk, say things he'd kept to himself for so long. Maybe because he could trust an apsara, or maybe it was just Manisha. Something about her chased away his loneliness, his feelings of worthlessness, and brought a way of thinking of himself that he hadn't known since Pritika passed away. He took pride in knowing how to tell who was lying and who was trustworthy, and Manisha, although she was hiding herself from him, was trustworthy.

When she looked at him with those emerald eyes, he saw strength but also sadness, and he wondered why. What had made her anything less than joyful? Why wasn't she carefree and happy? What had happened to her? He wanted to know everything.

While the King made sure to impress upon everyone how *he* saved the realm from monsters, and how his men were tools only as good as the one who wielded them, Pratyush questioned whether Manisha would ever tell him anything about herself. If she, an apsara, would ever trust him, a killer—much less love him.

The General asked, "Did you miss these?"

Pratyush snapped back to the present and ate.

"Tired, eh?"

"Yep," he muttered. He could've bypassed the pleasantries and traditions of the King, gone straight for a bath, and slept for three days. In fact, he would have preferred it. *Soon.*

Pratyush had known the General since his arrival. He had been there in the courtyard when the King first told Pratyush to fight. The General was only a soldier then but had taken Pratyush under his wing and helped train him. Yet they weren't friends. A slayer knew when to be careful.

He drew in a deep breath, smelling hints of the temple on the General, but also the recent bath he'd had before this meal. It was a confusing combination: the General's scent, the temple, mixed with...Manisha? Or was he just remembering Manisha too much, associating her smell with the temple?

Damn, he was too tired to think straight.

"What happened to you after I left the floating mountains?" he asked, eyeing the General.

"I misplaced something," he replied with a shake of his head.

"What was it?"

"What?"

Pratyush watched him carefully. "The apsara won't allow anyone to stay past dark. What did you misplace that made them bend the rule?"

The General chuckled, looking ahead at the others eating and drinking. "I already forgot."

"Did you, though?"

The General swallowed as he met Pratyush's stare and held it. In turn, Pratyush took note. He watched as the General's pupils dilated, expanding just the slightest bit. Sweat beads pushed out of his pores. A vein in his neck pulsed harder.

"How could I lie to you, Slayer?" he asked, his tone level. "You're far too perceptive."

Was he having an affair with one of the apsara? Bargaining illicitly with Sita? Searching for something?

"The Head Priestess knows me after so many years of service. I arrange for anything they need on behalf of the King and always deliver. Sometimes with extra. Those devout women want for nothing thanks to me. She had the kindness in her heart to allow me to return and search for it. While I don't remember what I thought I'd left behind, it turns out that I didn't have it on me in the first place." He laughed and bit into a diamond-shaped cashew sweet dusted in edible silver. "This brain. But don't tell the King. I don't want to lose my job if he thinks I'm getting forgetful."

"When you remember what you thought you lost, let me know."

"Of course!" He slapped Pratyush's shoulder.

Pratyush grunted and pushed back from his seat—he couldn't take any more music or food or drink. "I'm exhausted," he told the King. "Will you excuse me?"

"Ah! Yes! I know exactly what you need!" The King snapped his fingers and invited two beautiful young women to the table. Lavender silks draped their slender bodies, and strings of gold hung from their necks and wrists. Each wore her long hair braided over one shoulder.

Some watched with envy.

Pratyush didn't argue with the King. He was too tired to even think at this point. He let the girls lead him out through the double gold-rimmed doors, their faces encrusted with flowers made from jewels instead of paint. They quietly, quickly, led him to a room with a private bath. A pool the size of three beds was already filled with hot water. Steam curled upward, warming the air. Whole lotus flowers and rose petals floated on the surface, lacing the bath with fragrant oils.

"Did you add the rose oils like last time?" he asked, peeling off his shirt. He loved that stuff.

"Yes," one of the girls said.

He waited for them to turn before completely disrobing. The General thought it was a ridiculous thing, to be embarrassed getting naked in front of others, but whatever. No one was going to laugh at him over it. He'd mastered the deadpan look.

He quickly walked into the water, sighing as he sat down and sank into the most soothing bath he'd been in since leaving to kill the bhramari. His muscles went slack between the soothing scent and the heat.

Next to the steps, on the lip of the pool, sat a silver tray with a lavender bar of soap and a towel.

"Can we offer anything?" the second girl asked.

He cleared his throat and replied, "No."

"Are you certain we can't offer more this time?" she asked timidly.

He kept his eyes ahead, attentively listening to their movements in case they moved toward him. He could never be too careful. "No. You don't have to worry about that. The King doesn't ask you about me, does he?"

He glanced at them from over his shoulder. He could tell better if someone was lying by seeing them.

"No, Slayer," the first said, taking his clothes into her arms and heading toward the door.

The second lingered and bit her lip. "Slayer. Can I ask a question?"

"Sure."

"Why don't you take advantage of us the way the King offers?"

"I'm not interested."

"Oh," she said, disappointed. Rejection etched across her features with a deep blush.

"Not—not you in particular. But I don't condone taking someone against their will."

"But you have our consent."

He scowled. "Do I? Or does the King give you to me like anything else he owns? Did he ask you?"

"Actually, yes."

"What?" He watched her, surprised.

"He asked who among us would like to be dedicated to you, and we volunteered."

He raised his brows. "You're dedicated to me?"

She tilted her head and smiled invitingly. "As in no one else touches us. So, if you don't touch us, we go untouched forever."

"Oh . . ." Heat singed his cheeks.

"We do . . . want to be touched," she clarified.

He immediately turned back around. "No, thanks. But good to know this was your choice."

"Oh. Okay," she said. "Anything else we can do before we leave?"

"Yes. Please ask about these rose oils. I want to take some with me."

She laughed before stopping herself. Clearing her throat, a subtle sound that echoed against the surface of the water, she asked, "Where would you take oils to? Are you not only between here and errands?"

Errands? What the actual hell? Was that how people saw him? No longer a fierce slayer worthy of all glory and rivaled only by kings? But an *errand boy*, going to and fro at the King's dainty demands?

He closed his eyes and huffed out a breath. This wasn't right. None of this had ever felt right.

He didn't have a home, a house, or property. He came to the palace where the King fed him and clothed him and gave him food and rest. But he didn't own anything. He didn't have anything other than the clothes on his back at any given moment.

He'd worked to the edge of death, to the limits of the kingdom and back, and for what? He, just like everyone else, was at the mercy of the King and his far-reaching arm. Well, not for much longer. Not if Pratyush had anything to do with it.

EXPECTING TO SLEEP FOR THREE DAYS STRAIGHT WASN'T AN exaggeration. Not when Pratyush had gone weeks without a bed. Not when he'd gone weeks without a rose-oil-scented bath drenched in flowers. Stars, he loved that stuff. His callused, dry, wounded skin healed overnight, now as supple as that of the bored Queen herself.

After another giant meal, Pratyush walked alongside the King through his royal maze of magnificent gardens of towering trees and blooming gardenia bushes, terraces covered in flowering vines, and shrubs of lavender and marigolds and every color imaginable.

Amid the gardens, white peacocks strutted around, rare and prized like everything else here. They reminded him of the mayura from the floating mountains. He wondered why the King hadn't captured any to bring here. Maybe the apsara had rejected him?

He scoffed. Yeah. Right. If the King decreed, they couldn't deny him. As the most powerful man in the kingdom, the King was the only thing protecting them from the monsters below. He took what he wanted and kept what he needed.

"What are you frowning about, boy? Haven't you heard a word I said?" the King scolded.

"I was just wondering why you don't have a mayura."

He laughed. "Those wild things! They only listen to the apsara, and no temple priestess is allowed to leave the floating mountains. To tame an animal is one thing, my boy, but taming a fire-breathing creature is near impossible. I still don't understand how they do it."

"What's their origin? How did the sacred temple of the floating mountains and fire-breathing creatures tamed only by priestesses come to exist?"

The King waved his hand through the air, dismissing the question. "Eh. Who knows! I just don't want any fire hazards that can fight and fly around my palace. They tend to be temperamental."

Pratyush shrugged. "Fair enough."

"You've done a fine job with the bhramari. I heard you lost a few soldiers."

Pratyush recoiled as images flashed through his thoughts. Fighters snatched by vines and devoured by giant bloodthirsty pitcher plants. Ram eaten and burned alive.

The King went on, "I can't keep losing soldiers like this. At this rate, we'll end up sending out women and elderly, easy pickings for a monster resurgence."

Said a man who'd never walked onto a battlefield. Pratyush replied, "We die to protect the realm. We're the last barrier. Monsters are hard to track down and even harder to kill. It's not like I throw soldiers into waiting claws while I sit around eating mangos."

"Watch your tone." The King raised a brow.

Pratyush gritted his teeth, but he knew better than to aggravate the King. The first (and last) time he'd done so, he'd been severely whipped.

"Best to watch your words with me, boy." The King glared at him; his stubborn, royal jaw clenched so hard that his teeth might crack.

Pratyush wasn't as afraid of him as most, but he knew his place.

The King went on walking, and the slayer silently followed.

They left the gardens and entered manicured fields. In the distance, rare white rhinos with ivory horns grazed without a care. They were side by side with kapila: cows that glistened with short, shimmering golden hair. They were the King's most prized of rare creatures. Legend said that the kapila granted their owners whatever they desired. But the King would never admit that. As always, he laughed and brushed it off with a "Beautiful cows, bad milk. Sometimes not worth the maintenance."

"What a collection," Pratyush muttered. Ugh. Why was he here?

"You haven't seen my newest additions, my boy. White elephants! And a winged horse! My men in the north captured one."

"Ah. Congratulations," Pratyush said, bored.

The King beamed but then murmured, "Flying creatures are valuable, sacred. I could frequent the floating mountains more often. Yes ... yes. The amrita is somewhere...."

Pratyush slowly looked at the King as madness descended over him like a pall. A lascivious gleam shone in his eyes. Amrita was lore, and many had lost their minds in search of it—the so-called elixir of immortality. But madness ran in the royal family.

"Do you think the kingdom is safe from monsters now?" the King asked.

"Safer than it ever has been before. By the way, I have something to ask of you."

The King paused beneath a neel mohar tree. With its vibrant splash of deep purple flowers, it stood out against the distant pale green field. Servants had set up a table and chairs with a platter of nuts and figs and cheese, along with drinks, set on a display of steel bowls with intricate, colored carvings of peacock feathers. He sat down and nibbled while two servants catered to him.

Pratyush stood over him, his mind writhing between anxious and angry for no reason . . . yet. He hadn't been this nervous since trying, and horribly failing, to ask the King to reconsider Pritika's engagement, which had ended badly. Pratyush had immediately been sent away and his sister immediately betrothed. He could still hear her cries for him. And he could still feel the burning lashes on his back for trying to resist.

He continued his practiced speech, though he'd rather be slaying monsters than telling the realm's undisputed ruler, "I've worked hard and tirelessly for the kingdom most of my life. Monsters are manageable now. I think it's time for me to have my own place. I'm old enough. You promised it to me. It doesn't even have be a large estate—nothing like a palace or a nobleman's home. Just some land someplace quiet. I don't even mind fixing up a house, plowing land to clean it out. Maybe my father's land? Isn't it my inheritance? I need space to relax, even for a short while. It's not a lot to ask for. Half the guys my age are married and live on their own plots of land. If you value me, like you always say you do, then why am I without a home, without belongings?"

The King chuckled. "Do you think a boy like you can—what? Take care of property and garden and tend to broken things? Sit around a farmhouse all day and not get bored?"

"I'm *tired*."

"You're only seventeen," the King growled. "How tired can you be?"

Pratyush's chest burned as he reeled in his anxiety. "I'm tired of fighting, of killing, of tracking, of watching people die gruesome deaths, of trekking back and forth across the kingdom. I want to settle down and *be* bored."

"Huh..." The King continued to nibble and drink, enjoying his afternoon. "A slayer who doesn't want to slay. That's all you're good for, you know."

Words that the King had spoken on the day they'd met, and words that had been repeated to this day, particularly at times when Pratyush dared to ask for something or had the gall to think for himself.

When he'd first started training, the generals and commanders would ridicule him to the King. "He'll never be an asset like this."

"Are you certain he's a slayer?"

"Was he never taught to fight?"

"Not even competent enough to dodge hits."

The King had lifted his hand, ending a young Pratyush's beating. Pratyush had thought this ruler who claimed to be like a father would protect him. Instead, he'd told him, "You must kill or be killed. There is nothing else for you."

The King had turned to walk away, but he'd looked back at the boy wiping blood from the gashes across his face. "Do better. If you cannot slay, then you are no slayer. And if you are no slayer, then you are worthless. By extension, your sister is worthless, too."

Pratyush might've been young at the time, but he knew what that meant. No one would care for Pritika if he failed. Therefore, he could not fail.

Now, the King ate nut after cracked nut. "I saved your life when you were a child. People would kill to be in your position, in the good graces and presence of the King. You owe me many more years."

"I want to get married," he blurted.

The King slapped his hands together. "Ah! There it is! A girl! It always comes down to riches or women, doesn't it? They fell men all the time, every time. You know what I want? A golden serpent. They're even rarer than winged horses."

"Mm-hmm," Pratyush grumbled, agitation snaking its way through him. If the King denied him, then he was going to lose his temper. He felt the heat building up in his gut.

"Girls are fickle. You've yet to learn that. You've never even been in a relationship. It's not the life for a slayer."

Pratyush thought of his family and the farm where they'd lived, of his father's words about how loved ones could be used against him.

"Besides, I'm the King! I decide who my most important men marry. Just like I gave your sister to a nobleman's son to tie a treaty, so shall your union be used to further the kingdom."

A hot breath escaped Pratyush's nostrils, his jaw hardening. Yes, like property. The King gave his sister to an abusive boy, no matter how much she'd protested. No matter how much Pratyush had begged for her freedom.

"I haven't decided *if* you can marry, much less *whom* you will marry. That is the end of that. But this girl? Just have your way with her and be done with it. You're enamored because it's first love, or perhaps lust. Get her out of your system. You're the slayer. I'm sure she and her family will be more than willing to allow it. It would be their honor, her privilege. I'll allot you time to have visits with her. Ah... young love. Doesn't last, I promise. And since we're on the topic, you should breed."

Pratyush stilled. *Breed?* Like an animal?

"We need more slayers; yours is a dying kind. You've got good stock, and it doesn't take a lot of work on your part. In fact, it shouldn't be work at all. Haven't you, uh...?" The King waved his hand in the air.

Pratyush didn't respond.

"A virgin slayer?" the King teased. "I promise that once you get into it, you'll love it. And the permission to bed as many girls as possible will gain the envy of every man in the kingdom. Are my girls not good enough?"

Pratyush tensed, worried over what the King might do to them now that he knew they hadn't succeeded in bedding him.

The King added flatly, "They're not meant to take your laundry. They're meant to bear your children."

"Wh-what?"

"Must I spell it out? I need more slayers. I can have an entire generation of them if you do your part and take the girls. The kingdom is more than willing to offer one girl after another until we have an entire army of slayers! Imagine that! Why leave it to chance when we can ensure our future?"

Pratyush couldn't believe his ears. The King really did mean to breed him.

"Yes, yes. Then I will have more command and more power, and we will expand into new territories, creating an empire, and maybe even into other realms. My plan would move along much faster if you would just sire more slayers." He sighed. "At this rate, they wouldn't be ready for another fifteen or so years. We're very behind."

Before Pratyush could argue, the King dismissed him with another wave of his hand. "Now, to more important things. One more monster. Then we can discuss giving you property if it makes you happy," he promised begrudgingly.

Pratyush blinked at him, dumbfounded. "So, I *am* the errand boy others make me out to be."

He frowned. "Why ever would you think anyone sees you as an errand boy?"

Really?

"I pay you well, don't I?"

"You feed me and clothe me and give me a bed and a bath when I'm here." Pratyush looked around pointedly. "You've never paid me. Where are all the riches I've earned?"

"I'll release them to you after this new threat is taken care of, along with a property for you. It's for the good of the kingdom that you slay this monster first."

Pratyush didn't know what overcame him when he said, "You can keep your riches, then. I'll leave without them, and without *breeding*."

He'd turned to leave when the King called out, "You think I won't hunt you down?"

He paused.

"Oh, naive boy. Don't think that you can run. There is no place in this realm I cannot reach. There is not a single person alive who will die for you. Even all these lives you've saved. All it takes are a few rumors. The minds of the weak are easily manipulated. It takes time for people to honor a hero, but they are quick to loathe. One lavish bounty on your head, and it's all over. For you. For this girl. For any future."

Pratyush pressed his lips together, his breath fire in his chest. How far could he fight the King and still get a peaceful life with Manisha?

Maybe this was why his father had taken his mother and run. Why they lived in the borderlands so close to where monsters thrived. Papa must've loved Ma so much that he risked everything for her. He must've valued his life and freedom so much that he went against the King. He must've braved every new fear just to have a chance at a normal life.

Anger drained from the King's voice. "My boy. We will say our piece, and you can take a short time off. Only after you slay this monster. There are others out there, but they, for the time being, stick to their territories. This one doesn't. She's wreaking havoc across villages, a deadly and quickly spreading poison. You *could* walk away now, and I may not have my men come after you, but you'll lose my good graces. In the end, that's all you truly have. More importantly, if you don't slay her, her toxic touch will eventually reach you. It's already infiltrated the southern region. Some are even calling her their queen. They've become possessed by her lies. We can't have that. A monster cannot tear apart the kingdom, much less build her own."

Intrigued by this beast's strange fandom, Pratyush let curiosity get the better of him. A monster was a monster, but one who could turn the hearts of humans into followers was far deadlier. "What sort of monster is she?"

The King looked over the rim of his glass as he drank. "The reports say she's a nagin."

"That doesn't make sense. I thought the naga were just a people. Not monsters."

The King grunted. "You know so little."

Maybe, but he would've known about a human who could turn into a monster. That seemed important.

"Whatever the case, she exists. And she's coming for us."

Pratyush narrowed his eyes as the King continued, "They call her the Serpent Queen—so powerful that she commands vipers and so vile that she can turn men into stone. Bring me her head, and I shall grant your request."

TWELVE

MANISHA
(TWENTY-EIGHT DAYS AGO)

Kumari made a small fire, then cleaned banana leaves and fruit in the river.

Manisha sat a few feet from her, close to the fire, and pulled her knees to her chest. She didn't have any other clothes, so she'd had to dress in the same soiled sari.

Now that she no longer needed to hide her family's bangle in her blouse, she wore it around her wrist. Seeing the gold luster, touching the bands, feeling its weight glide down her arm, made her feel closer to her family, and with that came a surge of hope and revival.

She found herself wondering where the slayer was, if he would return for her, and what he would do when he discovered that she was gone. What would Sita tell him? Obviously not the truth. Maybe that she was defiled, and Sita sent her away. Or that she wanted to leave, and Sita allowed it. Either way, the slayer wasn't going to be happy. Would he forget about her? Would he track her down? Did he even truly care about her?

From what she'd learned at the temple, no one liked defiled girls.

The slayer wouldn't want to marry her now—not that she wanted marriage. She'd made it to the ground; she didn't need him. But... her thoughts kept wandering back to the warrior boy. He'd been so kind and genuine with her. More than that, he made her feel like her true self might be okay. Well, except the naga part.

She groaned as a throbbing headache came on.

"Are you all right?" Kumari asked, furrowing her brow as she turned a stuffed leaf over the flame.

"Headache," Manisha said, biting into some fruit. She'd watched Kumari very carefully to make sure she hadn't meddled with the food.

"Eating will help." Kumari laid out two of the larger leaves and looked out to the water.

Manisha faintly smiled. Whenever anything was wrong, her mother had always given her food because her mother, grandmothers, aunts, and aunties had claimed that eating helped everything. It didn't matter the cause: sprained ankle, ruined dress, unfortunate haircut, subpar grades... food was the remedy. Food was love. Feeding was their unspoken gesture of hospitality, affection, and bonding.

"There he is!"

Manisha startled when a wave came at them, full of the makara. She nearly screamed, scuttling backward as the water dragon, a giant crocodile-like creature covered in curved horns, rushed out of the river. He stopped inches from Manisha's feet, his swooping head filled with hundreds of sharp teeth, some bigger than her hand.

Her heart had never pounded so hard!

She sat petrified, water lapping at her feet, her eyes wide, her limbs trembling as she and the makara stared at each other.

He growled something deep and guttural, as if to announce that he could eat her whole in one move.

She believed him.

"Who's a good boy?" Kumari said, throwing her arms around his neck and hugging him.

Manisha had never seen a woman so happy, much less attached like an extra limb to a monstrous beast.

"What did you fetch for lunch?" Kumari asked, sitting on her haunches beside the makara. His pensive yellow eyes never leaving Manisha, he unclenched his jaw to reveal six floundering fish.

"Ooh, what a delicacy," Kumari said, her entire upper body bent into his mouth.

A nervous twitch started in Manisha's eye. How could Kumari so calmly—giddily, even—place herself in a monster's mouth? One chomp and she would be two dead halves.

Kumari plucked the fish from his mouth and deftly cleaned the catch in the river. The makara snapped his jaw shut, the sound of thunder. Manisha jumped.

He watched her carefully until Noni slithered forward. She had grown big enough to raise herself above Manisha's head.

The two beasts faced off in a tense moment, with Manisha dead center.

"Oh!" Kumari said when she returned with cleaned fish faster than a snap of her fingers. "What is that?" She eyed Noni in absolute awe.

"N-Noni," Manisha replied. "Could you, maybe, ask him to move back?"

"It's all right," she told him. "Thank you for lunch."

The makara growled and slipped backward into the river, leaving the tips of his thick, grayish horns above the surface to remind Manisha of his presence.

Noni lowered herself and coiled up beside Manisha as Kumari wrapped the fish in banana leaves and tossed them into the fire.

Embers danced in the air and settled down, and just like that, a full meal was on its way. Manisha's stomach rumbled. She couldn't take eating nothing but fruit much longer.

"A golden serpent? So rare..." Kumari commented, her voice drifting off.

"I think so." Manisha blinked at the water, waiting for the makara to jump out again.

Kumari waved him off. "Don't worry about him. He's a curmudgeon during the day. He's a nocturnal creature and prefers to nap during lunch. But this serpent. Where did you find her?"

"She found me. Introduced herself from the brush."

"Huh..." Kumari said, watching the two of them.

"What? Do you know something about her kind?"

Kumari flipped over the pockets of fish with her bare hands, as if the flames weren't searing.

She confessed, "I wasn't sure if they even existed. I heard they come from teardrops and the purest droplets of water straight from heaven, and hatch from eggs made from stardust under a full moon during the passing of falling stars. They grow to insurmountable sizes and are loyal to the death. They can spit venom and fire and split their heads into seven."

Manisha glanced at Noni resting peacefully, so innocent and wholesome. "I don't even know if her fangs have poison, much less fire."

"Seems like you're special if this one is attached to you. Fish is ready." Kumari snatched the pockets out of the fire and gave Manisha two while she took one. "You must be famished."

"Thank you."

Manisha handed a cooled lump to Noni, who slowly consumed it in one swallow. She couldn't imagine eating so much, but in a matter of minutes, her two fish were gone.

"Where are we? Where's the nearest village?" Manisha asked, glancing at the tip of the floating mountains far beyond the canopy. It had once been a spectacle to admire, now something to loathe.

"We're at the basin of the great Yamuna River. The floating mountains are to the north, the King's palace to the northeast, with a few villages just south of here. Which village are you from?"

"I don't remember everything. We were attacked when I was young, and I've been on the move since."

Kumari regarded her as she ate another bite of fish. "You're not dressed like a village girl."

"No." Manisha kept her eyes low.

"Silks and glimmering threads. Did you run away from the King? Are you part of his collection of maidens? Or do you belong to a noble?"

Manisha shook her head. "I don't belong to anyone."

"Are you an apsara?"

Manisha gaped at her.

Kumari shrugged, as if it weren't a surprise. "Once in a while, they're sent into the wild, to fend on their own. But the temple usually keeps their clothes. They look expensive. They probably don't grow silkworms and make their own clothes up there."

"What happens to those girls?"

"Sometimes they've been sold to a soldier and try to get away. Usually, they get taken by someone else. I'd avoid the villages for the most part if I were traveling alone."

"Why?"

She gave Manisha a sad look. "Men."

Manisha frowned.

"If I were you, I'd take my makara and seek vengeance," she said so plainly that it scared Manisha.

"I'm not a vengeful person," Manisha protested.

"Says the young woman with clenched fists."

Manisha glanced at her white-knuckled hands, not realizing that she had them balled into fists.

"Perhaps I misspoke. It's not about vengeance. It's about accountability. If someone hurt me and went about their life like nothing happened while I suffered, well, that's not right, is it?"

"Men get away with anything they want. It's not easy to go after one."

Kumari scoffed and tilted her chin toward the sky. "In your world. In mine, everyone is held accountable for their actions."

"What sort of world do you live in?"

"The underwater cities are a world where women have power, too. It's the only world worth living in, if you ask me. I couldn't live in the kingdom, in one of the towns or villages, much less the palace. I've seen and heard of women being taken advantage of, sold or traded, used for nothing more than cleaning and cooking, bearing and rearing children. There's no point in them otherwise. They have no authority. Their voices crushed, their passions denied, their gifts subdued. Do you know why?"

Manisha shook her head.

"Because those in power seek to control what they fear. We're strong and intelligent and compassionate and resilient. We're scholars and warriors and rulers. Imagine what would happen if women ruled the world. Or at least, if everyone were truly equal."

Kumari clucked her tongue. "This kingdom is sad. So much is lost by silencing women. They could be truly great and advanced and thrive. But they choose not to."

Kumari snapped her fingers in the air. "This place, the kingdom, needs a queen. A queendom. I'm tired of their idiot men bringing ruin so close to our world."

"Do you have any nominations?" Manisha asked dryly.

She smirked. "Overturning a patriarchy that's ruled the realm for generations isn't easy. It's the calm after the storm to strive for. And every storm begins with a droplet. But maybe . . . this storm needs to start with a flame."

"That doesn't make sense."

"People in power stay in power because the balances favor them already. They guard their wealth and prepare for uprisings. They know what to do when a storm comes. But they expect a storm of water and wind. Show them a storm of fire and vengeance, and they won't know what to do."

Maybe Kumari was right. Maybe this kingdom needed to burn to be rebuilt properly.

"I must leave soon. This is for you." Kumari handed her the rest of the fish, tightly packed in the leaves they'd been steamed in.

Manisha's heart warmed. "Thank you. I don't think I would've been able to get food like this on my own."

"It's nothing. The river is full of fish. I'd invite you to come with me, but, well . . . unless you can breathe underwater?"

Manisha shook her head, wondering if Kumari was serious. Did she really live underwater?

"Are you sure you don't want a ride?"

"No, thank you," Manisha mumbled, imagining the makara diving into the depths of the river with her attached to his back, bubbles of air escaping her lungs as he dragged her to a watery grave. She didn't think *that* was the vision her ancestors had given her.

"Still don't remember where you came from?" Kumari asked.

Manisha bit her lip. She hadn't said her people's name aloud in so long, as if her mother's warning to keep it hidden had tied her tongue in a spell. She couldn't utter the name. "Have you heard of the Fire Wars?"

"Who hasn't? They ended years ago. If you think my makara's

grumpy now, you should've seen him then. The fire and smoke, noise of battles, and encroaching invaders drove him restless. He'd rush the riverside to chomp into a soldier or two in his agitation."

Manisha winced. "That seems like an awful way to perish."

"It is. After a few soldiers were snatched, they learned to stay away. But sound carries over water, you know? We didn't get relief until they left."

"Why did they leave? Did they accomplish what they set out for?"

She shrugged. "They wanted to subdue scattered peoples and were looking for someone in particular, I think. Maybe a leader? Obviously a threat. I think they stopped when they'd killed all they could, or when they reached the river. But I can ask my elders if they know."

Manisha was shaking, her eyes brimming with tears.

"Was that what happened?" Kumari asked softly.

Manisha bit her lip and nodded. "I was separated from my family during the Fire Wars. Most of my people were killed. I don't know what happened to the rest."

"I think many went into the waters. Some drowned; some made it to the other side."

Manisha's heart grew heavier. Escaping a fiery death in exchange for a watery one? "Do . . . do you know anything about an island on the back of a giant sea turtle?"

Kumari stilled, but her expression didn't give way to surprise or guardedness. "Sounds like a legend."

"Yeah. Too fantastical to be real."

"Why do you ask?"

"Well, if you live in the water, you must know a lot about the water world. Maybe some survivors were able to stay hidden because they aren't anywhere the soldiers would look."

Kumari regarded Manisha for another minute. "Where did you hear about such a creature?"

Manisha stumbled over her thoughts. She knew to keep her guard up, but if true to lore, a yakshini was tied to her body of water. Kumari couldn't force Manisha back to the temple to find the scrolls. "I read about them. Not much. A drawing, really."

Kumari didn't probe further. "I'll ask my elders about your people and the creature."

"Why would you help me?"

"Because I'm not cruel. If it's as simple as asking around to find an answer that's so important to you, why wouldn't I?"

Manisha smiled.

Kumari added, "No matter what pain you go through or whether your life is perfectly balanced, there is always healing to be found in helping others. It will open your eyes and your heart. Trust me, there's nothing more dangerous than a dark heart, for dark hearts lead to dark times."

Manisha nodded, even though she didn't quite understand. "How would you find me, though?"

"If you're near the river, just call out and ask if I have the answer. I'll hear you. I'll find you."

It had been so long since anyone had been genuinely kind to her, not due to temple rules or court politics, that she didn't know what to make of Kumari's offer. She replied, "I'll ask the water. I should get going, too, and keep searching for my family."

"I hope you find them," Kumari said, a sadness in her voice. "If you follow the river down about a two-hour walk, and then go deeper into the jungle another hour, you should come across the central point of the Fire Wars, the last battle before the final scattering. I heard the boars ran through that battle and gored soldiers."

Manisha knew that area. She remembered the weeping willow trees and had seen the boars impale soldiers. She took some comfort knowing it was the last battle, that it gave survivors time to flee.

"I can't say if anything's still there. It's been a long time, and the jungle regenerates."

"It's a place to start."

Kumari rose as ripples appeared in the water. "Travel safely."

"You too. And thank you so much for your kindness and company." Manisha stood as Kumari walked into the lapping waves.

"If you ever need any help along this river, you can call on me. Like I said, sound travels on water, and I'll hear."

Manisha nodded and climbed onto a nearby boulder, Noni on her shoulder, to watch Kumari calmly walk into the river. Knee deep. Waist deep. Shoulder deep. Until she was fully submerged, and the last bubble of air popped.

As it turned out, yakshini were real, and they could breathe underwater. Maybe she was telling the truth about underwater cities and a kingdom where it was safe for girls.

THIRTEEN

MANISHA
(TWENTY-EIGHT DAYS AGO)

Digging toes into the sand and dirt was preferable to walking on pristine marble floors. Slouching with knees apart was more comfortable than rigid, upright posture. And wandering the jungle without having to worry about what others thought was equally small and liberating. All things that had slowly begun to draw Manisha back to her past self.

Vines had choked out the vaguely familiar sections of jungle where Manisha had spent her last months with family. The trio of weeping willows' limp curtain of branches and leaves swayed back and forth, caressing grave sites long forgotten by the jungle.

The grave where Eshani had hidden Manisha had sprouted colorful flowers. It was a tradition among their people to use the decaying bodies of their loved ones to nourish the rare blue rose, the color as rich and dark as a post-sunset sky. Maybe Eshani had planted them. She'd always been a gifted grower, termed the Little Goddess of Spring for her touch that could give life to any plant.

Before these violent times, the naga lived peacefully in the city of Anand, nestled in the canyonlands on the far edge of the rainforest between massive waterfalls. Her people, so much like Eshani, had turned the parched land into flourishing, fertile orchards. Every rock balcony had transformed into a hanging garden. Every corner burst with fruit trees and flowering shrubs, canopies of vines, an overflow of vegetables and grain. A beautiful, bustling city where no one went hungry.

They buried their loved ones in the plains just beyond, a day's travel, and planted a blue rosebush on top of each grave. The plains had become a field of blue, growing strong and hardy, nourished by friends and family. One couldn't differentiate between queens and farmers. In life, they tried to be as equal as possible. In death, equality was absolute.

Manisha missed those blue rose fields where the sunlight touched the wheat in the plains, creating a golden halo across the flatlands. They had turned mourning the dead into a celebration, their beauty for everyone to enjoy.

All she wanted was a home, a house with her sisters and mother. No politics. No fear of someone coming in and taking everything. No worry of having to be prepared for intruders.

Maybe ...

Maybe what the slayer offered hadn't been so bad after all. *If* he was telling the truth. *If* he was truly invested in her as a person, as a whole, as a future, and not just spinning sweet words to taste the forbidden. She'd seen over time what made the apsara so alluring. Beauty and talent, sure, but many men just wanted what they couldn't have. An apsara was like a conquest.

She wished she hadn't denied him. Then maybe she could've escaped when he'd offered marriage. Maybe he could've helped her, and maybe the General wouldn't have violated her.

But there was no point in thinking about that, as difficult as it was. She wiped away tears, hatred growing in her heart.

Manisha clenched and unclenched her fists, the scars on her hands now fully closed in marred, dark ridges. There was an unsettling mix of despair and darkness brewing inside her. It gnawed on the confines she'd been taught to set, chomping at the bars and borders her brain had created to keep emotion in its place.

It coursed through her veins, new and terrifying. Potent rage and violence were urging her, but also, she just wanted to crawl into a cave and hide, wither away and become like moss-covered stone. Emotions were leaking out of their cage. And she didn't know how to handle them. She scratched at her arms. Her vision blurred, her breathing erratic and thoughts spiraling.

"Enough!" She had to focus on finding her family. It was the only way to stay sane, the only way to control the darkness rising inside her.

The sun was descending, pitching final rays across the sky, prying through the canopy in glimpses. Her shoulders slumped as a mild breeze cooled the perspiration on her forehead. She'd forgotten how humid the jungle was, having grown used to the cold in the sky.

Dropping her head, Manisha walked on, touching trees with burn scars, remembering the heat of the fires. All the people who'd died. All those poor creatures that were burned alive. And for what? To extinguish the indomitable spirit of the naga by feeding them to the Blood River?

Manisha squinted, noticing an etching on the weeping willow tree. It stood so tall that she had to crane her head all the way back to look at it, and even then, she couldn't see the top of the lime-green dome of swaying branches.

Even when they were on the run, the sisters found time to play every now and then. Eshani was the leader, settling into maturity faster than the rest of their generation. Sithara was full of focused rage, determined to become the most famed nagin warrior in the jungle. But for a brief season, they were just young girls adapting to new lives as nomads trekking through the jungle in search of a reprieve.

The sisters would climb the weeping willow trees and pretend the vines were curtains of elegant threads of flowers. The branches the cradles of their charming beds. The tree itself their palace.

Sithara had taken a blade to the middle weeping willow tree and carved out the image of a snake. First one, then two, then three.

"You shouldn't do that!" Eshani had rebuked her, but Sithara was the most rebellious of the sisters. She pushed every boundary. Eshani thought through every point of logic. Manisha . . . obeyed. She hadn't found her voice then, and even now questioned what her voice was supposed to be, if she'd ever have one.

"The tree is sacred," Eshani had said.

"It doesn't feel anything," Sithara had countered.

"How do you know? Have you found a way to communicate with it and ask?"

Sithara had rolled her big jade eyes.

Eshani had placed a palm over the freshly carved images and closed her eyes to sense what it felt. She had that ability. Not just with trees, but with animals, too, if she could get close enough. Maybe that was why Lekha had never left her side.

Eshani had pouted. "The tree feels everything. Why would you mutilate it?"

"It's us. A reminder. To the tree and to others that we were here, and we won't be forgotten. We are three. Three sisters of the serpent."

Now, Manisha pushed away the vines that were wound tight against the trunk. Sithara's handiwork appeared, faded and chipped, but deep enough of a scar to last the hands of time.

There they were. Three serpents for three sisters.

Her hand hovered in place for seconds, minutes, as if touching the tree would throw her into an avalanche of memories. But this was just a scar. This was just a tree. It wasn't as if it could speak to her. After all, she wasn't Eshani.

She pressed her palm against the roughness of the bark, closing her eyes and clearing her thoughts, the way Eshani had done. Maybe Manisha didn't have the gifts of her sisters because she had been too young.

She imagined her thoughts detaching from her mind like ethereal tentacles pushing through the bark, searching the heart of the willow tree for answers.

But she felt nothing. No pain or remorse or contentment. Just bark.

Noni awoke from around Manisha's neck and slithered across her arm and up the tree.

The tree wasn't telling her anything!

Frustrated, Manisha ripped vines from the trunk, cursing her lack of abilities and her entire situation. This was a wistful moment locked in time, a tormenting memory where her sisters were ghosts wandering this wretched place. Nothing more.

Manisha croaked, "What?" when she caught sight of another etching beneath a fisted bunch of torn vines. It was a crude depiction of the granite pillar opening to the city of Anand. Was this a sign? Had they gone south? Had Sithara left this note after Manisha was sent away?

"Why can't you tell me more?" she mumbled, looking for clues that weren't there. Whatever secrets this tree had, it wasn't giving them up.

Defeated, she stepped back and did a full circle to view the blue roses.

Wait. They'd only dug *four* graves.

There was a fifth shrub growing in the root clutches of the central willow tree. Her people didn't usually bury so close to trees because of the roots. But this bush tried its best to climb up the trunk.

Manisha dropped to her knees and dug around the shrub.

She must've dug forever with bare hands, the dirt embedding beneath her fingernails and the smell clinging to her nostrils. She gnawed off a broken nail, ignoring the taste of soil, spitting it back out. She didn't have time for snagged nails.

She dug and dug and dug. The hole got deeper, wider, until finally her fingers felt something solid and leathery. Not a root, not a snake, and thank goodness, not a centipede.

Yanking it out with a grunt, Manisha victoriously held up a scroll. Sithara *had* left a message!

Before night fell, Manisha had a fire going. Forget sitars and sweets, these were real life skills! By now the jungle had descended into total darkness. Noni had vanished to do whatever it was snakes did.

As packets of steamed fish heated up on the fire, Manisha cradled the scroll with reverence. This cloth might've been brittle and could easily fall apart, but it was also something that had last been touched by her sister. And that was more precious than the finest silks.

The scroll was written in Sithara's handwriting, in the ancient language of their people that no outsider could decipher.

Manisha's fingers trailed over the black ink letters and symbols, her eyes misting.

In Sithara's harsh, rushed brushstrokes was written:

Little one. I hope this scroll finds you and leads you home. We fled the area, and even crossed the Great River with the help of some questionable new friends. We came back once the soldiers gave up on us. I'm sorry we couldn't get to you when it was safer, but I know you found a way. We got separated, but don't worry, we're resilient, and Death will have to try harder! Return home, our true home. We will be together again. Be careful. Be safe, little one. May the blood of our foremothers keep you strong and bring us together again. —S

Manisha clutched the cloth to her chest and wept.

As the fish popped and sizzled, her mind contorted the bars keeping her emotions and thoughts under control. The pressure built up, like an explosion waiting to happen. Everything was unleashed in a wild, uninhibited torrent.

Sorrow. Images of the rocky structures of Anand crumbling under attack, trapping innocent children.

Grief. Facing the possibility of never seeing her family again.

Isolation. Locked away on the floating mountains without a person to truly trust.

Rage. Undiluted rage. For those who sought to dismantle the naga. For those who attempted to annihilate them. For those who forced them to scatter. For those who betrayed and wounded them.

She shook uncontrollably, her hands appearing like talons through a layer of tears. The ridges of her bites seeming more like scales than scars. The fire flickered strong, but its heat faded. The call of the night and cold at her back more welcoming than ever.

It was like splitting into two. The squelch of muscle and membranes as they separated filled her ears, sent shivers down her spine.

The darkness shuddered, and bioluminescent plants came to life with a colorful glow. But everything looked different. Clearer. Sharper. The owl on a branch with jerky head movements. Monkeys in distant trees. Worms in the dirt, digging for nourishment.

Everything sounded crisp. The flutter of mosquito wings. The pitter-patter of rodent feet. The crunching of caterpillars munching on leaves.

The splitting sensation crawled down the back of her skull and down her spine. She gasped, falling onto her hands, trembling with terror, and clenching her jaw to keep from screaming.

Was she literally splintering into two beings? Or was her mind fragmenting?

Was she just imagining everything? Was none of this real?

Maybe . . . she was still lying in a ditch full of vipers, half dead.

FOURTEEN

PRATYUSH
(PRESENT DAY)

The King had given Pratyush nearly fifty fighters to hunt down the nagin and bring back her head. He'd wanted to go alone—it was easier and faster to look out for himself instead of worrying about others—but the King had been pushy. Did the King think he would run off? That he didn't care about the new threat inching closer to the countryside, jeopardizing all the people he'd worked so hard to protect?

Pratyush *wanted* to save lives. He wanted a united, strong kingdom. He wanted peace, eventually, somehow. And the King knew this. He always had.

"If you want to do your father proud," the King had told him as he trained, "then protect the people. That's what he did and that is what you're built for. Why you exist."

At least Dev volunteered to come along. Dev was smart, fast, and strong. Neither trusted most, but they wholly trusted one another.

"What crawled down your roti hole and died?" Dev grunted.

Pratyush's scowl disintegrated. Dev was as amusing as he was terrifying. "What makes you think something's wrong? I'm living my fantasy out here."

"Your fantasy involves sharing a tent with me?"

Pratyush tried to hold it together, but he laughed. "You'd be surprised."

"Or is this just your usual pissy mood after meeting with the King?"

"This is why you're in my fantasies; you always understand me."

Dev rolled his eyes.

Ras walked by. He'd volunteered, too. He was young, but he had a lot of potential and was shrewd enough that Pratyush didn't mind. His gaze skimmed across the others.

Wait. Why the hell was the crotch-punch guy here?

Dev eyed him as he walked ahead and muttered, "I don't trust him."

"I love how we're always on the same page," Pratyush said.

Dev grunted. "I should've just eaten him. Less stress."

"High in salt. He probably tastes gamey, too. A little tough."

Dev snickered.

"How was your stay? Do anything not boring?" Pratyush asked.

"Oh yes. Went shopping at the bazaar for gold and silk, attended a music festival with marigolds in my hair, saw a play where I wept, and crashed a wedding just to eat ras malai. You know," Dev added with a wave of his hand, "the usual."

"So, you just stayed in your room and slept?"

"Hmm," Dev conceded.

"Just once, I'd like to do normal-people things. Like go to a tailor and get fitted for a sherwani. Or mojri. I don't understand what those fancy shoes are for other than weddings, but I like the curl on the toe. And the sparkly style. You know, the glittery threads and shiny round things . . . I don't know what they're called."

"Zardozi is the metallic thread and sequin work," Dev replied flatly.

"My wife likes them, too. She would be thrilled to know she has that in common with the mighty slayer. All things glittery."

Pratyush grinned. "I wear dirt and mud all the time. Forgive me for wanting something nice. I'm still a little annoyed that you didn't invite me to your wedding. I was looking forward to dressing up for once."

Dev rolled his eyes. "For the last time, you wouldn't have been able to handle our customs."

"Meat off human bones . . . yeah, yeah. I don't honestly believe you're cannibals. I've seen you eat nothing but vegetables and grain."

"It's the only thing keeping me from eating annoying soldiers," Dev grunted.

Ras walked alongside them now, his complexion turning green at the tail end of this conversation. Pratyush chortled. He had to have fun where he could, right?

But with another near them, Dev quieted. He preferred to keep to himself and hold on to the stony, tough-guy persona. Ras, on the other hand, was a younger boy who'd barely even grown his first facial hair. His voice was a little higher, his cheeks plump with youth, and he held an air of new eagerness and inexperience.

That naivety showed when he asked, "Did you go home during the stay? My mother made my favorite dhal, with peppers and tindora from her garden."

Dev didn't react. Pratyush shook his head. "We don't have families here."

"Oh. Where are they?"

"Not here," Pratyush said, and left it at that.

Ras was young enough that his parents still doted on him. Pratyush could imagine the boy's mother trying to feed him, saying little blessings for him making it home one more time. He imagined his father fixing up their home for Ras to sleep comfortably in, inviting his friends for a small party. He imagined Ras's siblings tackling him to the ground and listening to all his otherworldly adventures.

Ahead, a scout returned from survey, his horse slowing to a trot as he cut through the soldiers and approached the slayer.

"What's the verdict?" Pratyush asked.

"The bridges are flooded from recent rains. The streams have turned into a raging river. We either wait for it to dry or go around."

"Monsoon season will be here, and it'll get worse. What about the elephant bridge to the south?"

"I checked there, Slayer. Also flooded. The closest route across is to head far north where the stream is at its narrowest and cross there . . ." the scout said nervously.

Pratyush groaned. The easiest way through something, in this case, was the most dangerous. Not the crossing itself, but what lay waiting in the meadows on the other side.

He thought about the decision as they trotted along. There was no way around it. Heavier rain impeded progress. Time lost was time gifted to the nagin. But could these guys keep their wits and obey him for once and not get killed?

Pratyush jerked his chin toward the new path.

"Are you sure?" Dev asked.

"We keep our eyes down and move slowly when we cross the fields. Get everyone ready."

Dev moved across the group as instructed.

"What's wrong with the meadows?" Ras asked.

"Hopefully, we'll pass before sun fall. If we don't, then make sure you stay calm and keep your eyes on your feet. Head east. Never head north."

He gulped. "Very foreboding."

"The vetala have been spotted there. Known to chase prey into the labyrinth north of the meadows. Those who enter never return. It's believed to have once been the old kings' project taken by the vetala to be their breeding ground."

Color drained from Ras's face, turning his light brown skin pallid and sickly. About what he would look like if the vetala sank their venom into him.

"Do you want to go back?" Pratyush asked. "This is the most dangerous mission you've been sent on."

Ras's gaze jerked up. "M-more dangerous than the bhramari?"

"You didn't even face her. You barely made it through the Flesh Fields. It's okay, you know. No one will think less of you. You're still very young."

His face hardened, chasing away fear. "No, Slayer. I'll go with you. I'm brave. And I'm not that young. You're barely a couple of years older than me."

"Don't be impetuous. We're not the same. I have the bloodlines to battle monsters and years of experience. You don't. It's best to know your limits to fight another day. Better to be a smart soldier than a dead one. You don't have anything to prove to me, not yet."

"I can help, and I'm smart."

Pratyush sighed. "All right. Just remember you can't fight the vetala. Don't even try. You can only avoid them."

Ras nodded, looking like he might turn back any minute now. And that was fine. He'd rather Ras grow up a little more and be a better soldier later than die tonight.

Pratyush mounted his horse, a beautiful onyx beast with ribbons of silk for a mane, riding him to the front. Fat raindrops fell, splashing against damp grass. The group trudged through mud, the air filled with the scent of fields—air, rain, grass, and mud. It was a nostalgic smell, taking him back to his childhood, memories of sitting on the window or on tree limbs as rain poured on the family farm. He had always liked the rain before that night.

For a farmer, rain meant nourishment. For a slayer, it meant mud-slides and slipping soldiers, grimy steeds, wet and sticky clothes, sneezes, and cold, irritating rivulets running down faces and obscuring vision. Rain was annoying as hell.

They crossed the soon-to-be raging stream and stood at the entrance to the meadows. The fields looked peaceful and calm, unassuming in the daylight—even if they were filled with corpses.

A few trees sprouted up here and there, and short grass covered mass graves. The kingdom burned bodies within a day of death for funeral rites. It prevented the spread of illness and the stench of rotting corpses. Burning bodies also prevented the superstitious from descending. Some said the dead were rejected by the Nightmare Realm and returned as reanimated corpses springing back to life to feast on the living.

Those were silly beliefs that had never been proven. But beliefs were strong vices.

Some of those sayings went as far as skeletons reanimating without flesh. That was why they burned the dead until the bones turned to ash. They kept the ash in special, tightly closed pots and sent them to be buried in these fields. It was a dangerous job, but the King paid well for it.

Across these meadows were small, disrupted patches of dirt above buried pots of ash. Some argued this was the reason the vetala came here in the first place. Others argued this was why the vetala hadn't come any farther.

"What are you thinking?" a soldier asked.

"We can't all make it through the meadow before dark," he said, dread in his gut.

The monsoons had brought whorls of agitated clouds and a pall of darkness that spurned the sunlight. Night would come sooner, so they had to move fast or retreat until morning.

"Look around. It's already dark," the General stated, trotting toward them. "We move through," he ordered.

"Soldiers will die," Pratyush contested.

"Vetala aren't monsters or lore, just ruthless men we can fight. We can't lose an entire day to sleep in safety. That's not what we're paid to do. These soldiers know what they signed up for."

In the end, it didn't matter if Pratyush was the slayer, the one who had slain endless monsters for the good of the realm. In the eyes of the King, he was still a boy—the General was in charge, and that was why people were going to die.

Pratyush grunted, trying to take whatever control he could. He told the scout, "I need riders to take the horses as fast as they can through the meadows and not stop until they've reached the other side. And then keep going for another mile."

"We only have ten horses, and half of those are carrying supplies for the entire trip. What about the rest of the soldiers?"

"We'll have to walk."

He dismounted, securing his father's trusty parashu to his back, and handed Ras the reins. He took them, perplexed, as Pratyush explained, "I need you to get on my horse and take him across. Keep him safe. Make him run the entire way. Horses are too fast for the vetala. And if you fall off, just remember that if the vetala get near you, stay calm and quiet. They're attracted to sound but sensitive to booming noise. Don't argue. We don't have time."

Ras nodded and mounted the horse.

"What about you?" the General asked.

"Obviously I'm walking," he replied, annoyed. "I'm the only one here who's dealt with a vetala and lived, because, you know, they're real and not just men. But I know you; you're entitled. Plus, you hate walking. So . . . hurry the hell up. Keep my guys safe on the other side."

The General scoffed as if the truth insulted him, but apparently not enough for him to get heroic. He didn't dismount.

Pratyush asked for volunteers. There were plenty to choose from, almost everyone. The General and crotch-punch guy weren't among them. Big surprise.

Instead, the General said, "One of us should make sure the mission succeeds. If you want to play hero and die in a field, then you leave me no choice but to ride."

Deflecting jackass. What did he think he was going to do without the slayer? Just walk up to the nagin and behead her himself? But now wasn't the time to start a fight. Pratyush gave a sarcastic smile and slapped the General's horse on the hindquarters, sending the General jolting forward when the steed took off with a whinny.

Pratyush cocked his chin at Dev to go with the horses.

"No. I'll stay with you," Dev replied in typical Dev fashion, always doing what he wanted.

"I need you to live."

"I need you to be less dramatic."

"Oh my stars . . ." But there was no arguing with him.

The rest of the riders followed, Ras among them.

With a few deep breaths, his hand shaking on the hilt of his parashu—let's be honest, running through a field full of monsters was never going to get easier—Pratyush led the fighters through the meadows.

"If you come across vetala, keep your eyes down and head low. They're attracted to movement and slight sounds, repelled by loud sounds, and faster than most of us."

"Why didn't we just have two riders a horse?" a soldier asked nervously.

"That's way too much weight for them to handle with supplies while running. We might as well just lie down and let the vetala carve out *all* our brains."

The soldier nodded, understanding. It wasn't a bad question. He was just afraid. But if Pratyush could smell fear on him, then so could the vetala.

The thorn wall to the labyrinth loomed along the skyline to the north—a death trap. There was no way around the labyrinth, only through. And once through, no one ever returned. No matter what, they could *not* be herded that way.

Twenty soldiers marched into the meadow.

The insidious question was how many would walk out the other side.

The sun had been absorbed into the night sky. Rain clouds moved across the sliver of a moon. The slayer's vision adjusted to the night. Everything was bright enough to see in outlines of blue, as sharp as his daytime eyesight. Every outline of tree and limb, every vein of every leaf, silhouettes of every blade of grass.

The others followed him. It was a hell of a lot to know that he was responsible for them and for everyone in the kingdom. Enough weight to break his shoulders and shatter his spine.

He never bothered to learn every soldier's name because it removed a layer of attachment. The guilt. The dread. It was better for his sanity not to think about them as individuals with families, children, wives, or first loves waiting for them back home. Because once he started to think that way, there was no stopping the fall down a jagged hole of misery. He could barely carry his own grief—how could he carry theirs, too?

The King thought *his* life was stressful, making decisions that could impact thousands. And yet, he didn't feel the haunting pain of his subjects. Their lives didn't torment him in his dreams, didn't add burden to his shoulders, didn't make him feel unworthy of happiness.

Maybe Pratyush *wasn't* worthy. Maybe he'd failed too many people and didn't deserve to return to Manisha. Maybe he needed to slay more monsters to make up for past shortcomings. Maybe the King was right, that slaying was all he was good for.

A slayer lived in cycles, in varying degrees of anguish. Death was the only way out.

But *not* tonight.

His footfalls were silent, a perfected way of walking, like floating over the ground. His fighters were almost as quiet, moving as quickly as possible.

Crossing the meadows at night was the absolute worst idea. Between the vetala and the darkness—plus sheer exhaustion from a long day's travel—this made for a bad call. But they had to follow the General, as asinine as he was.

Pratyush looked behind him, guessing they were about halfway across with no sign of danger. Ahead, as far as his hawkeyed vision could see, a torch had been lit in the far, far distance. The others had made it into the jungle.

Yes. That was a handful of soldiers he'd managed to keep safe. But relief was short-lived. Gray fog swept across the expanse of the meadow, prowling like a deadly predator, concealing the worst. It rose behind them, coming from every side, closing in, *herding* them.

The vetala. They knew humans were here. And they were coming for them.

The fog was unlike any other, more than just a mist of suspended water. As kids, Pratyush and his sister used to run through fog on the farm with their mouths open, tasting water.

This fog? It *felt* them. A million tiny particles searching over their bodies, tasting their skin to send information back to the vetala, to decide if they were worth the hunt.

Pratyush raised his hand to his face, observing how the fog swarmed around his fingers, touching his skin before jumping back, startled.

His skin was thicker than human skin, maybe harder for the fog to read? Or maybe the fog knew what he was by the way it hovered around his body like polarized magnets, unable to get any closer. If the fog knew what he was, then the vetala knew.

His vision blurred and split. Pratyush shook his head. He fought a mental assault, like fingers prying through his thoughts and forcing him to see and hear what wasn't there. He knew this wasn't real because a girl materialized in front of him and he couldn't smell her, couldn't sense her. Which, to be honest, was far creepier because how the hell does one fight something inside of their head?

She was cloaked in darkness with a crown of shattered glass, a wall of thorns rising behind her.

"It's you," she said bluntly.

He'd never seen her before, so she wasn't a past slain monster making him lose his mind like the Famed One.

Her eyes glowed green, reptilian slits like a viper. Her face and body were shadows, but her carmine lips flashed when she snarled, *"You."*

"What?" he croaked, despite knowing better than to speak to this mirage.

She squinted, digging deeper into his thoughts. He couldn't fight her off. She gasped when she reached his mission, his concept of the Serpent Queen: her hair snakes, her body half serpent, her teeth fangs, and her hideousness enough to destroy men with one glance.

"Don't you dare touch her, Slayer, or *I* will be the death you keep seeing."

He fought her invasion, setting up all the monsters he'd slain as a wall of thoughts she couldn't get past. The mirage splintered, and the last thing he heard was her fading words: "You can't outrun them anyway."

And then she was gone.

What was *that*? No, no, no! The vetala didn't communicate, they didn't speak, they didn't pierce thoughts. She was something new. Stars, could the world calm the hell down for one minute and not come up with new monsters every day?

The air chilled several degrees, his breaths releasing like ice from parted, panting lips. Their lungs would freeze at this rate. They had to hurry, but carefully.

A soldier beside him shivered, his teeth chattering, his lips turning blue. He dry-heaved and fell to his knees. Pratyush dropped beside him, swinging his hand toward the rest.

"Keep moving and do not stop," he ordered.

Then to the trembling boy: "Get up. Get up *now*."

He crawled onto his feet as the slayer helped him. They fell behind the others when someone to the right, veiled by the fog and darkness, pierced the quiet with a startling scream. The kind that could splinter bones.

Pratyush's adrenaline spiked as he yelled, *"Run!"*

But it was too late. They were here.

He turned toward the soldier, but the boy was on his knees again, shaking like a bush barely withstanding a windstorm. Beside the soldier, a figure materialized out of the mist. Bending down at the waist, it tilted its head in jerky movements.

The vetala was tall and slender, the color of this grayish fog, with reptilian skin fragmented into armored scales. It had large, oval voids of darkness for eyes and long, thin strips for lips. It possessed three sharp talons for fingers, its hands dragging on the ground.

It smelled of rotting death and had the soldier gagging.

"Do *not* move," Pratyush told him in a loud whisper as other vetala emerged from the fog. The soldier was too close to outrun this one.

Screams erupted in the distance, but it was hard to see through the fog.

Damn it.

The soldier convulsed, caught between cold and fear, his mind distraught on the threshold of death. It wasn't an easy order to follow.

Just obey.

His hand eased toward his sword. Pratyush tried to keep his attention, shaking his head and mouthing, "No."

Could the boy even see him?

The vetala froze. The soldier froze.

The beast let out a low clicking sound and began inching away. It was working. It was losing interest when there was no movement, no sound.

The young soldier should've taken this victory by default and lain low, maybe even stuck himself to the ground until daylight.

But he didn't.

The beast chittered and leaned in as the soldier slowly withdrew his sword.

And with that, his life was fated to end.

It happened fast, yet not fast enough. Pratyush, shaking, knew he was too far to help.

On the heels of the soldier's arm extending, on the metallic sound of blade dragging against scabbard, the vetala jerked back, suddenly in the boy's face. Its eyes glowed red with bloodlust, bulging with hunger. In a blink, it knocked the sword from the soldier and gripped his head with its massive hand, pulling him off the ground like he weighed no more than a small goat.

A long forked tongue unfolded from its mouth and struck. Like lightning. Right into the boy's gaping mouth as he gasped for air. The tongue went into him farther and faster, licking, tasting, feeling past his oral cavity, and pushing its way into his brain.

The soldier's eyes rolled into the back of his head. His screams gurgled in a mouth full of two tongues, and now a third as a second vetala appeared beside them to join the feast.

Pratyush clenched his eyes and said a fleeting, silent prayer, but even inner thoughts were difficult to hear with all the brain slurping. There was nothing he could do.

He backed away as another soldier screamed. His wails were so loud and horrific that it snapped the blood in Pratyush's veins. He shivered, clenching his eyes shut. If they were screaming, they were already seconds from a brutal death.

Pratyush swung his head toward a stench, coming face-to-face with another vetala gorging itself on a soldier with its tongue rammed into an ear.

I'm so sorry.

He couldn't help them at this point, even if he could kill every vetala. The damage was done. Once a vetala sank its tongue into the brain, the victim went insane. Those who were screaming were the ones who fought and got away, driven to madness and now running past, tearing off their clothes as blood ran down from their eyes, leaked from their noses, mouths, and ears.

The meadows, so serene and beautiful during the day, had turned into a chilled hill of nightmares.

Pratyush's breaths rushed out of an icy, numb chest, his legs finally moving. Ahead, a vetala chased a soldier. The soldier was fast, but the vetala almost floated in their movements to gain on him.

Pratyush drew his battle-axe and hurried his pace, shoving the blade straight into the beast. The sharp, shrill wails of a dying vetala were like banshee cries, alerting others.

Oh crap. He'd given himself away to a horde of angry, menacing, ghostlike monsters. All around, bodies thudded as the vetala dropped their meals and united to come for the slayer. But not before he beheaded the one at his feet.

"Thanks a lot," he grunted, chopping its thin neck. He braced for the absorption. Like a wailing ghost driven by primordial hunger, the vetala's life force rammed into Pratyush's mind, nearly knocking him over. His head felt like it was about to explode and lay waste to his brain matter across this bloody field.

He heaved, allowing himself one hard blink before roaring to all those who were left, "Run! Now!"

He ran headfirst toward two vetala. He pushed off from the ground and swung his parashu to behead both at once. Thin necks made it easier.

He landed behind them but hit the ground still running. While Pratyush focused on one coming up to his left, another appeared to his right, shoulder-butting him so hard his teeth rattled.

He skidded across the ground, the breath knocked from him, but jumped to a crouch as a vetala pounced. Its sheer weight had him sinking into the mud. It grabbed his jaw and tried to pry open his mouth, its tongue snaking out, its crimson eyes bulging like they were ready to burst.

Pratyush felt across the cold, wet ground for his battle-axe. With one forearm propped against the beast's collarbone, he grabbed his dagger out of a side pocket instead, wrapped its tongue around his fist—three times, that's how long it was!—and sliced it off. Leathery and tough. Then he rammed the dagger into the vetala's temple.

Pratyush rolled off to the side before any of its blood touched him. He cradled his head as the life force of the vetala invaded his mind. He roared into the fog, wanting to claw open his skull.

Another two vetala dove for the slayer in his weakest moment as a crash sounded ahead: clanking and trumpets. Pratyush didn't understand the tradition of having at least one musical soldier to laud their procession back home, but he'd never been happier to hear the sound. It drove the vetala back.

Just enough noise to render them disoriented, giving him enough time to grab his battle-axe a few feet away and slice one head while

Dev came out of the fog like an apex predator and took the second kill.

"Now who was being dramatic?" Pratyush said between pants.

Dev grabbed him by the arm, pulling him up. Together, they sprinted.

Pratyush stumbled, his teeth and eyes tightly closed as he fought through the shrieking cries careening through his head. He wanted to smash a rock into his brain. But he had to keep running. He had to save these soldiers. He had to protect the kingdom. He had to get back to Manisha.

Monsters and mortals died in different ways. There were some who could live without limbs or with half a heart. Some monsters regrew body parts while others continued life disfigured. Then there were head kills. The slayer had yet to meet a monster who'd survived a severed head or pierced brain.

Pratyush sensed enough footfalls, the difference between panicked, harsh ones in sludge and ethereal ones, to know that four soldiers ran with him and six vetala advanced behind them. He couldn't kill them all, and he just couldn't absorb another monster right now.

Torches and trumpets blazed just ahead, hazy lights at the end of their fight. If only they could make it past that line!

The only thing that sounded sweeter to his frigid ears was the buzz of flaming arrows. For once, he was glad his fighters hadn't listened to him!

A spray of fire lit the night sky, pierced the mist, and filled the air with the agony of wounded vetala.

FIFTEEN

MANISHA
(TWENTY-SIX DAYS AGO)

Manisha dragged herself along jungle paths. Her feet blistered, her ankles hurting with every step, her legs and back aching, her eyes sore from crying and restless nights. She was sure she'd had nightmares about the attack but was thankful she couldn't remember them. Focusing on her surroundings and trying to read the riverbank to stay on track kept her from thinking too much about the last few days.

Still, she had nothing but time to think. She tried her best to reflect on positive things: happy memories, all the things she wanted to tell her family, all the things she hoped to plan with them for a future together. Kumari was right. While reflection didn't completely heal her, it softened the jagged edges of her reality. If only by a little bit.

With no one to talk to, walking through the pain while foraging for food and water were the only things she could do. The quiet rang in her ears, made her head thrum. Her chapped lips twitched with the need to speak.

Loneliness was a strangely unnerving thing.

Towering trees and monstrous vines loomed in the jungles. The sound of the river's rapids raged to the right, and Manisha traveled toward it. Noni had left her side the day before, probably to feed. She knew they'd find each other again, somehow. They always did.

On the floating mountains, days were filled with duties, and the sounds of others were constantly nearby. Here? Her thoughts wandered.

Had her family forgotten about her? Where were they? Hopes of reuniting withered like petals in the heat. Did they have too much to worry about to add Manisha to their list? Did they think it was best to forget her if they couldn't reach her?

Did her mother miss her after so long? Was she sad? Was she... even alive?

Manisha swallowed, her eyes burning with tears. There were no signs of her people. Had any escaped, or was she the last of her kind, chasing family that was long gone?

Limping along, she licked dry, cracked lips, ready to drop from dehydration, when the sound of rushing water rose above the noise of the jungle. She hurried toward it, shoving aside ferns to see a glorious riverbank. She fell to her knees, not caring that her sari got wet, and drank until her face was smothered in precious cold water.

It wasn't until she was heaving, water trickling down her chin and neck, that she looked to her left to find two girls staring at her. One had a wet piece of cloth twisted around her arm, bent at the elbow, while the other was holding the opposite end.

Manisha startled, a hand to her chest. "Oh my stars!" Her voice came out shockingly hoarse. She hadn't heard herself in days.

"Are you all right?" the older girl asked. She was probably sixteen or seventeen. She unwound the cloth from the younger girl's arm and wiped wet hands on her shirt. Her hair was braided and coiled into a bun, but strands snaked out, damp with river spray and sweat.

The younger girl, maybe thirteen, had her hair braided into a single rope down her back.

Manisha shook her head. There were no words for seeing another person after wandering the jungle alone for days. And if there were words, they'd dried up and lodged themselves in the back of her aching throat.

She kept drinking, wishing she had a container to fill, but kept an eye on the girls and surroundings. They couldn't be too far from a village, which meant other strangers were nearby. Maybe kind, maybe not.

"Are you lost?" the older girl asked.

Manisha nodded.

"Maybe we can help. My name's Rayna. This is my sister, Rani."

The younger of the two waved cautiously, making it clear by her stern expression that she did *not* like strangers. She kept watch over their laundry as if it were gold. Maybe it was. By the looks of their stained, worn clothes, they probably didn't get a lot of clothing merchants coming through.

Never mind that. What she should really keep a watch out for was the makara in the river. Possibly plural.

"Where are you headed?" Rayna asked, her voice deeper than what Manisha was used to hearing among the apsara, but kind.

Manisha touched her throat, shrugging, and returned to gulping as much water as she could. But an empty stomach filled with water turned queasy. She might just throw it all up.

"Do you want to come with us to Vansol, our village?" Rayna asked carefully.

Rani furrowed her brow in warning to her sister.

Manisha hesitated, not knowing what to do. She needed food, and if they could give her a container for water, they might save her life. But she didn't know them, couldn't trust them.

Argh. She grunted, frustrated, and wished she'd remembered more of her life-on-the-run skills.

In the end, the need for nourishment won. She didn't have a choice and wheezed, "Water first."

Rayna nodded. "Why don't you rest and keep drinking? We'll finish washing our clothes, and when you're ready, you can walk with us. We don't have much, but we can give you some food and a place to sleep. Maybe some clothes and . . ." Her eyes drifted to Manisha's feet. "Shoes."

Manisha glanced at her bleeding soles, her shoulders slumping over. "Oh. Thank you."

The sisters returned to whatever it was they were doing with soaked cloth. It looked like Rayna was showing Rani how to hit someone's arm so that the cloth wrapped around their arm and entangled them. The slap of water-laden fabric against skin sounded as though it would hurt. When Rani tried it on Rayna, she yanked the cloth toward her, jerking her older sister so that Rayna fell, her arm bound by the cloth and unable to get free from it in time.

Manisha winced, but Rayna smiled and got to her feet. "Nice job. We'll practice another time."

"What were you doing?" Manisha quietly asked, curiosity getting the better of her.

Rani looked away as if being caught red-handed, but Rayna explained, "I try to teach my sister how to use anything around her as a weapon."

Panicked, Manisha croaked, "Why? Is it dangerous here?"

"It's dangerous everywhere," Rayna replied. "Which is why we must be able to defend ourselves and always stay alert. Right, Rani?"

Rani nodded, but not convincingly. Manisha recalled how her line of defense had been born from items once used for hunting and gardening and building. But maybe not everyone had those resources. She found herself admiring their ingenuity and wondered what other survival skills they knew of.

They went back to washing garments, whispering, and studying Manisha.

By the way the sisters were dressed, in muted green-and-brown knee-length kurtas and leggings, they probably belonged to a *civilized* village if they lived in the jungle. A word the apsara used that meant approved and in accordance with the kingdom. Manisha would have to be careful if they were part of the enemy territory.

Visitors to the temples had regaled the apsara with stories of how most of the jungle and outer regions had been "pacified." What they meant to say was they'd either assimilated into the kingdom or been subdued into oblivion. While the apsara cheered and fluttered with relief over that news, Manisha had wanted to vomit. She remembered how hard she had tried to hold it in until she was alone in her room.

Did such news mean the naga had been obliterated, or forced into submission, becoming shells of their ancestors?

Manisha stretched and massaged her legs, wincing at every uncomfortable ache and pinprick. She washed what she could without disrobing.

Rayna suggested, "There's a small cove down a bit, secluded enough if you want a bath."

Manisha eyed her suspiciously.

"Up to you. We'll be a while longer. Lots of clothes." She jerked her chin at the saturated heaps. "We won't bother you, and hardly anyone tends to be out here during the hot hours, which is why we're here at this time."

Manisha stretched her neck, every crack ricocheting in her head. She needed their help, but also a bath. With a grunt, keeping her eye on the sisters and her ears tuned to their surroundings, she wobbled past them to the cove. They didn't move from their spot.

After pacing the area and checking for any signs of danger, Manisha quickly bathed and dressed back into the dirty clothes that reeked of the General. She wanted to burn the sari, and him while she was at it.

She knew that she couldn't just ask for things, but what could she give the sisters for clothes, shoes, and a water container? The only thing of value was her sari, and it was shredded. And her bangle, but that was never coming off.

Maybe she could offer work? "Can I help?"

The sisters looked at one another and then back to her from their squatted positions, their leggings pulled up to their knees, the tail of their slit kurtas tied off to the side to keep their clothes from getting sopping wet. They squinted in the light.

"Sure. Thanks. It'll help us finish faster," Rayna said, despite her sister's frowning objection.

Manisha pulled up her sari, tucking it into her lap to squat beside them. Not too close, though. They worked without speaking for a long time, the only noises coming from cawing birds and scurrying animals in the jungle, the river at their feet, the brush of bar soap against cloth, and the slap of water-laden cloth against rocks. It was nice. Relaxing. *Normal.* A stretch of time not wondering about next moves, abysmal scenarios, and horrific pasts.

"What's your name?" Rayna asked.

"Manisha."

"It's nice to meet you. Make sure to drink plenty of water. It's okay if you need a break. You don't have to clean so much."

"This is enough clothes to dress an entire village," Manisha said instead, happy to help and even happier to occupy her thoughts.

"Yeah, it *is* for the entire village."

They finished washing and wringing, and laid the clothes out on rocks to roll up into a manageable pile for the woven baskets. A bunch of garments were heavy enough, but soaked ones could break backs. But the sisters, although slim, had broad shoulders and were stronger than they looked.

"Have you decided?" Rayna asked with a welcoming smile.

"Rayna..." Rani objected. "We *don't* know her."

Rayna pressed her lips together and asked Manisha, "Are you trouble?"

Manisha shook her head, desperate for any sort of help.

Rayna looked her up and down and told Rani, "She's a girl and all alone out here. We can at least give her some food and supplies and send her on her way. She doesn't even have shoes."

Manisha took a step forward, hesitant, and clenched her eyes shut. She didn't want to go with strangers, but she didn't have much of a choice. She didn't want to be alone, and she at least needed shoes.

She insisted, her voice returning, "I'm not trouble. I promise. No one is with me. No one is after me. I can pay you back, by, um... carrying this for you? Working? I know how to cook and clean."

Rayna jerked her chin at her sister. "I'd want someone to help you if you were alone."

Rani huffed and walked ahead with a smaller load balanced on her head. She didn't argue with her elder sister. They reminded Manisha of her own sisters. Eshani was always comforting but decisive. She'd been wonderful with divvying up mental and physical burdens by taking on someone else's load to help them. Manisha found herself smiling. She supposed that was what elder sisters did. There was nothing like a sister's love.

Rayna handed Manisha a basket. She carried the heavy load against her hip. She imagined she'd break her neck if she tried carrying the basket the way the sisters did.

"Don't worry about her," Rayna said. "Rani's careful, that's all. We all have to be, you know?"

Yeah, she knew. "Thank you."

"She's wary of strangers," Rayna explained as they headed toward the tree line.

Manisha calmed her beating heart as they entered the shadowy darkness of the jungle, jerking toward every sound in case this was an ambush. "That's wise. You never know what strangers are capable of."

"Where did you come from?"

"It doesn't matter. I can't go back."

"Oh, I'm so sorry to hear that. What happened?"

Manisha's eyelids fluttered, her body turning mushy and weak. "I was violated," she replied, using the word Kumari had taught her. It somehow gave her a tiny bit of strength. Violated, yes, because she was a victim. Not defiled, because it shouldn't determine her worth.

With this, the steps of the sisters slowed. Even Rani kept glancing over her shoulder at them, engrossed by this sordid conversation that Manisha didn't want to have.

"Is he—is he near us?" Rani asked with a tremble to her voice.

"I don't know," Manisha replied. "I don't think so."

"You'll be safe with us," Rayna reassured her.

"As long as we keep ourselves out of situations that place us in harm," Rani added, like a rehearsed chant.

Manisha's first instinct was to agree. Simplistic words of warning. A person shouldn't tempt fate. But then . . . she hadn't always felt this way. She'd never felt unsafe with her people, even when she snuck out at night with her sisters to watch meteor showers or fireflies or wanted to know what the older kids did. A hint of yearning seeped into her.

Her people weren't the only ones who'd created happy homes. Kumari had said her underwater city was like Manisha's. She wondered how Kumari would handle herself here, in the silence of the jungle paths. What would she have said in response to Rani?

Manisha couldn't help but to dwell on alternate scenarios. She could've been working on the fig harvest and waiting on the slayer to return if she hadn't chased the General. She was a stupid girl. No wonder her family had sent her off.

Rayna's village appeared in a clearing dotted with a handful of mud and wood huts with frond roofs, each with a firepit outside. Strewn lines of dried food hung from branches. Small children played on the ground.

Villagers stopped whatever they were doing to stare. All conversation hushed. All movements stilled.

An oddity walked among them. A lone girl in torn, dirty clothes, half wet, and improperly carrying a basket. The sari was destroyed, but there was enough of it to tell that it had been expensive. Pink and metallic gold designs shimmered in the sunlight. Which meant the girl wearing it wasn't a typical villager.

Two women approached to retrieve the baskets, taking a good look at Manisha. Rayna and Rani hung the rest, so Manisha did the same. She kept glancing over her shoulder. They were still glowering, but there were no men. Thank the stars.

"Who is she?" an elder asked. She wore the same muted brown-and-green kurta with leggings, a dupatta covering her ashen hair.

"Ma, this is Manisha. We met at the river," Rayna answered.

Rayna's mother had the same cautious reaction as Rani.

"I don't mean to intrude," Manisha said, her voice raspy. "Could I . . . ? Do you know where I could find new clothes and shoes? I could work for them, clean and—and cook?"

Manisha swept another gaze across the village. They were poor and probably didn't have anything to spare, but maybe they could tell her where to find supplies.

"We don't have much," the older woman spat. "We can give you some food and water, and then you can be on your way."

"Ma," Rayna protested. "We can't send a girl alone into the jungle

so late in the day. Something could happen to her. Something...
already happened to her."

Rayna turned to Manisha before her mother could rebut, offering,
"You can stay here if you'd like, for the night. Please, don't go out
alone so late. We don't have much, but you can wear something of
mine and I can wash your clothes in the morning."

Manisha's chest warmed at the small offering that wasn't really
small at all. It was obvious they weren't fond of strangers, and she
wondered why.

She replied, "Thank you."

"Can you finish the rest?" Rayna asked Rani.

She took Manisha to a hut, pushing through a crude door made of
arranged sticks plastered together with mud. It was smaller than her
room at the temple and smelled earthy.

"You can sleep on the floor," Rayna said, sweeping the dried mud
floors with a broom made of ferns. She grinned. "I haven't had visitors in a while, sorry about the mess. We only have one sleeping
blanket. Maybe my betrothed has an extra."

"You're going to be married?"

Rayna shrugged, not seeming particularly pleased. "I have to."

Manisha's smile slipped. The life in Rayna's eyes vanished.

"You're not happy?" Manisha found herself asking before she could
stop. Inappropriate!

"It's life. I used to think about leaving. I want to be an explorer,"
she said dreamily. "There has to be more than generations living in
this small village, doing the same thing over and over."

Manisha bit her lip, wondering if Rayna would join her on her journey until she added, "But Rani's here. And she's too scared to ever
leave. So. Here I am."

Manisha didn't probe. She'd already stepped too deep into a history
she didn't have the right to be in.

A bow and a quiver full of red-feather-fletched arrows against the curved wall caught Manisha's attention. Their song drew her toward them. "Do you hunt?"

"Sometimes. I'm learning. Usually, the boys hunt for food or fish, but in the past few years, we've had to learn, too."

"Spreading out the chores?"

Rayna set aside the broom, her shoulders drooping, and quietly confessed, "There's a neighboring village that has chosen to torment us. They've already killed or wounded most of our men. With men diminishing, we've had to adapt. Hunting, foraging, fishing, and climbing trees for fruit, not to mention all the things *we* have to do as girls. You know? Bearing and rearing children, cooking, cleaning, sewing, planting, harvesting. Here."

She handed Manisha a pair of dark green leggings with a matching top and dupatta. They were worn but looked newer than what she was currently wearing. "You can change in here. I'll be outside. And you can use the shoes by the door."

Manisha blew out a breath. "Thank you *so* much."

Rayna gave a soft smile. "Of course. Girls have to stick together."

Manisha watched the door for a second.

Girls have to stick together.

Such a contrast from her life on the floating mountains, where everyone was out for themselves and no one could be fully trusted.

She smiled. She liked this saying. It seemed like something that fit right in with the nagin sisterhood.

Manisha quickly unraveled the long fabric of her sari, folding it neatly. She took off her skirt and blouse and donned clean clothes and shoes for the first time in over a week. She dropped her head back with a sigh. While saris were pretty, there was nothing like leggings and a long top, the kind she'd worn as a kid—what she was wearing when her family sent her off. Her legs had room to move, to run, and be anything other than a "proper and pretty lady."

She was overcome with the urge to climb trees and jump from limb to limb. She hoped Rayna would let her keep the outfit, which was *much* easier to travel in.

When Manisha emerged from the hut, everyone watched her every move. She rubbed her arm and walked to the first large tree she could find. She gripped the tree and hoisted herself up but slipped. She tried again and again, her skin flaring as everyone watched her make a fool of herself. But no one laughed or snickered.

Bark scratched her skin and her palms caught splinters. She reverted to her childhood to remember how she'd been taught. The trick was getting the right grip with her feet and toes in combination with her hands, plus speed. After several more clumsy, exhausting tries, she was on the first limb, laughing and ignoring her sore throat. Finally!

Manisha looked down, expecting to be far off the ground. Instead, she was still within a person's long reach. Everyone was watching her, perplexed. She ignored them and climbed higher and higher into the canopy until she was barely hanging off the top branch. She caught her breath, her arms and legs sore. A cramp started in her foot, but she didn't care. She could see so much, yet nothing at all. A sea of trees. The underside of the floating mountains. The river.

So empowering. So freeing.

Gnawing on her bottom lip, she took another leap, and hopped from one tree to another with shaky landings, giggling like she was eleven again.

Like time hadn't passed.

Like the soles of her feet weren't bleeding.

Like her sisters were right behind her.

SIXTEEN

MANISHA
(TWENTY-SIX DAYS AGO)

The canopy darkened overhead. Manisha had been resting against a tree high in the branches pondering where Noni could be when the men and boys returned. She watched the villagers as they made dinner. Rayna called her down to join them.

For the first time ever, she thought twice about being near men. A frightening new fear took root in her thoughts, sprouting from the seed the General's actions had embedded. Second-guessing. Apprehension. Hyperawareness. A need to know every escape route. Locating every ordinary item turned weapon.

Her stomach was eating itself at this point, and she couldn't hide much longer.

Rayna must've noticed her hesitancy, because she said, "The men and women eat separately. You're safe."

There were only a handful of older men and several boys ranging from ten to twenty, but they were as cautious of Manisha as the women had been. It was easy to keep her distance when they sat and ate farther away. With her back to the huts, she kept an eye on them without worrying about anything sneaking up behind her. They sat around the central fire but could be heard discussing irrigation and fixing someone's home.

The women, girls, and children sat around a smaller fire. Communal meals were nice, something she took for granted growing up. There was always noise and clanking dishes as everyone pitched in to cook, ate together, and cleaned together. There was no shortage of food, just like there had never been a shortage of company. Not with three sisters, numerous relatives, friends, and neighbors.

Manisha, unaware of the people's customs, waited her turn. She didn't speak unless spoken to. Didn't move unless guided. The men and older boys ate first, then the children, then the older girls and women. While they ate, a few guards were positioned at the edge of the village.

Food felt good moving down her aching throat and filling a painfully empty stomach.

The group ate quietly, staring at Manisha. She hadn't felt this awkward since first arriving at the temple, wondering if anyone knew what she was . . . and if they would send her to the King.

"Don't worry about them," Rayna whispered. "Here, eat."

Manisha's stomach growled louder than a leopard, but she didn't take much since there wasn't much to share.

"I'm sorry it's not a lot," Rayna said. "Sometimes we feast, but most times not so much. We aren't the best archers. That's why we're trying to grow our own food."

"Maybe I can hunt something for you?" Manisha found herself offering, but could she even hunt? It'd been so long, and it wasn't as if apsara were allowed to practice weaponry.

"Really?" Rayna asked, her eyes lighting up in the firelight.

"Well, I haven't hunted in a long while, and I need practice. I used to be a skilled archer. My parents taught me when I was young."

Rayna beamed. "Tomorrow is my turn to hunt. We can head out early morning."

Across the circle, Rayna's mother poured murky liquid from a pot into a cup. She took a sip, fluttered her lashes, and passed it around. Manisha watched quietly as each girl took a sip, even the youngest ones. They cringed the most.

Their mothers scolded, "It's for your own good. Make sure you drink this every night."

The girl directly to Manisha's left nodded, her face as sour as the drink looked. She offered the cup to Manisha. Manisha took it, wary but curious enough to smell the strong tartness. A medicinal drink, maybe? Made from roots?

Rayna took the drink from Manisha. "That's not for you," she said and quickly took a sip, tamping down a cringe and passing it to the next girl.

"What is it?" Manisha asked, not that she was going to drink anyway.

The women glanced at her while they portioned out food for the children.

"It's poison," Rayna said matter-of-factly.

"Wh-what?" Manisha sputtered.

She explained as she fed a little girl beside her, "If you want to drink it, you'll have to start with a weaker ratio, diluted with water. Then build up tolerance; otherwise, you'll get deathly ill."

"Why would you drink poison?" Manisha asked, horrified.

Rayna ran a hand down the girl's hair. "The neighboring village we're at war with like to kidnap us. To violate us," she said in a whisper as if the words were unfit for conversation, or might conjure up evil to carry out the words. "We harvest poison from a type of oleander. If there's enough poison in us, then those who violate us suffer. Some have even died. It seems fitting."

"That's horrible," Manisha breathed.

"That they die?"

"No! That you live in this fear. That you have to drink poison to safeguard yourself."

"Oh, it doesn't stop them from taking us. It only creates a consequence they otherwise wouldn't face."

Manisha's skin turned hot, her gut twisting. She'd never heard such a thing. She wondered if this actually worked, and if so, what prevented their husbands from suffering. Did they drink, too? Or did they ingest an antidote?

The conversation in the men's circle escalated into angry shouts.

"What are they arguing about?" Manisha asked, hoping they wouldn't turn their anger at her.

"We asked for a small hut in the center of the village to use for a toilet so we don't have to go into the jungle. That's usually when girls are taken. In the middle of the night when they have to go or clean themselves during menstruation."

"They don't want to have a toilet in the middle of the village because it's unclean," Rayna's mother explained.

"That's a dumb reason," Rayna grumbled, her eyes set on her empty leaf plate.

Rayna's mother chided, "We must learn to control our bodies. Weaker ones must learn to become stronger."

Manisha balked. How...how was that being weak?

The woman went on, as if anyone had asked her to, "It's the only way to stay safe. Smart girls keep themselves safe."

Rayna stiffened, her nostrils flaring.

Manisha's eyes turned blurry with tears. Was it her fault she'd been violated by the General? Was she just another irresponsible girl? Kumari hadn't seemed to think so. But...who was right?

"We could learn to defend ourselves better," Rayna said quietly, as if she were speaking out of place.

"That's absurd. The girls have more important things to learn, like cooking and sewing. Don't put foolish ideas into their heads," her mother spat. "We move forward the best way we can, without losing more."

Manisha kept her eyes downcast as tension brewed around her.

Rayna cocked her chin at Manisha and asked her, "Is it like this where you're from?"

"Of course it is," her mother replied.

Manisha gritted her teeth and said, "No."

"What was it like?" Rayna pressed, eagerly wanting to know more.

"We—we had different teachings to begin with, respect, but also consequences."

She glanced at the unmoving facade of the elder women, then back to Rayna's hopeful expression, and went on, "I felt safe by myself and with men. Men and boys sought to be kind to everyone. They understood and respected that we're people and equal. There was a balance. They didn't seem to feel any less like men, or like they had something to lose by living that way—"

"Sounds like a nice place to live, but it is *not* here," Rayna's mother interjected and went back to eating, ending the conversation.

The group turned dead silent, save for the flickering flames. All eyes turned downcast.

Manisha blinked back tears as she thought, *Yes. It* was *a nice place to live. . . .*

MANISHA SLEPT IN A TREE THAT NIGHT, SOMETHING SHE'D done with her sisters growing up. They'd pretend to be watchers of the night. If they were lucky, they got to play with leopards or tree fairies, whisper secrets to bioluminescent flowers, and weave tall tales to monkeys.

She woke up in a startle, gasping for breath, her heart racing as her nightmare dissipated—barely there fragments of the General's attack but also, strangely, conversations with Eshani. Manisha desperately clung to her sister's words, but they faded within seconds.

Gathering herself before she toppled off the tree limb, Manisha took in the early morning sights of the jungle. Peaceful and calm with no signs of Noni.

Her feet were covered in salve and wrapped in leaves. The bleeding had stopped, and by morning, the wounds had vanished. Either her healing abilities had miraculously sped up, or that was one incredible ointment.

Rayna fetched her for the hunt early in the morning, handing her an extra bow and a quiver of arrows. Manisha took the weapons reverently. It'd been so long, and the anticipation didn't disappoint.

The girth and smoothness of the bowed wood was like a lifetime ago rushing to the present. It had been five years since she'd last held a weapon—kitchen knives didn't count—but she immediately found completeness, feeling more like herself instead of the shell the temple had made her.

Pieces of Manisha had been shattered when she left her family; the shards floating around slowly faded over time. Now one piece after another floated back, reattaching to their rightful places as if they had never been blown away. This was more than a weapon, more than a means of survival and food. It was home.

"Are you all right?" Rayna asked.

A slow smile made its way across Manisha's face. "Yes. It's been a while since I've used a bow and arrow."

"Well, I hope you remember enough to help with the hunt. But if not, that's okay. It's scarce sometimes."

Manisha checked the tautness of the string and slipped the slender quiver of arrows over a shoulder. She'd expected to take to her favorite weapon with ease, tapping into muscle memory, but frustratingly, she needed a *lot* of practice. Her skills were wobbly at best, and a growing pressure rose inside her knowing that Rayna was watching. Maybe Rayna thought she was joking about having been a good archer once?

Heat crawled up Manisha's neck as she quietly rebuked herself to get it together. Her palms were clammy and her arms shaky.

"Sometimes, what helps me to focus is humming my favorite song," Rayna suggested.

Manisha could only think of the songs she'd learned as an apsara. Eloquent and soothing. But they weren't songs of the heart. She closed her eyes, trying her hardest to think of songs from home. She struggled to remember the melodies her mother and aunts would hum while working, or the ones that Sithara belted off-key. But the naga—the men of her city—had an impeccable harmony. Papa and cousins and uncles would sing from high to low.

Manisha smiled. Yes. That was a healing balm for her emotions as frayed edges of her skills slowly came together.

One miserable shot turned into a dozen irritating ones, which turned into a heap of annoying misses, which eventually turned into a singular hit. Not perfect. Not even close to the center of the big tree. But at least she'd hit the tree.

Rayna applauded as if she hadn't waited what felt like an entire day for Manisha, the so-called archer, to hit her mark.

After more practice, Rayna took her to hunt deep in the woods. Rayna explained this and that about tracking prey, like hiding places, nests, the type of food each prey was drawn to, footprints, disturbed debris, rubbed-off moss on the sides of trees and rocks, and droppings. Manisha did her best to absorb the knowledge.

Rayna killed small prey, but it wasn't much for even one family. So Manisha went after bigger game. A boar. Not the monstrous kind that had knocked down trees during the Fire Wars and ruled the jungle with arm-length tusks, but an average one. Large enough to feed the entire village.

Boars were fast and hid in shrubs, forcing Manisha to move into the trees and, many times, fall off limbs.

"Maybe we should head back?" Rayna suggested after Manisha's third fall.

"No. We need this," Manisha grunted, ignoring the pain screaming down her back and limbs.

She tried again. She calmed the rising level of frustration, found her footing and balance, and hunted a little slower this time. Spotting a boar below, she stalked it from the branches, signaling to Rayna. Manisha put her weight into her legs for balance so that she could stand straight, pull back an arrow, taut against the resistance of the bow, and look down the shaft to the tip.

The boar snorted and pushed dirt around with its snout.

Manisha released, but it wasn't a clean kill. The boar squealed, startling birds and sending smaller creatures scurrying. She climbed down, and Rayna ran out of hiding to end the boar's life with a single, deep slit to the throat. She held the creature down and smoothed a hand over its convulsing body, cooing to it as one would to a baby. Then she bowed her head and mumbled prayer and thanks.

Rayna had tears in her eyes, as if hunting wrecked her soul. Maybe it did. Maybe she preferred to let animals live. But in hard times, she had to make sure her people survived. Maybe the villagers would be better off moving toward the prairies where farming was better, and they wouldn't have to worry about being attacked or killing animals for survival.

Manisha knelt beside Rayna and touched the boar's side as its last breaths escaped in pained pants, its eyes jerking back and forth, terrified. Manisha felt it, too. It hurt her to kill after so long, to see the pain she caused in another creature.

"I'm sorry," she murmured to the boar as its chest rose and fell for the final time.

Once the boar died, they rolled its enormous weight onto a mat of ferns and giant leaves and dragged it back to the village.

"Teamwork," Rayna announced with appreciation.

Teamwork. Ah, yes. Not instruction to be followed with the fear of being reprimanded. But like home. Rayna had been so patient that Manisha had forgotten what a burden waiting on her must've been.

The village cheered. Older ones went to work prepping the animal. Manisha couldn't watch. And when the time came to eat, she couldn't bring herself to consume it.

Instead, she foraged for roots and vegetables, anything other than fruit. She found enough to make a meal for herself.

Giving an entire village food for days was enough for the villagers to welcome her. She supposed if someone slept in trees, did laundry, and brought food, she'd want them to stay, too.

"You're a true blessing!" Rayna exclaimed, joyfully watching others eat.

Manisha smiled. Although she hadn't enjoyed killing the boar, helping others made her feel less lost, less broken. Kumari's words rang true.

Rani interjected, "But the real blessing is that neither of you were taken."

Rayna nodded, her mood dampening with such a depth of sadness that it turned palpable.

"Will you stay longer?" Rayna asked Manisha. "I'd have a worthy hunting partner."

"Thank you, but I need to find my family. I should get going in the morning."

She frowned. "What can I prepare for you? Your clothes are dry, but they're ripped. A sari doesn't seem comfortable for traveling."

"It's not. Maybe...do you think I could keep these clothes?" Manisha asked.

"Of course! You can keep the shoes, too."

"Oh! Thank you!"

"We actually have something else for you."

"Really?"

Rayna excitedly went to her hut and returned with a single-strapped bag. "A satchel. Friends donated items for your travels. A small pot of balm for your feet, a water container, and food. Mainly dried fruit, figs, dates, and nuts. Also roots, which will last longer in case you run out of food. Best to boil them, but you can eat them raw. Plus, a knife. You can't be without a knife in the jungle by yourself."

Manisha's heart swelled with gratitude. The bag fit perfectly over one shoulder, the strap across her chest to the waist. "I—I don't know what to say. This is too much."

Rayna shook her head. "They're things that can be replaced. I can make another satchel from this boar. You've given us so much food with just one kill. I'm hoping that maybe you can hunt with me in the morning before you leave?" she asked, her eyes big, pleading.

Manisha nodded. Well, she'd wanted to leave that day and didn't look forward to killing again, but with so much given to her, she felt obligated to hunt. But tomorrow, she absolutely had to leave.

"Look!" a little girl nearby exclaimed, pointing at something golden protruding from a thorny bush.

Rayna walked toward the unusual clump and pulled it out. She held it above her head, unrolling eight feet of golden snakeskin.

Everyone gathered, oohing and aahing. The men crowed, "That could be worth a fortune!"

Manisha flinched. That could only be from Noni. So quick to stab a monetary value on her best friend? Where was Noni, anyway? She hadn't seen her in days.

The villagers ran hands down the *long* shedding.

Either another rare golden snake had been nearby, or Noni had doubled in size. Neither seemed plausible, but both seemed incredibly fantastical.

SEVENTEEN

PRATYUSH
(PRESENT DAY)

Dev eyed Pratyush, a hint of concern cracking his stony features. "Ever going to tell me what happens when you slay a monster?"

"What?" Pratyush heaved out. His hands were shaking, his fingers stretching in and out of fists. He hadn't been able to save his men, and now their deaths added weight upon weight to his shoulders. He felt responsible for every one of them. Soldiers who'd gone out to slay a nagin and faced monsters of another kind. Sometimes he wondered what the point was, anyway. Death was at the end of the tunnel no matter where people turned.

And that mirage...*what* was happening? It didn't make any sense. He wished there was a library of knowledge for these things.

"You looked like you got physically hit in the head. It nearly took you down back there. You could've died," Dev said, clearly worried.

Pratyush took in a long breath and calmed himself. "It's nothing."

Dev allowed a few seconds before adding, "You can... always talk to me about these things."

Pratyush glanced at him. Dev never talked about his feelings. No soldier did. They were trained to keep it in and move on, that no one really cared about their feelings.

"Emotions make you weak," a training commander had told them as young soldiers.

Pratyush scowled, unable to form the words *I need help. I'm in pain. I'm filled with anxiety and loss, and nothing helps . . . except maybe Manisha.* She allowed him to feel, to hope.

His father had never been afraid, or at least he never appeared to be. Even when monsters had attacked their family, Papa was decisive. He fought. Pratyush aimed to be like him, but he kept falling short. Had Papa had depression, anxiety, paranoia? If so, how had he dealt with any of it?

No one could sleep after the vetala attack, so they traveled through the night. Numbers diminished by nearly a third, energy sapped, morale low. Not to mention the memories that now haunted them. Those sounds—brain slurping and warning trills—weren't going to be easy to forget. Nightmares for days.

The only surprise the jungle threw at them was a curious leopard in the trees. It startled a soldier so badly after his encounter with vetala that he was ready to kill the animal.

Dev lowered the older boy's bow and arrow as the leopard yawned, knowing full well it had nothing to fear from them. But frazzled nerves and sleep-deprived reasoning made for dumb decisions.

The team reached the Great River and set up camp in the moonlight. The soldiers rested in scattered clusters on the riverbank, a few taking turns to keep watch. The General, as pompous as the King, stationed himself in a tent. Pratyush could've punched his diya out. The jackass didn't *believe* the vetala were a threat because he'd never walked the meadows at night. Pratyush should've thrown him into a vetala's clutches to show him what they were.

The General's level of idiocy was growing, at speeds so rapid it made Pratyush question reality.

They'd gone through plenty of missions together and survived, but now Pratyush saw *how* the General had survived. He battled men, not monsters. Bring a monster around, and the General was out of sight. Fine, whatever, but don't tell anyone the monsters weren't real. There were a handful of newly brainless corpses in that field because of him.

Pratyush spent the rest of the night alone, on top of a tall, flattened boulder overlooking the river, the fighters, and the surrounding area. He felt strangely connected to Manisha, as if she were standing on this exact same spot. But that was foolishness.

The quiet quickly gave way to all that was wrong.

Depression was descending around him like shadows. He didn't even try to fight it off.

IN THE MORNING, PRATYUSH SAT ON THE BOULDER AND ATE a ration of roti, pickled mango, and large white radishes. He'd planned on snacking on makhana in between meals. The puffed lotus seeds were good for digestion. He'd save the savory, crunchy chevdo for his travels back since the snack would last the longest.

He kept an eye on the others and tried not to think of the dead soldiers or whether he could've fought the General's decision.

Which sucked for him, because the guilt was a darkness rising in his gut and contaminating his soul with toxic fumes. If he wasn't careful, it might snuff him out. Guilt wasn't easy to shake off or forget. Maybe in the beginning it'd been easy to ignore, but over time, it grew into this insurmountable cloud hovering over his head, choking out the light.

Speaking of insurmountable things...

Pratyush craned his head back and looked up at the shadowy undersides of the floating mountains, wondering if Manisha was awake, sitting on her balcony, drinking chai. Did she ever think about him? Maybe she wasn't interested in a person as ruthless as a slayer.

He scoffed, dipping a torn-off piece of roti into chutney. *Yeah. Who would be?* Even his mother had married a "retired" slayer. Most slayers never settled down with one person, much less in one place. Maybe this was just fate, and kismet's rules wouldn't bend.

He'd just hoped that, well, maybe Manisha would give him a chance if he could give her freedom. Maybe she would like him enough then? She seemed open to the idea of leaving her perfect, floating palace. The only reason someone would want to leave all that behind was if they weren't happy. But if she wasn't happy, then why couldn't she leave on her own? Maybe her freedom had been bought by the apsara.

He grunted. Ugh. Why was he so concerned about her when he might not make it back in time? Would the King withdraw his part of the deal if hardly any soldiers survived?

"Can I join you?" Ras asked, climbing up the steep, curved boulder.

Pratyush shrugged, chewing on his last bite as the sharpness of the white radish mellowed out.

"Wanted to see the view from up here. Wow . . ." Ras took a huge breath. "Are those the floating mountains?"

Pratyush scrunched his nose. "Well, they're not floating figs."

"Oh, right. I . . . I've never seen them this clearly before. From the inner cities, they're small and covered in clouds. From the jungle, can't see them at all unless you get above the canopy. They're amazing."

"I guess."

"Heard it's paradise up there: magnificent animals, clean air, bouncy grass, an overflow of good food. Sacred temples built from marble and gold with jewels embedded into sculptures, curated by the most beautiful, purest women in the world. Soft skin and divine eyes."

"Control yourself, there," Pratyush said dryly. "You make apsara sound like heaven itself."

"Aren't they, though?"

Pratyush shrugged. He didn't know about the rest of the temple priestesses, just the one.

An angel. Meek and meant to run around on errands for another, quiet and meant to be hidden? No.

A goddess. Powerful and all-consuming with the ability to both create and destroy worlds. Yes. *That* was what he smelled on Manisha. Power.

Other apsara smelled the same—human women and girls, clean and doused in oils. They sounded the same when they spoke, taught from the same teachers. Not Manisha. She smelled, looked, and sounded like something else. This wasn't infatuation, but the senses of a slayer. She made his skin tingle like a rainstorm before the first droplet fell. She was the beginning of a storm.

"You've been there, right?" Ras asked, cutting through his thoughts.

"Yeah."

"So. The apsara?"

"I don't know much about girls. I don't get a lot of time to think about them or look at them. I go there for the King and straight back. Why are you thinking about them, anyway?"

Ras flinched, his face pale. "Better to think about something poetic and serene instead of last night."

Pratyush sighed. "Yeah. I get that. I wanna say it gets easier, but . . . no. It doesn't."

"I thought everything was easier for a slayer."

Pratyush shook his head. "Everyone has their hardships. We just see the outside of someone, never knowing what's happening inside. Maybe they seem okay, undeterred, strong, successful, happy, whatever. Probably doesn't match the inside. It hardly ever does."

Ras regarded him, but Pratyush quickly changed the subject. "Do you have a girlfriend? Or is that why you're asking about girls?"

Ras almost choked on his laugh. "Ha! Girls like stronger, older boys. . . . I still have a way to go. There are a couple back at my village that my parents like for me. But they keep saying I'm like a brother. They even insist on giving me rakhi."

"Ouch . . ."

"If that's not telling the entire village about brother material, then I don't know what is."

Pratyush chuckled. Pritika used to tie a rakhi thread around his wrist, a symbol of sibling love and unbreakable bond. Even though he was younger, it signified that he would always be there to help her, to protect her. He had been foolish to think that he could.

"Are you really the last slayer?" Ras asked, catching Pratyush off guard.

"It's what I'm told. Haven't seen or heard of another in a while."

"Ah. Well, that's a shame. Would be helpful to have more."

Innocent words setting off cruel memories. There had been more. There would've been another, had his father not died. There would be an army of them if the King got what he wanted.

Below, the soldiers packed and loaded the horses, the younger ones being given the grunt work. No surprise that the General had his own help and had already mounted his steed, ready to get on his way. As impatient as ever without lifting a finger. Wow. Seemed like a great, annoying power of his.

"Thanks for getting my horse safely across the meadow."

Ras swallowed. "No worries."

"Why didn't you stay at the point I told you to stay at?"

Ras responded carefully, as if the slayer might smite him for disobedience. "Well, I went toward it at first. But then I heard screams, and we turned back. I'm a good archer."

Pratyush eyed him. "Did the General command you to return?"

"No. We did it on our own. He, um, actually ordered us to continue on."

Pratyush scoffed. Unbelievable. Was the General trying to get him killed? What did he plan on doing if the slayer died? Kill the nagin himself? He didn't stand a chance. Unless . . .

Wait . . .

Unless this was an impossible mission, and Pratyush wasn't meant to return alive. Was there even a monster out here to slay? He'd come across all sorts of creatures and had spent hours studying others, but none that turned men to stone. That just seemed impossible.

The slayer was supposed to be the golden ticket, the weapon of weapons, the one to be protected until a monster needed slaying. But the General let him literally walk through "monster meadows." Did the King have a new weapon against monsters—one better than a slayer?

No. No. No. That was definitely paranoia talking. But . . . his father had seemed anxious about something bad happening minutes before it destroyed their world. Was it paranoia or premonition? Was it a suspicion to be denied, or a sense to be heeded?

Ras had been saying, "When we refused to leave and made a line, he took control to lead us. Are you mad at me for disobeying?"

"No. You helped save us! I mean, I *should* tell you to obey your superiors, but sometimes you gotta make life-and-death decisions. There's a lot of gray in what we do."

"Really?" he asked. "There shouldn't be, right? Monsters are evil. Kill the monster, save the kingdom."

"Nothing is ever that simple," Pratyush said, kicking a pebble off the boulder when Dev climbed up.

Dev said, "Some of the soldiers are headed off. A few are trailing behind, and one is watching your horse. We should get going."

"So nice for the General to alert me," Pratyush told him, his tone dripping with sarcasm.

"Aren't you best friends?" Dev teased.

"The way falcons and rats are, I guess. What's going on down there?" Pratyush jerked his chin toward a group of four older boys laughing and playfully punching each other's shoulders as they peered through the bushes separating the jungle from the riverbanks.

"There's a woman out there," Ras said, pointing at the water.

Pratyush pivoted to face the river. Huh. What was a woman doing out alone in a behemoth river?

She slipped out of a yellow dress and walked into the water like the current wasn't dangerous.

"Oh!" Ras said. He spun around, his cheeks red.

"Why'd you look away? Not interested in naked women?" Pratyush asked, narrowing his eyes at the group of four.

Ras shook his head. "Th-that's not right."

"A soldier with morals? What have you been doing? Hanging around Dev too much?"

Dev cracked a smile, flashing those sharp teeth.

Pratyush yelled down to the group to get going, but either they didn't hear him or they didn't care. *The nerve.* They weren't out here to be harassing women. Besides, that wasn't the kind of soldier Pratyush wanted in his keep.

He grunted, "Let's go. We don't have time for this."

The group of four emerged from the bushes and snatched the dress. The woman, with her dark hair flowing in the breeze beneath a flower crown, chided them, concealing her breasts, her back to the soldiers. But they continued to tease her, laughing, whistling, and edging closer to the water. Were they possessed, or were they really this stupid?

"She looks like a yakshini," Dev said, barely looking at her.

"What's that?" Ras asked.

"A water nymph, protector of rivers. They're benevolent people." Dev crawled down the boulder, muttering, "How many guys I gotta punch in the crotch?"

By now the group was sloshing into the river, waving her dress, trying to surround her.

Pratyush's blood ran hot as he started to climb down. Then something moved in his periphery. He froze, searching the greenish, murky water.

A shadow serpentined beneath the surface. A very *large* shadow, twice the size of an adult crocodile, headed for the group. With his slayer vision, he could penetrate a shallow level of the water to see this wasn't even close to a crocodile, not with those razor-sharp horns and massive green tail.

"Get out of there!" he yelled.

The soldiers either didn't hear him or chose to ignore him. Again. The group swam farther out trying to catch the yakshini. But she also swam farther out, fleeing... or luring.

She dipped below the ripples and vanished.

Had the water beast snatched her? Had the currents taken her under?

Pratyush seethed.

"Look!" Ras said, pointing at the unmoving shadow in the water.

The yakshini resurfaced. The dark sheen of her sopping hair plastered over her head appeared first. Her eyes came next—angry and vengeful—then her downturned lips. Her breasts were covered by her hair as she leaned forward, her body emerging on the back of something big. The shadow.

It was a goliath makara, one with a multitude of tapered projections lining its head and neck and sides. And it, like the woman, was *not* pleased.

She clutched the backward-angled horns alongside the beast's neck, its eyes glowing yellow.

Pratyush yelled, "Retreat!"

They weren't quick enough.

The woman smirked. The makara, with her still attached to its back, sank into the water. A tight, forceful ripple rushed toward the group of four faster than an arrow.

Pratyush wouldn't have been able to get down the boulder and into the water in time to save them. Even if he'd jumped. Dev had barely reached the edge of the riverbank when the makara attacked.

The soldiers screamed. The creature, sinking its teeth into them and thrashing them back and forth like toys, dragged them down into watery graves.

"Dev! Stop!" Pratyush waved his hands to get his friend's attention at the same time Ras was also yelling for Dev.

Because now, as if one giant water dragon wasn't enough, others appeared. Shadows beneath the surface of the water, ripples racing toward the group.

The waters turned dark with blood, bubbling over in a feeding frenzy until, finally, everything stilled.

The silence after an attack was like quiet nightmares. A ringing, eerie silence: the sort that engulfed entire worlds and drowned them in blood.

EIGHTEEN

MANISHA
(TWENTY-FIVE DAYS AGO)

Manisha listened to the villagers debate over the golden snakeskin.

A woman suggested, "Some say there are medicinal properties to snakeskin, and if so, surely the rare golden serpent has potent capabilities."

Manisha eyed her.

Another said, "I don't know. Have you ever tried it? What if this one is too potent, poisonous, even? Also, the idea of eating snake is unappealing."

Manisha gagged.

A loud commotion started from the village behind them. An older boy came storming toward Rayna. He was short and gangly with a hardened face.

"What's going on?" Rayna asked him.

Manisha gripped the strap to her new bag as he replied, "I'm sorry to tell you, but . . . Rani was taken."

Manisha's gut dropped. Flashbacks of the General crowded her thoughts, splitting her vision between the past and the present, blending faces and ferns.

"What!" Rayna screamed. "When? Where?"

"That stupid girl was in the jungle by herself!" Rayna's mother howled, panic driving wedges through every member of the village while they stood around, shooting blame at everyone except Rani's attacker.

Rayna's face flared red as she spat, "She was probably just cleaning. It's her menstruation time."

The boy cringed.

"*What?* Does the vital blood of life displease you?" Rayna snapped. "Can a girl take care of her hygiene without being preyed upon! What are you waiting for? Go get her," she screamed, her fists trembling.

He took her hands and said in an even tone, "You know that's not going to happen."

"Why—why not?" Manisha found herself asking, her voice quivering, sweat pushing out of her pores.

The boy glared at Manisha. "Said so simplistically from an outsider who's been here for two days. You know, the clothes you were wearing were very nice silk, expensive. You were dressed like an important person."

Manisha stared at him, confused.

He went on, "You won't tell us where you came from, nothing about you except for a name. But your sari suggests you're from a high place."

She swallowed.

He narrowed his eyes. "Do you belong to a noble? Maybe a royal family? A palace worker at the least? There are stories about girls who work around royals dressed better than anyone in the towns, much less a village. Your clothes, your posture, the way you speak . . . you're not a jungle girl."

Manisha bit the inside of her cheek to hold back the fear bubbling up in her gut.

"If you want to help us..." He looked to Rayna and added, "We can trade her."

Blood drained from Manisha's face.

"What?" Rayna gasped. "No!"

"You're unwilling to trade a stranger for your own sister but want to send me to my death?"

"You're my betrothed. You're supposed to protect my family! What if they'd taken me? Would you even go after me?"

"Quiet your voice," he growled, glancing around as if he were mortified that he was being yelled at in front of everyone.

"Trading Manisha won't solve anything," Rayna hissed. "It makes things worse. They'd just take her and keep Rani. You're just handing them more girls. What a terrible suggestion!"

"Isn't it worth a try?" he asked.

Manisha looked around for an escape route.

"No," Rayna said, dejected. Pain was etched so deep in her features and in her voice that Manisha could feel it. And it was devastating. "We're not interchangeable pots to be bartered with. If you trade Manisha, then how are you any better?"

"Then let it go. There's nothing we can do," he said. "We can only hope that they release her when they're done. I'm sorry."

Rayna gulped and looked skyward, her eyes glistening, her jaw clenched.

With pressed lips, determined in his lack of resolve, her betrothed walked away, leaving Rayna to shatter into sobs beside Manisha as, one by one, everyone left.

Manisha caught Rayna before she collapsed, lowering her to the ground.

Rayna took several minutes to calm down enough to respond, her words tumbling out in hiccups. "This happens too often. What are we supposed to do?"

Manisha blinked back tears, wishing she had an answer.

Rayna wiped her cheeks. "I tried to teach her how to defend herself, but in the moment...She must be terrified. They might get tired of her and let her go, but she'll have to find her way back by herself. Or they like her and keep her."

Manisha's entire body shook.

Rayna's mother came to comfort her, moving Manisha out of the way.

"What do we do?" Rayna asked again.

"Nothing," her mother said softly, her voice quivering. "They might group together and take us all. There are too many of them." She sighed and shook her head, her jaw hard but her eyes glistening with pain and loss. "She shouldn't have gone out alone. She knows the risks. Reckless girl."

"She had to clean herself!" Rayna cried, her breathing ragged, sharp. "You can be worried about leopards and tigers and stinging ants and spiders, but not men."

"Hush!" her mother rebuked, wiping her own tears as her dupatta slipped from her gray hair.

"This is *Rani*!"

"I know. I know, beta. But what can we do? We can't fight them; they'll kill us all. We can't rescue her, there's no way."

"I hate this!" Rayna screamed, storming to her hut before her mother could react. Manisha followed, numb from trauma, reliving her own attack, even as the iciness in her skin crackled above the increasing heat in her veins. She knew exactly what Rani was going through, and it made her sick. Worse was not knowing what to do.

Rayna paced the hut. "What do we do? What do we do?"

Manisha gnawed on her lip, clenching and unclenching her fists, her knees shaking, her breaths fast and hot, and her head buzzing like a pack of wild bees.

Rayna jerked her chin. "What would you do?"

Manisha stilled. Her thoughts tripped over themselves. Words refused to form. Her mouth turned dry. She had no answers. Her parents would've known what to do. Her sisters. Kumari. If Kumari were here, what would she do?

Manisha's eyelids fluttered as her vision went in and out, blurry, then *crystal* clear. She saw the freckles on Rayna's nose, the speckles of dirt under her fingernails, the rush of blood in the vein at her throat.

What was happening? She was sick to her stomach.

She shoved aside the darkness pulsating in her head, saturated with the memory of the General's touch, and stuttered until actual words bubbled out of her mouth. "I'd do anything to have someone try to save me."

Rayna regarded her, her hands dropping to her sides. "This must bring back so much for you."

Manisha gulped, blinking back tears. "When it happened to me, I *wished* someone would've tried to help."

Rayna bit her bottom lip as she contorted her face to keep her sobs in.

Manisha wiped her own tears as they fell faster. "I don't know what to do. I don't have answers. But my mother used to say that life is like a ripple: cause and effect. Sometimes you have to be the drop in the water that causes a ripple that makes a change. She'd say: 'Beta, be a boulder, not a pebble, when you hit the water.'"

"Don't drop into the issue but splash so that the shores might feel it."

Manisha nodded. "You've heard the saying?"

"Hah," she conceded.

Manisha slackened the anxious energy seizing up her muscles. "I'm scared."

"Me too." Rayna's face hardened with determination. "I'm going."

"What can one girl do?"

"A girl can try."

Despite the tremors in her body, Manisha knew she couldn't just walk away. "You won't stand alone. I'll help."

Rayna's tears fell. She didn't bother brushing them away this time. "Thank you."

"Teamwork," Manisha said.

"We're a team. We can do this." She dropped to her knees and shoved aside a cloth on the floor. "We have a few daggers."

Manisha jerked her chin at the bow and arrow. "Give me those."

They tied their hair back, strapped weapons to their bodies, and snuck out in the dead of night so that no one could try stopping them.

Their footfalls were quiet. The firelight from the village faded behind them as they entered the dark, so absolute that it could petrify. Ahead, vines, flowers, and mushrooms began to glow, showing them the way in glimmering shades of pink, red, purple, yellow, and white. Things that had never glowed before lit up the jungle.

"I could've used your sari to cover myself and scare them as a booth," Rayna mused.

"A booth?"

"A ghost. Those men might not respect girls, but they fear superstitions."

They hurried over rocks and uprooted roots in a narrow trail, made even narrower with overgrowth. Creatures hissed in the night, rustled in the trees and bushes.

"Wait," Rayna said, grabbing Manisha's arm and pulling her against a tree.

Manisha flinched against the touch, momentarily thrown back into the General's clutches. She had to control herself. She had to push past her own trauma, at least for tonight, to save Rani.

"There's movement," Rayna said, releasing her hold.

They inched closer to the bulky, broad shadows on the ground, toward squelching. Feathery predators jerked their heads to the side in one-inch movements until their heads had twisted halfway around to glare at the girls.

"Crow pheasants..." Rayna announced with a sigh.

They feasted on something so mutilated it was impossible to tell what the poor creature had been. They were known for ripping apart prey and consuming organs, leaving the rest. Which explained the gut-churning squelching sounds as they sopped up brains and intestines.

They were also extremely territorial while eating, even if others had no interest in getting between them and their meal.

The girls went all the way around them, moving so far from the trail that it was a miracle they even found it again.

They walked forever. More than once, Rayna complained about not being able to get her bearings. One tree looked like the next. One fern looked like a million others.

"Do you see the glow?" Manisha asked, lifting her fingers toward a trailing pink vine speckled with purple hyacinth-type blooms. These were not the same blooms she'd seen on the trail. They hadn't back-tracked or gone in a circle.

"What?"

Manisha furrowed her brow, hyperaware of a new clarity embed-ded in her night vision. Eerie but wonderful. Down to the veins on each leaf, the patterns on bark, the types of vegetation, the scars and markings, the shapes of rocks.

As acute as this new eyesight was, her hearing was even more so. The light buzz of fireflies above. The gentle swoosh of an owl's flight. And...footfalls. Hushed conversations. The crackle of flames on resin-soaked torches.

"They're over there," Manisha whispered, listening for Rani's voice through the sounds of the village ahead.

Something else. Muffled cries. Manisha froze in mid-step. Pain and terror floated on the wind, scratching her skin, pressing into her brain, clawing at her entire being. At first, it was an assault of emotions, an onslaught of her own memories. The General's disgusting hands all over her, pushing, hurting. The suffocation. The coldness of her exposed skin. The agony of forced penetration.

Then it turned into Rani's story, her pleas and horrors, because they were in the present where *she* suffered.

Manisha shook off the lingering dread from her trauma, finding breath and stability, and fought through the agonizing immobility the General had left within her. She managed to tell Rayna, "She's in that hut on the edge."

"How do you know?" Rayna asked, craning her head to see. The glow from faraway torches fell on her face.

"I can hear her." Manisha tilted her head, listening. "There's only one man in the hut with her. The nearest is farther into the village. We can get her. The two of us can take him."

"How could you know this?"

"I can hear them. Trust me."

Rayna jutted her chin, brows lowered, nostrils flaring. She didn't seem to care too much about how Manisha could hear all that, or even if it were true. She just wanted her sister, and she was ready to fight for her.

A man walked out of the hut wearing only pants. He was smoking and looking around like some ordinary person enjoying the night, not like an insidious predator who had a terrified girl trapped inside.

Much like the Fire Wars, the girls teamed up to outmaneuver the enemy in a time of great distress. To save a life.

Fear and anger warred within Manisha when she stuttered, "One— one of us can pretend to stumble into the clearing. He won't suspect anything. The other in the trees can shoot if he doesn't hand her over. I'm sure he won't. Or we can wait until he's asleep."

Rayna's anger contorted her features as she volunteered herself. "No. We can't risk anything else happening. She's *my* sister. I'll walk into the camp. Besides, I'm faster on the ground and better skilled with a dagger." She held up her weapon, the metal catching the torchlight.

"Okay. Give me a minute to get into position. But only go if he's alone. If others come out, we'll have to wait."

Rayna nodded. They had their backs to the jungle as they checked the clearing for signs of others.

Manisha had been so busy between studying the edge of the village and keeping her dread under control that she hadn't registered the silent footsteps approaching from behind until five older boys were upon them.

NINETEEN

MANISHA
(TWENTY-FIVE DAYS AGO)

"What are you doing here?" Rayna demanded, a hand to her chest. She gawked at her betrothed and four other boys.

His face hardened as he took her by the elbow and dragged her away. "What are *you* doing here? Don't you know how dangerous this is? What if they captured you, too, huh? Get home. *Now.*"

She struggled against his grip. "Not without my sister."

"Shh!"

Panic descended on Manisha. Still, she took a step toward them, an explanation on the tip of her tongue. They had a plan—maybe not the best one, but a plan. And everything would work out better if they would just help.

The other boys stepped in between Manisha and the bickering couple, pointing the sharp ends of spears at her. She swallowed hard and tentatively stepped back.

"Remove your weapons and satchel," one of the boys ordered.

"What's going on?" Manisha gripped her only source of defense.

Behind them, Rayna's wide eyes filled with imploring apologies. Her betrothed had a hand wrapped around her mouth and was dragging her off into the darkness. The other four stayed rooted.

Manisha could guess their plan. Her body turned limp, her throat drying as anxiety clawed down her spine. Her breathing was ragged, her eyes darting around to find an exit. But there wasn't anywhere to go, not when four spears were pointed at her, jagged tips inches from the tenderness of her throat.

She huffed out a breath, trembling, and slid off the satchel, the quiver and bow, dropping them to the ground. She pushed them into the underbrush behind her with a foot.

"This—this is a mistake," she told them. She'd meant to be bold, brazen, but her words came out shaky and weak. "We had a plan. I can get Rani out. Let me try."

Instead of listening, or even volleying excuses, they shoved spears at her, closing the small gaps, poking her bare neck and collarbone. But her skin didn't break.

She hissed at the sharpness flicking against her skin and jumped. They forced her to walk backward little by little, her hands up, until she stumbled into the open area, now fully visible to the man smoking in front of his hut.

Manisha slowly turned to meet his curious scrutiny. She shuddered, flashbacks from her own attack razing her thoughts.

"Keep walking," a boy behind her demanded, poking her back with a spear.

She grunted, lurching forward.

"We have an exchange for the girl you took from our village tonight," another boy behind her declared.

The man at the hut flicked his smoke onto the ground and snuffed it out with his bare toe. He was tall and thin, with sharp cheekbones and the right side of his head shaved. He approached them in commanding, confident steps and stopped several feet in front of Manisha. He swept his gaze down her body, as if deciding whether she was worth an exchange.

Manisha was so petrified to the spot that she couldn't even ball her fists.

"You've used the girl already?" the boy behind Manisha asked.

Her heart sank into her stomach. She wanted to vomit remembering the General's callous touches.

The man nodded with a grunt. His lip curled up as if Rani had been simply *okay* and nowhere near as gratifying as he had expected her to be.

"We offer this one for her," the boy behind Manisha said, commenting on her soft skin, full lips, and silky hair.

Manisha couldn't manage to even avert her eyes.

The boy tossed her sari to the ground in front of her as proof. "She's a stranger, a wanderer. But obviously of high breeding. She's bound to be worth something if you can find her owner."

The man picked up the sari and examined it, sliding the fabric between grimy fingers and sniffing. He nodded and said, "I'm done with the other one, anyway." As if Rani were disposable. As if girls were just objects to be used and discarded.

Manisha's stomach churned something vile and deadly. It wasn't the urge to vomit this time, but something dark and menacing that whispered, *Let the anger flow and forget the terror.* The call of vengeance she'd first realized with Kumari. It whispered to be unleashed, a seductive plea caressing her brain and slithering down her spine, ready to take control of her body. It promised her that fate could be changed, and she could be the force behind it.

If only she could let go of the fear.

The man went into his hut and returned with Rani in tow, dragging her small body out by her bony elbow. Her hair was disheveled, her braid undone and wild. Her face was marred with purple-and-green bruises, and her haggard eyes red and swollen from crying. Her clothes were mangled and sullied, her pants nowhere to be found, but her slit kurta was long enough to cover to the knees.

Residual trauma mixed with a growing, searing fire deep within Manisha's bones. Indignation? Hatred? Vengeance? No. What had Kumari said? *Justice. Accountability.*

Rani's captor shoved her forward, and Manisha caught her. Rani wobbled in her arms and Manisha hugged her, held her tight, forgetting that Rani must've been in so much pain. But the embrace only lasted seconds before the boys took her.

In that moment, Rani looked up, flashing red-streaked eyes glistening with tears. Blood gushed from her mouth, spilling over her quivering lips. There was a *lot* of blood, more than there should've been. A river of red.

A deep horror sank into Manisha, twisting her stomach. Had Rani's tongue been cut out? To keep her from speaking, yelling, screaming?

Manisha reached out for her, to protect her or save her, she wasn't sure. Rani vomited blood at Manisha's feet, speckles of crimson marring the grass.

Manisha gasped, her eyelids fluttering as she looked up, unable to help.

Rani could barely walk. Blood trickled down her legs so that every step left carmine footprints. Was this life in the kingdom? On the floating mountains or in the jungles, no safety, no security, no peace? Fire and blood steeped in hatred?

The villagers vanished into the jungle. Guessing from how much Rani was bleeding and the way her people had to drag her off, she might not survive after all.

Manisha reeled in an achingly deep sorrow and cast the most vicious glower at the last boy to leave her in the hands of this cruel abuser. This one, though, flashed his eyes as if maybe he was saddened and knew this was wrong. But he didn't stop. He didn't help her.

Manisha climbed out of her stupor, clenching her jaw and fists. There was no one here to help her. She had to save herself.

A horrid rage she'd never known consumed her. Even more feverish than what she'd felt after the General's attack. She turned to the man standing at his hut as his lewd, hungry gaze dragged down her body once more. She could practically see his plans unfurl across his face.

She was numb, but she couldn't quite tell if it was because of fear or anger. The two seemed the same in this nightmarish moment.

He was suddenly standing right in front of her, saying, "Let's go, and don't make a sound. Don't make me cut out your tongue, too."

He snatched her wrist and hauled her inside. Manisha yelped, digging her feet into the dirt, and clawed against his grip. But he only tightened it.

He yanked her forward and shoved her inside a disgusting, dirty hut stained in Rani's blood. The smell of her fear still lingered in the air.

Manisha's gaze darted around to find something she could use as a weapon. Anything. Pots, tinder, the rocks around a fire, the fire itself.

The man picked her up by the waist, strangling the breath from her lungs, and threw her onto a bed of dusty blankets. She grunted, gasping for breath but inhaling dust and a foul stench. She rolled over right as he fell on top of her, his pants already halfway down his thighs. He fought to draw her leggings down.

Something primal snapped in Manisha.

"*No!*" she screamed, the word tearing out of her throat like a feral growl. She floundered and thrashed, keeping her knees together at her chest to create a barrier, shoving his face away, scratching, punching.

He snarled, and when he couldn't part her knees, when he couldn't keep her hands pinned down, he threw a fist.

On instinct, Manisha's arms flew to her face to take the brunt of his brutal force. She expected this to be the end of her, on the verge of another attack, knowing that he'd be stronger and more violent than the General. One solid punch was all it would take to knock her out.

But something unexpected happened. Her flesh glowed a golden-bronze iridescence where his fist made contact. An alarming hum exploded on impact and faded just as fast. His punch didn't hurt nearly as much as she'd expected. Hardly at all, really.

But for him?

He hissed and jumped back, cradling his wrist to his chest like he'd hit stone.

Manisha stared at him, shuddering, perplexed. She kicked him in the stomach and then his crotch, which seemed to be the only pain to rival his face.

Rage careened through her. The whisper in her head grew, telling her to let it take over. She did, welcoming the darkness that felt so right, luscious, and intoxicating. Most of all, empowering.

The apsara had drilled into her that anger was a weakness and emotions clouded judgment, but in this moment, she'd never felt stronger. Anger that had been tamped down for *years* unleashed in mighty torrents, ignited by the General and fueled by this abuser's detestable crimes.

Manisha spat at him. Wherever her spit touched, his flesh melted like it had met a splatter of acid, a potent venom. His skin bubbled and popped, exposing red, inflamed muscle.

She paused, bewildered and terrified, but found a new calm as understanding dawned on her. She was not only stronger than before, but she had power.

She spat in his eyes; his eyelids were eaten away in seconds before he could cover his face. His yells turned into manic sobs as he rolled from side to side in a curled position, his legs tied by the pants cuffed halfway down his thighs.

The apsara in Manisha sympathized for him, even felt bad about the pain she'd caused. The scholar in her wanted to understand everything, from catalyst to reaction. But the victim in Manisha? The girl? The human? Indifference swept her away.

Eye for an eye. Genital for a . . . genital?

Could she be so bold, so vengeful? With shaking hands, she yanked up his long tunic and flinched with memories of the General, the pain this man had put Rani through, and all the terrible things he must've done to others.

Manisha gagged. "The sight of you makes me want to vomit."

His words garbled in his mouth.

"You think it's your right to force that thing into helpless victims? But you know, it's a pitiful, vulnerable mass hanging off your body. Weak and exposed, and so easy to hurt," she said, her voice trembling.

He glared up at her with one eye, but his anger had been diluted with pain.

"You wanted intense sensation, the kind that only comes when you hurt girls?" Her voice became level, even.

She was shaking harder, her vision blurry with tears, her fists clenched, her gut spasming.

"How about the kind that can only come from me?" she said, her voice low and dangerous.

Manisha gathered as much saliva as possible and spat on his greatest "weapon," inciting the worst screams imaginable. The kind that shattered eardrums and ruptured brains. Yet it was nothing compared to being his victim.

He grabbed and released and grabbed himself again, like he needed to console his wound but couldn't bear touching it with this flesh-melting agony.

Manisha could relate. All who'd been violated could relate. But for all the horror this man was going through, Manisha wasn't exactly enjoying this. She was fraught with bewilderment and terror. First the pit of snakes and now this? *What* was wrong with her?

She hopped over the man's convulsing body and ran outside. Shadows and voices trickled through the village.

She hurried to the tree line and found the items she'd been forced to drop. Thank goodness the villagers hadn't taken them. She scrambled up the nearest tree and leapt, branch to branch. She could easily vanish, but already this village's men gathered to attack Rayna's village in retaliation.

Manisha groaned and dropped her head. She should flee. Take her chance at escaping. After all, those villagers had done this to her. But she couldn't leave Rayna and Rani to this fate. Or any of the others.

She crept across a few more branches, intending to slip away, but her thoughts warred. Of course she should run! She was just a scared girl! But the others didn't deserve this, not because of her.

She groaned. *No.* Leaving them vulnerable would never sit well with her. No matter the fear clawing down her spine, Rayna and her village didn't deserve this.

She aimed an arrow at one of the villagers. It was a clean shot through his shoulder blade, turning the group around. He cried out and fell forward, another man stepping away instead of catching him.

"Are we being attacked?" one asked.

"Get him inside," another said, dragging the injured one into the now quiet hut.

She didn't think they'd spot her, not in the dark, but she was close enough to the glow of the torches to be seen.

"There! Someone in the trees!" a man shouted.

Panic drove Manisha to move quickly. She huffed, sweat pouring down her temples, as she made her away across the trees, her movements jerky, her footing uncertain.

The villagers' voices eventually faded. Thinking she'd escaped without any more incidents, she allowed herself to relax.

She leapt onto the next branch of another tree only to come face-to-face with the watchful amber eyes of a leopard resting on a limb, a lazy growl exposing sharp teeth. But Manisha was already in its tree. She gasped and slipped, hitting branch after branch in a rough descent to the ground. Tree limbs snapped beneath her, and she stifled a howl when she hit hard ground studded with sharp rocks.

Pain seared into her bones and screamed across her back. She struggled to get up but pushed herself. She did *not* want to become a leopard's next meal. She limped away, keeping an eye on the beast as it sank back into the shadows.

Manisha trudged over fallen leaves and jagged rocks buried in dirt. Her breaths short, rapid pants. Her body hot, filled with trepidation. But she couldn't stop running, not when voices faded in and out.

Heaving, she slid behind a wide tree, her back hitting the trunk as she caught her breath. Could she climb again with the throbbing pain in her back? Probably not. It hurt to breathe.

She had a few arrows left. They weren't the splitting kind she'd once been accustomed to. These were primitive, rudimentary. One meant *one*.

With the wooden shaft of the arrow against her forehead, Manisha remembered her youth. She mentally scrambled for the whispers swirling through her thoughts, the ones she'd tried so hard to repress as an apsara. Not whispers of the rising darkness, but whispers of her foremothers, memories of family, anything to make her feel one with her weapon and her surroundings instead of this isolating fear.

Please help me, she thought.

Her mother's voice sang through her, reached her in the night like prowling shadows breaking open the mist of her nightmares. Her mother's voice was so ethereal, as if ghostly whispers were speaking directly into her ears.

Mama had once said, "We have the tradition of dipping arrowheads in the blood of our foremothers to grant a quick death to our enemies. A poison, potent and deadly. The blood of your foremothers flows through your veins."

Manisha scrunched her brows and glanced at the dark green vein in her wrist, the one that wove in and out of view all the way to her inner elbow.

Could it be? I mean . . . could my blood possibly be the same?

It was a far-fetched, implausible idea. Still . . . Manisha took an arrow tip and cut through her wrist, hissing. Even with her newfound strength, it took a surprising amount of pressure to cut through.

A trickle of blood appeared as her skin split. She heaved when her skin spread open to reveal the river of red flowing beneath her flesh and, just as quickly, fused back together. She swiped up the small amount of blood left on her newly closed skin and smeared it over the arrow tip. She'd have to process this later—when she wasn't fighting for her life.

She startled at a sound, a subtle rustle shaking the ferns. Manisha immediately drew the blood-tipped arrow taut against the bow and aimed.

A man emerged. Then another. And another.

She huffed, consumed with panic, her eyes wide and darting from one man to the next. She stilled, listening for others.

"Put that down," the man in the middle snarled, holding up a torch.

"There's three of us and one arrow," another snapped.

Manisha's vision blurred, splitting into two. Ah, now wasn't the best time! She fought the urge to curl into herself.

Her resolve hardened. She desperately needed it to. She couldn't go through another assault. She blew out a breath and stilled. Her nerves, and her arms, stopped trembling. The arrow readied for release.

From the tree limbs above the men, a slithering, lean form eased down, shimmering gold in the moonlight.

Noni! After so long, she'd found Manisha! She was okay! But... *stars*. Noni had *grown*. She was almost as thick as Manisha and at least three times as long.

"Don't take another step," Manisha warned.

The men chuckled, a twisted and malicious sound churning her insides. She didn't falter, didn't cave to the dizziness or light-headedness. She couldn't let her body shut down.

Noni hovered over the third man. She was as silent as unmoving air. She turned her head and watched Manisha with those entrancing moss-colored eyes, her forked tongue slithering out. Beautifully frightening.

"You killed our brother!" the first yelled.

"He violated girls," Manisha snapped.

"And that was worth killing over?"

She scoffed. She had no words.

"You have to pay!" he demanded.

But not his brother who'd kidnapped Rani? Who cut out her tongue and violated her to near death? Who was more than eager to do the same to Manisha, and probably others?

She replied, "I didn't kill your brother."

"Liar! Put down the arrow. You might injure one of us, but not all of us."

Manisha aimed at the first man, the one speaking, the most belligerent of the three. Apsara had been taught to use soft, gentle voices, to be subservient and pleasing. Her tone dropped, level. She'd heard men do this to appear authoritative, commanding, intimidating.

"Last warning," Manisha said, feeling the power of air in her throat.

She no longer sounded like a scared little girl. "Go back to your village and change your ways. Ask for forgiveness. Or die."

He snickered and lunged toward her. His foot wasn't even fully planted on the ground when two things happened at once, forever changing Manisha's entire world.

Manisha released that arrow, coated in her blood—the blood of her foremothers that flowed through her veins. It cut through the humid night air and right into the man's thick neck, that big artery that meant certain death. He gurgled and stopped dead in his advance, his eyes wide in terror as he dropped to his knees and clutched his throat where blood spurted out.

At the same time, Noni hissed and struck faster than any viper, opening her jaw wide and sinking her dripping fangs into the third man's head. Her gobbling jaw muffled his scream as she deftly lifted herself back into the shadow of the tree, taking his kicking limbs with her.

The man in the middle jumped, swinging the torch so that flames danced across the air.

While Noni coiled her massive, muscular body around the man in her jaws—crunching his bones—the man with the arrow in his neck had barely moved.

At first, his hand had flown quickly to his wound, but then his movements slowed, froze. Petrified. Gaping eyes stared at Manisha. Her eyes had widened just as much. She tilted her head, equally perplexed. Her head hurt trying to make sense of so many things.

She hadn't been sure what to expect using that arrow other than an artery kill. Her foremothers' blood was poison offering quick deaths to enemies in battle. Manisha had never thought that her blood could be poison, too.

But hers was different. It hadn't instantly killed him.

Instead, he solidified. Gray scales skittered across his flesh, changing him into stone, a statue in his final, frightened position for eternity.

Manisha panted for a breath.

Her blood didn't just kill.

Her blood turned men into stone.

The man in the middle screamed, "Nagin! Nagin!" and ran off into the jungle.

He would wake up his entire village with a fantastical tale of the nagin who turned men into stone. Of a nagin who had mastery over giant serpents.

Well. His tale was *absolutely* true.

Noni slowly descended and slithered across the dewy ground toward Manisha, her middle section full and round with a heavy meal. Her hooded head rose to face Manisha as she gently ran a hand over the space above Noni's nostrils, between her hypnotizing speckled eyes.

For the first time in five years, Manisha could no longer keep the name of her people silent. For the first time in a long time, she spoke secret names and lineages.

And it felt *incredible*. Freeing. Powerful. Immeasurable.

The words rolled off her tongue, like releasing a breath she'd held for far too long. She closed her eyes for a moment, reopening them to stare into Noni's steady gaze. The vision from her ancestors finally began to make sense after so long, a deluge of understanding.

"I am Manisha," she said aloud. "She who turns men into stone and commands serpents."

Every word came louder, stronger. "I am from the lost naga. Daughter of Padma. Granddaughter of Padmavati."

Her chest heaved with every proclamation. "I am a nagin, and I. Am. *Venom*."

TWENTY

PRATYUSH
(PRESENT DAY)

Pratyush, Dev, and Ras trailed behind the others in a solemn daze. Ras was still pale, poor guy. He probably wasn't used to seeing people get eaten. The squelching, the violent thrashing, the ripping apart of flesh from bone, the smell, the blood and guts . . . Ras had thrown up twice now, and he looked like he was going for a third.

"It's not your fault," Dev told Pratyush.

"Still weighs on me."

"You can't go down that road. Taking every death onto your shoulders will break your back. How can a pile of broken bones save anyone then?"

Pratyush didn't respond. He couldn't turn his feelings of responsibility on and off.

His head was full of dead monsters, his shoulders sagging with dead soldiers, his back cracked beneath dead villagers, and his heart skewered from losing loved ones. What was left?

Dev was still watching him. What did he see? A slayer going mad? A boy crumpling with guilt?

"Sometimes the perceived strongest among us are the most vulnerable," Dev grunted.

"I'm not weak," Pratyush protested.

"*Vulnerable* doesn't mean weak. You truly cannot take everything alone. You're not alone."

Pratyush wouldn't wish the weight of his burdens on anyone, even if he *could* share them. But everyone had their trauma. How could he unload on someone if they were dealing with their own issues? Didn't seem right.

The group traveled for another day. They set up camp once more, ate, and slept. Well, Pratyush mainly simmered over how he could've prevented more from dying. Doing this, or that.

The next day lent to long travels.

Pratyush rubbed the bridge of his nose, a habit he'd seen the King do when he wanted to convey an extraordinary level of exasperation.

He asked, "Is there *any* real proof of this monster? Because if you haven't noticed, we've lost a lot of people already. Why should we keep risking lives for some stories about a fanciful beast that no one has ever heard of before?"

"Because the King decreed it," the General replied matter-of-factly, because of course that said it all. The King was lord and god, et cetera et cetera, into every pit of lies.

"His timing was interesting." Tell the King you want a break from fighting and suddenly there was a magical serpent queen wreaking havoc?

"Let's say he *was* sending you on a wild, pointless chase. Why would he send me along? I have important matters to tend to."

"Why don't you tell me?" Pratyush narrowed his eyes, suspicion, even paranoia, sinking deeper into his thoughts like grubs burrowing beneath dirt.

"What do you mean by that?"

If Pratyush voiced his suspicions of this being a ploy to get him as far from the kingdom as possible and kill him off without anyone left alive to witness, then it would leave him without an upper hand in what was feeling more and more like a trap.

"You'd tell me anything that I should know, right?" Pratyush asked as they walked through dense jungle.

"Of course."

"Do you believe this rumor? This nagin slithering around, turning innocent men into stone?" Pratyush asked skeptically, one brow quirked.

"Some things seem impossible. When we were kids, we believed everything. We grew older and learned to rationalize. Legends were always a part of our existence because we knew people who faced monsters. We heard a thousand tales, and they had some truth. Then we fought the legends and knew, one by one, this legend was real, that legend was real. It's best to check in case it's true." The General paused.

"And . . . ?" Pratyush asked, rolling his hand in a gesture for him to hurry up and get to the point.

"*And* it's a known fact: Monsters exist. We've brought back heads, corpses, clipped wings, and artifacts. People tend to believe the legends because they know there's a high probability of them being true. It's uncommon for people to make something up with this sort of fast-spreading consistency, to take it directly to the King *and* the slayer. Your time and skills are valuable. You wouldn't be sent on a wild chase for nothing."

Pratyush shook his head, still trying to wrap his thoughts around this. "We've all heard of the naga legends. The blood-tipped arrows and invincible winter-steel. Their ability to create nature from nothing, to grow vegetation from dry rock, and their harmony with serpents. Even myths about vast caverns filled with treasures and astra, maybe even amrita, even though no one's found celestial weapons or the immortal elixir. But nothing like this. How far are we going to travel without proof?"

"At least to the location of the sightings..." the General replied, pulling back a curtain of vines and stepping into a small clearing. In that clearing was a single statue of a man.

Pratyush tilted his head, scrutinizing the statue as he walked around it. He scratched his neck. "Well, that's a new way to stone someone, I guess...."

There was nothing off about this carved rock. Except he was on his knees, clutching an arrow through the neck, his expression pained and horrified. Stone blood oozed from the wound in interesting dark trickles. Macabre, if anything. Detailed to the last strand of hair. Magnificently created.

Pratyush came prepared to argue. Craftsmen had the ability to carve detailed statues out of stone. It was nothing to fear. If anything, others were moved to worship this kind of precision and beauty.

But it didn't make sense for this to be in the middle of the jungle. As heavy as it was, there were no tracks or a path around it to indicate it had been placed here. And it hadn't been here long enough for tracks to get covered in overgrowth—the statue looked new, clean, untouched by weather or moss.

Ras and another soldier examined the surrounding area and then the statue, shuddering at the unknown. Superstitions were easy to succumb to. It was why they were so dangerous.

"It's just one unexplained statue. Did an entire legend come from this one thing? A dozen soldiers dead for it?" Pratyush asked.

"No," the General said, jerking his chin at an approaching band of villagers. "Stop right there. Who are you?"

The soldiers went for their swords, hands on hilts, but didn't draw.

The villagers were dressed similarly to the statue, in loose pants and bland shirts, and they held spears.

"Were you sent by the King to save us?" one asked.

"Save you from what?" Pratyush asked instead.

"From the she-demon that descended upon us!" another cried.

"What demon?" Pratyush pressed, trying to find answers instead of assumptions.

"The one who did that." He pointed at the statue.

The first villager slowly approached the statue, dropping his head, and reverently touched the stone shoulder. His hand trembled. "I'm the one who sent word to the King about her."

"Did you actually see what happened?"

He glared at Pratyush, and Pratyush glared right back at him. He wasn't in the mood to deal with villagers with imaginations as wild as this jungle just so soldiers could die.

Pratyush growled, "You know sending lies to the King is a serious offense, don't you? We've lost many soldiers trying to get here. You better give me proof this monster exists, because if not, someone is going to pay."

The villager looked from Pratyush to the General and back to Pratyush. "We—we don't want any trouble, or—or any more contact with the kingdom than what's necessary. Even my own people were afraid of disturbing the King. But she can't continue to live! Not after this!"

"Then tell me everything that happened."

"We were in our village, a normal evening, minding ourselves after dinner. Some of us had retired to our homes for the night. Then she comes speeding through our village and into my friend's hut. She . . . she did something to him. His skin had melted off by the time we found him."

Ras stifled a wince, but Pratyush caught it from the corner of his eye. Melted skin was a new one. What *couldn't* the nagin do? She was basically a super-monster at this point, larger than lore.

"Most of his face was exposed. The skin had bubbled off. You could only see muscle and jaw and teeth on one side. I still have nightmares. His ... privates ..." He gagged. "Were melted off, leaving gaping, blistering, oozing holes all the way through."

Even Dev cringed, and it took a lot to disturb him. But yeah, a decimated dick wasn't the best way to go.

"Well, where's he now? Is he alive? Let us talk to him," Pratyush said, oddly curious to see a man with melted-off flesh.

The villager replied, "He died from his wounds before the sun rose. As soon as he started screaming, the she-demon ran out of his hut and into the trees like a monkey. My neighbor, brother, and I chased her here."

"And three grown men couldn't take her?" Pratyush asked incredulously.

He shook his head. "We tried to. We didn't have much time. She moved so fast, like a viper striking. She turned him—my brother—into stone." He glanced mournfully at the statue. "While we were distracted by the impossibility of what was happening in front of us, she descended as a giant snake and snatched my neighbor into the trees and—and ate him. In the blink of an eye. I'm the only one left."

Pratyush crossed his arms and narrowed his eyes, trying to follow this story. How could she be in two places at once? *Super-monster* was becoming an understatement. "And how did you get away from a venomous, half-viper, incredibly fast she-demon?"

"I *ran*. I'm no fool. I knew I wouldn't be able to fight her or even get near her. I ran back to the village to tell everyone what happened. I returned to a crowd around my friend's hut. She'd killed three men in one night like it was nothing. We searched days for her. Not just that. We traveled to a neighboring village. They spoke about a stranger who came down the river. They said she was traveling south to find her family."

"Family?" Huh. Was this monster heading south toward the canyonlands? Toward the decayed ruins of the naga? Were there more like her? Were they banding together to plot a rebellion against the kingdom?

"We asked," the villager went on as if he'd read Pratyush's mind. "They didn't know how many are in her family, but—but there might be an entire horde of them! A mass of monsters!"

"Calm down. Where's the village that spoke to her?"

He swallowed before replying, "Vansol. Three hours' walk from here, to the west toward the Yamuna River. But...they're no more."

"Well? *Why?* What happened to them?" Stars, if this guy could stop pausing dramatically every other sentence, it would be great.

"The nagin," another man said, his tone a little higher, like he'd been practicing. His pupils dilated, like gaping black voids for a slayer to look straight into and pry open his thoughts. "She returned to them, to Vansol, and killed every last one for revealing her."

"How would you know that she killed everyone?"

His eyes darted to the others. "We found a few as they were dying. They told us."

So much blood rained onto this land. The Nightmare Realm was probably overflowing with the dead.

Pratyush paced the area around the statue, noting the blood trickling from its neck. Interesting that it appeared wet. He swiped a finger across it. What was this? Thick, sticky blood. He brought the drop close to his nose and took a tentative sniff.

His eyes widened at the onslaught of information: pain, anger, desperation. He could almost see the man's final moments unfurl in panicked scenes. Slit snake eyes in the shadows. An arrow careening toward him.

But also...something else. Was it fear? Dread? Resolution. The blood had a drop of the nagin's venom mixed in. An unfurling scroll of lineages, of potent, deadly venom. But not like that of an animal or insect or any normal serpent. Something far worse.

He heaved out a breath, his skin crawling. Whatever *this* was, it was real. Not stories or fabricated lies. Blood didn't lie.

He told the General, "Let's send some soldiers out there to report if the other stones are like this one."

"Other stones?" the villager asked.

"If she turned them to stone like this one. Or...melted their *privates* off."

"No, Soldier."

"Slayer," he corrected.

For a moment, all three villagers froze, startled.

What did they expect? They told the King there was a ferocious monster, so who else would he have sent?

"The slayer?" he whispered. "But—but you're so young. Still a boy."

"A boy who could slit your throat before you even blinked," Pratyush said flatly. "You were saying?"

"Ah. Yes. Yes. Sorry, please. You won't find their remains."

Pratyush quirked a sharp brow and took three long strides to stand in front of the man. Even though the slayer was several years the man's junior, he towered over him by a foot. And the villager *did* cower. "Why not?"

The man blinked a few rapid times, his pupils big, his body shaking when he replied, "She—she didn't turn them to stone, just killed them like our friend in the hut. This was weeks ago. We had to burn the bodies."

"Convenient, isn't it?"

He gulped. "Not convenient at all, Slayer. It took a lot of work to properly burn all the bodies, which didn't even belong to us. But we had to pay them respect. There was no one left to do it."

Pratyush twisted his mouth and stepped away. Something felt off. Was it a kind thing to take care of all those dead bodies? A necessity to ward off superstition and stench? Or something else? The slayer's senses prickled down his spine, telling him to pay attention to details and the unseen truth.

With his back turned to the villagers, Pratyush quietly spoke to Dev and Ras. "Take two horses to Vansol and report. We'll swing back toward the river but keep heading south to the canyonlands and we'll meet along the way."

They left the clearing with two horses.

Meanwhile, the rest traveled with the men to their village to interview others. It was an exhausting but uneventful trip, giving Pratyush plenty of time to ruminate on what the hell was going on. Who was this nagin, and who was that vision in the meadows who warned him not to pursue? Was she a nagin, too? Nothing made sense.

Every villager confirmed the same story. Most had seen something rustling in the trees, but the creature was too quick to get a good look at in the darkness. Everyone had heard of the firsthand account of the brother, and with one witness, there wasn't much factual dispute.

The General snickered after speaking with the last villager. "Look at them. No ambition. No desire to do more, be more, add to the kingdom. Just exist. In their little mud-and-straw huts. In their plain clothes and simplistic shoes. Dirty. Ruthless. Rats."

"Anyway," Pratyush grumbled. "Where are the women?"

"Maybe they don't allow strangers to see their women."

"Nah. That's not going to work. Besides, women who don't want to be seen wear head coverings." Pratyush signaled the brother over.

"Yes, Slayer? Will you be on your way to hunt down the demon?" he asked eagerly.

"We need to interview everyone."

"You have interviewed everyone. Unless you want to ask children, but they were all asleep when this happened."

"I mean the women, the girls."

He gaped at the slayer quizzically.

Pratyush snapped, "The *women*. Where are they? And don't tell me they're all off on some pious pilgrimage to some temple even deeper in the jungle. I don't have time for that."

"We don't allow outsiders to view our women."

Pratyush crossed his arms and sighed, working his neck side to side so that it cracked. "Listen. We're on a time-sensitive hunt for a creature *you* called *us* to capture."

"To kill," the man corrected.

"You do realize I'm in control here, don't you? Don't let my age fool you. I can't be easily pushed around. But I'm impatient and getting irritated, and if you don't bring out all the women and girls for us to interview, then I'll most likely get annoyed and go home where I can enjoy decent food instead of rations and sleep in a comfortable bed instead of on a rock and take a nice bath with rose oils. Yes. Rose oils. I said it. Do you know who I'd kill for rose oils right now?"

The man shook his head, confused.

Pratyush slapped an irritant on his neck, making the villager jump. "Well, I'd kill you. If you're wondering. Because you're the reason I'm out here battling to the death with bloodthirsty mosquitos instead of eating jalebi and watching butterflies in the garden. Because that's what I'd always rather be enjoying, in that order: rose oils, sweets, butterflies."

The villager didn't respond, didn't move.

Pratyush sucked in a breath. "Soldiers *died* getting here. Some had their brains literally sucked out of their heads. Like your friend over there with that coconut." He jerked his chin at a guy leaning against a tree and trying his best to get the last drops of water out of a coconut. "Some were eaten alive by *water dragons*."

He paused and asked, his voice dropping, "Do you think I'm going to waste time with you? Deliver the women and girls. *Now*. Or things will go one of two ways. I'll leave with my soldiers and abandon your call, or I'll kill you out of annoyance and abandon your call."

The villager gulped and nodded, backing away and running to his kin to round up all the women and girls. They'd been in their huts, and while Pratyush understood why some villages kept women out of view, they knew he wasn't going to harm them or violate their beliefs.

The women and girls came out, and there was a surprisingly large number of them. A lot, in fact. The ratio was too skewed to be normal.

Some wore long brown dresses with leggings, their clothes dirty at the hems with holes here and there. Most wore lighter brown clothing: long kurtas and leggings. Some had dirt smeared on their faces, maybe soot from working over fires. Several were pregnant. Some wore large head coverings. In fact, all the kurta-adorned girls had their heads covered and their chins tucked so low that he couldn't see their faces. Maybe they were younger? Unmarried? Engaged?

He interviewed them individually. They cooperated until he arrived at a division in the line, the dresses versus the kurtas.

The first girl only nodded or shook her head in response. As did the second. The third. The fourth... None had anything to add or detract. But he did smell something strange. Infection? Rotting?

Finally, Pratyush said to the girl in front of him, "Don't nod or shake your head to answer. Speak. Please," he added, softening his tone.

She trembled but didn't lift her tucked chin to look up at him, just like the others.

"*Can* you speak?" he asked, his head listing to the side.

When she didn't respond, he dipped his head low to get a view of her from below the head covering. All the while the villagers watched, the men anxious. One or two took a step forward.

Pratyush held up a hand, signaling for them to stay in place. He whispered to the girl, "I would never touch you or force you to remove your head covering, but there's something awful going on here. Are you all right? You can nod or shake your head."

It took several seconds before she slowly nodded.

"Are you certain? I can help you."

She nodded again. With every tilt of her chin, she flashed minuscule bits of her face. Bruises. Swollen, busted skin. And... crawling lips?

He heaved, sensing much more than injury in the blood oozing off her face. "I'm going to need you to remove your head covering."

She didn't fight or argue, but instead looked to the men. One walked over and opened his mouth when Pratyush reminded, "I'm getting impatient while you're hindering."

The villager turned red and ordered the girls, "Pull up your covering."

They slid their shawls halfway up. The General audibly gagged, but Pratyush stayed stoic, unmoved even though his gut twisted in agony for them. He'd seen too much to gag over most things. But this was a fist to the gut. Fast, hard, and lingering with a sort of pain that had him wanting to sit down.

Most of the girls' faces, still partially covered, were pounded with fresh bruises, swollen cheeks, and scabs from recent bleeding. They'd been beaten. Severely. But if that wasn't enough, the most unnerving thing was their mouths.

Their lips had been sewn shut, left open just enough to sip water or push in a sliver of food. There was no way this could be long-term.

They would starve in a matter of days. Not to mention dehydration and pain.

The redness and swelling around the lips indicated the sewing was fresh. The skin above and below the mouth where a needle had been shoved in and out was crusted with dried blood and greenish scabs—signs of infection.

He leaned closer to the girl in front of him, and when she jerked back with a slight gasp, the threading on her lips quivered, and she winced.

This was not thread, fabric, or plant fiber.

The writhing came from long, slender grayish-white worms feeding on her lips with tiny, gnashing teeth every time she moved.

"Are—are you in pain?" Pratyush rasped. What a ridiculous question. Of course she was!

She shook her head. Lies stained the air.

"What's your name? Can you speak?"

She tried so hard to mutter. He leaned in and made out the panting syllables, a ghostly confession: *Rayna.*

Every movement goaded the worms into a feeding frenzy, and she winced, tears falling. He wanted to cut them out, but these were flesh worms, and harming them would only drive them to burrow deeper. They might lodge into her cheeks and travel to her eyes, her brain. It was a death sentence, and he hated that he didn't know how to help.

"Why are they like this?" he demanded, grabbing the villager by his shirt.

"This—this is our custom!" he claimed.

"Your custom is to beat and mutilate girls?" Pratyush croaked, losing the control over emotions that he'd been trained to forcefully keep in check.

The villager's tone elevated. Sweat beads formed on his dirt-freckled forehead. There he went, sounding practiced when he spoke. "All cultures are different and strange to outsiders. Do you dare remove the Queen's head covering? Or demand why the inlanders devour sacred animals? Or look down on men who shave their heads and tattoo their skin?"

"The difference is consent versus abuse. Purpose versus domination. What's the reason for this? Why do only some have them? Why are they all girls? And don't lie and tell me it's due to age or occasion. There's no consistency. The older ones don't have scars to show they've gone through this. *Why* are you lying to me?" Pratyush snarled, his blood running hot, livid.

"They—they were rebellious. We have punishment standards for all. Boys have their fingers cut off for stealing, kids get whipped for misbehaving, girls are—"

The General cut him off with a loud grunt. "All right. I don't care. We don't have time for this. I think we've gotten all the information we can. Let's go."

Pratyush sputtered over his thoughts, glowering at the General, but the truth was, he was right. This wasn't what they came for. They'd be acting beyond their authority if they intervened. They didn't have time. Every moment spent here was another opportunity for the nagin to get ahead. Once the nagin slipped into the canyonlands, she might never be found. There were too many tunnels for her to move through, too many caves to hide in.

Pratyush clenched his jaw, turning one way and then another. If the King were here, he'd smack Pratyush in the back of the head for showing indecision.

Much to Pratyush's distress, they moved on and met back up with Dev and Ras.

"Was he lying?" Pratyush asked, his soul seething after seeing the girls like that.

"We found the village. It was burned to the ground, just like he said."

Pratyush frowned. The monster could kill so uniquely. . . . Why burn a village?

TWENTY-ONE

MANISHA
(TWENTY-THREE DAYS AGO)

Noni was now *much* bigger and wider than Manisha, able to easily swallow a man whole. As was apparent when she, well...swallowed a man whole.

She was incredibly fast, too. A yellow flash zipping down a tree and fully coiled five times around Manisha, her perpetually grinning face inches away. A single, involuntary twitch could leave Manisha in a pile of crushed bones and pulverized organs.

Noni was a powerful creature born from a magical bangle, but Manisha knew Noni would never hurt her. She'd known Noni when she was the size of a grain of rice in a golden egg cushioned between the bands of an heirloom. The curved formation that Manisha had caressed every night and spoken to in case there had been a real snake inside. Noni was like...her child?

Manisha, Mother of Serpents had a ring to it.

Noni's long tongue dashed out, tasting the air, then again to lick Manisha's face.

"Ew...*Noni*..."

Her coils dropped to the ground in a heavy thud. She rolled her upper body partway, presenting glimpses of her underside. Manisha rubbed Noni's throat until she went limp.

"You're just a big baby, aren't you? Where are my belly rubs, huh?"

Manisha was feeling exponentially better. Her aches and sprains had vanished. She moved faster, more nimbly. She'd adjusted to heightened senses. Her welts were still there, marring her skin, but they didn't hurt.

The pair continued southbound. Being with Noni gave Manisha a sense of safety and friendship, but Noni couldn't speak, and that left Manisha a lot of time to think.

At night, the colorful glow of mushrooms and ferns lit the jungle paths, making it easier to see. Owls hooted above and small animals of all sorts scurried around. Monkeys, perched on branches, chattered and nibbled on bananas.

Without another person to talk to, her thoughts wandered back to everything that had happened. Her hands shook as she realized that *she* was the strongest weapon she'd ever heard of. She didn't know if that meant she was immortal, if she no longer had weaknesses, or if the poison was rotting her insides and slowly killing her. All Manisha knew was that she would never again allow someone to hurt her or others and get away with it. If she could be this deadly, then she had to use her gifts to protect. As Kumari had said: There was healing in helping others, an opening of hearts.

Her entire life, she'd known that her sisters had gifts. Eshani could open the threads of communication by touching any living thing. She was a born leader and healer. She was the daughter of life.

Sithara could see how actions would unfurl before she fought. She was the most warrior-like, fearless. She was the daughter of vengeance.

Manisha had always thought her sisters had gifts because they were twins, rare, and she was the baby they had to make sacrifices for. She'd always thought she was the obedient one who hadn't found her voice, her strength.

She'd finally found her legacy. She was the daughter of death. And while that seemed dark and dreadful, the more Manisha considered the benefits, the more she realized how empowering this was. Her gift was not a curse, but a blessing.

Many might argue that she was a monster to be destroyed. Death was rarely welcomed. But death was a victory, a justice to those who'd earned it. She wasn't a monster, but a harbinger of equality. And venom was a powerful equalizer.

Yes. The more she thought about it, the more she accepted it. She was the balance in an unbalanced world, in a kingdom where the greedy ruled with iron fists. Where love was considered a weakness and girls were treated like nothing more than property or breeders.

She gently touched the welts on her skin and embraced them as marks of beauty and ascension. They weren't ugly mars to be ashamed of. They were the reason no one would ever hurt her again. Seeing things that way? Well, she wasn't so afraid anymore.

As an apsara, she would've been a tiny pebble dropping into the sea creating an imperceptible and fleeting ripple. But as . . . whatever she was now . . . she was a meteorite surging into the water, creating a larger-than-life impact.

She could make a difference. Maybe her actions had taught those villagers a lesson.

May they regret taking Rani and Manisha and countless others. May they never kidnap or violate another girl, and may they leave Rayna's village in peace.

Manisha smiled to herself. Yes. She believed she'd made a difference.

MANISHA AND NONI HAD BEEN TRAVELING FOR DAYS. WALK-
ing was the slowest way to travel, but what else could she do? She
trudged alongside Noni, knowing that her pace slowed the serpent
down.

"My legs are cramping. I'm sorry. I'm tired. Go on without me. Or
show up out of nowhere miles down the road. Whichever suits you,
my friend."

Noni whipped toward Manisha in a zigzag motion, startling her.
Manisha tumbled and landed on her back, on Noni's midsection.
Noni didn't stop but kept slithering along, faster now that she didn't
have to wait on Manisha. Manisha's stomach fluttered at the sensation
of riding a snake, and the oddness of lying on her back while doing so.

"Oh no, Noni! Aren't I a burden?"

Not according to her speed and smoothness. It was like she was
gliding on air.

Wind whipped through Manisha's hair, a refreshing coolness on
her face. "Ah. Actually. If you insist, this is *very* nice. A girl could get
used to this. You make me feel like a princess in an open palanquin."

Noni vibrated beneath Manisha, a shudder like laughter. The way
Lekha purred when Eshani showered her with pets and nuzzles and
praise. Sometimes Lekha would even roll over for belly rubs and
scratches. She'd never thought a wild giant tiger and a colossal serpent
could be so similar.

She set her head back and watched the canopy move by. "Hmmm.
I wonder if you and Lekha would get along. I think you'd like her."

Noni trilled, for lack of a better word, a rapid succession of clicks
and hisses.

She slithered for miles, fitting in between tight spaces, until she
spilled out from the jungle and into open fields of waist-high grass,
sporadic trees, and sparse shrubs.

The full light of the sun washed over Manisha, and she immediately sat up. There was always something hiding in tall grass. Giant boars, crocodiles, leopards, tigers, snakes. She glanced down at Noni. Oh, right. She probably had nothing to fear.

The sun descended, and Noni stopped in the middle of a vast field of tall grass.

"Are you tired?"

Noni stretched her neck, craning it back in an elegant, classical dance, and unhinged her jaw in a yawn. Manisha gawked at that gaping mouth, at a set of impressive fangs and a row of serrated backward-curved teeth. There was a series of four elongated holes alongside her lower jaw. Fascinating, eerie, beautiful.

"Serpents yawn?"

Noni curled up into a massive coil, leaving a platform of muscle for Manisha to stretch out on.

She sat on her serpent bed for a while, skimming the vast open. Out here, nothing glowed. It was pitch darkness save for the subtle glow of the moon and stars. Behind her, the floating mountains hovered like a dark cloud. She'd never hated a place so much, and yet feared it. Had the slayer returned? What had Sita told him?

It didn't matter.

Manisha slipped off her bow, quiver, and satchel, keeping them within reach, and ate.

"This is sort of nice." She ran a hand over Noni's head. "But also, a bit unnerving. Out in the open like this. But maybe this lets you sense things coming? The rumbles in the ground beneath you? Do you feel better out in the open?"

Noni eyed Manisha. Or maybe she was asleep. Since snakes didn't have eyelids, there was no way to tell.

Manisha studied her companion in the fading light. Beautiful and strong, loyal and understanding. "I wish I had more friends like you."

If only people were as trustworthy as Noni. If only human friendships were this easy.

Exhaustion took over. The world, with all its unfairness and cruelty, was perfect and still when it was just the two of them. Anything seemed possible, even disappearing into the world beyond the kingdom's boundaries and living a peaceful life.

Manisha's eyelids fluttered open. She stared into the night sky sprinkled with stars.

Peace wasn't for her.

She had a family to find.

She had vengeance to claim.

The blood of her fallen ancestors scorched hotter than the Fire Wars.

And every drop was calling her name.

NONI HAD WANDERED OFF, PROBABLY TO FEED. SHE WAS BIG enough to take down boars and crocodiles and leopards. Maybe even all three at once!

Manisha cringed. She didn't want to think about Noni unhinging her jaw around something crunching to death in her coils. Her feeding out of sight was a blessing, but it also left Manisha alone to wander farther south. Noni's ride the day before had alleviated aches and sprains. She was able to move much faster today.

The Great River raged to her left, so wide that she could barely make out trees on the other side. She wondered if any of her people were there, looking at the river in this very moment. There was so much beyond this kingdom, and she wanted to know more.

If she called Kumari, would she hear and come? Did she have any news about the naga? The spot where they'd met was so far away. Kumari probably wouldn't hear her.

She moved on.

Ahead, the rocks and crags beside the river forced her to move into the jungle again, cutting off the true path. She pushed herself to continue, drowsy, hungry, aching. Every step away from the floating mountains was one step closer to finding her family.

She yawned. The day was humid, the sun hot. Her eyelids started drooping, her body relaxing, her heart rate slowing—until a scream shattered her calm.

Manisha froze. Another unforgettable cry cut the air. Birds trilled in the canopy.

She searched the area before edging closer to the tree line, toward the noise.

She hadn't intended to stumble through the brush and into a village clearing. She honestly thought there was more vegetation to buffer the area. But she was here now, and several pairs of eyes landed on her. She stilled, staring back at a handful of older boys.

Why were they ignoring this bawling girl and the boy beating her?

Other boys stood nearby with crossed arms and watched, like this was a spectacle, a play to be seen. This *wasn't* a play. This girl, maybe a couple of years older than Manisha, was on her knees begging, her face bloody. Rivulets of tears turned into raging streams when the boy who had been beating her snatched her hand and snapped her finger back.

Manisha gasped, clutching a breath in her lungs as a crunch echoed. Her entire body shook, the sound so resounding that even *she* could feel the bones breaking.

The girl's screech reverberated against the boulders behind her, the only thing drowning out the haunting sound of cracking bones.

Manisha's breaths went in and out of her chest, faster, harder, shorter. Adrenaline surged in her veins, her skin flaring. And that darkness rising inside of her, whispering to be let free? It returned.

The boy lamented, "Why are you making a scene? Why can't you be quiet?"

The darkness inside her whispered louder. *Darkness doesn't run, doesn't cower. Darkness devours.*

"Hey!" Manisha yelled, startling the boys. *"Stop!"*

She meant to be commanding, but her demand came out as a shrilling cry.

The girl on the ground sobbed, cradling her hand to her chest. The boy kicked her, triggering Manisha's memory of being kicked off the floating mountains. She *felt* it. Whatever indecisiveness or trepidation she'd felt turned into rage. She let the darkness take over. If no one else was going to stand up for this girl, then *she* would. She'd told herself that, hadn't she? That she would use her gifts to protect others. Now was her chance.

Manisha marched toward the boy. He, along with his friends, faced her. Nearby girls helped the injured girl off the ground, half carrying her through the small fields of crops and into their village, hopefully to reset her fingers.

The boy ordered, "Move along."

Manisha huffed out a breath. He was much taller and broader than she'd thought, and maybe even a bit older. She couldn't tell, and it didn't matter. She wasn't going to be intimidated. She was venom; he was nothing. "Who do you think you are? Beating her?"

"I can do whatever I want to her. She ruined my best foraging supplies and had to be punished. The smallest mistakes can lead to starvation when winter comes. It's within my rights to punish her. Not that I have anything to explain to you, stranger."

"Can she beat you, too, for humiliating and hurting her?" Manisha scowled.

He cackled. "Stupid little girl! What sort of idiotic questions form in that tiny head of yours? No wonder your brains are so small. What's the point of having brains if you can't think straight, huh?"

He called to the group of girls, "Bring her back!"

They paused, glancing at one another and at the whimpering girl in their hands.

"If you don't bring her back, you'll get punished, too. You know that."

They slowly turned.

"Leave her alone," Manisha demanded.

"Shut up," the boy spat. "You don't live here. You don't know better. What sort of wilderness were you raised in?"

Manisha blinked back memories of her loving people who had been forced to become raging warriors. She came from a world that had shown her love, and then a world that had taught her to fight back.

She said, "You should apologize to her and take care of her."

He scoffed, running a hand down his face, annoyed. He cocked his chin toward Manisha, signaling for the others to . . . what? Subdue her?

Manisha didn't move an inch, no matter how much she wanted to. She was stronger than them. "You don't scare me. You don't even know who I am."

"You don't care about your safety, do you? Girls have their place, and when they step out of it, they have to be taught a lesson so they don't think they can start doing whatever they want. Maybe you should learn that lesson, too."

"You don't want to do that," she replied, her voice steady as she slipped the bow off her shoulder.

"But it seems that we should."

"Okay. Lessons should be taught," she replied, and nocked an arrow before realizing it was the one coated with her blood. Was this worthy of death? Or should she use a regular arrow to disarm them?

No. Why was she hesitating? Doubting herself? Her sisters had always taught her to be decisive. Sithara had particularly stressed the importance of making swift, calculated decisions in battle.

Ah! But they didn't deserve to die. It was too late to change the arrows. She really hoped they wouldn't push her. Her nerves lit up, her legs shaking. *Please don't make me use this arrow.*

Another boy joined in. Really? They needed this many to stop . . . what was it they'd called her? A stupid little girl?

A level of trepidation crawled through Manisha. She was outnumbered, hungry, tired, and a little weak, but none of that could show.

A rumbling grew beneath her feet. The boys mumbled and looked at the shaking ground. The tremors didn't deter Manisha, not even when a gush of wind whooshed up behind her.

The boys stumbled backward, gaping in horror at whatever was looming over Manisha.

Her calm returned. She knew, and she didn't even have to turn to see for herself. She and Noni had a deeper connection now. Strange, surreal, but magnificent. Manisha could almost see through Noni's eyes, a double vision—Noni saw in contrasting reds, blues, and yellows—and could almost decipher her thoughts.

She shook off the wave of nausea that came with being so in tune with Noni and looked straight up. The camouflaged underside of Noni quivered several feet above her. Lines and shapes of trees and ferns blurred and solidified into a tower of gold.

Noni had camouflaging abilities now? Was there anything this wonderful creature couldn't do?

Noni didn't seem to be in the mood to deal with strangers advancing on Manisha. She pulled her lips back, opening her jaw a fraction to hiss. Not a normal serpent hiss, but the kind that made skin crawl, the sort of nightmare that reached into a person's soul and squeezed.

The boys, who should've fallen to their knees in fear, or at the least run off if they had any sense, called out for weapons.

Manisha clucked her tongue. Noni did *not* like that. Her upper body, hooded over Manisha like a cobra, shuddered. Her head split into two, leaving a trail of slimy membrane in between.

"Well," Manisha muttered. "That's new." Honestly, could Noni be any more amazing?

Most of the boys fled. Noni was lightning fast, gliding over Manisha, trapping two against a boulder—including the breaker of fingers. The boys immediately dropped to their knees. They had nowhere to run, caught between a rock and four fangs. Not that they could outrun Noni. A serpent head glared at each boy. They clasped their hands and begged for mercy.

Noni opened her jaws, unhinging them as if she were about to swallow them whole. Her fangs, two immense tapered incisors in each head, curved down, dropping out of her upper jaw. A mixture of venom and saliva dripped from those fangs. It was all incredibly fascinating.

"Please. *Please*," the boys begged, tears streaming down their faces.

Others skidded to a petrified stop to Manisha's right, weapons in hand. She aimed an arrow at them without hesitating, warning, "Don't."

Don't mess with Noni.

Noni shrieked, her saliva sputtering onto the boys trapped against the boulder. Wherever droplets touched their skin, little eruptions bubbled. They cowered and cried.

The boy to the right put his weapon to the ground and backed away.

Manisha lowered her bow and arrow, relieved. She didn't want to kill anyone else, although the darkness inside her did. Thank the stars it was retreating. She slipped from beneath Noni's arched body, running a hand along the length of her. As Manisha approached Noni's heads, the one farthest from Manisha stayed trained on the boys, while the other head swerved to watch Manisha, her jaw closing and her fangs narrowly missing Manisha's face.

"Why did you have to upset her?" Manisha asked.

"We didn't mean to," the older boy blubbered, his eyes glued to Noni.

"Why did you have to threaten me? You really shouldn't be beating anyone. And you really shouldn't attack a stranger in passing. You never know who they might be."

"You're right. We're sorry. Please accept our deepest apologies, O great serpent."

Noni's two heads snapped back into one, mucus splattering on the boy's face and chest. He flinched, his lips curled in disgust, but he didn't move.

"You should apologize to the girl, too, and for the right reason. Not just because you were about to get eaten."

Noni snarled and slithered away, returning to the colors of the jungle, melting into the scenery. *Ah! So amazing!*

"If only you cared for girls the way you do for your friends," Manisha grumbled to the others, who hurried to help the two boys.

They didn't respond, but kept their stares staked to where Noni had been.

"Don't be fooled. Just because you can't see her doesn't mean she's not there," Manisha promised.

They nodded.

"And don't be delusional. Even if I'm without her, I'm just as dangerous."

"Who are you?" the girl with the broken fingers asked, two others at her side, holding her up as she pressed a cloth to her face.

"Manisha," she answered. "Are you all right?"

"What do you want?" one of the girls helping her asked instead.

Manisha's gut twisted. Maybe they didn't want her help. Or had she made things worse for them? "Nothing," she said quietly. "I'm just passing through."

"Wait," an older girl called. She rushed past the crowd of boys, chasing them off with a rope in her hand. She cradled the girl's arms as she told the others, "Set her fingers and tie them with a stick to keep her bones in place as she heals. Give her plenty of water and medicine. Heated rocks, too. When you're done, tell me who did this so I can deal with them."

Manisha pivoted toward her.

"My name's Mitali. Thank you," she said. "For helping my cousin."

The injured girl nodded and clasped her hands together in front of her in reverence, two fingers bent unnaturally backward, before the small group hurried her away.

Manisha grimaced and replied, "It wasn't anything to help. I just hope no one retaliates after I leave. I honestly didn't mean to cause trouble."

Mitali hurried to Manisha's side, her mouth hanging open, her eyes searching over her shoulder. "What was that? The serpent?"

"Oh, that's just Noni," Manisha replied in a heartbeat, like Noni was her best human friend and had been a part of her life forever. Maybe she had been, in bangle form. Noni was just Noni. Beloved and beautiful. Deadly and daring. Protective and powerful.

"I've never seen such a gigantic creature. Is Noni a—a pet?"

Manisha laughed. "No. She's her own, free self. She's ... more like a friend."

"Ah. So, what—*who*—are you?"

"I'm just a girl passing through."

Mitali smiled. "Well, friend of Noni's who's just a girl passing through, can I repay you with a meal?"

Manisha studied her with a scrupulous sweep. Mitali *was* a stranger, but she wasn't giving off a strange vibe. "You're not trying to deceive me, are you?"

"Oh, no! I would never. I don't even know what to deceive you for."

Manisha twisted her lips, her brows high. "No one's going to try to harm me or trade me into servitude? That sort of thing?"

"Oh stars, no! What awful things have you been through?"

Manisha glanced at her worn shoes caked in dried mud. "You don't want to know. But I'd really appreciate a meal." Her stomach rumbled and she flinched. "Hunger pangs are actual pangs."

Mitali nodded. "We know that pain too well these days, since the kingdom absorbed us."

"What do you mean?"

"We have to pay the King. Usually with food, since that's all we have of value. Always at the mercy of feeding any soldier who comes by no matter how much food we have or don't have. We didn't have any food for ourselves during the Fire Wars; the soldiers took whatever they wanted. Many of us starved to death."

Manisha frowned. "I'm so sorry. The kingdom is awful."

"Shh." Mitali was quick to hush her. "We mustn't say those things about them. The King has spies everywhere."

Manisha walked alongside her, aware of everyone watching them. She picked up on muted conversations about her, both awe and fear of Noni and the girl who accompanied her.

The village was large, sprawling, consisting of dirt roads and homes made from wood. Grazing water buffalo roamed here and there, their wide eyes watching everyone. Children played with baby goats, corralling them into a pen.

"Welcome to Bharoda." Mitali lifted a hand toward one of many small fields where workers hunched over crops.

"Are you sure it's okay for me to be here?" Manisha asked.

"Yes. It's not every day a girl archer shows up, or, you know... a fantastic beast," Mitali said with such awe that she had Manisha grinning.

"Okay. But... why did those boys do that your cousin?"

Mitali swallowed. "They're arrogant and trying to assert dominance, I think. Walk in the way of the kingdom. I'll take care of them later."

Manisha didn't press, but she was glad that Mitali would do something about them.

They sat outside of a hut, surrounded by older girls and children wanting to know everything about the stranger. There wasn't much to tell, at least not much that Manisha could share. Instead, she listened to their stories as she ate snacks of fried lentils and chana. It was just nice to hear voices, normal conversations, and happy children who weren't constantly told to sit down and be quiet. This was more like home than the temple. There seemed to be a pattern. The farther away from the palace she traveled, the happier the people.

"Sorry, we don't get many visitors," Mitali admitted, trying to calm down a little girl.

"I don't mind." Manisha laughed as the girl threw handfuls of petals into the air and danced beneath the floating colors. Manisha touched her fingers to her lips.

"Are you okay?" the girl asked. "Am I making too much noise?"

"No. I just... haven't laughed in a long time. Thank you for that."

She shyly shrank into herself and sat in Mitali's lap. Mitali said, "This is my sister."

"She's so full of life."

"Papa doesn't like that," the girl admitted, and then begrudgingly glared at a younger child behind her. "He's worse, and Papa's okay with him."

Mitali gently slapped her sister's thin arm, chiding, "Don't speak badly about others. Besides, we can't compare."

The girl scowled. "Why can't I run and be loud? I want to play in the mud, too!"

Manisha remembered wanting to run and play in the mud when was little. She'd gotten into trouble, but mainly for making a mess. Sithara was incredibly loud, yelling and sometimes singing, and she'd gotten into trouble, but that was usually because someone had a headache or just wanted a break from her. Manisha didn't ever remember being taught that boys could do different things because they were boys.

Mitali sighed and hugged the girl to her. "Boys are different."

Manisha frowned but focused on the village's hospitality and eagerness to welcome her.

Mitali prepared a meal of ghee-basted roti, jeera rice, and curried bhinda and tindora grown just several feet away. As they ate, Manisha enjoyed the little girls who eagerly told grand stories and young boys who dramatically acted out the tales. She giddily took in their larger-than-life energy. They made her feel like a kid again, wrapping her in tall tales.

She hadn't been this content in so long.

TWENTY-TWO

MANISHA
(THIRTEEN DAYS AGO)

Mitali had offered Manisha her family's private bathing area. A large hut had been built alongside a creek for privacy while still utilizing fresh, running water, a firepit in the center for warmer baths. Most importantly, it was a safe space.

Manisha quickly bathed. The less vulnerable, the better. No matter how strong she felt knowing she had power now, her body quivered every time she touched her privates for cleaning. Delicate touches, clenched eyes, gritted teeth.

Would this ever change? Would this ever be normal again?

There was a trickle of blood. Manisha numbly finished bathing, drying, and dressing. Her thoughts faltered. She hadn't bled in days, not since her first bath after being violated.

Mitali was waiting for her outside, all smiles. "There! Isn't that better? Nothing like a good cleaning after long travels. Glad my clothes fit! Yours will be dry by morning."

Her expression fell flat when Manisha didn't respond. She instead gazed absently into the distance.

"What's wrong?" Mitali asked.

"I'm bleeding," she uttered.

"Menstruation?"

Manisha nodded.

"Oh, no worries. What do you need?" Mitali called over some girls. With them came a couple of young boys. "Please gather menstruation items."

Manisha startled as the small group went to work. How could Mitali so plainly announce something this personal to everyone? And to boys!

"I'm sorry. Is this taboo where you're from?" Mitali asked, leading Manisha to a more secluded area.

"We don't talk about these things."

"The literal blood of life."

"What?"

"It creates and supports new life in the womb. Without it, no baby would be born. It's literally the blood of life. Sacred."

"I never thought of it that way." She'd been too young to experience menstruation in her homeland before the war, but she remembered older girls and women speaking openly about it.

The temple, which followed the customs of the kingdom, decreed that menstruating girls were unclean. Anything they touched was considered defiled. They stayed in their rooms and didn't associate with others, much less attend worship.

In a matter of minutes, the boys had returned with a bag filled with hot rocks.

"For your cramps and aches," one said, handing her the bag.

"Th-thank you."

They smiled and off they went.

Manisha's cheeks flushed when the girls returned with undergarments and a bag full of white pods. She thanked them, and off they went.

Mitali explained, "Our elders long ago adopted a custom from faraway villages. When someone menstruates here, they're left alone but cared for. Others pick up their work, and family looks after their children until they're well. Hot rocks ease the pain. The fibers in these undergarments and inserts soak up the blood. They're made from a sponge gourd. We harvest them, boil them to sanitize, and let them dry. They're very absorbent, and if you rinse them out, boil, and dry them again, you can reuse them!"

Mitali opened a small pot. "This is a powder made from ground bark. It does two things. Purges the bleeding so you menstruate for a few hours instead of days. And helps with the really bad pain. But pregnant women can't take this . . . unless they mean to purge."

Manisha blinked away tears, her hand landing on the flatness of her belly. The temple didn't speak about sex, since the act was forbidden, but she'd learned from naga teachings about bodies and babies. Menstruation meant she wasn't pregnant. And if she was, she had a choice? A decision all her own?

"What's wrong?" Mitali asked.

As soon as Manisha uttered, "I'm not pregnant," she fell to her knees and sobbed. An intense wave of relief rocked her body. She'd been attacked, raped, and didn't know how long she'd have to face lingering trauma. That vile man had severely harmed her . . . but what he did would *not* be the end of her.

Mitali landed beside her, a hand going to Manisha's shoulder. She paused and asked, "Can . . . ? Is it all right if I hug you? To comfort you?"

Manisha wrapped her arms around herself and shook her head. She couldn't be touched. Not yet.

"Then I'll sit with you for as long as you'd like."

MANISHA HAD BEEN INVITED TO SPEND THE NIGHT, NOT only by Mitali, but at the request of the village elders. She slept in the trees, on the highest of the thick limbs, cradling her weapons. How different this village was from Rayna's, where she knew to keep her guard up and had sensed the hostility the moment she'd arrived. While she knew some of the boys here had been trouble, she didn't think they'd betray her the way Rayna's people had. Mitali seemed like a clear-headed thinker, a negotiator, a planner. Her people probably would've helped.

She relaxed her shoulders. Things seemed a hundred times better this morning. Maybe one day, she could return here. A simple thought that warmed her chest.

From her perch, Manisha's gaze swept across the village clearing, landing on a handful of people around a large tree in the center of the village. She'd heard of those growing up. Anand had one, too, although she couldn't remember the term for it. It was a central gathering point for elders to sit and chat at all hours of the day. Typically, the sitting area around the central tree was occupied by the older ones taking the lead. It was the center for discussion and politics, but children were also allowed to sit and listen.

There were several older men around this village's central tree, but the eldest were women. There were three, all dressed the same in ash-pale saris, their heads covered.

As morning light grew, Manisha returned to the bathhouse. The products had worked. Her bleeding had ended, her cramps gone, leaving nothing but relief.

Mitali offered a soft greeting. "Are you feeling better?"

Manisha smiled. "Yes. The remedy worked."

"I'll write down the plants for the pods and the medicine, and the process for each. You can keep the extras if you'd like."

"Thank you. That's so generous."

Mitali didn't press for more. Instead, she asked, "Do you feel up to walking the gardens?"

Manisha eagerly nodded and followed her into the fields, toiling beside her.

"You don't have to help. I meant for you to sit and keep me company."

"I want to help, considering all that you've given me."

"Small gifts of hospitality. Besides, you helped my cousin," Mitali argued.

"I don't mind. It's relaxing."

Mitali gave her a doubtful look. "I've *never* heard anyone consider this relaxing. Backbreaking? Yes."

"It's normalcy. You're close to your family. It's nice."

"Nicer now that those boys were dealt with." Mitali offered what Manisha had been waiting all day to ask about. "He got a beating from me, and I hit hard."

Manisha's eyes went wide imagining this tall, slender girl beating that tall, broad boy. "What did you hit him with?" she asked, curiosity getting the best of her.

"My broom. Then I made him sweep every house as punishment in humility. He's also going to take on my cousin's chores and workload—she works in crafts and needs her fingers—and he's going to serve her until she heals."

"Wow. How did you get him to agree to all that?"

She seemed reluctant to confess but said, "The elders approved it."

Manisha nodded in awe.

Mitali stood, swatting dirt off her dark green salwar kameez, and stretched at the end of their modest harvest of corn and long green beans. Her clothes were more vibrant and darker than those from Rayna's village. Newer, even. Her leggings were puffy and cuffed at the ankle. Manisha imagined that sort of style allowed better air flow and was easier to squat to do gardening in.

Manisha held up a foot-long pod and grinned, feeling all sorts of nostalgic. "My mother loved these. We had vines growing over trellises with curtains of green bean pods. Her basket would be piled high with every harvest. The pods never fit, so they always hung off the ends. My sisters and I would help clean them and break them into smaller pieces for cooking and sneak a bite or two. Which always led to ten."

Mitali laughed. "We're the same. I have to resist and make sure others are fed first. I eat last. If there's anything left."

"Oh no. And here I was eating so much this morning."

She shook her head and looked lovingly at her younger siblings at the end of the field. They were studying baby corn that was still too small to pick. "We have food right now. Don't worry. And it's my honor to make sure others are fed first. I enjoy taking care of others."

Manisha smiled sadly, fighting back tears remembering how Mama would make sure the three sisters ate first when they were on the run, even when it meant she went days without food. Whenever they were safe enough to cook food, she'd take the burned pieces, making sure the girls had the best picks. Eshani, being the eldest but also the most affectionate, would do the same. Essentially, Manisha, although not traditionally spoiled, was spoiled the most in the situation they'd been given.

Mama had loved them so much, and she loved feeding others even before the war. Manisha saw that same fierce, unselfish love in Mitali.

"Where are your parents?" Manisha asked.

"Papa's out on a big hunt, and my mom died during the Fire Wars . . ." she responded somberly.

"I'm so sorry," Manisha said, regretting that she'd asked. Maybe her mother had been one of those who'd died from starvation.

Mitali forced a smile and said, "You were probably wondering why I act like a mother?"

Manisha nodded, not knowing what else to say.

Mitali went on, "It was my duty to help my dad with my siblings and the house. He wasn't able to handle it on his own, but also, I needed something to focus on. I'm happy to help, especially to see my siblings enjoy themselves. I don't want them to know so much pain. Because soldiers and the kingdom pushed us to our food supply limits so often, we learned. We store food in hidden places so that our own people won't starve ever again."

Manisha thought back to her people and Eshani in particular. She could make things grow before she understood how they grew. "My parents built a place to grow seedlings," she recalled slowly.

Mitali watched her. "You mean in the ground?"

"It was like . . . a house meant to grow seedlings. We grew them in small pots until they were strong enough to put into the ground outside. I think it helped the plants grow better. The house had lots of windows and the roof was made of glass. It kept birds and insects out and made the house humid. Maybe you could try that? Cut back some more trees and build a house like that? Also, I think smaller crops had netting above the field, to keep out birds and insects, too. I wish I knew more. My sister was the one who knew."

Mitali nodded. "If that worked for your people, maybe we can try it. I'll bring it up with my aunt. She heads the fieldwork."

Manisha smiled, overjoyed that she could possibly help someone with her faded memories. Maybe her people couldn't get back to their seedling houses and netted fields, but these people could try out the practice.

A few minutes later, a woman approached and whispered something to Mitali. Mitali thanked her and said to Manisha, "Our elders want to meet you."

"Is that a good thing?"

She shrugged. "Difficult to tell."

"Okay. I should at least thank them for inviting me to stay."

Manisha nervously followed Mitali out of the field, handing their harvest to the woman.

"They're a little unusual," Mitali explained a little farther out. "Please don't react unkindly."

"Oh, I would never."

"Our elders are women."

"I didn't know village elders in the kingdom could be women. Has it always been that way here?"

Mitali replied, "No. They're the first. Their father had been the anointed village elder. The triplets were his only children to survive birth. Back then, there was a punishment when women didn't have sons."

Manisha cringed. "Do I want to know?"

"Several days' trek from here, where the jungle flattens and dries out, there are large crevices, ravines. There are insects, arachnids, centipedes, lampreys, and so forth bigger than either of us. They'll eat *anything* within reach. Women who failed to provide children were taken there and sacrificed."

Manisha gulped. *Awful* wasn't a strong enough word for such a practice.

"Now the elders go there to pay homage to all the sacrificed women. The former elder's wife, in her case, was given honor for having triplets. The village had never seen three children born at once before, or since. Because the elder couldn't produce a son, he married the girls off to the next appointed leader."

"All three have the same husband?" Manisha croaked.

"*Had*. They didn't give him children, so he beat them in public since he couldn't sacrifice them—their father was still alive and was still the elder."

"What happened to the husband?"

"Oh, they killed him," Mitali said matter-of-factly, like she was talking about corn.

"*What?*" Manisha choked out.

"Shortly after their father died—when their husband had barely taken control of the village. The triplets lived in one hut where the husband bedded each every third night, one after the other, forcing the other two to stay in the hut. He wasn't kind to them. It was when he threatened to gouge out their eye that they struck him with a torch, smashing his head against a rock and then setting him on fire," Mitali said, watching the elders with a sort of awe when they came into view in front of the central tree.

Seemed like Mitali found the act more heroic than gruesome.

She looked back to Manisha and said, "I suppose those sorts of things happen when one is pushed to their breaking point."

"Weren't they punished?"

"Oh yes. They had their teeth pulled out. One by one over the course of three months to extend their suffering."

Manisha recoiled.

"Some of their gums were eaten away by infection, showing the jawbone. But they survived. They're incredibly resilient," she added with definite reverence. "No one has questioned them since they survived their ordeal, and no one has harmed them since. We call them the Dosi Sisters."

"*Dosi?* Like old woman?"

She chuckled. "Yes. Can you believe they looked like old women from the day they were born? Wrinkled, pale skin, gray hair, and white eyes. At least, that's what everyone says."

"Were they sickly?"

"Sort of. They always had hunched backs and frail bones. Also, they're blind. Except one. She has one functioning eye. But the strange thing is that all three sisters can see through that one eye."

Manisha watched the elderly women hunched over the fire, wrapped in a blanket despite the humidity. They stared into the flames like the flames were showing them something.

Manisha followed Mitali as she cut through the small crowd that had parted for them.

The sisters wore pale old saris. Their wrists hung over knees bent to their chests. Their shoulders hunched as if the weight of a thousand suns burdened them. Their skin was pallid and wrinkled, covered with dark spots, and hung from protruding bones. One dragged a long, sharp nail across her forearm, slowly cutting her skin. Dark red blood seeped out in a single large droplet.

They had concave collarbones and long necks with pulsating veins, like they could explode any second. Their lips were thin and down-turned with no teeth to hold them up. Their eyes, sunken and hollow, were clouded white, like ghosts, trained on the stranger as if they could see her.

The woman in the middle had one clouded, all-white eye and one all-black eye. She watched Manisha in the most unnerving way. Manisha shivered.

"*So,*" the elder hissed. "The nagin returns?"

Mitali jerked her head toward Manisha, her stare incredulous.

"Such surprise when all clues forged a path?" the elder asked.

Manisha wasn't sure if she was speaking to her or to Mitali.

"The one who controls the golden serpent, the one who fears to speak her own name," the sister to the right said.

Manisha lifted her chin, unafraid for the first time in a long time, declaring, "My name is Manisha. Daughter of Padma. Granddaughter of Padmavati. Descendent of the naga."

"You were not killed in the fire," the sister on the left stated, her voice croaky. Then she leaned into the middle sister and added, "Instead, rising from the ashes."

"Impossible, fleeing without a trace," the one on the left argued.

"Where has the risen hidden?" the middle one asked.

"I was sent to the floating mountains," Manisha answered, not understanding why she revealed so much, so easily.

"Hens inviting the snake into their nest?" the sister on the left asked, her voice high.

"They didn't know who I was," Manisha explained.

Then all three stilled, their lips simultaneously curving upward into toothless grins. "So, the risen has returned. Things fall into place," they said in unison, a haunting echo bouncing off Manisha's ears. "To reunite the people and restore lost grace."

"What?"

"The golden serpent," said the one on the left.

"The blood of vipers," said the one on the right.

"The wrath of gods," said the one in the middle.

"I—I don't understand," Manisha muttered.

"You have no idea who you are."

"Or what you're capable of doing."

"Or what you will achieve."

"Do you somehow know the future?" Manisha asked, skeptical and eyeing an equally confused Mitali.

"We may have one eye, but we see more than anyone," the middle sister replied.

"Do you know where my family is, then?" Manisha asked, hopeful.

"Your twin sisters will meet you near the canyonlands," she said.

Manisha's arms dropped to her sides. Her throat turned parched. She could've fainted. "How did . . . ?"

"But others are coming," the one on the left added.

"So be on your way," the one to the right ended.

"Wait. Who's coming?" Manisha asked.

"Someone who incites passion," answered the one on the right.

"Someone who incites rage," replied the one to the left.

"That makes no sense," Manisha said.

"Hurry," the one in the middle said. "They're fast approaching."

Manisha shook her head at their riddles.

The sisters, as one, turned eerily to Mitali and jerked their chin toward Manisha.

"This is for you," Mitali said. She handed her a bag that had been sitting between her and the sisters. "Food and water for your journey."

Manisha argued, "But you don't have much food. And don't try to lie and tell me that you do."

"It's rude not to feed a stranger. And it's rude to send one off without food and water. We may have some customs that are lacking, but hospitality to strangers isn't one of them."

"Thank you," Manisha mumbled. She took the bag, opening it to find two containers of water surrounded by a pile of dried fruit, nuts, parathas, and corn.

"Thank you," she told the elders, who turned to her again.

The flames flickered reddish light across their clouded eyes, making them glow.

"You were buried once as a girl," said the one on the right.

"Sent away and raised an apsara," said the one to the left.

"And returned as a warrior," added the one in the middle.

A warrior? They thought so much of her, as if she were strong and resilient and mighty. They didn't personally know her, yet they knew so much about her. Such random, eerie sayings that made Manisha stand taller. Yes. She was a warrior now. She'd earned it and proven it and would carry that title like a special bestowal from these ancient, wise women.

Then, in their unforgettable, eerie unison, they added, "All hail the queens."

"Wait. What did you say?" Manisha stared at them, her mouth hanging open.

They lowered their chins and closed their eyes, as if falling asleep.

"What do you mean by that?" she probed.

They didn't answer, didn't move. Were they even breathing?

Mitali led her away and explained, "They don't often speak, but when they do, they always speak truth. Sometimes they speak in riddles to decipher later when you see their words come to life. But when they're done speaking, they're done speaking."

Manisha was still reeling over their words, their revelations, their insight into things no one should know. She kept looking over her shoulder, but the elders didn't move. Soon the crowds that had parted for them closed, blocking the elders from view.

Being called a warrior had been empowering, but suggesting she might be a queen? Was that the meaning? Or were they talking about someone else? But there was only one queen in this kingdom. A queen from another kingdom? Plural queens sounded promising—a light in this bleakness. Maybe queens ruled in other parts of the realm and would save this kingdom.

Mitali and Manisha paused at the southernmost edge of the territory. The village was barely visible from here, and ahead, there was darkness. Black trees and what appeared to be a sprawl of black vines and a shadowy canopy beneath dark clouds. The clouds sat in place. There was no wind or movement, even though the sky was piercing blue all around.

"I should be on my way," Manisha said. "Thank you for everything."

Mitali shrugged. "It really wasn't much."

It was so much more than Mitali would ever know.

"Will you come back for a visit?"

"I'd like that."

Mitali beamed like a child with a platter full of sweets. "I want to hear all about your travels, your home, your family. We can put on a real feast, a proper welcome. Like what we do whenever our friends return."

Friends? Were they really friends? *True* friends? Like Noni but in human form? Like the kind Manisha had back in Anand before the Fire Wars separated them? Telling each other secrets and giggling over goings-on, divulging tales, and catching up on news. Sleepovers and hair braiding, trying new foods and customs. Watching one another grow up and taking on expanding responsibilities.

Friends sounded nice.

"You're headed to the marshlands?" Mitali asked.

"Yes," Manisha replied, remembering how quickly her family had moved through them when they fled their home.

"Dark things lurk there," she said. As if Manisha didn't know.

"I have to go through. The path at the river is blocked off. It would take too long to go around the other way."

"Whatever you do, don't head west. It's a dead end. Literally. A drop into a ravine filled with creatures taller than trees that will snatch you and eat you before you can blink. The place where barren women were sacrificed."

Flesh-eating monsters to the left. A blocked-off riverbank to the right. Beyond that, raging waters filled with gigantic beasts.

The marshlands were the only thing that stood between Manisha and the canyonlands beyond. She had to keep heading south. There was literally no way around the darkness.

She narrowed her eyes and studied the faraway marshlands, knowing somewhere in the thicket awaited the shades. Shadowy apparitions that killed from the inside. There was no way to fight a shadow. One had to evade, run, or perish.

Some said the marshlands were the entryway to the Nightmare Realm, and the shades took the dead down the Blood River to meet their eternal fate at the hands of the Shadow King.

Whatever was there was enough to scare off the King's army. When they'd chased her family through, the soldiers had never made it to the other side.

What had to be done had to be done. Besides, the darkness lurking inside Manisha whispered that she didn't need to be so afraid. For darkness welcomed darkness.

TWENTY-THREE

PRATYUSH
(PRESENT DAY)

Rations of fresh food had almost been depleted by the time another village appeared. The General decided to take "what is ours, by decree of the King."

Ahead, women worked in a modest field picking and pruning vegetables with sickles, and men worked on homes. Young children were playing while older ones helped with the labor.

The village of Bharoda, tucked into the edges of the jungle, gave Pratyush ideas for a future home. He would build with stone, brick, wood, and even marble—he deserved it—with plenty of rooms and indoor plumbing. Maybe even two stories, with the bedrooms and a study on the second floor. A study, yes. A place to read and relax. His future wife and children could read their hearts out or sew or paint or compose or whatever *normal*, creative thing they wanted to do. He wouldn't set limits on them. He wouldn't tell the girls they couldn't be educated and artistic. He wouldn't teach the boys they couldn't cook and clean. Just like his parents had raised him and his sister. Equals.

He would have a courtyard for his children to safely play in. A garden to grow flowers and herbs. A small field like this one to grow vegetables. Another, larger field for steeds and maybe goats or water buffalo for milk and cheese, or whatever his family wanted. Sure, maybe that sounded like an old man's dream, but he'd do anything to re-create the home his parents had made for him.

Pratyush could almost taste that new life. It was so close. Lay down his axe and sword and pick up a harvesting scythe and pruning shears.

And best of all? If she ever believed him...if she ever agreed... Manisha would be his bride. Maybe not right away, but hopefully one day. Those eyes, which must've slain a hundred guys before him, would be the last thing he'd see every night. Sleeping side by side in a real bed, a mattress filled with gossamer feathers and fitted with silk sheets. Not a cot or a pile of blankets on the floor. He'd run his fingers through her hair as it fell over her shoulders. She'd smile and everything would make sense again.

Damn. He never thought in all his life he'd want something as domestic as a wife and children on a secluded piece of farmland. Yet here he was, pining like a lovestruck fool over her.

After he beheaded the nagin, he'd get land and build a house and garden and take trips to the floating mountains to see her and woo her and win her. And when the house was complete, he'd ask her to marry him again, but properly, like how nobles proposed with an engagement bracelet. They'd have a ceremony and he'd show Manisha what he'd built for her.

He'd have to work on socializing, but he could do that if it meant she would have friends near their new home.

The villagers met the soldiers with baskets of freshly picked beans, corn, and gourds.

"Bread. Cheese. *Cooked* food. *Now*," the General commanded with a snap of his fingers.

While the villagers scurried to feed them with parathas and curried vegetables, Pratyush and the General interviewed everyone.

The women kept their heads covered and their eyes downcast, but they seemed to be better treated than the last village...as in not mutilated.

"Women don't know anything," the General grumbled. "They can't even speak."

"No," an older girl said loudly.

The General pushed through the crowd to find her. "What did you say?"

"We have *not* seen a monstrous woman who turns into a serpent or who turns men into stone. Whatever you're looking for doesn't exist," she said.

"What's your name?"

"Mitali."

"You speak so boldly for a girl," the General barked.

"Well, it seems you're complaining when we don't speak and questioning when we do speak. Make up your mind."

"Insolence!" His voice boomed.

Pratyush stepped around him and asked her, "Have you seen anything out of the ordinary or had any visitors recently?"

"No."

Her eyes dilated and her pulse raged a little faster. "Hmm. Are you sure? Or are you afraid to say something?"

She shook her head. "No threat has come by, especially one like this monster you're looking for."

About that, she wasn't lying. Strange.

They moved on to the few men present and then the older boys, who also seemed reluctant to speak. They were afraid of something. But what? Averted gazes, dilated pupils, pulsating veins, perspiration, and a tremble in their slightly elevated voices said they were lying. All of them.

"I don't like being lied to," Pratyush announced.

"We have no news for you, boy," a man stated.

"Slayer," he corrected.

That seemed to get their attention. But now none of them wanted to talk. Why was interviewing witnesses about this monster *so* hard? This had never happened before. Usually, people were quick to spill any information, down to the irrelevant color of the sky that day, if it meant killing a monster.

Mitali said, "You'll be fed shortly. Once you've eaten and rested, you can be on your way."

He scowled. "No one's ever pushed me out so fast."

"You're the slayer. You're hunting a monster. We don't want to get caught in the middle of your fight."

"We need to speak with your elders before we leave."

"That's a problem, then," she said matter-of-factly.

"Why?"

"Our elders left yesterday for sacrificial offering."

"All right. Where?"

She pointed to the west. "Toward the ravines."

"Then we'll go there."

Elders rarely lied to those sent by the King.

SLAYERS COULD GO DAYS WITHOUT SLEEP, BUT HUMANS needed it. Which was why, after partaking of a hot meal, they'd made camp several hours from the village. The soldiers tucked in for the night.

Pratyush climbed into a tree and leaned against the trunk, pulling one knee to his chest, his battle-axe at his foot. He liked high places. Less chance of getting attacked.

Below, Dev emerged from the camp and looked around before

escaping into the woods. Ahead, the jungle opened up to flatter grasslands. To the right...

Hmm. They must've been close to Dev's village.

Pratyush jumped down and followed him. Maybe he was just taking a piss. *Way* out in the wilderness.

He followed, walking a parallel path to Dev. But Dev was a better soldier than any other guy out here. He knew when he was being followed. He suddenly stopped, turned around, and waited.

Pratyush walked out of the brush. "Ways to go for a nightly piss, isn't it?"

Dev grunted.

"We're close to your village. If you leave to be with them, I wouldn't blame you, honestly. If I had someone waiting at home, I'd want to see her, too."

"I haven't seen my wife in months," Dev growled, irritated.

"I know. Your sacrifice for your people is great. I hope they appreciate it."

"I'm revered as a hero," he said in that sharp tone of his, as if Pratyush's words had been condescending instead of genuine.

Pratyush nodded. "I think of you as a hero, too. If you leave, I won't stop you. I won't help them look for you. In fact, I feel sorry for anyone who tries. But you know the King won't stop searching for you, and his treaty with your people will be void."

Dev dropped his shoulders, looking longingly in the direction of his village. "I know."

"I'm sorry you can't be with her. Not that you need my permission, but you should go and stay as long as you want. I'll try to cover for you. But the longer you stay, the more likely the King will find out. You know how he is with this stuff."

"I *hate* being in servitude to that pompous, gluttonous bag of meat."

Pratyush snickered. "Same."

"Should I have my bride send me back with zardozi fabric?" Dev asked, his expression deadpan.

Pratyush guffawed. "Of course! I'll make my own mojri."

"And wear them back to the palace with the nagin's head in a bag? The King's sure to marry you off right then and there."

"Nah. There's only one for me."

If ever Dev had looked surprised, this was it. He stared at Pratyush, his mouth gaping open but with no words to request answers.

Pratyush rubbed the back of his neck, nervously laughing. "Ah, yeah. Guess I haven't mentioned her?"

"I didn't think you knew how to talk to girls."

"You're so funny," Pratyush said sarcastically.

"When have you had time to even meet a girl?"

"At the floating temple."

Dev's look of surprise turned into shock. "That's walking a dangerous line. An apsara? Really?"

"Really. I asked the King for permission to marry her."

Dev's expression fell. "Be careful. He'll use whatever he can as leverage against you. What did he ask in return?"

Pratyush sucked in a breath. "The nagin's head for a little bit of time off with her. He's more concerned with breeding me."

"Is that why he throws palace girls at you?"

"Apparently."

"Be even more careful, then."

Pratyush nodded, but he didn't fully understand. It wasn't like the King could force him to father children . . . right?

As if Dev could read the question on his face, he huffed. "You're skilled and brave, but still young. If the King wants your offspring, he'll make them and take them."

"No. I would never let him."

"It's not a matter of letting him. There are ways. Ranchers breed water buffalo and horses the same way. Drugs and toxins so you don't know you're doing it and can't fight back, or make you forget it happened. You think girls are the only ones who get violated?"

Pratyush froze. Dev placed a hand on his shoulder. "Don't let your guard down. Everything about you is valuable, and some people will stop at nothing to keep you, to replicate you."

Pratyush nodded and Dev stepped back. Well, this was a whole new level of badness to think about.

He said to Dev, "Well, that conversation got dark. I'll remember your warning. You better get going. We'll be at the ravine by dawn. And past the marshlands by nightfall. Meet us there if you want. Otherwise, it was an honor fighting alongside you."

"Don't get sentimental."

Pratyush smirked. "I'll get sentimental if I want. You're truly the best fighter among fighters, and a friend."

"Thanks, Slayer. You too."

And with that, they parted ways.

TWENTY-FOUR

MANISHA
(EIGHT DAYS AGO)

Just how creepy were the marshlands? Creepy enough to make even Noni tread carefully. She'd found Manisha halfway and kept looking at her as if asking, *Are you sure you want to venture here?*

Noni slithered behind Manisha, like she was literally watching her back. Her gaze flitted every which way, flashing the emerald specks in her eyes, catching dull gray light.

"It's all right," Manisha said, trying her best to reassure Noni. "We'll be safe. But . . . if you don't want to come, I understand—"

Noni interrupted her with a gentle nudge, as if saying they were in this together to the end.

"Thank you." Manisha hugged her around the neck, and they traveled onward.

The jungle had been humid, wet from encroaching monsoon clouds swollen with flood rains they could barely hold back. The marshlands started out humid, but as they traversed the strange, cryptic land, the temperature dropped. Breath formed into fog. Manisha hadn't felt this sort of cold since winter on the floating mountains. In fact, strange snow fluttered down in sparse flakes the size of almond blossoms.

Manisha closed her arms around herself and shivered. Why didn't Noni zoom by? Why didn't she stay camouflaged? Did this place inhibit her abilities? Or was she that afraid?

Noni moved slower and slower. Her shimmering gold scales turned dull, her eyes glazed over, and she became lethargic. Manisha frowned, a stab of worry riling up her insides. She slowed down to Noni's pace, rubbing the serpent's forehead, and hugging her around her freezing head. Why was she so cold?

Manisha blinked away snowflakes from her lashes.

"Not much farther," she assured Noni, although she had no idea. Every map Manisha had seen showed this place as a small circle in comparison to the canyonlands. The truth was no one knew this area. No one stayed here, no one explored, and if someone got through, they were considered fortunate.

Ahead, the quiet awoke with warbling birds and babbling water. The gray turned vibrant olive, dotted with snow. A ray of sunlight hit evergreen water, what many called the marsh ghost light. The eerie yet beautiful glowing iridescence came from nowhere. The sky was blanketed in dark gray whorls, preventing sunlight from filtering through.

Manisha had passed through the marshlands when her people were fleeing soldiers. Mama had told them to keep their eyes down and never look up, to hold hands and run.

Manisha had only seen curled black vines, things that might've been plant or creature. But she'd never slowed down enough to take a better look. She didn't remember the icy cold. Or the snow. Just the darkness and silence. Even now, her footfalls were hushed, not a leaf crunching or a pebble scraping.

"Maybe you need water?" she told Noni.

Upon closer look, the pond and surrounding streams weren't shallow. There was an unsettling depth cloaked in inky darkness.

A harsh chill descended, falling around them like a pall of smoke. Manisha's teeth chattered and her fingernails turned blue.

"We sh-should go."

She forced herself to move faster. This seemed like the type of place where something was lying in wait, ready to jump out and snatch a morsel like her.

A *click, click, click* sound echoed through the air. Was that her chattering teeth? Noni chattering? Did snakes even chatter?

Noni raised her head and stilled.

A tall, slender creature tilted its head to watch her from behind a tree. A tree that had been clawed apart by its talons, each finger a razor-sharp, double-edged blade.

When still, the beast blended into the inkiness of the marsh and water. Until it opened its large, elongated eyes of pure white. Until it grinned. Its thin lips pulled back to the sides of its head, revealing long, sharp white teeth. Between those claws and mouth, it could probably kill its prey in one fell swoop.

The rest of its body was sleek, shiny black. A large head. The shoulders and body of a muscular man. One leg bent, with a long foot digging into the muddy bank, the other leg ankle-deep in water.

Manisha's heart rammed in her chest, but she was more worried for Noni. This wasn't the time for her to get sick. She wasn't a baby snake that Manisha could hold in her hand and run with.

Manisha didn't make any sudden moves. The creature curiously watched her walk by, snarling and snapping its jaw. Manisha's hand moved to her bow, slipping it off her shoulder as she reached for an arrow.

She stopped in front of the beast, stood as an armed barrier between it and Noni so Noni could slither by. Was Noni unaware of the creature? She barely turned her head toward it, didn't snarl or hiss or raise herself in defense. She kept moving, flashing her eyes. There was a strange opaqueness growing there, replacing their usual mossy green with a bluish hue.

The beast screeched, a mixture of enraged hawk and territorial boar, showing all its teeth—and there were many teeth. Strings of saliva lashed out. Manisha covered her ears. She felt the screech dig deep into her ears and curl down her neck.

Noni startled and swerved her head toward the beast, baring her fangs and hissing in warning. But she didn't get into an attack position.

"We're just traveling through," she told the beast, trepidation rising. "We don't want any trouble."

It watched with ravenous energy, snapping its jaws and swiping the air, trying to reach them. But it didn't move from the spot. The creature seemed to be tied to the stream, stuck, or maybe its foot was caught in the water beneath the boulder.

When Manisha didn't budge, the creature quieted. The shrieks of terror turned into stomach rumblings. It fell to one knee, the leg that wasn't stuck to the boulder, and dropped to its hands, heaving.

Noni struggled to move, and she needed to get out of here to safety. Manisha could buy time. This creature wasn't an immediate threat. There was a sad heaviness in its hunched, forsaken body and twisted ankle.

Some considered Noni a monster because she was of monstrous size and different. People feared what they didn't know. But Manisha knew her, and she was deserving of life, peace, and freedom. She had a heart as golden as her scales, a soul as bright as her eyes.

Manisha would want someone to help Noni if she were trapped.

She sighed and replaced her bow and arrow. She carefully, slowly approached the creature, her hands out in a gesture meaning no harm. "Are you trapped? Hurt?"

The beast moaned, like a wolf crying to the moon.

Oh my heart. It was in pain. It shivered.

"I'm going to move the boulder," she said, peering into the water and hoping this wasn't a mistake.

The beast stayed on its knee but swung at Manisha, narrowly missing her face.

"Hey!" she yelled, jumping back. "Settle down! I'm offering help, and if you don't want it, swipe at me again and I'll be on my way. Curmudgeon..."

Those big eyes, like teardrops turned sideways, frowned and drooped, and Manisha had never seen anything look sadder.

"All right. I'm going to push this boulder."

She pressed against solid rock. The boulder barely moved, but the creature flinched. She put her entire weight into it and pushed. It budged little by little.

"How can one rock be so heavy?" she grumbled, hitting her back against the boulder to use her legs.

There. It moved. More and more. Until it slid off the creature's ankle.

The beast howled, but finally, the weight was fully off. Manisha slipped on wet rocks but caught herself before touching the water.

The inkiness in the stream's depths blinked back at her.

Oh! She yelped and scrambled backward. There was most definitely something in the water!

But now she was closer to the beast. She hurriedly crawled away, jumping to her feet as the beast limped toward her. Towering higher and higher, growing.

It appeared as a shadow of a shadow, darker than black. When it moved, it turned into the fabric of nightmares. If this place was an entryway into the Nightmare Realm, then this creature seemed like the kind that would fit right in.

It watched Manisha, studied her with a blink. It took one step after another, tall and gangly with talons for hands *and* feet. Spikes rose from its back, skittered down its spine in waves. It cawed like a ravenous bird, a call that shook the trees and ground and made its skin shudder.

When it dropped its head back and howled into the sky, its jaw opened all the way, an expanding void cutting clear from one side of its face to the other, revealing rows of those long, sharp white teeth and a forked reptilian tongue as long as its head. Sticky saliva stretched from the top row of teeth to the bottom.

Manisha's heartbeat pounded, and her gut dropped into her stomach at the sickening, terrifying sight. Her skin crawled, and she was sure this was her end.

But the beast didn't come after her, even when she backed away.

It grunted and calmed down. Huffing, it flicked a flower off a nearby bush like it had forgotten she was there. A yellow butterfly landed on the beast's head. It scratched the air, capturing the butterfly and bringing it to its face. The butterfly spread its wings, brushing them against the beast's slender nose. The beast... laughed.

Manisha nervously laughed under her breath. "All right. You're free. Please don't hurt me, though. I'll be on my way now."

It looked from her to something behind her.

Oh, please, stars, please don't let there be others.

She gulped and slowly turned, her icy hand on her bow. She sidestepped so that the creature she'd helped wouldn't be positioned behind her, primed for an ambush of the fool who thought it needed aid.

Her heart was beating so hard that it knocked the breath from her lungs. She wheezed, the air suddenly thin. Her pulse gushed like a river behind her ears. She blinked a few times to make sure her eyes weren't giving out, that she was actually seeing this phenomenon.

No wonder Mama had told them not to look. This was the stuff of nightmares.

Manisha had heard tales of ghost light. The eerie, greenish light that seemed to come out of the marshy water, descending from nothing above. The light that seemed to shimmer and whisper and move with you. Mystifying and beautiful, rumored to have powers that could kill a person in agonizing, twisted ways a thousand times over with a single twinkle.

But what she saw made the stories of the marsh ghost light sound like children's bedtime stories.

Not light at all.

But darkness.

Sheer, maddening, infinite, cavernous darkness.

Like looking back at herself and yet seeing the void as it twisted her mind.

Not a mirror or even a form. Four hovering clouds of black fog, so dense that she couldn't see through them, had appeared.

She gasped for air, realizing that she'd stopped breathing beneath the intensity of their presence.

The shades. Creatures of darkest lore that dragged people to the Nightmare Realm's Blood River.

They were real.

And they were here.

She stood petrified as they advanced. She couldn't feel anything, not a single sensation, not even the cold. She couldn't hear a single thing, either. No crickets chirping, birds warbling, brush rustling in the breeze, or water dripping into the stream. Where was that darkness inside her now? Telling her to let it take over so she could fight?

Noni appeared at her side and hissed. Poor girl tried her best to seem formidable, but they both knew this marsh had debilitating effects.

The shades, all at once, careened toward Manisha faster than a blink, somehow silent yet screeching louder than a hundred ghosts.

Manisha gasped. But nothing went in or out of her lungs when they hit her.

She felt every particle of the darkness gush into her, swirl around inside, and levitate around her. Her body pulled out of itself. Her insides turned fiery hot and icy cold at the same time. Her legs turned into liquid but screamed with the pain of a million serpent bites.

The darkness that had been rising inside her? The shades *found* it and pulled it out, like they were looking at a pet they'd drawn out of a cage. She couldn't move, couldn't breathe, couldn't think.

Noni wrapped herself around Manisha, cocooned her using her thick, muscular body as a shield. But as quickly as she'd positioned herself to protect Manisha, Noni turned heavy and limp. She slowly fell.

Manisha's body was returned to her, along with her rising darkness. She dropped to her knees and held Noni's limp, leaden head against her chest.

"Leave her alone!" she demanded.

The shades hovered over them. They could've killed her, but she wasn't about to let that happen.

Manisha gathered as much of Noni's massive body into her arms as possible, namely her head and upper part, and dragged her out of the marshlands. She'd never been particularly strong, but in this moment, she had newfound strength. Enough to drag a colossal snake.

The shades, for some reason, didn't come after them. They floated in place with the inky black creature beside them curiously watching, that yellow butterfly still on its head. The beast jerked its chin from Manisha to the Shades and then back to Manisha, as if they were having a conversation about why they chose to let her go.

She didn't wait to be out of sight before trying to run with Noni's weight. She huffed and ignored the pain in her body. Every minute felt eons longer than the last, but finally, they emerged from the marshlands in grueling agony.

Her palms clammy, Manisha lost her grip on Noni. Noni kept slipping out of her arms, and her worst fears descended into madness.

"Come on. Please..." *Please don't die.*

Noni didn't respond. She tried to push herself along. She tried her best, she really did.

But the thing Manisha had learned from this world was that sometimes one's best wasn't enough.

TWENTY-FIVE

MANISHA
(EIGHT DAYS AGO)

The edge of the marshlands was a steep downward hill that sent Manisha tumbling into a sprawling valley. She cried out in surprise, the ground suddenly taken from underneath her. Noni seemed to come alert for a second, but not enough to stop herself from falling.

Manisha landed at the bottom of the hill, her skin burning and damp with blood. Noni landed on top of her, knocking the breath out of Manisha. Her entire body screamed in pain.

"You weigh a million suns!"

She used her feet to push herself out from underneath Noni, her back hitting uneven surfaces with the satchel, bow, and quiver. A final grunt, a final push, and she was free from Noni's weight. She panted, staring at a blue sky dabbed with pearly clouds and then over to the stark delineation against the marshland's cloudy whorls. She shivered at the thought of what the shades had done, and what they were capable of doing. *Never* again.

Her cuts healed. Her skin snapped back into place. She wasn't sure if she'd ever get used to the pinching, pulling, and sharp flicks, but she was grateful for her healing abilities.

She crawled onto her knees and cradled Noni's limp head in her lap, rubbing a hand over her head, between her eyes. They were still opaque and bluish.

Manisha's heart broke. "Did I sentence you to death by making you travel through the marshlands?"

She stilled when the sounds of a stampede roared to life behind her. The ground shook. She twisted around and squinted into the distance. What else could possibly happen?

"*What* is that?"

Fast-moving blurs materialized, encroaching quickly. Manisha placed Noni's head on the ground and crawled onto her knees, aiming one of the blood-coated arrows at three charging rhinos. It wasn't until they came to an abrupt stop some feet away, kicking up massive amounts of dirt, that riders popped up from over the wild beasts.

Three older girls with half-shaved heads covered with black-and-green tattoos. Silver rings pierced their bottom lips, and silver bracelets adorned their wrists. They wore tan, sleeveless tops and pants.

One grinned, showing teeth filed to points. "Looks like dinner for days."

Manisha shook her head in warning, pulling the arrow back.

"Let's say you're an outstanding archer who could hit us even if we ducked behind our beasts. You can't strike all three of us."

"Do you want to test that?" Manisha asked.

The girl rested her forearms on the rhino's head and leaned forward. "What are you doing on our land?"

"Moving south, no trouble to you."

The rider glanced to her left. "What's out there?"

"Maybe family."

"You don't know?"

"I'm just trying to get home," Manisha replied.

"While dragging that magnificent meal?"

"She is *not* a meal," Manisha growled.

The girl regarded her for another moment. "What's wrong with it?"

"I don't know. We stumbled out of the marshlands, and she's been like this since."

She guffawed. "The marshlands! What were you doing there? Don't you know that you can go around?"

"To the ravine?" She did *not* want to get eaten by giant spiders, thank you.

"There's a hidden trail just before the ravine, but it's an extra four days' walk. No matter. You're here now, somehow surviving the marshlands."

"It's a snake, right?" the girl on the left asked, her gaze intent on Noni. While the older girl's voice had been deeper, this one had a softer, higher voice.

Manisha nodded.

"Looks as though . . . it's in brumation."

Manisha quirked a brow. "What's that?"

"Semi-hibernation. Snakes become lethargic. But that happens in winter."

The older girl sighed. "Our most scholarly scholar knows all."

"Don't get mad at me because I like to read," the younger one taunted, bouncing her shoulder-length hair with a palm. "But animals *are* fascinating."

"The marshlands were freezing. Does that explain her eyes and scales?" Manisha asked, desperate for answers.

The girl on the middle rhino swung her long leg over and jumped down. Patting the beast, she walked toward Manisha. She didn't have a weapon on her, but still, Manisha shifted the arrow to follow her.

She was tall, maybe six feet. She held her hands up. "Can I take a look?"

"Look, but don't touch," Manisha said dryly.

The girl smirked. Manisha's gaze flitted between the three strangers.

She didn't touch Noni when she bent down to study her. "If it's anything like a regular serpent—"

"She," Manisha corrected, standing watch over Noni.

"If she's anything like a regular serpent, then it seems that she's in brumation and also shedding."

"Oh." That would explain why her scales had dulled. Noni had recently molted and emerged much larger than before. It was incomprehensible to think how much bigger she might get. "Why are her eyes like that?"

"Don't you know anything about the animal your lineage is tied to?"

Manisha shook her head. How did this stranger know that Manisha was a nagin?

"Snakes shed from their eyes to their tails. They don't have eyelids like us, just scales. That's why her eyes look so strange. Don't worry. She'll shed her skin in its entirety and be back to normal in a few days to a couple of weeks."

Well, that explained why Noni had disappeared the last time she molted, but she hadn't taken weeks. Hopefully, she wouldn't take that long this time, either. What a relief to know that Noni wasn't dying!

The girl stood upright.

Manisha took a step back. "We'll be on our way now."

"No, you won't."

"Is that a threat?"

"No. But how you will carry this monstrous creature? She's not going anywhere. Moving her isn't wise. Not until she sheds."

All right. So Manisha couldn't drag Noni all the way to the

canyonlands. They would have to spend the night here. Under the stars. In the open. Exposed to potential dangers.

"We're not a threat," the girl said with a grin, flashing sharp points.

"Nice teeth."

"Oh, these?" She curled her upper lip and touched the tip of her tongue to a jagged tooth. "Better for tearing flesh off bone."

"We're *not* your meal. Let's make that clear."

"Don't worry. While we enjoy a good boa every now and then, this one looks a little too tough for our discerning tastes."

Manisha squinted. "Are you the infamous cannibals of Skanda?"

The girl narrowed her eyes, as if her existence was supposed to be a well-guarded secret. She leaned toward Manisha, her chin nearly touching the deadly blood-tipped arrow. "Yes. We file our teeth to make it easier to rip flesh. Cooking meat makes it tough and dry."

Manisha didn't waver, didn't blink. She wasn't afraid. One thrust at this range and this girl would be dead, venom-tipped or not.

She regarded Manisha for another second. "Aren't you afraid of us? That we, who outnumber you, could eat you alive?"

Manisha clucked her tongue and said without missing a beat, "I've been through worse."

The girl's impassiveness cracked into amusement. She, along with the other two, laughed, turning their entire demeanor from foe to friend. "Oh. I like you! My name's Deepa. What's yours?"

"Manisha," she replied bluntly, confused.

"You can put the blood-rusted arrow away. Why do you have blood on there anyway? Is it poison?"

"Observant, aren't you?"

"Incredibly. I know that bangle on your wrist signifies the naga."

Manisha swallowed. "What do you know about them?"

"Our people tried to protect one another during the Fire Wars, but our village succumbed. We had to send some of our men into servitude to the King's army in exchange for being left alone. Your people didn't negotiate. The last that I heard, the naga scattered across the plains, jungles, and some crossed the Great River. Somehow. Are you the one they're waiting for?"

"What?"

"A nagin came by a while back, looking for her sister. Is that you?"

Manisha lowered the arrow, relaxing the pull but keeping it in its notch. "Maybe."

Deepa smiled. Something that should've been so kind turned incredibly creepy with those teeth meant to shred flesh. "Finally! Where have you been?"

"Occupied?" croaked Manisha.

The girl glanced at Manisha's exposed arms, at the welts and ridges. "Were you enslaved?"

"Something like that."

"Well. You know what they say. What fails to kill you will make you much, much stronger."

"Sometimes what fails to kill you weakens you to a shell of your former self."

"I doubt that's true in your case."

The skies thundered in the distance behind the girls. They glanced back.

Deepa commented, "The monsoons have started. Soaking the snake's shedding skin in water may help, but you shouldn't get caught in the rains."

"I'm not leaving her."

Deepa sighed and nodded to the other two. They dismounted and went to work, foraging giant leaves and ferns from the edge of the plains.

"What are they doing?"

"Building you shelter. Your serpent might take days to shed."

"Oh," Manisha muttered, perplexed. "Th-thanks. But why would you do that for me?"

Deepa walked around, searching overhead for the best spot to set up. "Your people are friends. Particularly your sister."

"Really?" she asked skeptically. "What's her name?"

"Sithara. She has a twin named Eshani. Which makes you Manisha, the youngest."

Manisha faltered, closing her eyes. She hadn't heard anyone say her sisters' names in so long. It made them more real and less ghost. Her heart ached for them.

Deepa added, "I heard tales about you. I thought they were exaggerated stories. The girl who was buried alive during the Fire Wars and rose from the ashes. The girl who was sent off to hide in the open. Where did they hide you?"

"In the open," Manisha replied dryly.

"Up there," Deepa instructed the others. "The trees will be the safest area. It'll rain heavily tonight and for the next few days. Do you know how to climb?"

Manisha nodded, returning her weapon to her back in order to help carry leaves and vines.

"Good. You'll be able to gather water up there, too. Do you have a water container? Food?"

"Yes."

In no time, they'd built a small but sturdy shelter in the trees on the thickest limbs. Just high enough to withstand monsoon floods.

"What do you know about my sister?" Manisha asked as Deepa tied the last of the vines.

"She was focused and strategic. She didn't give a lot of information or get chatty, but she looked like she was in a hurry."

"What did she say?" Manisha asked, eager to know anything about her family, to find a clue as to what happened.

"Not much. Just to keep an eye out for you."

"Nothing about what happened to the others?"

"No."

She frowned. Manisha was hoping for more, but she could understand why her sister had been guarded.

"Why would you help?"

"Why wouldn't I? People looking for family because war drove them apart? I'd risk the King's wrath to help them. He has my husband in his army. At any given moment, he could be killed by King or battle. His death or desertion would render the agreement null. And we'll end up like your people. My husband is literally the only thing that prevents us from entering total chaos."

She touched her belly. Only now, as her touch flattened her loose top, did Manisha notice that she was with child. "We see one another illicitly when he happens to be nearby. It's been months. Your people did everything to fight and survive. Your family did everything to protect you. I don't really know much else of them, but I respect them. You can consider me a friend."

Deepa cocked her chin at the girl behind her. She handed Manisha a bag of food. "We carry this on trips in case we get caught outside of the village longer than expected. You should have it. Water buffalo paneer, paratha, chevdo, and nuts. I don't think you want leftover boa...."

Manisha cringed. "No, thanks. But thank you for this."

"You're headed to the canyonlands," Deepa stated rather than asked. "Be careful. The place is deserted but might be filled with dangers." She squinted toward the pall of darkness heading toward them. "We have to get back. Are you sure you want to stay here?"

Manisha glanced at Noni and nodded. "She needs me. I have to protect her."

"Noble." Deepa climbed onto her rhino and said, "Farewell, Manisha the Nagin. Stay high and dry. We'll check on you after the rains."

"Wait! Did my sister mention where she lived or if my mother's alive?"

Deepa gave a sad smile and shook her head. "She was guarded. I never asked, and she never told me."

"How . . . how long ago was this?"

Deepa sighed and thought for a second. "It's been at least . . ."

Manisha bit her lip, silently begging for something, *anything* that could support hope.

"At least several months. I can't remember how long ago exactly, but it was before I realized I was pregnant."

Manisha shuddered out a breath, holding back sobs. "Thank you for everything."

"Of course. Be well."

Manisha waved as they took off. They fled into the horizon, engulfed by sheets of rain. When they were out of view, she nearly collapsed to her knees. She covered her face, sobbing into her hands and overcome with a torrent of emotion.

Sithara was *alive*.

TWENTY-SIX

PRATYUSH
(PRESENT DAY)

Slayers didn't dodge questions any more than they dodged fights. Pratyush, however, *had* mastered the art of ignoring people. It was a gift, really.

"Where's Dev?" the General demanded for the twentieth time the following day.

"How should I know? Am I his better half?" Pratyush asked calmly.

"Isn't it your job to know where your men are?" the General spat.

"My job is to slay monsters."

"Isn't he your friend? Your best fighter?"

Pratyush rolled his eyes and rode faster uphill to get in front of Ras, who had Dev's horse tied to his.

Ras carefully glanced over his shoulder at the General before asking Pratyush, "Is he all right?"

"The General? Probably not. Dev? Probably yes."

The color had returned to Ras's face, but he had bags beneath his eyes.

"Are . . . you okay?"

Ras startled. "Yes. Why?"

"Calm down. Just wondering. You look tired and unnerved."

"No. I'm fine," he replied, as if trying to convince himself more than anyone else.

"It's okay if you're not."

Ras nodded, an acknowledgment out of respect, but didn't respond.

"Listen. I need my guys to be strong, brave, skilled, and smart. But they also have to recognize problems and take care of them, including asking for help or stepping back. A frazzled soldier is as good as dead. Do you need to step back?"

"No, Slayer. I'm good. I promise."

They were the first to mount the hill where golden morning light touched the horizon. There, in the distance, stood Dev. Pratyush smirked. For a minute, he thought he'd lost him. But Dev was true to his word. He would never risk endangering his village.

"Are your eyes not working as well as they used to?" Pratyush called back to the General. "Dev is *right* there."

"Where have you been?" the General roared.

"Scouting," Dev replied bluntly, his posture relaxed and unthreatened.

"Without your horse? Without telling anyone?"

"I went out for a piss and followed a trail. Before I knew it, I was halfway to the ravine. There was no point in going all the way back to camp. And I'm sure you wouldn't have liked your rest interrupted."

"That's a good point," Pratyush conceded. "You're obnoxious when you don't get your beauty sleep."

The General huffed, asking Dev, "Anything ahead?"

"Three hooded figures. Possibly the elders."

They hurried to the clearing, leaving jungle and stepping onto grassy flatlands. Open. Exposed. With nothing ahead except three hooded figures and a deep, dark crevasse splitting the grasslands into two. Above, scavengers floated in circles. Waiting.

The horses refused to move ahead. Something wasn't right. A few soldiers stayed back to guard them.

The skies darkened with rain clouds. The winds howled, chillingly eerie. There was a scent in the air, of dirt, mud, and erosive fluid. The kind arachnids and poisonous centipedes secreted.

Strange. Why was the air so heavy with it?

Pratyush and the soldiers fanned out around the three elders. They didn't move, just stood there staring ahead at the gorge.

"Who cares if they're worshipping or in the middle of a sacrifice?" the General snapped. "We don't have time to wait on heathens."

Three fighters walked around to the front of the elders and gasped, covering their mouths as the figures turned to Pratyush.

He swallowed and didn't react to the decayed, ashen skin and haunting white eyes, long nails, and hunched shoulders. The elders were frail old women.

"Are you the elders of Bharoda?" Pratyush asked.

They didn't respond.

"Can you understand me?"

They blinked, flashing those odd, milky eyes.

"We're from the King's army, tracking a threat. We need to ask you questions."

The woman in the middle, with one white eye and one completely black eye, turned her chin up to him.

"Answer him, you crones!" the General roared. "We haven't got all day!"

The elders didn't even flinch. They couldn't care less about the General, which made Pratyush like them.

The General stomped toward the trio, like he was going to snatch their arms and shake the truth out of them.

Pratyush stepped in front of him, gripping his battle-axe. "Don't touch them."

The General paused, casting an annoyed scowl at the slayer and then to the elders.

"I'm—" Pratyush began before they cut him off.

They began speaking from left to right, and then back, their voices shuddering and cryptic.

"The slayer."

"The one sent to behead the nagin."

"Who is not what you think she is."

"And is everything you didn't expect her to be."

"To slay..."

"Or not to slay..."

"When you discover the truth."

"Which is what?" Pratyush asked, mesmerized by the cadence of their voices flowing as one between them.

"That you know this monster."

He frowned. What did that even mean?

"She's poison and darkness."

"From fate told long ago."

"She's vengeance and light."

"From fate bestowed."

"So, the nagin *did* come through your village and your people lied?" the General said. "You understand that lying to the King's army is punishable by death?"

"Where is she?" Pratyush asked, wishing the General would just stay out of the way.

"The monster that you must slay to obtain the life that you most desire..." one of the elders started.

"Is the life you desire from the true monster you must slay," another ended.

"That . . . makes no sense," Pratyush mumbled.

"They speak in riddles," the General said. "It's nonsense. Where did the nagin go? What did she look like? What did she say and do?"

They ignored him and stepped toward the ravine. The soldiers found themselves in front of the elders, between them and the gorge, and automatically moved into position, their swords unsheathed as if these frail, old women were dangerous.

"A sacrifice must be made," said one of the elders.

"To a new queen," another added.

"Born from the ashes," the third said.

"To reset the tilted crown," all three intoned.

At first, Pratyush thought the subtle rumble was him scoffing. Then he realized that it hadn't come from him at all. He turned toward the movement.

Behind the soldiers, two giant, crooked, hairy arms crawled out of the ravine. An arachnid the size of two houses peered up and over the lip of the cliff, all eight eyes black voids gaping at the men. Pincers snatched up the soldier directly in front of it before anyone could react.

His cries were like banshee screams as the arachnid lifted him high off the ground. He swung his sword at the monster, but the blade broke and rattled to the ground.

The arachnid dipped back into the ravine as the other two soldiers rushed to the ledge.

"Wait!" Pratyush called, but it was too late. He'd barely managed to throw out an arm in time to at least stop Ras.

Dev knew better.

A string of thick white webbing cast out, landing on a soldier's face, covering his nose and mouth and parts of his eyes. He clutched at it, but it was no use. The webbing went taut, and he went flying into the crevasse.

One didn't need to look over the edge to know what had become of him. His screams were gone faster than a blink.

The third soldier had the good sense to run, but not before a gigantic lamprey lurched up and swooshed down. Its gaping, round mouth, full of oscillating teeth, latched onto the fighter's arm, biting it right off.

Pratyush grabbed him by his uninjured arm and yanked him away, swiping his battle-axe across the beast's eye. It moaned and dropped back.

Pratyush wasn't going to stand around, oblivious to the situation and wondering what happened to the beast and the two soldiers. He wasn't a hero. He wasn't the guy who went flying into the night to save every soul. He had *one* job. To slay monsters, the nagin. Not rescue every living person from here to there.

A part of him wanted to skid into that ravine and slay them all—what he imagined his father would've done. But Pratyush knew better; he knew what was there. He smelled it in the air: mucus and slime, blood and poison. That ravine was filled with dozens of horrors. He wasn't invincible. He also wasn't impetuous enough to jump into their territory without a plan or a way out.

Instead, he ran to the tree line, dragging the soldier behind him and shoving Ras ahead of them. Toward the horses who knew better than to have gotten that close.

The remainder of the soldiers gathered around the injured fighter, who rolled on the ground. Some tried to hold him still. Someone else shoved a stick into his mouth for him to bite on.

"Give me the torch," Pratyush huffed, stretching his arm out to an older boy.

They held the soldier down while Pratyush set one knee on his shoulder and used the torch to cauterize his arm. The robust stench of burning flesh and sizzling blood gorging the air faded out all other smells. Both nauseating and sweet. Sure to linger in their nostrils for days.

The soldier's cries faded as he passed out in a blanket of dark smoke, convulsing with the last of the shock. His skin turned pallid, his eyes sunk, like the life force had been drained from him with that one bite. Maybe it had. Maybe he was as good as dead.

Pratyush crawled off and released a ragged breath, gulping and shaking.

The elders had never moved. But they watched him. It was all so eerie and weird.

They'd gotten their sacrifice, all right.

The injured soldier couldn't continue with them. He couldn't even wake up. They had to leave him and hope that they'd carried him far enough into the jungle that the creatures from the ravine wouldn't sniff him out and finish eating him.

The horrifying thing, though? Many creatures did just that. Injected poison to slow down their prey so they could track them later, for sport or for ease.

The group couldn't spare a person to stay behind with the soldier, either. So they reluctantly said their solemn farewells and moved on, some offering prayers, including quick funeral rites. They all sort of knew his fate wasn't going to end well.

Numbers had dwindled. Now there was a horse for each soldier to ride.

They were heading back when the General broke the grueling silence. "There's supposed to be a hidden trail here to get across."

Pratyush glanced at Dev. He knew that trail; it was the one leading to his village. Dev wasn't about to let the King's army use it, and neither would his people.

"Let's just hurry," a soldier demanded, terrified.

Crotch-punch guy?

How the hell had he even made it this far? Unless he rode a horse across the meadows, helped the General with his tent to leave the yakshini's territory first, and stayed behind with the horses at the ravine...

Yep. Sounded about right.

Pratyush contemplated a way to argue with the General about cutting across the hidden trail to protect Dev's people. When, suddenly, something spooked the entire herd of horses, and they took off running. It took a while to them get them under control, and by then, the group was far from the hidden trail.

"We can go back!" crotch-punch guy complained.

In the next second, his horse whinnied, kicking up its front legs and bucking him off. Something long, slender, and hairy stomped right through crotch-punch guy's head. His skull exploded. Blood and brain matter splattered against the ferns.

The horses broke into a gallop right as another leg stomped down beside Pratyush, catching his shirt and snatching him off his fleeing horse.

He grunted when he hit the ground, his back slamming against uneven terrain and rocks. He was pinned but still able to get his battle-axe from his back. The thing had sliced his leg, and his blood would attract more. He had to end this quickly, if he could stop shaking from the pain ricocheting from his wound.

He looked up at the underside of a behemoth spider, its eyes trained on him. It didn't make sense for it to come out into the open, to enter the jungle.

Pratyush grunted and swiped clean through the spider, barely missing getting doused in its—probably toxic—blood.

The thing screeched, stomping with its other legs as Pratyush chopped it down, section by section. It cast a web at him, and he dodged, flinching every time he landed on his shredded leg. If that web got him, he was done for. In a matter of seconds, it would have him rolled into a neat cocoon so it could drain his insides.

And then . . . a spiraling headache hit. *Really?* Now? But this wasn't a normal headache. He'd felt this before. His vision split, and *she* appeared. That girl from the meadows with the thorns to her back, her eyes glowing green and her lips red like blood glistening in the moonlight.

"I told you not to go after her," she said.

"Who are you?" Pratyush shouted, then dodged. He almost got decapitated by another leg!

Focus! Stop talking to strange girls and kill the monster!

Arrows whooshed through the air as Dev called out, "Duck!"

Didn't have to tell him twice. Pratyush hit the ground as a cloud of fiery arrows hit the beast. With half its legs cut off and the rest set on fire, it should've retreated to the ravine where these things usually stayed. Yet here they were.

There was an agonized look in its many eyes, not the typical vacant kind. Like maybe it wanted to retreat but couldn't.

Pratyush jerked toward the mirage and swung at the girl. His parashu went through, leaving a disrupted cloud of smoke in her wake. She was gone. And finally, the beast screeched and retreated.

Pratyush dropped to his knees. Panting, he watched the creature until it was gone. Dev and Ras and a few others ran to him, helping him up. But first things first. He had to tend to his injury, or the thing would hunt him down.

"Thanks for coming back for me," he told them, knowing the General had nothing to do with the help.

"If you die, I'll never hear the end of it," Dev said.

Pratyush meant to smirk but ended up grimacing.

Dev helped clean the wound while Ras searched a bag for supplies.

"Looks like we'll have to go through the marshlands after all, but I don't think that thing will follow," Pratyush told the General.

"Fine," he barked from his horse, annoyed.

"You're welcome," Pratyush grunted. Next time the General could get speared in the face by a giant spider leg, then.

Ras and Dev wrapped up his leg. Ras flinched when he realized how close he was to Dev.

"What?" Dev growled.

Ras carefully looked at him and asked, "Do you, um, ever think about eating me?"

Dev scowled. "You're not ready."

"Oh. Like . . . aged meat?" he asked with a wretched look.

Dev grinned so that his filed teeth gleamed. "I could always try a bite, though."

"No, thanks," Ras replied dryly.

Dev laughed. "I like him," he said to Pratyush.

"Yeah. Do me a favor and watch his back," Pratyush said with a sigh as he leaned back for a second, his gash under control. He felt his scraped bones healing, the veins snapping back together, and his skin fusing.

∽§∾

THERE WERE A FEW DISTURBING THINGS ABOUT THE MARSH-lands, aside from the unusual bitter cold and frost nipping at any exposed flesh. Pratyush had traveled through these parts a few times. He knew to keep his eyes low and not react to what was around him, or what he thought was around him. Most of this was an illusion.

But the cold and darkness were real.

The marsh ghost light was *not* real. It couldn't be because there was no opening in the canopy or clouds for light to shine down.

Only darkness lived here. It was why people believed this was the gateway to the Nightmare Realm. The squirming mass of black in the river and streams were clumps of flesh-eating hagfish. As long as a man was tall, shaped like an eel, with oval mouths filled with three rows of muscle-ripping teeth. They were like lamprey but cast nets of slime to entrap and confuse prey.

"Stay away from the water," he warned.

By far the worst things in the marshlands were the shades. They nibbled away at the insides and made people go mad.

"Keep your chins down," he ordered.

They walked through the marshlands instead of riding on horses. Thankfully, Pratyush's leg had healed enough for him to go on foot. Shades could easily peer into their eyes if they were that high on horses. Even if they didn't, horses spooked easily, and one outburst could send a horse kicking them off into a place they didn't want to land.

They came to a dead stop when a towering figure cloaked in gleaming black peered at them from around a tree at a bend in the stream. It was in the shape of a muscular man, tall with a bulbous head. It had two oblong white eyes and thin lips spreading from nonexistent ear to nonexistent ear. Those lips slowly curled upward in a maniacal, cryptic grin. Saliva dripped from razor-sharp teeth filling half its head.

The soldiers removed their swords to fight.

Pratyush put out a hand, palm facing the ground, indicating they back down.

The beast suddenly ran at him, but Pratyush didn't move. His heart hammered in his chest. He sucked in a breath. The thing stopped inches from his face. He didn't look it in the eye, but lowered his gaze to its claws, which curled and uncurled with faint snaps and cracks of its bones. He wasn't going to lie; it was unnerving as hell to be so close to razor claws that they could flick the hair on his arm. One wrong move on his part, or even annoyance on the beast's part, would end him. If no one provoked it, maybe it would let them pass without a single soul lost.

The man next to Pratyush unsheathed his sword, drawing its attention. The beast moved over to stand in front of him.

"Don't," Pratyush murmured.

"Kill it," the General ordered.

Ugh. The General always undermined him.

The creature threw its head back, mouth agape, and hissed, shooting stringy saliva across the soldier's face. Instinctively, he attacked the beast. And naturally, the beast swiped at the soldier. Its wide claws slashed the man clean through, four cuts from its four talons: across the forehead, nose, mouth, and throat. He dropped to the ground, his blood gurgling. The beast stepped onto what remained of the soldier's head, crushing his skull. His brains and fluids squelched with the most nauseating echo.

All around, fighters slowly unsheathed their swords.

"Don't," Pratyush growled.

"Prepare," the General countered.

The soldiers glanced from the slayer to the General, confused. It didn't matter now. It was over.

This inky creature was a harbinger of the darkness to come. And the horses knew. They broke free, rearing onto their hind legs, front legs kicking the air above the soldiers' heads. Their eyes wide and frightened as a battle cry of neighs exploded.

They took off, whinnying all the way.

The shades emerged. Four smoky creatures that killed by being inhaled, making victims bleed from literally every orifice and pore. They turned insides into tar. And if you weren't that lucky, they'd drag you to the Nightmare Realm.

The shades were impossible to kill. But they were also slow.

"Run!" Pratyush yelled.

TWENTY-SEVEN

MANISHA
(FIVE DAYS AGO)

The winds were howling louder than a pack of wolves.

From her small shelter, Manisha hadn't taken her eyes off Noni in three days. She'd managed to move Noni closer to the trees so that she wasn't soaked with monsoon rains the entire time. She'd also managed to arrange her into coils to keep her head at the top just in case the valley flooded. That'd been grueling, and now her entire body was sore and achy, but she would do it again.

While she was anxious for Noni to wake up and be okay, to get back on their journey, it was nice to sit. But *rest* was a relative term. The marshlands (and everything creepy about them) weren't terribly far away. Any of those dark creatures could venture out. And being in one place allowed Manisha a lot of time to think about Sithara.

Where was she now? What had she been doing out this way again? Had she returned to the canyonlands like her letter had implied? Were other naga there, too? Where were Eshani and Mama?

Manisha grunted, pulling her knees to her chest. She pressed her forehead to her knees. Anxiety was climbing back up. She was so close to her family, and yet so far.

She shook off the woes and worries and what-ifs and went through the food rations. The water buffalo paneer made her eyelids flutter with delight. She hadn't had this kind of cheese since before the war. It was as tangy and rich and wonderful as she'd remembered. Back home, someone was always making paneer. Sometimes eaten like this, but most times lightly fried with leafy palak or marinated and roasted with potatoes and onions. Paneer was a hardy cheese that didn't melt and was very filling.

This small portion lasted Manisha a while, which was good because the rains were keeping her and Noni in place.

Monsoons reached the canyonlands every year, too, turning dry valley beds into torrential rivers. The city of Anand sat higher up and didn't face immediate danger. Manisha fondly remembered running around barefoot, splashing in puddles and ignoring scolding parents. Papa always had a warm fire in their stone home. Mama always had dry clothes for the sisters to change into as soon as they came inside, coupled with blankets and hot broth.

They would sit on the floor or in bed and listen to Papa tell stories while Mama snuggled them. Sithara would whine that she was too old to be hugged like a baby, but everyone knew she loved it the most.

Manisha stretched out her legs. Although it was midday, it was as dark as twilight. It was impossible to hear anything other than the rain and thunder, and nearly impossible to see through the rain. But something moved across the empty space ahead.

They came from the left, from somewhere between the marshlands and the jungle. Maybe from the hidden trail Deepa had mentioned.

They didn't look like Deepa's people. They were lighter-skinned, shorter, and wore brown clothes like the men from the village that had taken Rani.

Had they followed Manisha here?

She knelt near the edge of the shelter where rain rolled down from the roof. Mindful not to slip or destroy the precarious vulnerability of the makeshift shelter, she grabbed her weapons.

"Is she here?" one man yelled over the rain when they were closer.

"I don't see her! No way she would be nearby! There's no huts or caves or high ground," another called back.

A third man bellowed, "She must've left the beast!"

Manisha steadied her breathing, finding a calm, as they crept toward Noni.

"Or she *is* the beast! Isn't that what your cousin said? We need to kill it for what it's done!"

The other two roared in agreement. Manisha clutched the bow and took an arrow tipped in her blood.

"Then off with her head!"

"Yes! Who does she think she is, attacking us?"

That isn't right at all, she thought. How could they not see that she was defending herself against unspoken horrors?

"It doesn't look great. Is it alive?" the second asked.

"Are you sure this is the one?" the first asked.

"Don't be stupid! How many monstrous serpents are out here?!"

"What's wrong with it?" the third asked.

"Who knows! Maybe it ate something that it shouldn't have!"

"Not taking chances! We have to kill it! Now, while it's vulnerable!"

The third carefully trudged through the mud toward Noni. Manisha readied her arrow. He poked Noni with a spear either too gently or with a blunt spearhead, or maybe Noni's molted skin was tough, because she didn't move or bleed.

He snarled and pushed the spear harder. The spear bowed and snapped.

The others sloshed around Noni, her head sitting on a pedestal of coils. Could she detect their heat in this cold or hear them above the rain? Was she playing asleep to protect herself, or was she really locked in that deep of a brumation?

They stood in front of her snout, her coiled body slightly higher, forcing them to look up. Yet they didn't see Manisha perched in the trees directly in front of them through the downpour.

"We can defang it so it can't bite! Then break its jaw so it's unable to swallow us. It'll be in so much pain that it won't have the strength to escape or hurt anyone. Then we pierce it from inside its mouth. Surely its insides are more vulnerable!"

Manisha grimaced.

"Are you sure about this?" another asked, blinking through the barrage of rain weighing down his face.

"Yes. Two of us will need to climb up and pull its head back, the third to pull the lower jaw down."

"We need rope! Vines! We can't have our hands in its jaws!"

"Gouge out its eyes first!"

Two of the men pulled out daggers.

Heat pulsed through Manisha: fury, vengeance, unbridled loyalty.

She aimed the blood-tipped arrow and called down in a voice so booming that it made her throat ache, "*Don't* move!"

"Who's there?" they demanded, tilting their heads up. But they couldn't see through pouring rain.

Manisha glared down the shaft of the arrow. Her eyesight sharpened on minuscule sections of light cutting between falling drops of incandescent rain. It was as if the monsoon, and the rest of the world, slowed down just for her. "*Final* warning. Move one step closer to the serpent, and this'll be your end."

"It's her!" one cried. "The nagin!"

"Cut the snake before she gets to us!" another yelled.

And with that, all three raised daggers to plunge into Noni.

Manisha released with the decisiveness of her sisters. Arrow after arrow, faster than she'd ever been, with clarity and vision sharper than she could ever imagine.

The arrows went right through their hearts. Their movements slowed, like being underwater.

The first man screamed, his arm up in mid-strike.

The second man cried out, his arm lower, the blade close to Noni.

The third man yelled in pain, his knees bent, one leg slipping in the mud, the other leaning toward Noni. His dagger made it the closest to Noni, the tip inches from her eye.

All three changed in waves, stone skittering across them like scales, transforming flesh and bone into eternal statues.

Manisha heaved out a breath, one after another. Her hands trembled as she searched the area for others, but she didn't see or hear anyone else. No one emerged. That didn't mean she was alone.

She stayed in place, hidden inside the shelter, ready to defend Noni to the end. Nothing moved her. Not sleep, cold, hunger, or dampness. She stayed in position.

Two more days of infuriating rain passed. Manisha eventually fell asleep.

In this rain, Noni's molted skin had softened. She moved on the third day when Manisha had finished the last of her food and refilled the water containers. Her heart spilled over with joy and relief. She hadn't been this happy since Papa had rewarded her with a pomegranate the morning before the kingdom attacked.

Noni shifted under the blades held by stone men, rubbing aggressively against the ground and the statues to snag her skin. She writhed out of her shedding.

Manisha gleefully climbed down and sloshed through the mud. She carefully anchored her knife into the dead layer of Noni's skin and peeled, helping her emerge from the cocoon of opaqueness. Noni's shimmering golden scales were dazzling, and, in that moment, the rains ceased. Sunlight filtered through thinning clouds, easing their agitation.

Noni looked at Manisha with those beautiful moss-speckled eyes, no longer a sickly bluish opacity. Her mouth was curved upward as if she were smiling.

Manisha threw her hands around Noni's neck and hugged her tight. She wept, "I thought I'd lost you! I was so worried."

Noni nuzzled her, as if saying she'd missed her, too. Did Noni have any idea what had happened? The brumation, the attack, how Manisha defended her?

It didn't matter.

Manisha would grapple through a hundred more days protecting Noni if it meant saving her.

When Noni finished shedding, Manisha created a pile and burned the molted skin, leaving no trace of her precious Noni.

Just in case others were hunting them.

TWENTY-EIGHT

MANISHA
(TWO DAYS AGO)

Manisha and Noni had been traveling for what felt like forever and yet no time at all. Exhaustion mixed with revived hope warped her sense of time. Sithara had been close by not too long ago.

Ahead, the tops of the flattened canyons appeared. Granite and limestone and marble surfaces dotted with sporadic trees and bushes across the topmost ledge. Something warm and memorable gushed through Manisha's soul. A sense of home, familiarity, happiness, much needed family, and people. *Her* people.

She ran. Her heart racing, face beaming, skin thrumming. She sprinted past Noni, who wistfully watched and slithered after her.

"We're almost home!" she cried, bouncing into the air like a little girl chasing butterflies.

With renewed energy, Manisha ran faster, harder, almost keeping pace with Noni. Wind whipped through her hair. Her shoes pounded against pebbles and dry ground. The looming surface of the canyonlands appeared, stretching higher into the skies like a yawning giant.

Home.

Manisha was finally home.

MEMORIES FLOATED AROUND MANISHA LIKE HAUNTING
ghosts clashing with reality.

A long, winding path lined with sconces—bowls atop seven-foot
slender pillars—stretched out half a mile ahead. This was the road
into Anand.

Instead of being filled with brush and flammable sap and oils to
light the way to town, the sconces were filled with bioluminescent
plants. During the day, dark green ivy cascaded to the ground. At
night, the ivy glowed lime green, speckled with pulsating yellow
blooms like twinkling stars.

In this ascending twilight, the colors of day and night melted
together in a spectacular glow that had Manisha's eyes teeming with
tears, with unfathomable longing.

The entrance to Anand was a massive archway in a wall of granite. Once etched and sculpted into magnificent stories of serpents
and stars, the stone had eroded. Heaps of crumbled granite, broken
images, and shattered tales gathered dust.

Manisha closed her eyes and let memories guide the way. They rustled through her thoughts, awakening from a deep slumber.

The entrance opened around the town square with a massive, dried
fountain at its center. Structures built into the canyon walls loomed
all around, some as high as four stories. Endless balconies had once
been full of color in curtains of climbing vines and gardens. Broken
carts were scattered across the splintered streets, partway overgrown
with prickly shrubs. Shards of vases and containers, pieces of frayed
fabrics and toys, and all sorts of marketplace remnants were scattered
around the once-dazzling bazaar. Above, open windows gaped—
empty homes in an abandoned town.

Manisha's skin tingled. Her house was ahead to the right, calling her from the depths of buried memories. The last of the fading sunlight showed the way to what could only be described as a stone palace around a dusty courtyard. The greenery had faded along with her people.

She pushed through the gates and stood at the threshold to her home. The place where she'd played with her sisters, where they'd been raised, where their grandparents had lived with them. Where they were loved and nurtured and had only known happiness.

A once-great city brimming with prosperity had eroded into fragmented emptiness.

She touched the crumbling, cracked walls, closing her eyes as memories pulsed through her palm. Laughter, hushed conversations, joy. Women with long braids adorned with hibiscus and jasmine blooms, tending to children, sitting in the courtyard beneath flourishing plum and fig trees. Girls with unruly curls running around fruitful pomegranate trees twice their size. Men with commanding postures grinning and hoisting their little ones onto their shoulders. Boys and girls exchanging shy smiles as their families contemplated their unions. Young women round with child. Elderly ones knitting and sewing on steps, chattering about life.

It had been a place of knowledge and skill, a happy, warm place where everyone knew everyone and hospitality reigned.

Tears streamed down Manisha's face as she held back sobs. The stories of her people poured into her soul, clashing for attention, bubbling over the rim, expanding until she nearly combusted. Fulfilling yet painful as pressure built. Too many emotions, too many strings of various lives intertwining, excitedly sharing their stories as if these voices had been muted for the past five years. Torture rose and filled a depleted void.

They were ghosts—memories—but in their company, she finally felt whole.

This city had once been pristine, with sleek marble floors and walls stained with art and stonework. Filled with statues of serpents climbing ever higher. Depictions of peacocks and tigers and elephants. Roses and jasmine and ivy climbed trellises and archways. Fountains were dotted with fish and lotus. Canopies of crawling vines crossed the tallest fruit and nut trees.

They'd been at peace, more concerned with bringing life to the canyonlands than waging war. They weren't perfect and had problems, but they didn't fight among themselves. They upheld amicable hospitality with other peoples, trading goods and knowledge.

Until the kings rose to power.

The kingdom didn't want peace. It wanted dominance.

The kingdom didn't want to exchange goods and knowledge. It wanted to own them.

The kingdom didn't want to learn new cultures. It wanted to snuff them out.

The King wanted an empire of subservient loyalty. An army to destroy anything he deemed a threat. He wanted riches. Always riches.

Maybe the King believed too much in myth. That the naga were hiding the location to a cavern filled with celestial weapons called astra, the immortal elixir of life known as amrita, and riches beyond anyone's wildest dreams. Enough to adorn the world in beauty or control the world with greed.

Legend spoke of the Chelamma—a scorpion goddess who guarded the entrance to the caverns. She commanded and rode giant beasts with scorpion tails and pincers strong enough to cut a boar in two with one clench.

She lived in a fortress atop a winding labyrinth leading to the treasures. Legend said that each tower in her home was topped with statues of men with wings and talons for hands and feet. They were made of stone, perched on high to watch for invaders, but came to life at night or when called upon by the Chelamma.

Had the King annihilated the naga over this rural tale?

Manisha's footfalls were a soft cadence reverberating against splintered walls, hitting dusty tapestries and shelves, pedestals, and broken ornaments. Tall, fractured floor vases were filled with wilted and dead stems, some with faded peacock feathers dredged with debris.

She walked upstairs to her room, the one she'd shared with her sisters. Her palm smoothed over rumpled and dusty bedspreads and a quilt made by her mother and aunts. Maybe she could wash it without it falling apart, to preserve *something* from long ago, last touched by Mama's hands.

Toys slumped in the corner, covered in a layer of thick dirt. Leaves splayed the floor and surfaces from years of wind pushing past open windows and faded curtains, now riddled with holes.

She searched the room for clues. If her sisters expected her to return here, they would've planted a clue in her room.

There wasn't anything beneath the mattresses or beds, behind dressers or in closets. There were no hidden compartments in the floors or walls.

Manisha desperately clung to hope. She planted her hands on her hips and looked out the window. She used to love sitting at the window, picking custard apples from the tree right outside. That tree had kept growing, its dried leaves dancing across the floor of her room.

The curtains fluttered in the breeze, but the heavy tassels behind it did not.

Hmm. She didn't remember having tassels in the house.

She touched the leather. It wasn't a tassel, but the long end of a whip that curled across the top of the window, on top of the worn curtains. She brought it down, wiped the dust from it, and smiled at the three serpents etched onto the handle. Sithara's handiwork.

Coiling it, she hooked the holder to her waist and moved on. She took in all the memories of her home, ending in her parents' room.

Two vases were left intact on the bedside table, filled with decrepit plants that would turn to powder with one breath. She hiccupped, holding a hand to her mouth. Like ghosts swaying across the room, she could see her mother filling vases with fresh flowers, arranging them just so. And Papa, a man who adored color, pulling out a rainbow plumeria to tuck into Mama's hair. They'd laugh and dance and fill the house with love.

Manisha cleaned off the bedspread and turned it upside down, brushing off any unwanted things. The mattress, once fluffy and filled with feathers, was flat and lumpy.

She crawled into her parents' bed, curled up, and wept enough tears to fill the Great River.

TWENTY-NINE

PRATYUSH
(PRESENT DAY)

They'd run for their lives through the marshlands. Not everyone had escaped. That was the cost. The shades could be preoccupied with victims. They could capture some or chase the rest; they couldn't do both.

Pratyush jumped from the cold clutches of the darkness nipping at the back of his neck and skidded down the steep side of a hill, ignoring the pain in his injured leg. Some soldiers fell behind him, others leapt, and one even ran all the way to the bottom with unstoppable momentum.

They all ended the same way: at the bottom of the hill in clusters, panting and searching the tall, thin trees for movement. The horses, having escaped long before the team, stood in the distance grazing as if they hadn't just been spooked by insidious creatures.

"How many did we lose?" the General heaved.

"Four," Ras replied after a head count, his own chest heaving.

At this rate, Pratyush would be facing the nagin alone.

THE TEAM CAME ACROSS A SET OF STATUES NOT FAR AWAY. Pratyush studied the trio of stone men. Three perfect engraved images, carved with incredible detail, from the individual hairs on their heads and beards to the wrinkles in their soaked clothes. Rain trickled down every ridge in rivulets. Beauty and pain. Their expressions of determination and agony were palpable. Three men with three angles of attack, each closer than the last in an artistic arch of the arms and lean of the legs.

"What do you suppose they were attacking?" Ras asked.

"The nagin, obviously," the General spat from his horse. "What else is turning men into stone? These brave men, perhaps avenging their fellow villagers or fighting off an attack or even preemptively striking, turned to stone. They're heroes."

Ras and Dev gave Pratyush a look, like *Were they really?*

Pratyush walked around the statues, noting the dried mud on their shoes and the depressed mud in front of them. It hadn't been long since she'd been here, the snake in women's clothing. Maybe a day or two. A circular, heavy thing had sat in front of the statues but had moved on, leaving a trail. Was the nagin truly also a serpent? A gigantic one, at that!

The statues had been in the process of attacking something directly in front of them. That much was obvious. Something heavy and large, possibly coiled into a circle. A serpent was beginning to form in his thoughts. He could see it better now. Towering height, immense weight, incomprehensible strength, and incalculable speed all wrapped into one frightening monster.

But the arrows? Pratyush sniffed. They smelled faintly familiar. Like jungle and dirt and blood. Memories thrashed around in his thoughts. Where had he smelled something so close to this scent before? He tried and tried, so close, but still, he couldn't pull out the specific memory to solve this mystery.

Agitated, he growled underneath his breath.

The arrows had come from directly ahead of the statues, piercing their hearts from the front. But not at eye level. The arrows were slanted down. He gauged the angle and looked ahead, then up.

The creature hadn't raised itself and released arrows. Whatever had been directly in front of the men was too close to have shot arrows. Which meant someone, maybe the nagin, if she wasn't the serpent, had been in the trees and shot them from above.

Was the accomplice alone? How could they shoot three arrows so quickly if the men attacked together?

There were a lot of questions here, but no more clues.

"Let's go," he finally said.

The dwindling team was just moving on when something yellowish, buried in the mud, caught Pratyush's eye. He picked it up and held it to the sun.

"What is it?" Ras asked, leaning in for a better look.

Opaque, rigid, oblong, and longer than his hand. "A scale, I think."

"*One* scale?"

"Yeah. Maybe it molted."

"Monstrous," Ras whispered with a shudder.

The scale fell from his hand and fluttered to the ground. While the others were wondering how big this serpent truly was, Pratyush was wondering where the rest of its shedding went.

Behind them, across the valley, was the village of Skanda. Had Dev's people seen anything?

Pratyush mounted his horse and rode side by side with Dev on the wide trails leading down the valley. He asked, "Did your people mention the nagin?"

Dev eyed him. "Simply that things are not always what they appear to be."

"What does that mean? Is the nagin a twenty-foot serpent who turns men into stone or not?"

"There *is* a very large serpent out there. As for the rest of the tale? I'm unsure. Every story has at least two sides. I don't plan on attacking this creature without knowing why I'm attacking."

"What? You want to give her the chance to turn you into stone?"

Dev didn't respond. So, his village *had* met the nagin. Why hold back information on a monster they were about to face? Did he even know more?

As they traveled, Pratyush caught glimpses every now and then of footsteps in the dried mud. Small feet. Who else had been on this path? Was the nagin changing between snake and woman? Or were the two traveling together?

As mud turned into dirt and grass, the trail faded.

Ahead, the peaks of the canyonlands rose from the depths of the valley like a welcoming beacon. Or a call to battle.

They were closing in on the nagin. The fight he'd been waiting for was approaching. And once he clutched her severed head for the King to see, he would have his property, his rest, and maybe even Manisha.

THIRTY

MANISHA
(PRESENT DAY)

Manisha picked fruit alongside abandoned homes, a medley of custard apples, figs, and apricots. She took her breakfast to the top of the canyon peaks by way of steps that had been carved into the outer wall near a guard's tower.

The valley was beautiful from here, the river behind her alive with the sounds of gushing water. A gentle breeze cut through the humidity with a subtle taste of faraway rain. Birds chirped from trees, white butterflies danced around scattered blossoms, and trickling water echoed from cracked roofs. Manisha enjoyed the moment of rest, even past memories spilling into a joyful sadness. All was peaceful until a line appeared in the distance, advancing quickly and heading straight for Anand.

She lay on her stomach and watched, chewing her last bite. Her hearing picked up subtle sounds. Birds, animals, the hooves of galloping horses. As they neared, their voices carried, bubbling up the granite wall.

"The tracks continue south," one of them said. He sounded so familiar.

"Yes. Just as the villagers said," another confirmed. He also sounded familiar.

There were several intruders, too many for one girl to handle. They didn't look like villagers, not with their dark-colored clothes with silver patches on the chest, swords and scabbards inlaid with silver, and heavy boots. Many had trimmed hair with short beards.

When the boy in the lead turned his head, a flash of his profile sparked Manisha's memory. *The slayer.*

Her heart cantered in her chest. A fleeting sense of relief and familiarity. Someone she knew! Someone who had been unerringly kind to her, who had encouraged her true self when it wasn't very apsara-like. After all this time, Manisha never thought she'd see a familiar face again, much less the one person who had brought her some sort of joy during her time at the temple.

Maybe he would help her. After all, he'd wanted to marry her. He said he loved her. But why was he here? Was he tracking her? Was he searching for the girl he claimed to love, or for an enemy of the King? Did he know what she was?

Whatever spark of optimism she'd had fizzled.

Her gaze drifted to the man riding beside him. And all hope slipped away.

The General.

Her body turned heavy, instantly petrified. Heaving, she sank into the tower and wished she could disappear. No matter how powerful she'd become, or that others called her a warrior—despite whatever resolve she'd set for herself... the only thing she knew in this moment was immense terror.

NONI, BEING HER SWEET SELF, HAD MANAGED TO FIT through narrow corridors and side streets to find Manisha and was slithering up the building. But while many naga structures were made from granite, they'd taken a lot of damage. Noni, with her enormous weight, crashed through the roof, startling Manisha back to reality and forcing her to move.

She rushed toward the crash, which was probably loud enough for the encroaching army to hear. She found Noni shaking her head and whining with a long, restrained hiss. Jagged edges of broken granite and wood had shredded her side. Bright green blood oozed from her many cuts.

"Oh my stars! Don't move!"

Manisha ran to her house in a panic and gathered sheets for bandages. She wrapped one layer over another around Noni's midsection to stop the bleeding.

Noni suddenly stilled, and Manisha followed suit, her heart racing.

"They're here, aren't they?"

Noni gave a sweeping nod. She could probably feel the vibrations in the ground.

"We must go and not leave a trail. Can you move?" Manisha asked, rubbing Noni's head above the eyes.

Noni rose slowly, dazed, and moved ever so carefully. She followed Manisha through the tight corridors to the decayed ruins of a partially covered amphitheater. They could hide in here for now, until Manisha figured something out.

They went down winding stairs. Pieces crumbled and fell beneath them from their weight. Some steps fell away completely.

Tattered theater curtains were piled up in one corner, sitting pillows in another, and broken pottery in yet another.

"Keep going," Manisha told her, retracing her steps up the stairs. She tiptoed across the room until she spotted them.

The soldiers walked with quiet footfalls, some with swords out, others armed with bows and arrows. Definitely hunting.

Manisha stole a breath, and then another, her hands shaking. With her back to the wall, her breathing even, she considered options. She couldn't keep hiding. They knew she was here; she could tell by the way they'd quieted and split to comb the area. They were soldiers. The slayer was a tracker. He would find her.

Were they looking for Manisha because she'd left the floating mountains? Were they searching for her because they knew her truth—what she was capable of, what she'd already done? Or were they hunting Noni? *What* had those villagers told them?

Manisha had to protect Noni. She had to hide her, but where?

Ah! The labyrinths beneath the enclosed amphitheater.

She returned to Noni and said, "Come with me."

Manisha made sure every turn was clear. Dim rooms turned even darker as the duo trekked away from windows and openings. Manisha's eyesight was sharp, though, regardless of the dark.

They inched closer to the fractured edges of a long, large fissure. Manisha peered into its depths. Darkness lined with glowing red vines to light the way. What had happened here? An earthquake? A rumble powerful enough to split the earth in two, exposing the labyrinth below?

It was wide enough for Noni and deep enough for her to completely disappear into.

Manisha paused and listened. She didn't think there was anything down there, but Noni could probably take care of it if there was.

"Go down. Escape through the tunnels."

Noni swung her head toward Manisha and nudged her. Manisha's heart sank as she rubbed the space between Noni's eyes. "I can't come. If they're looking for you, then they won't stop searching. If they're looking for me, then they'll find me. I have to fight them off. This must end here."

Noni nudged her again, and Manisha's heart broke.

Her voice cracked as she pleaded, "Please. We don't have time. If they see you, they'll try to kill you."

Manisha hugged Noni tight and begged, "Please, go, Noni. I don't think you've fully recovered from everything that's happened. You're not as fast. You're injured. Stronger than all of them, I know, even at your worst, but I can't risk anything happening to you. I *will* fight them off and come for you. Don't worry about me. This isn't the end of our story."

She pushed her. "Go. *Now.*"

Noni moaned but slipped down the fissure, her long, heavy golden tail disappearing with the grace of a slow fall.

Manisha sucked in a breath, turned, and ran back up the steps where sunlight crested through jagged openings and shattered windows.

When she ducked through another section, a soldier jumped down through a hole in the roof and landed in front of her.

"Nagin?" he asked, perplexed. "You're just a little girl."

She gasped as he drew his sword and lunged, not even waiting for an answer. He would really, so easily, attack "a little girl"?

Her reflexes were swift, elegant, sliding to the side, dragging her shoe against the dusty floor. He narrowly missed, plunging his blade into the air.

He dropped the sword to his left hand, and with his right, he *punched* her. In the face! Bones cracked.

It hurt, of course, as one expected a punch would. Pain radiated through Manisha's face, down her neck and shoulders. Her head jerked back from the force. But not by much. A what-is-going-on look of surprise hit the boy's face. His expression of shock fractured into one of pain. Because those were *his* bones that had cracked. The hand he examined was distorted and twisted, broken fingers bent every way except the right way.

"See?" she heaved. "You shouldn't have done that. Don't you know better than to hit a little girl?"

Manisha grabbed his collar, yanked him toward her, and head-butted him.

The undeniable sound of his skull cracking shattered his shocked silence. He fell flat on his back, gurgling a cry.

Manisha landed on one knee beside him, ignoring the pain vibrating through her head, and demanded, "Why are you here?"

"D-death to you, n-nagin," he grunted.

They *were* hunting her. But maybe they didn't know about Noni.

He moved his unbroken hand across the ground, his fingers crawling in search of his sword. Manisha shook her head, whispering "I wish you would just stop," and spat in his face.

His wails were quickly stifled by the toxic saliva dripping down his mouth, eating his tongue and throat.

Manisha shot to her feet as another soldier rushed in. She'd already drawn her bow and arrow before realizing that he had his ready.

They released their arrows at the exact same time. Except Manisha's cut his, splitting it into two splintered halves that fell uselessly to the floor. Hers, on the other hand, pierced his eye socket.

He screamed and fell to his knees, clutching the arrow. Her blood transformed his flesh. Skittering patches of stone consumed his body, solidifying him in mid-scream.

A spray of arrows zipped through the openings ahead and from above. Manisha ducked and ran back down the stairs, looking for a way out as she readied another arrow. She inched closer to the fissure while searching for a way out, a way to lead them away from Noni.

With no exit in sight, she ran back to the base of the stairs for a running start and darted across the expanse. As she leapt over the fissure, an arrow pierced her leg. She tumbled into a roll, clenching her jaw to entomb her scream. She broke the arrow, pulling it through. Blood gushed from the wound.

She ripped a part of her dupatta, tying it over the gash, just below the knee, to slow the bleeding as she healed. She didn't heal instantly like she would with a superficial cut, and the pain sent a shock wave through her body. Her eyes almost rolled into her head. Her heart was beating so fast that she thought it would fail any second now.

Several soldiers attacked while Manisha fumbled for her bow and arrow, smearing blood across *everything*. It was hard to think through the pain, her entire body shaking, her slippery hands trying to get control of even one arrow.

A soldier leapt over the crevice to get to her.

Noni, that clever, disobedient girl, lunged up from the fissure and snatched the soldier in mid-jump, gulping him down whole: clothes, armor, sword, and all. She rose to intimidating heights, at least ten feet above the floor, and hissed angrily at the soldiers. The sound reverberated off the walls, making them shake. Pebbles and rocks fell.

The soldiers skidded to a stop at various distances from Noni's striking range.

To the far right emerged the slayer, who'd slowed down, eyes fixed on Noni. Manisha's breath hitched, and she didn't understand why. He was here despite their different fates. It truly was him—and with him, he brought a deluge of emotions, memories of the giddiness and the safety she'd felt with him on the floating mountains. Part of her wanted to believe that he truly loved her, that he'd help her.

But that was all a lie, wasn't it? It had to be—they were here for her because she dared to stand up to men. Maybe the slayer wasn't any different. How could he be when he sided with the General? How could he be when he was allowing these trained soldiers to assault her?

Noni roared, unleashing the most ferocious hiss as her head split into not two, but *seven* glorious, agitated, defensive heads snapping in seven different directions. Picking off soldiers even as others shot arrows and spears.

And then there was the General. The sight of him made bile bubble up Manisha's throat. She wanted to both hide from him and hurt him. She *wanted* to kill him. She wanted to damage him the way he'd done to her—and so much worse. Even more so as he catapulted a spear into one of Noni's heads, at the throat.

Manisha wailed.

The injured head went limp.

Oh stars. The sight of Noni going slack, the life fizzling out of one set of eyes, was heart-wrenching and *enraging*.

Manisha fumbled to get up. She struggled to focus as she released an arrow at the General. It missed by an inch.

At the same time, the slayer was running toward Noni. He launched himself onto her with his battle-axe in the air, ready to chop off her heads.

The darkness rising inside Manisha didn't wait for permission this time. It gurgled up her throat as she released a scream so chaotic and piercing that the slayer almost slipped, soldiers stumbled, rocks dislodged from walls, the ground splintered, and the ceiling rumbled, dropping stones.

Manisha half ran (mostly hobbled) toward Noni. Grabbing her knife from her boot, she swiped the blade against the blood dripping down her leg and launched herself at the slayer. She stabbed him in the calf, dragging him down the length of Noni's massive body.

But he didn't fall off in panicked pain. Why didn't he clutch the wound as he turned to stone? Why didn't he *turn* to stone?

As he slid, swinging his weapon back at Manisha, another soldier launched himself at Noni, windmilling until he could grab on to her. Yet a third soldier was yelling for him to stop, drawing Manisha's attention. He looked like Deepa, with staggering height and a half-shaved head, tattoos on his gray-tinged skin, and sharp teeth beneath curled lips.

"Ras!" the slayer yelled, sliding off Noni's body, slick with green blood.

Manisha climbed onto his back, locking her arm around his neck in a death grip. "If she dies, *you* die!" she growled.

He released Noni, falling backward and crushing Manisha between his weight and the floor.

The one who resembled Deepa's people charged Noni but paused, shifting left and then right and then left again. Noni didn't attack him. She slid into the fissure, taking with her the soldier attached to one of her necks. Dark green blood gushed from her wounds like a cluster of springs. Her body hit the bottom of the deep darkness with a crashing thud.

"*No!*" Manisha shrieked, crawling toward the fissure, fully prepared to tumble over the edge.

The slayer grabbed Manisha by the waist, hoisting her back from plunging to her death.

She fought him, his chest against her back as she desperately reached out for Noni. The entire room quavered behind a wall of tears.

Her heart pounded against her ribs. Desolation masked the pain, the realization that she was injured and in the hands of the boy sent to kill her. It muddled the fact that she had enough of her own blood on her hands to twist around in his arms and gouge out his eyes, sending her poison straight into his sockets.

Yet . . . here she was—fighting against him to get to her best friend.

THIRTY-ONE

PRATYUSH
(PRESENT DAY)

Pratyush had always felt the weight of grief and guilt when a soldier died during his missions. Sometimes it was their fault—let's face it—but sometimes, it was the turn of the fates, the fact they went up against larger-than-life monsters when they'd never really stood a chance.

He usually felt burdened but never desolate.

Until now. Until Ras. He was still young. He had an entire world to explore, a hundred alternative careers he could've chosen. He couldn't just stand back at the far wall and shoot arrows? Did Ras really have to come after him? Was he trying to help him? Save him? Emulate him?

Ras had been smart this entire time, but apparently not smart enough to know that he couldn't do what a slayer could. He wasn't supposed to be another fallen soldier!

And now, instead of climbing down to the remaining six jaws of death to see if Ras was alive—Pratyush wasn't a hero—he was on his knees grappling the nagin from behind. She was squirming . . . not to fight him, but to get to the serpent. Her tears wet his arms. Her sobs vibrated against his chest.

This monster was just a girl. But still a dangerous one.

He wrapped an arm across her throat in the same headlock she'd had him in moments ago. Her wrist flashed a familiar bracelet, four bands of a bangle.

Her scent rushed into him. Not volatile, pungent blood, but jungle, mud, earth, sky, and almond blossoms.

It shoved him back to those days watching her dance, sneaking in conversations, forbidden meetings on her balcony and in the gardens.

Wait...

His heart beat painfully in his chest.

Was this nagin...

A sickening nausea rolled up his throat.

Was it actually...?

The nagin was a girl. But not just any girl.

"Manisha."

She caught him off guard. He was *not* expecting her to thrash her head back, slamming his nose. Pratyush hissed, clutching at the pain roaring across his face. She scrambled out from his hold and ran off, limping on an injured leg.

He immediately went after her, ignoring the gash in his calf, the throb in his face, and the surge of pain down his neck. He chased her past the fissure and into another room, away from the stairs where they'd descended, away from the light.

She stopped and spun around. He halted, his battle-axe-wielding arm in mid-movement.

He barely missed cutting her as she ducked. Her torn dupatta fluttered up from the movement and caught the razor edge of his blade, slicing the fabric in two and tearing it from her head.

The parashu hung in his hand as he recognized her exquisite features. Albeit, in this moment, her expression was unhinged. Dangerous. And just as fast as his swing had been, so was hers. A fist. To his face. It sent him reeling with an unexpected, unruly force. Definitely *not* the dainty hand of a temple priestess.

Pratyush stumbled back and touched his jaw, his gaze flitting back to her.

Damn.

This nagin, so powerful as to turn men into stone, a queen of monstrous serpents . . . well, he supposed he'd expected more.

He'd expected a giant of a woman, hideous and wretched with claws for hands and talons for feet, with reptilian skin and the body of a snake. He'd expected a viper who slithered in the darkness, with snakes for hair. He'd expected to find her lair with a pendulum of skulls swinging back and forth at its gates.

Her legend had preceded her, larger than life. But what Pratyush saw was the girl he loved, in all her rage, beauty, and glory.

Wild. Angry. Afraid. *Manisha.* The same eyes that had slain his heart, the ones he'd do anything for. So full of life, mesmerizing and heartrendingly beautiful in a haunting daze of jade.

All slayers had breaking points.

Pratyush supposed . . . he finally faced his.

Love was painful. Duty was painful. In this moment, on this day, he had to choose his pain.

The sight of his beloved in the throes of an impending slaughter sent a shudder through him. Made him sick. A war brewed in his soul over how to handle this. He had his mission, his orders. She'd killed so many already. But she was his beloved, and this couldn't be. This *wasn't* her.

An impasse.

Manisha rose to her feet, unfazed, determination like sun fire in her eyes. Despite being cornered. Despite being injured. Despite going toe-to-toe with the slayer.

"Breathtaking . . ." Pratyush mumbled.

"Why are you after me?" she demanded, her voice quivering as she unlatched the coiled whip at her side. It unfurled, and seven ends in the shape of seven viper heads hit the floor, kicking up dirt in a rising cloud.

"Why are you... *What* happened?" he asked, baffled.

Behind her, three soldiers slowly, carefully appeared, dropping down from an opening in the upper wall.

The nagin was his. He wanted to speak with her, protect her. He needed to know what had happened in the past weeks since she'd been dismissed to the kitchens in a temple on a floating mountain so far away.

She clutched the leathery hilt of the whip, her head shifting in the slightest to the side. She sensed them.

Was Manisha... Could she possibly be a new slayer? A female slayer? That was unheard of, but could be the best thing to ever happen, honestly.

There was a jumbled mass of questions and puzzle pieces and scenarios rolling through his head, waiting to explode on his tongue. And none of them would get answered if those idiots trying to sneak up on her interrupted.

Pratyush went to lift his hand to stop them, but Manisha was faster.

She spun to the side with the full force of her whip, a blur of fire that raced all the way to the hilt. The jaws of seven serpent tips opened and slashed the soldiers in a fury of fangs and fire.

A flash of flames.

A blast of screams.

A slash faster than the blink of an eye sliced three soldiers into dozens of pieces. Blood bubbled across cuts cauterized by the heat. Then silence after chunks of flesh hit the ground.

Manisha slid the tips of the whip back to her.

"What have you done?" Pratyush yelled.

She spun toward him, her whip ready.

Pratyush lifted his chin in warning. "Don't. Put down your weapon and come with me."

She slapped the whip against the ground. Sparks flew up. "You need to leave."

"I want to help you."

"Really?" she retorted, her tone dripping with ire. "What sort of help is a group of armed soldiers chasing down a girl in a cave? How badly do you want to help me when I just killed three of your people? You saw them behind me—and you did nothing?"

He took a step toward her.

"Are we doing this?" she asked.

"Of course not. You don't want to go up against a slayer of monsters."

"I guess . . ." she started, as if thinking about her next moves, as if she might have the good sense to stop. Instead, she smirked, adding, "It's a good thing I'm a slayer of men."

The whip careened across the space between them. The fire blinding. The serpent heads hissing. The fangs sharp and as fast as lightning.

Thank the stars Pratyush was just as fast.

Ducking would only work once when she was this quick and had seven tips lashing out seven different ways. One sharp slash raked across his cheek, cutting and burning. The hiss had been so close to his ears that it sounded like a vat of vipers snapping at his head.

He rolled out of the way as her second strike came on the heels of the first. The rock floor split where the seven heads struck, spitting up pebbles, dirt, and sparks.

"Stop! I don't want to hurt you!" Pratyush yelled, chopping off two of the heads.

They hissed their final screams, writhing on the ground, bleeding flames, before turning into limp rope with a tail of cinder.

Manisha came at him again, her whip catching his axe across the wooden handle instead of the blade...and *breaking* his father's parashu. What in the actual hell!

But instead of jumping back, Pratyush sprang forward and grabbed the underside of the whip where it split into the five remaining heads. The flash of fire struggled to stay lit as he wrapped the whip around his leather-covered arm, bracing against the heat and snapping jaws. With his other hand, he yanked the whip out of Manisha's grip and jerked her into him, spinning her so that she was tied by her own weapon. The braided rope dug into her flesh. Her skin had, not too long ago, been velvety smooth, the color of sun-drenched bronze. Now it was marred with welts. A hundred scars upon a hundred scars.

His stomach dropped. He needed to know everything that had happened to her.

She huffed when her back hit his chest. He fought to control her and brought her to her knees.

"What happened to you?" Pratyush asked, out of breath. "Or were you never a temple priestess? Were you this monster all along, fooling everyone?"

In her panic, Manisha fell forward onto her face and gasped, heaving, lurching. "Let me up! Let me up!" she cried.

As soon as Pratyush finished securing her, he pulled her back onto her knees and knelt in front of her.

Tears streamed down her face as terror dissipated into rage. "Don't ever push me onto the ground again," she snapped.

He hadn't meant for her to fall. His heart was beating wildly, swollen with panic. He swallowed, studying her. "I'm sorry."

He helped her to her feet. "Just...tell me what happened to you. Manisha? It's me. The boy who proposed to you, who declared his love for you."

"And that same boy tied me up," she spat.

"Because you were attacking me with fire snakes!"

"Because you and your soldiers attacked me!"

"Because you turned men into stone and terrorized an entire village!"

"Those men?" she croaked.

Would she deny it? Or maybe she had nothing to do with these events, wasn't even aware of the decree for her head.

Pratyush pleaded, "Tell me you don't know anything about this."

"You slay monsters, don't you?"

He nodded.

She searched his eyes. "Then did you slay them?"

"Who? Those men in the village?"

"Yes."

"They aren't monsters. They're just men."

"Men who dominate. Men who steal girls from their villages. Men who *violate*," she said, her breath steady, even, despite the heave of her chest on every breath, heaves filled with hot indignation.

Pratyush's gut twisted. It was incredibly common. It had been done to his sister and left him seeing murderous red. The thought of some-one having done that to Manisha had his blood boiling. His fists clenched so hard that the skin of his knuckles turned white.

"I need answers," he said in a lowered voice. "I don't have much time before the rest of the soldiers find us and demand your death."

"As if you don't want to kill me." She struggled against her binds.

"I don't. I don't know what's happening here, except that I was sent to stop you from your tyrannical spree of turning men into stone."

She grunt-squeaked.

"But I know you. At least, I—I thought I did. I'm not going to let anyone take you, do you understand?"

She stilled.

He reached out to gently touch her cheek, the bruises, the tears. *Dangerous.* She was lethal, but he couldn't help it. She was Manisha. His Manisha.

She warned him, "You shouldn't touch me."

"You're not an apsara anymore, Princess."

"No. But haven't you heard? My touch kills."

"I'll risk it."

"I'm going to kill you all," she whispered bitterly.

Pratyush sighed. "Can I help? With them, anyway."

She narrowed her eyes as his gaze dropped to her mouth. *"What?"*

He stepped back. "I never lied to you. When I told you that I loved you, when I asked you to marry me, I meant it."

"Is this the new custom now? Boys tie up their loves and drag them into a temple for marriage?" she mumbled.

Pratyush groaned.

"Oh, is the bound hostage exasperating you? Should I flounder at your feet in response to your adoration? Fall for my captor, or, if you so believe, my savior? Be still my heart."

"You're still a smart-ass, aren't you? Now tell me what happened."

"Why does it matter? Are you going to free me depending on my words? What keeps me from lying to you, then?"

"I only tied you up to keep you from fighting me so we can talk. I know you don't lie. Evade and circumvent, yes. Lie? No."

She inclined her chin. "If you deem me a monster, you'll slay me. It's in your blood. If you deem me innocent, you'll free me?"

"I watched you kill soldiers. You're *not* that innocent. Although . . . there is a lot of gray area."

"Do you simply wish there to be gray area so you don't have to kill me? Will that make you feel better? To be the hero either way?"

He grunted. "Hell. You won't even let me free you?"

"I don't need your help. I'll escape and kill the rest of you."

"You can't kill me."

"Because you think I reciprocate your love?"

"I know you'll do what you need to do to escape. But I'm the slayer. We're hard to kill."

She blinked, but she was as perceptive as he remembered. "How's your leg?"

Pratyush swallowed. It wasn't great, to be honest. It was bleeding and hurting and shooting ribbons of pain. While his wounds healed fast, this gash stayed open. Lightning bolts of dark gray veins branched out from the wound unlike anything he'd ever had before.

"You helped kill Noni. You're going to die for that."

"Who's Noni?" he asked.

"My friend. The serpent you let your soldiers *murder*," she growled, trembling. Her eyes brimmed with tears, and it tore him apart. He did this to her. He hurt her, caused her loss. Her head fell forward.

"That beast was your friend?" he asked quietly.

"My *best* friend," she rasped, holding back tears.

His soul fractured. "I'm . . . sorry, but your friend killed half of my soldiers."

"Because she was trying to protect me," Manisha snapped, meeting his gaze behind a film of tears.

His gut contorted, feeling her every torment. He swiped a thumb across her cheeks. "She would've killed more. They had to protect themselves."

"And *me*? Are you going to kill me, too?"

"If you run, the King *will* come for you. You turned men into stone."

She scoffed, half laughing. "Just the ones I stopped from violating girls, the ones who also tried to violate me. I didn't know I could turn them into stone. I was defending myself. But that makes me a monster and not them, huh?"

Pratyush clenched his teeth, anger like volatile surges pulsing through his veins. "They tried to *violate* you?"

"Yes," she replied. "Was it wrong to defend myself? To defend others?"

"No. It's admirable." If she hadn't turned those men to stone, and had he known what they'd done, he would've killed them himself.

"We're not that different. We both slay monsters. It's just that *monster* is subjective."

"I'm going to get you out of this." Pratyush leaned down to untie the binds.

She watched him closely as he neared her. "You realize that I can melt your face off, don't you?"

He smirked. "Guess I'm a sucker for danger."

"Or you really are a stupid boy. You let me go, we'll both be hunted down."

Pratyush paused, gazing down at her tearstained face. "As long as we're together."

"I still might kill you. I haven't decided yet."

"You know I'm not afraid of you."

"You should be."

He grinned. "If I died by your hands, then it would be an honorable way to go."

"Hmm. You may be honored soon."

Pratyush hadn't finished untying her binds when she looked past him and yelled, "Behind you!"

He didn't move fast enough. Someone stabbed him in the neck, *hard*.

He swung back. The General! But he had already jumped out of the way. That weasel! Pratyush was going to end him. But one step turned a million times heavier than the last. He yanked out the needle and threw it across the room.

"Slayer!" Manisha cried, pushing through her binds as the General rushed behind her to tighten them again. She struggled in his arms as he rammed something into her shoulder.

She grunted. Her body convulsed as she collapsed in the binds *Pratyush* had put her in.

He tried to fight the drowsiness, tried to follow them. His tongue turned to lead, his eyes dropped, his limbs collapsed until he was facedown on the cracked floor. His fingers twitched, trying, willing, *fighting* to get back to Manisha.

His vision went blurry, then dark, all while the General took her away.

And it was all Pratyush's fault.

THIRTY-TWO

MANISHA
(PRESENT DAY)

Manisha gulped breath after breath, fighting to swim up and break through the ice. She knew this wasn't real—this was a dream—because she remembered losing Noni, vaguely felt the pain in her leg, and absolutely felt the sting in her shoulder blade.

She was in a place where her foremothers grabbed her wrist and pulled her out of frigid waters. The waters turned into caverns. She staggered through the riverbed, exhausted, and fell to her knees. She was tired and sleepy, her eyelids getting heavier. Sleep sounded like the best thing in existence right now. The final frontier, the last effort.

As she lay down, slumber blanketed her like a heavy mist, an invisible weight of a hundred moons. Her body sank deeper and deeper into the riverbed as the displaced sand rose around her. A grave of pebbles.

Manisha was ready for real sleep. Deep sleep. The final sleep. But her foremothers begged to differ. They dragged her out of the grave and onto her feet. Their faces were blurred. Their voices came from everywhere and yet nowhere.

Serpents made of gold, green, purple, red, orange, and bronze smoke slithered around them, floating through the air, while her foremothers spoke, one after another.

"This is not where you end."

"This is not how you end."

"Wake up and move on."

"Wake up and decipher."

"Maps abound."

"Water is dry."

"Darkness leads the way."

They screeched, "Rise, Daughter of Death!" as the serpents careened into Manisha.

She gasped, sucking in cloth and a foul taste.

"There she is," a voice coaxed—a familiar voice that had her stomach roiling.

Her blurred vision slowly clarified. She was bound. Her nose and mouth were covered with cloth. Her eyes snapped wide open, wild, panicked.

No. Not this again!

She was chained to the wall and lurched forward, trying to loosen her binding.

"Stop that. You're only going to break your bones. These walls and chains are still sturdy after all these years." The General looked around, impressed.

Manisha hated that he was in front of her. She hated that he still lived, that he had her bound and gagged again. Most of all, she hated that, despite everything she was capable of, despite everything she'd accomplished, his presence still spiked fear in her. The kind that festered the soul and devoured her strength.

She wanted to both hide from him and hurt him. To cry and scream.

She wanted to fall into this black hole of depression and shame yet rise out of its ashes having scorched every one of these emotions incited by him.

The General scoffed, examining Manisha from afar, his disgusting gaze undressing her. "So, *you're* the mighty nagin? The one who turns men into stone and melts flesh. A warrior. Where was all this back then?" He rolled his wrist above his head, indicating the floating mountains.

If Manisha could've done *any* of this back then, wouldn't that have been a glorious surprise? What if, instead of being pushed down, humiliated, and violated, she'd punched him, shattered his worthless bones, and melted his privates for daring to attack her?

What if, instead of being kicked off the mountain, she had kicked *him* off?

What if, instead of being betrayed by Sita, she had dragged her out and exposed her evil soul?

Manisha would be Head Priestess. She would rule the floating mountains, the sacred temple, and the horde of powerful, flying, fire-breathing mayura. The most coveted place in the world that held the most coveted things in the world.

But the biggest questions? What if the fall had been the catalyst to who she'd become? What if her body had to be broken to be rebuilt? What if she needed to be buried in a serpent nest to be filled with venom?

What if this journey was the key to unlocking who she was meant to be?

"You're gagged because I know what you can do. Your spit is toxic—melts flesh, doesn't it? And your words are equally toxic. No, you won't get the chance to melt my face or jabber on about...what happened to you."

Rotted truth infiltrated the air.

She fumed. Gathering saliva in her mouth, Manisha darted the tip of her tongue against the cloth to test if it could dissolve fabric the way it did flesh.

"How did you survive that fall? Even the most ruthless, powerful monsters couldn't have survived that. Which makes me wonder what's in your blood and how it can be used. I never thought I'd say this, not until I saw that it was you...but I can use you. Well, you know. More than I already have." His brows shot up in amusement, in twistedly fond remembrance.

The darkness inside her was a hot energy, spiking her temperature. It didn't need to ask for permission to take over.

"Using your body *was* gratifying."

Her stomach churned and pushed bile up her throat, but the darkness urged her to stay calm.

"Getting something from Sita in return for enjoying myself was extra."

She rode through her fear as the darkness unfurled into anger, latching onto vengeance.

"I might bring you back alive. Sedated and always bound, of course. I like you much better this way. You can't speak or move. It reminds me of that night. Do you remember?"

He smirked like a reincarnated ruler of demons. Evil dripped from his pores, so potent that Manisha could smell the vileness in his sweat.

He ran a disgusting finger down her temple to her cheek, across her mouth over the cloth where it was dry, where her saliva hadn't yet seeped through. She lurched at the General, trying to headbutt him, but he swerved back.

"Let's not do that," he said gruffly. "If you play nice, I can be nice. I do enjoy the thought of keeping you this way, doing whatever I want to you whenever I want. Repeating that night. Over. And over.

And *over.* I would be the richest and most powerful man in the world. Using your magnificent body for poisons. Imagine if I unlocked your secrets. I could turn anyone I wanted into stone, anyone who stood against me. I could win wars with that flesh-eating spit."

He stepped back. "Huh. Maybe you *are* a more precious tool to keep alive than to behead. I suppose I'll have to extract some saliva from that mouth of yours and kill the slayer first. He'll want to kill you himself. And sure, it's a bad idea to kill a slayer, but we won't need his kind anymore. Especially when one drop from you could take care of every monster."

Manisha felt sick to her stomach. He meant to kill the slayer, which meant the slayer was a threat to him. Maybe . . . had the warrior boy been honest with her this entire time? Had he been tracking her on the King's decree? Attacked Noni because Noni attacked the soldiers to defend Manisha? Had the slayer grappled with Manisha to force her to listen? Had he really intended to let her go—to help her now that he knew the truth?

She clenched her eyes shut, her lashes wet with tears. The slayer would, one way or another, die.

The General had been going on. "Think of that. You'd be saving countless lives. Well, not the slayer's, per se . . . nor the King's, as I've always wanted to be king, and now I have my way to the throne. Thank the King for this idea, by the way; he wanted you alive if you could be used. Won't he be in for a rude awakening when I use you against him, eh?"

Oh, was that the plan? The General would enslave her, violate her, and use her abilities to further his agenda. He thought he could be the most powerful man in the world because he had her? Didn't that make *her* the most powerful person in the world, then?

THIRTY-THREE

PRATYUSH
(PRESENT DAY)

Trying to pry open his eyes was like trying to push a palace off his face. Keeping them open was just as hard.

Pratyush's vision blurred, clarified, pulled apart, and realigned. It was enough to make him want to vomit, and not a lot of things could do that. Where had the General gotten this potion from, and why was everyone stabbing him?

Every muscle throbbed, especially at the back of his neck.

Where's Manisha?

The ground shook as he dragged himself back to the fissure. Past the exit, far-off sounds of battle echoed. Who was fighting, though? And *what* were they fighting?

Ahead, the crevice came into view, and then the air fluttered with distortion. Or was his vision still messed up?

Pratyush blinked and squinted into the dimness.

The air wavered and squiggled.

Maybe he was dead. Because the giant golden serpent, which Pratyush was sure had fallen to its—*her*—death in the fissure, formed before his eyes. She rose from the crevice, head lowered, glaring directly at him. She was a shudder of the air, camouflaged against the backdrop of sand and pink granite. The colors transformed into shimmery scales sealed over a winding tower of muscle looming above him.

Moss-colored eyes glared at him, bored into the depths of his thoughts with that hypnotizing gaze. Those eyes, with their complex blend of beauty and intensity, could only be rivaled by Manisha's.

Pratyush wheezed out a breath, his first instinct to find a weapon. There wasn't even a rock near him.

Roll and run? Punch and grab her jaws to pry them apart?

The only problem? Aside from the fact that he could barely move, Manisha called the serpent a friend. She'd cried over her, lamented when she thought they'd killed her.

"Noni," he whispered.

She watched him with one head instead of seven.

He struggled to fight off the toxins.

"I'm sorry," he told her, his words slurred. "I thought you were a threat—when *we* were the threat to Manisha. I'm sorry for attacking you. You're right to deal with me, but first... Manisha needs our help."

The serpent tilted her head as if she understood. Noni slithered toward him but stayed several feet away. She heaved and gagged, her jaw opening and closing, the lower half moving side to side. A large mass moved up her throat. Her jaw unhinged. Her fangs retracted into her head.

A gurgle accompanied a slimy yellow regurgitated ball. Noni's last meal fell to the ground with a thud.

Pratyush powered through his grogginess to sit up. That was one way to snap back to alertness.

Did Noni vomit so she could eat him instead? He wouldn't blame her.

Splatters of sticky saliva and stomach fluids gleamed on his boots. Ugh. Gross. He held a forearm against his nose. The contents of a giant serpent's insides weren't exactly roses.

"Why?" he mumbled, using his feet to push away.

The ball of sticky strings fell apart, revealing a curled-up body. One wearing soldier's clothes. A boy unfolded like a beetle and gasped for air, lurching up with a disoriented startle.

He spat out more slime. How much could there possibly be?

The serpent...chirped? A series of hisses mixed with clicks. Strange but hypnotic. Noni lowered her head to the ground, her body still partway in the fissure. She looked exhausted. He couldn't blame her, and regret scourged his insides.

The soldier came to full awareness. He jumped to his feet, slipping on the pebbles and falling on his butt. Hard. He scuttled backward, sliding right into the wall with an *oomph*.

Noni watched him before slowly turning her head to Pratyush. She didn't move.

"What the hell just happened?" the soldier squeaked, his eyes as wide as lemons.

"Ras?" Pratyush choked out.

Ras lifted his hands, horrified. "What am I covered in?"

"What happened?" Pratyush asked, fighting through the haze and taking control over his muscles.

"I—I don't know. Dev wanted us to stop attacking the...the serpent." He watched Noni carefully. "And I was trying to help him, but then you were on it, and I thought it was going to kill you."

"So, you jumped on her to save me?"

"Well, no. I jumped on it to stop you. I figured you didn't hear Dev. Next thing I know, we're both falling into the crater. I blacked out. Did it...try to eat me and vomit me up...or...was this its way of getting me out?" Ras looked at Noni, who passively watched him in return. "Does it know that I tried to help? No, no way it would know that."

As Pratyush watched Noni's sorrowful eyes and bloody green gashes, he knew she understood. She loved and protected Manisha, which made her a worthy creature with a heart of gold.

"She understands," he said.

"What now?" Ras wiped his face, not that it helped any.

"No idea, but we have to go."

Once Pratyush regained control of his muscles and got to his feet without wobbling, he told Noni, "I promise to help her. Stay here."

She chirped and sluggishly pulled the rest of her body out of the fissure in slow movements.

"Come on," he told Ras.

They crossed the fissure at the narrowest point, jumping across with a running start. Ras, still covered in slime, slid, while Pratyush's entire body felt like it had been pounded against granite, especially his leg. His wound still hadn't healed and hurt like a hundred stabs.

Ras grabbed a faded, tattered curtain, yanked it off its last hook, and wiped the slime off.

They emerged into a battle. The soldiers battled warriors. Tall, half-shaved heads, tattoos, piercings, and silver armor. He'd never been happier to see cannibals.

"Who are they?" Ras asked, wheezing.

"Dev's people. Find him! And do *not* engage in battle with his people!"

"Where are you going?"

"To save the nagin."

Finding her in the ruins wouldn't be easy, but picking up her scent was. Her blood left a glaring trail.

THIRTY-FOUR

MANISHA
(PRESENT DAY)

A
s it turned out, Manisha's saliva *could* melt cloth. The strings were falling apart while the General paced, muttering to himself. Manisha surveyed the room, spotting her weapons in the corner. The whip lay in the forefront and moved.

Interesting.

She blinked hard.

No, she wasn't seeing things. The whip came to life, just as it had when she used it on the soldiers. It writhed and slowly awakened, slithering behind the rubbish against the wall and toward her. She didn't know what this strange whip creature was, but she was eternally grateful for it.

Manisha remained still in hopes that the General wouldn't pay attention to her. As long he thought she was bound and helpless, he wouldn't need to look at her, wouldn't notice the whip coiling behind her, hidden by her legs. He wouldn't see it rise behind her or catch it eroding the binding. The remaining five serpent heads worked together until the rope fell to the floor, alerting the General. Manisha grabbed the whip and slashed his sword to pieces, igniting the room with fire and hisses.

The whip's flames faded when it hung in her hand, but the serpents were alive, watching him watching them. She yanked off the gag.

"What are you doing?" the General demanded.

"Whatever it takes," she said, wishing that she could stop trembling in his presence.

He went for the door, but the serpent heads were fast to snap at the handle, turning it red-hot to the touch. He jumped back, clutching his hand.

His steps matched Manisha's as she followed him around the room. She grabbed her knife from the corner while he searched for another weapon. She slid the knife's blade against the drying blood on her leg, coating both sides.

The General found his belt on the table and went for a dagger tucked inside, holding it out to ward her off. The tip gleamed in the light streaming in through a small hole in the upper wall.

"While I admire endurance, this is getting you nowhere. It's only angering me, and I should behead you here and now."

Manisha's shoulders deflated. "You're so full of pointless words. Does it ever hurt your head to hear yourself speak?"

"Get against the wall," he snapped.

"Why don't you make me? You should have to work for me, don't you think? Instead of having the slayer tie me in a neat bow for you. Are you so weak and pathetic that you have to literally slice my throat in front of your king's eyes for him to believe you're capable of slaying a monster?"

"I liked you better as an apsara. Silent. Obedient. Knowing your place."

"How are you going to convince him that I'm the monster he sent you to kill? Aren't I just a girl?" Manisha walked around the room, one foot in front of the other, closing in on the General even though he took a few small steps away. She wanted the door. She wanted an escape.

"I can extract your spit and show him what it does."

"But he didn't send you to kill a girl who has toxic saliva, did he?"

"I can force you to shoot an arrow."

"At an innocent person of your choosing? And which arrow? You don't even know. Even if I could turn a man into stone with an arrow, is it really me or the arrow? You have no idea."

He snarled and stomped toward her, wrapping his face with cloth, a barrier between her saliva and his skin.

She staggered back, holding up the knife, shorter than his dagger. "Stop," she croaked.

"Or what? You'll cut yourself and make my job easier?" He took another step.

She'd wanted an exit, but the darkness inside her swelled. "No. I just wanted to see if you knew the meaning of that word. I understand why you attacked me today; I'm a powerful girl, a threat."

He scowled.

"But you *violated* me, took something from me that was not *yours* to take. So this, really, is *your* fault."

His fist came at her first. Manisha let him hit her. She wanted his bones to crack. She wanted to see the surprise on his face, the moment when he realized that he'd severely underestimated her, that *he* was the one in danger.

He yelped. His expression was a horrid blend of confusion, horror, and pain as he cradled his broken bones. His tall, domineering frame suddenly turned small and withering, weak. Manisha imagined this was how he saw her when he violated her, as something so small, pathetic, and unworthy.

She shook her head. Her fear had finally ebbed away. He no longer held power over her because she had taken it back. And that power made her free, invincible, *unbroken*. She'd embraced her gifts, her rights, her darkness.

"I just needed to get you close." She swiped across the General's cheek. He stumbled back. The blade cut through the cloth and penetrated his flesh.

He hissed, touching his face with his unbroken hand. He fidgeted, jerked, as if he couldn't tell which pain was worse: broken hand bones or venom sluggishly trudging through his jaw, calcifying his mortal flesh into stone.

"It'll be slow, because the cut is shallow," Manisha told him, slicing his other cheek.

The General hissed again, falling back against the wall, leaning against it for support.

Her voice dropped. "How does it feel? Is your body shutting down? Does it feel heavy, achy? Does the gash scream? Can you feel the venom skittering across your nerves and digging into your bones? Do you feel the poison cracking your spine? Is it like a hundred tiny monsters devouring your flesh? Do you feel it gnawing at your brain, infusing you with the vengeance of a million agonized victims?"

He quickly unwrapped the cloth in a desperate attempt to wipe the venom off. When that didn't work, he clutched his jaw.

"Or does it just work on skin, entombing you, a living corpse inside stone?"

He shook his head, trying to stave off the venom.

Darkness spread through Manisha, warming her insides. "You can't fight it. But I enjoy seeing you try. Do you feel helpless, cornered, afraid? Still, there's no fear that compares to having your privates violated."

Manisha ducked and swept the blade, still plenty wet with her blood, across his crotch. With a little extra exertion, enough to cut through his pants, but not enough to cut off his privates.

The General screamed.

"*No*," she said firmly. "I want you to be quiet. The way you demanded I be quiet."

His left eye twitched as stone formed patchwork across his face. His eye drooped and hardened. Gray spread from the second cut as he gasped for air, heaving and clutching his crotch.

"How's that for hard?" she gritted out.

The door swung open. Manisha jumped back, facing both the General and the intruder, knife in hand and serpent whip alert.

"Are you all right?" the slayer asked Manisha, taking two long strides toward her. There was an achingly raw need in the way he rushed to her. A depth of concern in his voice and his expression, and how he didn't give one ounce of worry for the General.

Did the slayer truly care about her? Could she take the chance to trust him when it seemed there were very few people in this world who could be trusted?

"Stay right there!" Manisha warned him.

He immediately stopped and licked his lower lip. Her breath caught in her throat at the sight of him. The slayer was alive, and she couldn't understand why that made her so happy.

He watched her with the same longing he'd had on the floating mountains. All she could see was the young warrior boy who'd broken the diya holder and allowed her to laugh, the boy who'd visited her balcony just to talk, who told her about his family, who'd encouraged her to show her emotions, even if they were anger and annoyance.

In his imploring lavender eyes, Manisha saw the boy who'd confessed his love, who'd promised he'd return for her.

But . . . was any of it true? Or was she seeing things that had passed long ago?

THIRTY-FIVE

PRATYUSH
(PRESENT DAY)

Manisha had the General on his knees. Parts of his face were turning into stone . . . and yet he was cradling his crotch? Her eyes, brimming with tears, met his, driving panic deep through him.

"Did he hurt you?" Pratyush asked, wanting nothing more than to hold her.

"Behead her," the General rasped. "Another lifetime for your collection."

Pratyush didn't really care about adding lifetimes. Facing off with the one thing in this entire world he truly wanted, the only thing left worth fighting for, had him questioning his entire existence.

The General had no idea what slaying monsters did to him. The nightmares. The daymares. The voices. The hallucinations. He took the life force of monsters and added them to his, but with that came faint memories and wrathful cries. Having one or two buried in his mind was enough. Having dozens was a cacophony of nightmares, a tangled web of deadfalls and snares.

He couldn't carry Manisha's wails inside him to haunt him for eternity.

The elders' cryptic riddles at the ravine finally made sense.

"Don't you want your freedom?" the General murmured, leaning against the wall, panting. "I know what you asked the King, and what the King demanded in return. This is your only chance."

Manisha blinked at Pratyush, anger draining from her expression as she understood. She was fighting for the same thing. Freedom. A home in peace. Or maybe she was trying to overthrow the kingdom. Which, hell, he couldn't blame her.

She was silent. A tear fell down her cheek.

"Don't think that," the General warned, grimacing. "I know that look. You're probably wanting to wipe tears from her face. You can't be in love with her. Be reasonable. She used you. She lied to you. She played you like a game, and you had no idea you were a pawn. She's a monster. She's a killer," he rasped, every word more arduous than the last.

"So am I," Pratyush said. "A killer. To those I've slain and their families, *I'm* the monster. The one who comes in the night and destroys lives."

His shoulders slumped as he added, "I'm sorry, Manisha. You didn't deserve any of this. I will never fight you. I came to—"

"Rescue me?" She guffawed. "Haven't you heard? This is the legend where the princess saves herself."

Pratyush smirked. "So, you *are* a princess. I knew it."

At that, she almost cracked a smile.

The General hacked up blood, convulsing.

"What did you do to him?"

"Turning him into stone," she replied. "Slowly. For what he's done."

Pratyush crossed his arms and watched. "I agree with this method of torture."

"You don't even know what he's done to me."

"Beyond this?" He dropped his arms, narrowing his eyes, reading her face.

"You want to know what happened to me, Slayer?" Her hands trembled, one holding a knife, the other holding the whip where five serpent heads rose to watch him. "How I went from apsara to this?"

He swallowed hard, knowing that her next words weren't going to be easy to take. But there was no way to prepare for what she said. No way to stop the deluge of hate and indignation from surging through his veins.

As she unleashed the truth—the violation, the betrayal, the fall—he saw murderous red. His vision went from clear to shaky to scarlet.

His eye twitched. His pulse raged. Perspiration forged a line of beads across his temple and at the back of his neck. His temperature spiked.

He sucked in a deep breath and looked Manisha in the eye. She glared at him, all fury and chaos. But there was a hint of something else. Panic. Fear. Not for death. No. That had a certain smell: metallic and tart.

She was fierce and independent and *powerful*, indisputably the strongest person in this room. Yet this scum on the bottom of a rock incited fear in her.

Pratyush released a feral snarl, flew to the General, and punched his face.

The General howled into the air. He wasn't noble, or valiant. He was petty and worthless and didn't deserve to breathe the same air as Manisha.

Pratyush intended to pummel him bloody until he died, but with one punch, his face shattered. The stone fractured on impact, leaving jagged rock fragments and exposed jawbone, the clinging flesh still transforming into stone.

Pratyush had no doubt, by the cut in the General's pants and the way he'd been holding his crotch, that Manisha had turned his worthless dick into stone, too. So he stomped the General's crotch with his boot, feeling it crunch and shatter beneath the blow.

"Do you want to kick him the way he kicked you?" Pratyush asked Manisha.

When she didn't respond, he glanced at her from over his shoulder. Tears streamed down her face. The weapons fell from her hands.

He immediately went to her and swept her into his arms. She didn't fight him. The serpent heads didn't attack.

For the first time in their lives, they embraced. He only wished it was under better circumstances. Whatever rage he'd had melted into sorrow for all the things she'd endured. Her body shook with sobs as she clutched the back of his shirt.

He pressed his lips to her hair but didn't say a word. There were no words. What could he possibly say to comfort her?

Instead, he held her and let her cry. His heart broke, drowning in the pain of her sobs.

THIRTY-SIX

MANISHA
(PRESENT DAY)

Manisha wept into the slayer's chest, unsure of how much distance to put between them, if he was still a threat, or if she could finally trust him. She wanted to believe that he wasn't lying, that he loved her.

It wasn't until she pulled away that she realized she hadn't instinctively recoiled from his touch. He held her face and gently wiped tears from her cheeks, the glow of his amethyst eyes consuming her. So much concern and pain in them. Did he hurt for her?

He spoke in a soft, tortured voice. "I'm so sorry he hurt you. I'm so sorry I didn't watch him that night. I could've stopped him. I should've stayed with you."

"It's not your fault," Manisha hiccupped. Just like it hadn't been her fault, either.

His brow creased. He nodded and leaned down, forehead to forehead. Their breathing heavy. Their futures uncertain.

Her breath caught in her throat as she smoothed the hair from his face. She pressed a palm to his cheek and rubbed a thumb across his lips.

She wasn't sure how to feel, what to feel, or which of many emotions should be allowed to surface.

He loved her, and no matter what her focus had been on the floating mountains, there was no denying that the slayer, amid the hundreds of visitors, was the only one who stayed with her long after he'd left.

He wobbled back and she caught him, her arm around his waist.

"Are you all right?" she asked.

"That scum drugged me," he mumbled. "I'll be fine."

"You said you weren't easy to kill. . . ." She ran a thumb down his neck, turning his head one way and then another to check for the puncture. There it was. Dried blood over a closed wound.

His chest made the slightest of movements. In and out. Shallow breath after shallow breath. "You're touching me, you know."

She pulled back and said, "I—I have to go."

"Where?"

"I don't know."

"I have to show you something first." He held out his hand.

"Are you joking?" She gathered her weapons.

"Trust me."

"Trust?" She spoke the word aloud, a foreign utterance. She hadn't trusted anyone, truly, since her family.

He nodded once. "Had I known you're the Serpent Queen I was sent to kill, things would've been very different. I'm on your side. I always have been, always will be."

She blew out a breath. She'd once refused his touch but had desperately wanted to believe he was good and kind and honest. She'd never really been sure if she could trust him. But she knew now. She took his hand. "Fine, but be quick."

Together, they left the heap of crumbled stone in the corner. What remained of the General would one day be a pile of rocks, and no one would remember him.

Manisha and the slayer walked straight into a battle. Who were these people?

There were yells and laments. Metal clashing against metal, the buzz of flying arrows, the heat of bodies, the smell of blood and fire in the air. It made her stomach roil. Not because this was the heavy, acrid smell of violence, but because it reminded her so much of the Fire Wars and her last days at home before fleeing. How dare they bring war back here! Hadn't this place suffered enough?

The King's army was easy to spot with their uniforms, but the others were different. Glimpses of tattooed skin and sharp teeth reminiscent of Deepa.

"Kill her!" a soldier cried, cutting off Manisha's thoughts. He surged toward her with a snarl, blood dripping from his temples. His face bruised and his eyes wild.

She drew her bow and arrow, but the slayer had stepped between them. He warned, "Stop!"

They didn't have time for this. Manisha released an arrow. Fortunately for the soldier, it wasn't one coated in her blood. The arrow dug deep into his shoulder socket, forcing him to drop his sword. It hit the ground, and he fell to his knees.

The slayer jumped back and looked at her from over his shoulder. In her periphery, another soldier lunged at her from the alley. Another arrow met him in the arm in one fluid movement.

"We do *not* have time for this," she said.

The slayer's brows shot up in surprise. Then he pressed his lips together and nodded in reverence. He jerked his chin to the side. The courtyard was to the right, where so much noise and fighting abounded. The amphitheater to the left.

They went left, down the stairs. To Manisha's utter disbelief, the beautiful golden Noni was half crested over the fissure, struggling to lift the last section of her body out.

Manisha's heart went wild, her breath catching, and her knees buckled in her hurried rush. Her tears gushed like a wild spring. She could've dropped to her knees and bawled.

"Noni!" she shouted, skidding to a stop beside her.

If serpents could weep and express sorrow, angst, and suffering, this was it. Manisha didn't even want to touch her for fear of hurting her. Green blood covered her in large patches, in long smears.

She knelt beside Noni's head resting on the ground. Noni watched her with sorrowful eyes. Manisha gently hugged her. The serpents on the whip at her hip lifted to rub against Noni, too, as if they were long-lost family.

"You're going to be okay, sweet, sweet girl."

Noni eyed the slayer behind Manisha but didn't make a move to attack.

Manisha looked back at him. He crossed his arms and watched them with a sort of solemn but joyful gleam in his eyes.

"Did you know?"

He nodded. "When I came to, she came out of the fissure. I told her I had to help you. She seemed to understand and let me go. I told her I'd be back. I'm a guy of my word."

Manisha swallowed her sobs. "Thank you."

"She means everything to you, and I apologized to her for hurting you. Now that I know, I'm sorry to both of you."

She nodded, holding back tears. He understood. Amid the masses of the King's cruel servants, the slayer was like a sunflower refusing to be choked out by thorns.

"I'll get some water and sheets. She's bled a lot," he said, walking away.

Manisha wiped across Noni's smears, finding welts instead of open gashes. She sighed, slumping against her. Noni also had great healing abilities.

Thank the stars.

The slayer returned with water and helped her clean Noni. Surprisingly, Noni let him touch her. Manisha kept continuous watch over him, Noni, and the stairs.

Once Noni was all cleaned up, they stood. The slayer went to the steps to check the sudden calm.

"Can you move?" Manisha asked Noni.

She raised her head and gradually slithered toward the steps, following them as they ascended toward the exit.

The slayer had a sword ready, and his broken battle-axe stuffed into its holder on his back.

Manisha had her bow and arrows prepared, her whip at her hip. She didn't know what to expect when they emerged into the light, but not this. Not Deepa.

She stood beside an older boy. Manisha recognized him as the one who'd been with the slayer. He had his arm around Deepa's shoulder.

"Slayer!" he yelled.

"What's going on?" The slayer met him, his sword loose in his hand.

Deepa ran to Manisha but abruptly stopped when she saw Noni lurking in the shadows over Manisha's shoulder. "You're alive! Whose blood is this? Are you all right?"

Manisha stumbled over her words, shocked to find Deepa with so many others armed and walking around. "I'm fine. Wh-what's going on? What are you doing here? Who *are* all these people?"

"Oh, thank the stars, you're okay. I told you I'd return. When the rain cleared, my husband came to me."

"The one who's in the King's army?"

Deepa nodded. "He snuck away to see me. He told me that he was with the slayer looking for a nagin. I told him about you and to protect you."

"Wait…" Manisha searched her memories and jerked her chin at the older boy standing beside the slayer. He'd ordered the soldiers to stop attacking Noni during battle. "The tall one with a half-shaved head?"

Deepa nodded. "He said what you did was very serious, but he would judge for himself and protect you if the King was in the wrong. And we know, by plenty of experience, that the King will declare anyone powerful, or even someone he simply doesn't want to exist, an enemy. I explained you weren't a monster and probably had very good reason for doing what you did… that is, *if* you did those things."

Manisha nodded. "I did. I had to defend myself and help others, and the result was unexpected."

"I understand. We came back to check on you, warn you, but you were gone by then. We found your camp before the soldiers came and did our best to cover your tracks."

She sighed. "Thank you."

"But we knew the slayer would find you anyway. We returned home and gathered our warriors and came here when we saw that the army had picked up your tracks."

"All this? For me? Why?" Manisha asked, dumbfounded but incredibly honored.

"Because you don't deserve this. And there's something very special, very big about your fate. It doesn't end here. Besides, we're friends now, and I'd promised your sister." Deepa beamed, and Manisha grinned back at her. A friend? Such a foreign concept after so many years away from people she could trust. First Mitali, now Deepa? It seemed surreal to think that she had true friends now.

Manisha's heart warmed. She'd thought Deepa was spinning words to be kind, if anything. She never expected someone to actually rise up and fight for her. She blinked back tears, wondering if the fate of her people might have been different if more friends like Deepa had helped them before.

Her mother would say, "There's no point in dwelling on the past, for it cannot be changed. But the future? Then yes, let your musings flow, for the future can be altered in a hundred ways."

Perhaps with friends like Deepa and the slayer, Manisha could change her fate.

"Thank you. Thank you so *very* much. Is your husband all right?"

"Yes. My Dev, my love." Deepa jerked her chin at the tall boy explaining the same story to the slayer. The slayer kept his eyes glued to Manisha.

This did not go unnoticed by Deepa. "Oh my. What's going on here?"

Their eyes locked, and neither could pull away from the magnetic strength sparking between them. They were meant to be natural enemies, pitted against one another by men, but there was something deeper brewing, a calling stronger than either of them.

They were drawn to one another, bound to each other. One a slayer, the other a monster—yet each was both.

THIRTY-SEVEN

PRATYUSH
(PRESENT DAY)

Pratyush winced when Dev checked the back of his calf where Manisha had tried to gut his leg with her venom. The oozing gash of ripped muscle already looked infected with crusted edges of dark blood. Gray lightning bolts branched outward from the wound. The same color as the stone men. There was a dead weight feeling inside his calf, with sparks of snapping pain around the cut.

He swallowed hard. *Well, hell...*

Dev knelt behind him and cleaned the wound with a damp cloth while his wife prepared a local antidote for venom made from the nearby custard apple plant and then used needle and thread to close the gash.

Pratyush frowned, his heart thudding. His wound hadn't healed much. He'd never seen the sinewy surface of his own muscle like this before. A few minutes to several hours and his wounds always closed on their own, rarely leaving scars for very long, much less infection.

Would he fully heal this time, or would he turn to stone in some horrific, agonizingly slow way? Would this concoction work? Was there a cure? Did Manisha even know of one?

Dev woefully glanced up at him and then to Manisha as she took a bundle of fresh clothes from a girl. Dev was the only one here who knew something was wrong with him.

Manisha gave a kind smile to the girl, turning to walk away, when their eyes met. Her soft smile faded, her glance falling to Pratyush's calf. Color drained from her face, and he knew the answer. She did *not* have a cure.

It wasn't unthinkable for Manisha to be powerful enough to kill a slayer. Maybe he was on his way, descending toward a final sleep. But until that moment, he was going to protect her. Nothing would tear him away from her ever again. If the forces of the cosmos wanted to keep them apart, then death was the only thing they could throw at them.

He grunted. Hell. They had to try harder than that.

An older girl called Manisha over, and off she went to clean up.

Pratyush didn't feel the prick of the needle as Dev's wife sewed his flesh together, nor did he notice Dev patting down cloth dressing around his calf.

Dev stood upright when he was done and asked, "Are you all right?"

Few people had ever asked Pratyush if he was okay. They either didn't care or assumed he was strong all the time, inside and outside and all the way through. Dev asked every now and then, but Pratyush could never seem to let the truth slip. Even now, he nodded and thanked his friend.

Dev didn't push it. He merely said, "It's good to ask, and good to confess."

Pratyush rubbed the back of his neck. "Yeah . . . Hey. Are *you* okay?"

"I'm near my bride, which means I'm more than okay. My people have extra clothes that they brought for me. You can clean up and have them instead."

"Thanks. What are your plans now?"

Dev gave his wife a warm look of longing, and Pratyush knew they'd stumbled toward the end of their journey as a team brought together by bonds enforced by the King.

This was freedom. Pratyush hoped it wasn't short-lived for either of them.

THIRTY-EIGHT

MANISHA
(PRESENT DAY)

With Noni keeping watch, the slayer struggling to walk, and Deepa nearby, Manisha took the chance to clean up. A quick bath with washcloths, a change of clothes courtesy of Deepa, and quick swipes of a water-soaked towel against her whip and her bow. The blood-tipped arrowheads and blade would stay as they were.

The slayer had also cleaned up and was in fresh clothes—in a black kurta with the sleeves rolled up his forearms. Manisha took a minute, perhaps many minutes, to appreciate him. He looked more like a regular boy, albeit a very attractive one. His hair was under control, the top half tied with a loop at the back of his head. He stood tall, shoulders back, but leaned most of his weight on his uninjured leg.

She chewed on her lower lip with worry. Had she sentenced him to a slow death, or could he fight her venom? How would it affect him? Leave him with a painful limp that would never recover? Make him vulnerable? Lead to his demise in battle? Would his people shun him, strip him of his title?

Dread bubbled up her throat.

Manisha stood beside Deepa and said, "Thank you for everything."

Deepa shrugged. "It's what friends are for."

"You know what I'm capable of?"

Deepa nodded.

Manisha noticed the girls who'd built her shelter in the near distance. "Your companion from before? The one you called a scholar?"

"Hah. She was born during the monsoon rains, but the clouds broke during her birth and the elders said she would become a great scholar. So, they named her Manshvi, meaning intelligence. I suppose it's true. We try not to tell her because it goes to her head." Deepa laughed.

Deepa then called out the girl's name, waving her over. Manshvi trotted across the field, straightening her top as she approached.

"Good to see you, Serpent Queen," Manshvi teased.

Manisha's cheeks turned hot. "Oh, no. I'm no queen." Even as she said the words, she remembered the Dosi Sisters and their riddles. She shook it off and asked, "Do you know how to treat venom?"

Manshvi furrowed her brows as she thought. "All sorts of herbs, bark, spices, waters from various pools, incense soot...depends on the creature. Cobras, kraits, vipers—all serpents. Red scorpions. Hornets. Sea wasps and sea slugs. Centipedes. There are many others, but these are the deadliest."

She paused and looked from Manisha to Deepa, adding, "I suppose you want to know about your serpent's venom? We made a treatment for the slayer from the custard apple plant. Not that he needs it. Nothing can kill him, but for good measure."

"It's a start. But...I have venom, too."

The girls watched her with great awe. "I can search my books. But...you know..."

"What?" Manisha pressed.

"You are naga. Your lineage is tied to the great cobras. Your people, your books . . . should have answers."

Manisha nodded, glancing back at the crumbling buildings. Would the libraries be intact? Or had the King's army raided everything? She'd only heard of fantastical stories told from generation to generation, but she didn't remember anything like this.

"We'll work on it," Deepa said, touching her swollen belly. "But we need to return."

"I understand. Thanks again for everything, *friend.* . . ." Manisha said the word as if her mouth had to work to correctly pronounce it.

The girls laughed. What a strange, new feel to an old word.

Manisha sat on the grass in front of the gates. Noni sprawled out in a loose *S* shape, her head at Manisha's side so that the tip of her snout touched her lap.

"She's hungry and needs rest," Dev was telling the slayer of Deepa. "I don't know why she came. I told her not to."

The slayer glanced at Manisha from over his shoulder and said, "I do."

Manisha swallowed, heat rising to her cheeks.

Dev grunted. "She can barely ride a rhino, you know? The momentum forces you to lie on the stomach, and her stomach is swollen."

"She's pregnant? Congratulations!"

"Thanks. It's something to have a girl like that, a love, and now a child. I can't believe I have a family of my own." He looked wistfully at Deepa as she climbed onto her rhino, waiting for her husband.

Dev added, "This is where we part. Unless you have a problem?"

The slayer clasped Dev's arm and gave him a side embrace. "Nah. Be well. And be prepared for the King's backlash."

"The King will come for you, too."

"He won't be able to find me."

Dev grinned a sharp-toothed grin and climbed onto the rhino behind Deepa. She waved at Manisha. Manisha waved back.

The slayer hobbled toward her, eyeing Noni, who barely lifted her head at his presence. He sat beside Manisha with a grunt.

She bit the inside of her cheek, worry cresting over her. She was almost afraid to ask, "How's your leg?"

"Hurts," he replied, and then side-eyed her. "It'll heal."

She wasn't too sure about that, but she hoped he was right. The thought of him suffering ate away at her. "What if it doesn't?"

He smirked. "You sound like you care about me."

She shook her head even though he was right, because now she fretted over his fate. Her lips trembled and she looked away so he wouldn't see.

"Ah, don't worry. I always heal."

"You know so much about the world. Have you seen venom like this? Ways to heal it?"

He was quiet for a second before replying, "Not like this. But there's medicine that can stop snake venom, so there must be something."

She nodded, still turned from him. They would find something. They had to.

They watched a dozen rhinos covered in armor, horns painted with blood, leave in a stampede. On their backs were armed warriors. All fierce and formidable, yet the kindest people Manisha had ever come across. Her new friends.

"They really came prepared for war," she commented.

"Only to face a handful of soldiers. Since someone else took care of the rest."

Manisha side-eyed him and smiled.

Winds howled across the rolling hills in an impending, hostile future.

She asked, "The King won't stop looking for me, will he?"

"There'll be rumors that you died in all this, that only one soldier survived." He looked out to the bottom of the hill where Ras was standing, his back to them as he watched the rhinos take off.

"He's trustworthy," the slayer promised. "In case you were wondering. I mean, Noni saved his life. She seems like a good judge of character."

Manisha smiled at the serpent. "What about me? I heard you gain a lifetime for every monster you slay. Don't you want one more?"

"I just want a lifetime with you."

His hand found hers on the patch of grass between them. He brushed a finger over hers. It was a soft, gentle touch that didn't make her recoil. She wasn't sure if she could ever feel normal again after being violated, but maybe one day she could. With the right person. With him.

"A slayer and a monster? What an abomination..."

He laughed. "Not as if we're normal." He eyed Noni and asked, "Does she always do that? Stare like she's about to eat me."

"No. Don't be ridiculous. She would just eat you. She's never let anyone get this close to her, though."

"Think she'll be okay?"

Manisha rubbed Noni's snout. "She's strong, and this is just the beginning of her adventures."

"What are you going to do now?"

She shrugged. "I don't know. I need rest, but there's still so much to do, so much to figure out."

He nodded in agreement. He looked as worn and beaten as she felt.

"Noni could use the rest, too, and heal properly. It's safe for now. No one else is coming after us?"

"No," he replied.

"I want to look around for more clues about my family. I'm so close, I can feel it."

"Not at all tempted to storm the palace?" he asked, his shoulders squared. "I know I am."

"We both know neither one of us is ready," she said quietly, glancing at his leg, pained that he might be in serious trouble.

The slayer glanced at their hands before gazing into her eyes, his expression achingly raw, and asked, "Am I anywhere in your plans?"

"I barely know you."

He guffawed. "After all this time, that's still your answer? I know in the temples, being the little princess . . ."

She scoffed.

He grinned, flashing sharp canines. She'd missed his smile.

He said, "Now we have the chance to get to know each another. Or are you banishing me?"

"Pratyush—" Manisha started, then sucked in a breath.

His smile turned sly. "That's the first time I've heard you say my name. It's always been *Slayer* or *stupid boy*."

She laughed. "Maybe this is the first step toward a . . . a friendship?"

He conceded, "Hah. A friendship sounds like a great place to start."

Manisha's skin flushed. She might not have felt as strongly about him as he did her, but there was something brewing between them. She didn't mind figuring things out together.

"You realize that I'd follow you anywhere. All you have to do is ask. . . ." The slayer—*Pratyush*—watched her, hopeful. She'd have to get used to thinking his name now.

Manisha's heart warmed at the thought of having him near, of daring to trust another person, of allowing someone to get close after so many years of distrusting people.

"I'd make a great assistant, you know. I make the best lassis. Ever had jamun lassi?" He whistled, like his yogurt berry drink was the best in the realm.

"All right," she said after some thought, "I suppose you can stick around."

He seemed incredibly pleased, the way his smile reached his eyes. He finally looked like any other boy. Someone who didn't have the weight of the King's demands on his shoulders, a gruesome legacy, or a potentially fatal injury. But like a boy who had his entire future ready to be what he wanted it to be.

It couldn't hurt to have someone help her fill in the gaps of what had happened when she was sent away. He could help her find her family. After all, he was the best tracker in the realm.

But first...

"Two heads are better than one," she said. "Maybe there's a cure or a hint of treatment for you hiding in my city."

"It would be nice not to die," he joked.

Manisha bit her lip. They went quiet again.

"What do you suppose is across the Great River?" Manisha asked after a while, as if Pratyush might have all the answers about this world.

He furrowed his brow in thought. "I've never crossed. Heard it's a one-way move and most don't make it."

Her heart sank. "Oh..."

He quickly added, "But there are creatures and beings in the water who could help. And these things called boats."

She slapped his arm. "I know what boats are!"

"Ow!" He feigned pain.

Maybe if they could find a boat, she might be able to reach Kumari to see if she'd found any answers. Manisha bit her lip and confessed, "I found hidden scrolls in the temple."

Pratyush stilled. "As in, from the ancient ones?"

"Who else?"

"All right, smart-ass," he jested. "What did they say?"

"I didn't get to read much, or many, and there were lots. They're hard to get to. You could probably get to them easily since you're such a great scaler of walls."

"I am," he said proudly, and she was sure he was thinking back to all the times he'd climbed her balcony.

"The scroll I read mentioned an island on the back of a giant sea turtle."

"That's new. Well, maybe we'll find it while looking for your family?" He gave a soft smile, one without hostility or lust or ulterior motives.

Genuine was the word.

They enjoyed a few long minutes of serenity, but that seemed short-lived.

Something strange moved through Manisha. An aching sensation, a dizzy spell. Noni raised her chin to look at her.

"Are you okay?" Pratyush asked, brushing a finger over her trembling hand. "Your hands are like ice."

Manisha silenced a groan, suddenly bombarded with visions of her foremothers as if they stood in the valley right in front of her. Hooded figures, shrouded in shadows and dark mist, their eyes piercing green. A vast number appeared. Each one looked like the next. But three stood out, gliding to the forefront like mist rolling over the hills.

The first had a crown of bramble and thorns with spangles of red hyacinth blooms.

The second had a crown of fractured glass with spires tipped in gold.

The third had a crown of serpents, coiled with fangs bared.

The first began to speak, her face pushing out from inky ambiguity, her eyelids springing open in surprise, a gasp escaping her lips. She looked and sounded so much like an older Eshani.

"I'm here, little one," she said, her voice aghast, both a whisper and a screech.

And then they were gone.

Pandemonium writhed inside Manisha's soul like a caged animal trying to find its way out. It skittered beneath her skin, flooded through her veins, ached inside her muscles, and ebbed across her bones.

Kismet and karma clashed, a chaotic struggle until they emerged like a tapestry woven by the fates. A world of light drenched in darkness, set on fire. Vipers and bramble and jagged glass rose from the ashes, dripping in blood.

Pratyush fully turned to Manisha. "What is it?"

Manisha's breath caught in her throat. "It's *venom....*"

Meanwhile...

MITALI WIPED HER BROW AS SHE SWEPT THE CHOPAL—a platform around an ancient, towering fig tree in the center of the village—where the older men would soon come to gather once those from the hunting party returned. As always, the Dosi Sisters sat on the smooth rock platform, the fire crackling in front of them.

Once Mitali had swept all the debris, she leaned the grass broom against the tree and stoked the modest fire.

"The monsoons are coming," she said. The earthy smell of rain filled the air, and thick gray clouds blocked out the afternoon sun.

Mitali didn't mean to look up at the sisters from her crouched position, but she did. The normally impassive elders, who looked like slumbering statues uninterested in life, had raised their tucked chins one by one. The shadows from the faded, pale saris covering their heads lifted above hollow eyes—eyes clouded white for each of them except the sister in the middle, who had one clouded eye and one consuming black void.

Mitali rarely made eye contact with her elders, as it wasn't an appropriate thing for someone as young as Mitali to do. The one difference that kept anyone from rebuking her manners was the fact that the middle sister, the one with one functioning eye, was her grandmother.

"Nani?" Mitali asked, her brow furrowed in worry.

The sisters' hunched backs had grown bigger over time and now curved over their thin bodies. Nani scratched a long nail against one sunken, wrinkled cheek as all three suddenly grinned toothless grins.

They seldom smiled.

They looked like Death reaching out to Mitali as a pall of darkness descended, turning gray clouds into whorls of black streaked with silver. A chilling breeze swept through the village, rustling dried leaves off the ground and shaking tree limbs. The flames of the fire crackled and danced.

Mitali's skin crawled, like little centipedes skittering up her spine with pincers ready at the back of her neck.

With no one else around, the elders spoke from left to right.

"Future ruler of Bharoda, listen closely."

Mitali scowled. Ruler? Since when?

There was no time to ask what they meant, or even a second to think on it. The Dosi Sisters spoke as one.

"Granddaughter of mine, keeper of histories," began Nani.

"Befriender of new rulers, riders of beasts," added the third.

"A new queen, one of three," said the first.

"Risen from the Blood River," said Nani.

"Who walks through nightmares unseen," said the third.

"Ruby seeds clutched in her grasp," said the first.

"Such treasures sought by kings," said Nani.

"She who has walked the realm below realms," said the third.

"And lived to tell the tale," said the first.

"Who will snatch apart the court with vines," said Nani.

"That hum and speak secrets into her hands," said the third.

"She wears a crown of bramble dipped in red," said the first.

"The taste of blood fresh on her lips," said Nani.

"Walking among those once thought to be dead," said the third.

Just as quickly as they'd begun their haunting riddle, they stopped and stared past Mitali. Confused, she turned and stood. Something glowed in the distance above the tree line. She hurried toward the light, her frantic steps turning into a run as her people gathered alongside the southern border.

In the distance, above the marshlands, a spray of red mist crept up from the tips of the trees. The usually gray clouds turned crimson, and purple lightning struck the skies with a ferocity that had Mitali shielding her eyes. A heart-stopping thunderclap rocked the ground; the villagers felt it even from across the great expanse.

Voices overlapped in confusion and fear.

Mitali had heard the stories passed down from generation to generation.

The marshlands were said to be the entryway to the Nightmare Realm.

It had opened once, a call to arms against the vidyadhara long ago. And in that moment, the skies bled, terrifying creatures crossed into this realm, and nothing was ever to be the same.

As if the elders were standing right there, Mitali heard their voices carry on the breeze and whisper into her ear as one, eerie and foreboding.

"A touch of blood is all she needs. . . ."

ESHANI SAT CROSS-LEGGED ON A CLIFF OVERLOOKING THE Blood River, its glittery red mist stretching upward and choking off the view to the other side. Below, a riverbed of bones paved the ground in warning to never near the waters of the dead. Eshani knew all too well what crossing that threshold had been like, and she would do just fine perched here, high above.

Sithara's image faded in and out as her form hovered beside her twin sister. She was cloaked in shadows, her jade eyes a soft glow against pallid skin, and a crown of shattered glass on top of her head. She'd always been the dramatic one.

She was watching the river, but every once in a while, she glanced over Eshani's shoulder at the stonelike statues, particularly the intimidating one in the middle. A figure of dark gray dressed in a black sherwani made him difficult to see against the darkness of the Nightmare Realm, but his presence was consuming.

"Not much of a talker, huh?" Sithara asked.

He didn't reply, didn't move.

"Your gift is getting stronger," Eshani told her. "I'm nowhere near the Court of Nightmares, but our connection is solid."

"I *am* all-powerful these days," Sithara jested.

Eshani smirked, smoothing down the black-and-dark-red dhoti

draping her legs, unabashed at the glimmering black choli baring her midriff without a sari or dupatta to cover her.

"There," Sithara said, her shadowy form gliding over the cliff and pointing down at the river, at the new face drowning in the waters. "Is that him?"

"Yes," Eshani hissed.

"Are you sure?"

"I'd recognize the man who raped our sister anywhere," Eshani growled.

She stood and, with a flick of her wrist, called to the roots beneath the river and plucked the man out. A thick black tentacle squeezed around his waist until he spat out bloody water, wheezing. His hands flew to the grip crushing his bones, and it took everything in Eshani not to shatter him for what he'd done to Manisha.

She blew out a breath and silenced her anger, drawing him toward her as Sithara followed.

Parts of the man's face and crotch had crumbled like pulverized rocks. The twins were happy to see that he'd had a painful death.

"Where—where am I?" he asked, his voice tortured and his expression one of agony.

Eshani spoke. "You didn't think you'd get off so easily, did you? I wasn't going to just let you slip past me into perdition."

"No! I don't deserve—"

"Perdition is a picnic compared to me, General."

Another root wrapped around his neck to lift him to her eye level. He squirmed and choked.

She explained, "You can still feel pain here. I can choke you for lifetimes and death will never come because, well, you're already dead."

"Don't you know who I am? Stupid girl! Release me at once!" he demanded, as if he had any say here.

Beyond Eshani, a pair of wings unfolded to reveal a silent, dark statue. He breathed, coming to life. His claws curled, and a sea of flesh-eating critters trilled around him in the endless shadows. The sound echoed against rocks, promising that this realm was vast and deadly even if one couldn't see it. A smoldering heat, like a heavy fog, crashed into the man strangled by roots, his skin blistering. The darkest of eyes glared back at him.

The General stilled. The statue stepped forward, his footsteps like thunderous hooves. His face parted into a ridge of vertical, gnashing teeth as he growled. It was a ghastly sight, the sort that would make any mortal faint.

"You should watch your manners," Eshani warned the General.

"What do you want, you she-demon?!" he spat at her.

Eshani clucked her tongue. *Typical.*

A serpent necklace writhed to life around her throat, pulsating with an illustrious carmine glow matching her lips and clothes. Both the serpent's iridescent emerald eyes and hers flickered. Corporeal, yet ethereal.

"I'm not a demon," she promised softly. "But I *am* your worst nightmare."

ACKNOWLEDGMENTS

LET'S GO WAY BACK. TO WHEN I FIRST READ A NOVEL BY RICK Riordan and became enthralled by mythology. My love for fantasy was born, and my creativity was realized. Mythology has remained a powerful force in my imagination since.

Medusa was one of many characters, a small figure standing against legendary giants. But her story has always been captivating, tragic, and unjust.

The reality about popular legends is that these stories are one-sided, meant to distort veracities by expressing what society wishes to be. A hold on the narrative. Medusa was a prime example, always presented as the villain, the monster. Her assailant dismissed. Her curse justified. Her killer the hero. We know such stories. We've heard them told and retold through generations and across civilizations. Some of us have lived them, and oh, how we know the depth these scars travel.

Like many myths, this one has its fair share of flaws among the mutable landscape of storytelling. It felt broken. And I deeply wanted it to make sense.

Other myths helped forge this book, particularly one that had captured my imagination since childhood. The naga: a divine race of half-human, half-cobra beings. Benevolent and beautiful.

I put the two together, seemingly a natural pairing, but like mismatched puzzle pieces, they didn't quite fit. Over time, my vision of this story evolved. Nightmares and dreams. Blood and glitter. Venom and solace. Elements that fit perfectly together and were perfectly befitting. Still, floating pieces yet to settle. Something was missing.

In 2021, I came across the statue of *Medusa with the Head of Perseus* by Luciano Garbati in a reversal of the famous *Perseus with the Head of Medusa* by Benvenuto Cellini. This hauntingly beautiful statue, not of a victim or a monster but of a formidable woman having fought back and prevailed, ignited this dormant story, a call to all those floating pieces to assemble. And thus, *A Drop of Venom* was born in a flurry of words demanding to be told.

I took the idea of Medusa, picked up the shards of her beginnings, reexamined her origins, and placed her in a world steeped in Indian lore. I wanted to show how a girl can be changed by violence, how an assailant can take a victim, twist her truth, and make her the monster. But most of all, what it truly means to *be* a monster.

I never imagined this story exploding into the vast world it's become, much less taking this publishing ride. Eternal gratitude shall always be bestowed upon my agent, Katelyn Detweiler. When I pitched this idea to her, she said, "YES! WE NEED THIS STORY!" with such enthusiasm and heartfelt support for a story that means so much to me. Thank you for being with me through the ups and downs with this book, and for talking me off the proverbial ledge when I wanted to give up. We both knew this story's worth and stuck with it.

I told Katelyn: This is my dream book and Disney is my dream publisher.

Katelyn said: Okay. Let's do it!

And then we did it.

It was as magically simple as that, and you are simply magic.

We submitted to Disney not realizing that Rick Riordan Presents had expanded to YA. My editor, Christine Collins, loved the book as much as I did and saw how to make it great. I'm floored by her guidance and passion for this series. Thank you for championing this story. Thank you, Stephanie Lurie, for taking this project to Rick in consideration for RRP. I was quite shocked at this turn of events, knowing that *the* Rick Riordan was reading my words, that he knew I even existed. I was stunned when he welcomed *Venom* into his imprint. Full circle. I went from reading his books based on mythology to working with him on a book inspired by that love of mythology. This was a plot twist I never saw coming. Thank you, Rick, for not only embracing *Venom* but for conveying the importance of this book and its topics and how such a story can impact the lives of young readers.

I want to thank the entire Disney/RRP team for making this possible, as there are a multitude of people and moving pieces that go into publishing a book. And the spectacularly talented Khadijah Khatib for bringing Manisha and Noni to the cover in such a striking way.

I'm grateful for everyone who had a hand in forging this path.

I can't express enough gratitude to my husband for his support of this writerly lifestyle in which I tuck myself away into the recesses of our home, splendidly robed in an array of loungewear and fueled by coffee and cheese as I slip into the furthest reaches of my imagination.

To Rohan, who read the early draft and immediately demanded more.

To Meet, who learned that he can indeed keep a secret for many months.

To my parents, who tell every auntie and uncle about this book and actually said, and I quote, "Good job." I almost cried.

To Parth, who constantly tells me how proud he is of me. For which I did cry.

I hope you enjoyed Manisha and Pratyush's journey. And I hope you'll join me for Eshani's story next, where we dip our toes in a deeper, darker realm.

There's nothing like a just reckoning.

THE FOREST BEYOND

THE FLOATING MOUNTAINS

YAMUNA RIVER

VANSOL

YAMUN
UNDERWATER CITY OF THE YAKSHA

MARSHLANDS

THE VAST AND INFINITE SEA

CANYONLANDS

ANAND
HOME OF THE NAGA

KURMA